PRAISE F

MW01484166

"Jaime Stickle's d.   .y ..., ...ay... .... enjoyment.
Any former reporter can investigate murder, but Stickle's protagonist,
Corey Tracey-Lieberman, does it with a baby strapped to her chest
while fighting postpartum anxiety. Funny in spots, heartbreaking in
spots, Stickle brings the humanity—and lands the plane without nary
a bump."

—Tracy Clark, award-winning author of the Cass Raines and
Detective Harriet Foster series

"Jaime Parker Stickle's debut is both a love letter to the everyday people
of Los Angeles and a kick-ass mystery. Corey Tracey-Lieberman is a
vibrant, often-delirious, and surprisingly moving investigator who
never stops being herself, even in the most hilarious and harrowing
circumstances. Vicious Cycle is an absolute delight."

—Tod Goldberg, New York Times bestselling author

VICIOUS
CYCLE

VICIOUS CYCLE

A Thriller

JAIME PARKER STICKLE

THOMAS & MERCER

Published by Thomas & Mercer, Seattle

www.apub.com

Amazon, the Amazon logo, and Thomas & Mercer are trademarks of Amazon.com, Inc., or its affiliates.

EU product safety contact:
Amazon Media EU S. à r.l.
38, avenue John F. Kennedy, L-1855 Luxembourg
amazonpublishing-gpsr@amazon.com

ISBN-13: 9781662531781 (paperback)
ISBN-13: 9781662531774 (digital)

Cover design and illustration by Jarrod Taylor
Cover image: © Kristina Bilous / Getty

Printed in the United States of America

FOR ALL WOMEN

1

Listening to a police scanner is tedious work and habit forming and has nothing to do with me anymore except that I can't quit.

When we got pregnant, I promised Evan I would stop monitoring the criminal activity in our neighborhood: He assumed that was the cause of my episodes. He was wrong, but I went along with it. Now that our son, Jacob, has arrived, everything is fair game again. Except alcohol. No alcohol while I nurse. No alcohol to ease anxiety. No alcohol to enjoy life.

I flip on the police scanner.

A high-pitched chirp comes from my phone. A sound that I'm conditioned to respond to immediately—a new tweet.

NELAScanBoy:

Alert: Possible 187 NELA HLP area.

Debs Park/2F/Hispanic/17yo

NELA = Northeast Los Angeles. HLP = Highland Park. My neighborhood. Fuck.

LA News First with the Wake-Up Crew is shouting at me from the television, but I can't remember turning it on. I grab the remote to turn it down, not wanting Jacob to wake up yet. The scanner, the small TV, my laptop, the crib, and my baby are all in my office, now an office / nursery / investigative hideout.

LA News First: the place where my career started and ended. *The Wake-Up Crew* was exactly that—the early-early-morning anchors. Bottom-feeders who couldn't cut it with a mainstream audience—I knew because I had started there as a general assignment reporter fourteen years ago. Of course, the money worked in their favor, put them up in nice homes with decent cars, but there was no potential for prestige or fame. To Los Angeles, *The Wake-Up Crew* is background noise against the morning hustle and bustle of teeth being brushed, blow-dryers screaming, and juicers pulverizing. Or, in my case, the constant motoring of the breast pump as it *in*delicately attempts to milk me. I glance at Jacob in his crib, still asleep, swaddled in a muslin blanket decorated with giraffes in neat rows. His head full of red baby hair. It's easier for me to get ready to go to class while he's still asleep, not needing me. We'll be leaving after the weather report. Always after the weather, the same time every morning, and Jacob will be bright eyed and ready to teach spin with me.

"*. . . and I'm Courtney Wheeler. Two young women were found dead at the bottom of a trail at Debs Park in Northeast LA this morning. The women's names are not being released at this time. Sources say the deaths may be related to an uptick in gang-related activity.*

"*We'll be right back with your daily weather forecast. It's another hot September, folks.*"

I've lived in this neighborhood for six years. We were able to afford a starter home. Now the starter homes cost more than our dream home. I live on the east side of town, an ungentrified holdout, but they are coming: the gentrifiers, the hipsters, and the Realtors aiming to become reality stars, HGTV flippers. Only a few years ago, these same opportunists wouldn't even set foot in Highland Park, but after the federal gang injunction, it's now just an ordinary working-class neighborhood ready to be taken over by the white middle class.

There is no uptick in gangs. The only *g* word that is *up*ticking is *gentrification*. Anything labeled *gang related* is code for Latino/Latina—and only when they're from a marginalized community does the media refer to seventeen-year-old children—*victims*—as young women or men. Just another way we make it easier to victim blame and dismiss the crimes against them. Isn't that right, Courtney Wheeler? You're so very good at sweeping murder under the *gang-related* rug. It's guaranteed with the tag—*gang related*—that the girls would never be mentioned again.

"That's what you're doing, right, Courtney? Isn't it?" I say. Quietly to the TV so as not to wake Jacob.

Courtney was an intern at the assignment desk when I was the general assignment reporter. She's an ass-kisser. An idiot with no journalistic ethics. Zero integrity. A wannabe entertainment-television host building her résumé in local news. She sped through newsworthy stories just to get to her comfort zone—celebrity fluff pieces. Courtney is more *Playboy* Playmate than *Good Morning America* anchor—tan, blond, and perfectly coiffed. She's on her way to becoming *the* local TV hero, five days a week—an anchor who can barely read her prompts but will blink, smile, and flirt for LA.

"Being a morning anchor is as good as being syndicated. I'm a verified celebrity on Instagram and X." Courtney sang this fucking millennial tune to anyone who'd listen when she got the gig. I hate how much everyone loves her—I'd find a way to get her fired, if they'd offer me my job back. I used to imagine some form of tragedy happening to Courtney, something—anything—that would send her away: a drug problem, a cheating scandal, DUI. Those thoughts were simple whispers. Harmless. Almost playful. Happy hour jokes with those that felt the same way. I look at Jacob, stirring in his crib. Trying to free his hand from the tight swaddle. I want to pick him up and hold him close to me. I promise myself I will never hurt him. I swear I will protect him from anyone who would hurt him. My baby—I love him in a way that makes me feel primal and scared at the same time, all the time. My fight-or-flight instinct has been on constant overdrive since his arrival.

I was never a talking head reading someone else's words like the Courtney Wheelers of the world. I'm an investigative reporter—was. I wrote the stories that I told. I controlled the message. My focus and hard, relentless work ethic made me a producer at *LA News First*. Traits that also eventually cost me my job there.

My engorged breasts are resisting the relentless suction of the Medela pump again—top of the line, courtesy of my husband's premier health plan at his middle management marketing job—while I pine over chasing the "gang-related" murder. "C'mon, give me another ounce, please," I say to my left breast. "I'll give you a lanolin massage later, I promise." My husband's alarm beeps from the other room—I'm running out of time. If I can squeeze out another half an ounce, Jacob will be content while I teach the sunrise spin class.

I hate it. All of it: spin class, life, motherhood, marriage, the news . . . I zone out to the police scanner a lot. Sketch out the crimes in my head. Talk out the story—how I'd interview the prime suspects. Investigate the victim's social media before the accounts were made private. Tally my eventual wins and losses.

I should be happy I'm alive. Not dead. Not at the bottom of Debs Park.

I love Debs. Before I had Jacob, I hiked there four, sometimes five times a week. A pro at the steep climbs. It had been my sanctuary, where I would overlook the entirety of Downtown Los Angeles when I reached the top—accomplished, going places, my future in full view, bright lights and all. Now, after Jacob, two girls dead, probably murdered, *my* LA is looking down. Pressing me into the inevitable domesticity of life with Evan and Jacob. Evan, the man I was supposed to see the world with but never did. We settled on a weekend in San Diego for our babymoon. Maybe we should have another kid—that's what Evan's mother wants. She never bothers to help with the one we have but insists we need a second. My mother leaned into motherhood, initially. She had four kids but ended up drinking more and paying us less attention. She resented us the moment we could talk. Told my sister, after her first child was born, "Don't ask me to help. I'll pray for you." She didn't bother to show up to my baby shower. She didn't come for the birth or any time after. Her only visit with Jacob has been over FaceTime, which she says "is enough." My stomach lurches like something wants out whenever I think about life as a full-time mom.

Now I have a child and no career.

Last week, before the dead girls were found, a mom at the Sycamore Park playground lost sight of her child in the time span of a hug. I knew we'd searched long enough for the child to have been snatched—it's always too long when the downward spiral of *what-if* has its claws in a mother's imagination. She'd called out, at first. Yelled. Run in circles looking behind impossible places to hide—the little amphitheater, the restroom that doubles as a homeless shelter at night, the cement tunnel that leads to a set of stairs that take you across the freeway and into Debs Park. Holding back tears, keeping the *what-if* at bay. Then, she screamed. I stopped, the line of day laborers at the seafood taco truck paused, the other mothers stared, I covered my mouth and shook my head, pulled Jacob close, too close, too tight. The little boy clambered out from under a bush, unscathed. He'd been playing fort. Three minutes. That's how long it took for our worlds to collapse—so fucking fragile. My hands shook. I went cold. My throat was closing, fighting against bursts of breath. I couldn't die in the park with Jacob strapped to my chest. But I couldn't breathe. Couldn't stop shaking. And my son, looking into my wide, distorted eyes, was absorbing everything— me. The mother speed-walked away—son crying, pressed hard against her—toward the line of blue, white, and black Teslas. Safety. I wanted to fall to my knees, scream for help, anything to make me better, not be what I was in that moment, but the journalist buried somewhere under the fresh-turned earth of motherhood wasn't going to let me fall into a full panic attack.

Jacob hasn't been back to that park: all those places to hide, all the people who would take him.

I grab the diaper bag, my nine-month-old baby, the three precious ounces of breast milk and head toward the door, the outside world. Making it to the car, getting Jacob in his seat, and driving away without talking to any neighbors is a need, not a want.

"Morning, Mrs. Evan!"

Fuck.

The thought of idle chitchat with Pete, the eighty-year-old ex-pimp, makes me want to peel skin. Why the hell is he out and about before six a.m. on a Thursday?

Pete ("My friends call me Pedro") always refers to me as Mrs. Evan—not my fucking name. He's currently shacked up with Beatriz, a ninety-two-year-old widow with dementia. She tends her rose garden most days, and he hawks the block in short-sleeve button-downs and gray polyester slacks. He could pass for sixty with his thick still-brown mane. I tolerate him, Pedro, because he was the first person to recognize me from television—the news, my actual life—when we moved in.

"What's new this morning, Pete?" If I don't engage, he'd hold back on the avocados and mangoes hanging from his—Beatriz's—backyard trees. Their front yard is a cement slab crowded with potted roses, and the whole place is enclosed by a rusted black wrought iron gate.

"You be careful." He tilts a pair of knockoff Ray-Bans and looks past me at the horizon of the city coming to life against the sunrise.

I turn—even though it's against my nature to turn my back on a guy like Pete—and put Jacob in his car seat. Pete moves in too close, says, "Two dead girls up there at Debs." Seems Pete has been up listening to Courtney too. "When you gonna be on the TV again, Mrs. Evan?" He's close enough now that I can feel his hot breath on my neck.

"I teach spin classes now, Pete."

He looks around me at Jacob. "Mom's on the TV all the time." He scans the street, pulls a dollar from his pocket. "No life for a beautiful boy like yours. Here"—he holds the dollar out for me to take—"a gift for the boy."

Images of killings, brutal thoughts of violence, imagined ways of losing my baby to a kidnapping or death are constants in my new life. And these images almost never involve strangers. Pete would go down like a sack, not too heavy either. I take the dollar; there is no refusing Pete. He walks away without another word.

Admittedly, sometimes I do feel safer with Pete always watching the block. He lets us know the comings and goings of strangers and neighbors—more like a criminal informant than a friend. I don't want him playing grandpa to my kid, though.

"Corey!" Elsie—the other-side neighbor—yells from her porch. Elsie and I are the same age, but her youngest is in high school, eldest in college. I look tired every day, but Elsie is dressed, hair curled, face done—red lips and big lashes; she is polished and ready for the day before I'm awake most mornings. A single mom with her shit together.

I look at Jacob. He smiles at me—probably shitting his diaper. Fucker. I smile back at him and then to Elsie and say, "Hey, neighbor." She is already down her steps and halfway across her cement yard by the time I turn around. Grass is a scarce commodity in these parts. Cement, and colorful, chipped decorative pots filled with desert plants and lemon trees are the norm. The old parts of Highland Park are trying to hold claim against the new—crowds, and buildings that sprout up next to landmarks like the Highland Theatre. Historic murals celebrating the culture of migrants are being painted over with bold blues and stark white. There are protestors standing guard at buildings marked for destruction on a daily basis.

"I won't keep you. I only wanted to see Mr. Guapo." She pushes past me to coo at Jacob. "How about that Courtney Wheeler this morning?"

"Two girls," I say.

"Gang related? Bullshit." She crosses herself, kisses a gold crucifix necklace, closes her eyes, and mumbles something. "I'd pay for a little performative charity from the news."

"Manufactured virtue. Forget her," I say. "Courtney wouldn't know a South Side Crip from an Avenue." I open the driver's side door.

Pete struts back toward us.

I say goodbye, tell Elsie to have a great day, and get in my car. It is Thursday, and I want to scream.

I open the police-scanner app on my phone, stick it to the dash mount. It beeps with static—a traffic stop. A whiff and I know Jacob has definitely shit himself. "You won't be sitting in it for long, pal." I look at the seat-mounted mirror that reflects his face in the rear-facing car seat. "Mommy loves you." He makes wide eyes and grabs at a toy hanging above him, pulls it down, and puts it in his mouth. I can't remember if I've ever washed it. It's probably crawling with bacteria—*E. coli*. "Jacob, don't put that in your mouth, please." I should pull over and take it away, but I won't. He's content, and being late is not an option my anxiety affords me.

2

The Cyclone Spin Studio is dark. The sky a beaten blue, fading amber streetlights not nearly bright enough to vanquish the monsters in the shadows. The hairs on my back tingle like I'm being watched. Jacob flails his arms and legs in his stroller. The mood lights are on around the studio, but the harsh fluorescent overheads remain off. I stand inside by the glass doors waiting to unlock them until I see the first familiar face. I change Jacob's diaper there, on the floor. "It's a full one, buddy. Good job," I tell him. Proud of myself because he's eating well.

My riders, the dawn crew, are pros. Newbies don't last long at *my* hour—some type A's hang in there, but they eventually have something more important to do. My crew could coach the class if they wanted to. Half the time, I believe they're riding to the voice in their head. No one's pedal stroke is in sync, and no one sits when I sit—I'm not coaching; I'm babysitting. But I'm not sitting at home, and that's all that matters some mornings. Evan feels otherwise. Wishes I were content to stay home with our son and relish the title of Stay-at-Home Mom like our—*his*—friends' wives.

"Here we go, gang." The boom of my voice over the mic is startling. "We're going around the world in three, two, one, and up!" There are several regulars in my class this morning. I try to remember each one in my head as I scan their faces. I want to make sure none are missing, that none of them are at the bottom of Debs, dead.

Jacob is parked in his stroller next to me, noise-canceling headphones wobbling on his head while he sucks on an empty bottle. Always happy to be with me. Right? Smiles more with me? Laughs more? Eats the healthiest foods—brain food? Feels safer with me? The voices are wrong: He doesn't need Baby-and-Me classes; he's got me—showing him real-life experiences. Not curated Disney crap from strangers. Be Corey the Coach: "We're going back around the world in three, two, one, and up!" I make eye contact with a rider in the last row. My heart races. I look to Jacob.

I tried leaving Jacob at home with Evan once. When I got home I burst through the door convinced my son was dead. Not dead, but inconsolable in the arms of my husband, who was stomping around the house, bouncing my baby too hard. I snatched Jacob away. Squeezed him. Fed him. Told him I'd never leave him again.

The funny thing is, Evan used to console me the way I console Jacob. Bad day? Evan would scoop me up in his arms, feed me street tacos and beer. Tell me he loved me, that he'd never leave me—it was us against the world, together. But that day I screamed at him for being too rough with Jacob. I yelled at him for not calling me to come home, told him he was irresponsible. I didn't mean any of it, but I couldn't stop myself from saying it. I wanted him to hurt. To apologize and mean it. To believe he'd been wrong.

If Evan ever considered a divorce, it would be because of that day— he left without a word. After he'd been gone for an hour, I called him. I knew there was a plastic bag in the house—that would find its way over my head if someone didn't intervene. My brain, since the birth, convinced me that plastic bags, sharp knives, ropes, and belts were weapons I could use on myself. Somewhere in my kitchen. Hiding. Waiting for me. Teasing me—could be a knife or bag or rope. After six voicemails of me sobbing, begging my husband to come home and be the man I married, he calmly opened the door, stopped to look at the mess that I was, went to the kitchen, and dumped out every drawer—no plastic bags, no sharp knives left, and he lifted his shirt to show me once again that he'd rid himself and the house of belts. Left it all there for me to see. I made the executive decision to bring Jacob to work with me—no matter what. He needed me. Evan agreed, not because Jacob needed it, but because I did. He held me that day, the way I held Jacob, the way he held me before we became parents. He told me we were "permanently tethered." Evan also convinced himself that day that I needed therapy and took it upon himself to find me a psychiatrist.

"Hill climbs: for ten, eight, then six. Let's go!" In front of this crew, I am confident; my voice holds authority—even if it only shows up in spin class, it's there.

"No break. Active recovery!" The riders hustle out of their seats, legs quivering—quaking from the glutes down. Faces going red, some purple. Sucking air. Suffering because I said so.

"Let's get ready to pick up that pace right here! Let's-go-let's-go-let's-go!"

When I tried submitting a swabbed sample of sweat from the studio to 23andMe—from a guy that fit the description of a serial rapist—it was returned in the mail weeks later. *Sample compromised.* It had been a long shot, I knew. I needed a contact at a forensics lab again. And an expense account. Evan makes plenty of money, but I no longer have my own bank account. All expenses are now discussed. He questioned my PI-license renewal fee. "Why, Corey? You're not an investigator—you're not even a reporter anymore. You're a mom—isn't that enough?" No. "Let it go. You don't need it. You've got me." He took me in his arms and held me in an Evan embrace. One that should make a woman feel safe and adored, I think. I only felt lonely and small. "Hey, did you make an appointment with that therapist Heather recommended?" he asked.

Heather, one of Evan's friends' wives. Evan was talking about me, my *problems*, with other women and men. I did not ask for the referral. I do not need a therapist.

Cyclone had a less-than-part-time receptionist when I started, Abby. She was paid in classes. I'd watch Abby discreetly stuff handfuls of the studio's towels into her gym bag while I taught. When Cyclone began selling sweatshirts and leggings, the towels were all but forgotten in place of these new goods. She wore the clothes like a uniform. A walking billboard for Cyclone. She told me her family was from the Philippines. That was all I knew.

I walked Abby to her car once, insisting I needed to stroll Jacob a bit so he'd fall asleep. In Abby's back seat: a small flat-screen television, filled garbage bags, and caging it all in was a papasan chair.

I pulled Jacob out of the stroller, stalling Abby from leaving. "Where you headed?"

"Home," Abby said.

"Where do you live?" I asked.

"Other side of Debs," she said. I imagined she'd meant Hermon. "That's all junk for the Goodwill." Abby rolled the car keys in her hand. "I should get going. See you later."

I followed her on Facebook when I got home. Her most recent public post was from over a year earlier. No Instagram. No TikTok.

Abby disappeared.

I asked around at the time, but no one knew anything about her or where she'd gone. Her Facebook is still silent. Please, God, do not let one of the girls at the bottom of Debs be Abby.

◆ ◆ ◆

"Corey!"

I scan the thirty riders in front of me. Each obsessed with a different perceived flaw of their body, splashing around sweat—the smell of body parts permeates the room.

"Corey!"

Mary. She screams a lot.

Mary's internet profiles all read the same: "Happy, divorced, happily no kids, happily middle-aged-young, I love bar trivia!" All profile pictures ten years old or filtered. She has dyed red hair that she passes off as natural—some blondes can do that. She isn't skinny or chubby but fits the model on quizzes for "average" body type. I've tried digging for the *real* Mary. Nothing. Clean and boring as fuck. Her form on the bike—bent at the hips, gentle slope over her handlebars—is perfect. Where she fails is execution and endurance. Mary cannot be pushed, a perpetual beginner.

"Corey!" Her screams become breathless and begging. I like hearing her suffer.

"Corey!"

Fuck.

Jacob starts to cry.

My left boob, the one that wouldn't give any milk earlier while I pumped the shit out of it, lets down and flows like a spigot. Another piercing wail from the stroller and my right boob lets down. I am all milk and sweat, sticky and warm. Why don't the plastic bags hunt for Mary, the knives pine for her throat? Is it because she's "happily no kids"?

I turn the music up, drowning Mary out. I plug Jacob's mouth with a pacifier. I can no longer hear anyone screaming. I think about Debs. Where the bodies were found. Did the killer turn up the music to drown out the screams?

Debs is an oasis for all the towns of Northeast Los Angeles, a.k.a. NELA. My town, Highland Park, is divided by the Realtors into two sections: east and west. I proudly tell everyone I live on the east side, right near the Gold Line off Marmion Way. Cyclone is on the west side of town. Most of the studio's clients reside on the west side, a.k.a. the "good" side.

My small neighborhood has a front-row view of Debs's green hillside and bird sanctuary. Wild parakeets in the early mornings, hawks circling. Coyotes slinking around, forgetting their nocturnal nature. We are insulated from the violence of Los Angeles. Everything we need is no more than a block in any direction. Who would come into our neighborhood to kill? Especially kids. For sure not "local gangs." They kill for gain, power, respect—out in the open for all to see.

Debs is where I went to let it all out when I was fired from *LA News First*. It's been three years since Sam, my intern at *LA News First*, said, "Ms. Tracey, we need to talk." She was a college junior with ambition. Sam was petite, probably still wore GapKids, and easily hid in plain sight. It had to have been a Tuesday when she came to me because I was doing expense reports.

"Sam, c'mon, it's Corey," I said. I hit her with a bunch of questions, which was how I avoided being asked for favors like a letter of recommendation. "Is summer break already over? I can't lose you! You're my best researcher. Do you think you'll do more research projects back at USC?"

"Fullerton," she said.

"Right, home of the Titans. Why are they called Titans? Weird, right?" I dug my phone out of my purse.

"Ms. Tracey," Sam practically yelled. "I need to have a word with you in private."

Oh. "Of course," I said. "Let's go to the conference room."

Sam chewed her fingernails the entire walk. I took a seat at the oversize table. Sam stood by the door, hesitant. I waved her in. She closed the door behind her but remained standing.

"I've wanted to tell you all summer but felt it was important that I prove myself as a reliable worker first."

"Sam, you're awesome. You are among the best I've worked with—that includes full-time staff."

"Thank you. You've taught me so much. This is hard," she said. Her arms crossed tight at her chest.

"Sam, spit it out." I took a big gulp of my coffee. It was cold—bitter from sitting all morning. I picked up a leftover printed agenda from the morning meeting and mentally checked off each line item.

"Derek—"

"Our production assistant?" I looked at her anew.

"He's been making things difficult?" Sam said.

I set the agenda down, attention on Sam.

"You think or you know?" I said.

She dropped her head, tucking her chin into her chest. A long second passed.

"I know." She jerked her head up. "He's been harassing me."

"I don't mistrust you—but these are big allegations—let's be very clear. Was he sexually harassing you?" I couldn't believe I was about to bust a sexual predator. Finally. In all the years I'd been there, I'd never had the opportunity to take down a monster.

"Yes," she said.

"Start at the beginning." I pulled out the chair next to mine for Sam.

Sam pulled out a Moleskine notebook from the pocket of her pants and opened it to the first page. She leaned in, reading her own words next to me.

June 19, Derek asked if he could take me out for a drink. I said no thank you. Then he blocked me from being able to leave the copy room and said, "You have to say the magic word, 'YES, mmm, yes' in order to leave."

June 22, Derek came into the office supply closet where I was stocking supplies and trapped me in the closet with him. He asked if I preferred boys or girls. I told him it was none of his business. He said he wanted to show me how real men treat women. Someone opened the door, and I was able to leave because of the disruption.

The notebook was full of this shit. Every page. Top to bottom. Weeks of it—more aggressive toward the end of the summer. Sam, although composed, was too young to look so tired.

"Why didn't you say something sooner?" I asked.

But I knew. We're taught to tolerate the abuse. Taught by every woman who told us to put on a sweater, cover up, stop flaunting ourselves. We're taught by every man who calls us *sweetheart, honey, darling* in the workplace—openly. We're taught, as young girls, that this is the price we pay for being born a woman.

"I needed this internship." Her leg bounced while she bit her nails to nubs.

"I have to take this to Jay. You understand that, right, Sam?" Jay O'Farrell was the general manager of the station. He looked at numbers. He was an MBA, not a journalist. Old and built like a man half his age, but it's Hollywood.

"Isn't there something you can say to Derek? Fire him?" Sam asked. Begged.

"He doesn't report to me, Sam. I don't have that power."

"I don't want everyone to know, Corey."

"You have my full support," I said. I ushered her out of the conference room. My heart was pounding hard enough to hear.

❖ ❖ ❖

16

With Sam's notebook in my hand, I knocked on Jay's door. I could see through the glass wall he was with someone. I paced in front of his door until they walked out. I went in, almost clashing with the exiting editor—Ed—and closed the door behind me. We had an inside story here. A scoop. The news was happening in our own house.

"Corey, loved the piece on those kids," Jay said. He looked at the entire news staff as one person. I hadn't done a piece involving kids in at least two months. He had the only Herman Miller Aeron ergonomic chair in the building. There were daytime Emmys lined up on a bookcase and photos of celebrities shaking hands with him. He was handsome, Botoxed, with the build of a president—broad shoulders, thick hair, tall.

"Thank you, yes. I need to speak to you about a matter involving an intern. I'm pretty sure you're going to want to call in HR or legal."

"Don't do this to me today. A rape?" The ease of the word coming out of his mouth felt assaulting.

"Derek, the fucking PA, has been harassing my intern all goddamn summer."

"Let me guess. 'Let's get drinks. Do you have a boyfriend?' Come on, Corey."

"You know."

"So Derek likes the new girl. What am I supposed to do every time an employee is attracted to another employee at work? Fire them? I'd have to pay unemployment up the ass. I'll have a talk with her. Is she graduating? Why don't we offer her the assignment desk when she graduates?" He took a moment to glance at his computer and, without looking back at me, said, "Are we good?"

I didn't only want Derek fired. I wanted him prosecuted, made an example of. I wanted to show the world we would no longer tolerate this behavior.

"No. Look at this notebook, Jay. A record of escalating harassment. What about *that* lawsuit?"

"She's an intern. It's her word against his. They were flirting; it didn't go the way she liked. Did you vet her story, Corey? Find out his side yet?

You're taking one person's word and feelings before you do your job. You're an investigative news reporter and an executive producer, or do I need to remind you?" He looked older, in a way I had not previously noticed. His generation was mostly retired. "Corey, calm down. It's not that big of a deal. What did she want to happen by telling you and not HR?"

He was right; Sam didn't want anyone to know. She wanted Derek to be let go by me so no one would know. I couldn't go to HR without her corroborating. I couldn't fire Derek, but Jay was right; I was an investigative reporter, and I knew exactly how to vet the story.

Fuck it.

The next morning, early, I angled a camera in a hanging plant in the corner of the galley kitchen that doubled as a break room. Coffee was brewed hourly, and doughnuts were the one cliché the station took seriously. I put a mic on Sam, planning for her to wear a baggy sweater that morning, making it easier to hide. She stood in wait for Derek to show up, while I watched on my phone from an empty editing bay. It only took ten minutes, like a shark to chum. The little shit walked in with his short-sleeve button-down and Dickies khakis. He used so much gel, there was no way to tell if his hair was blond, brown, or dirty. He deserved no mercy.

"You look hot. You should take that sweater off," Derek said to Sam.

"I'm cold," Sam responded.

"I'd love to warm you up."

"I'm good."

He moved closer to Sam, stroking her arm with the back of his hand. Sam moved to avoid the touch.

"One drink. I promise to make it the most amazing night you've ever had. You, me, my king-size bed." He grabbed Sam's arm as she tried to leave the break room. "You'll like it so much you'll beg to come back." Sam tried to get her arm free. He pulled at her, too hard. Coffee splashed onto her sweater. His free hand on her back now pulling her closer.

I almost kicked the door in and tackled the prick. But I had a plan.

I had enough to edit together a piece for the 11:00 p.m. news: SEXUAL HARASSMENT REVEALED IN THE MOST UNEXPECTED PLACE.

The piece ran that night. And continued to run on the internet for what felt like weeks. TikTok, Reels, TMZ, BuzzFeed, YouTube. The story got me fired.

The *LA Times* and *Variety* dug up a history of Jay O'Farrell's poor leadership. There were more than a dozen former employees who had given interviews—there wasn't enough hush money to pay anyone off. The network needed to show a strong stand against sexual harassment, so they gave Jay O'Farrell a payout and release of his contract. While I high-fived my team, walked around smug and happy knowing we had done something big, Jay was negotiating his final acts as boss. The viral sensation only revealed a larger truth, that doing the right thing is rewarded with equal punishment as doing the wrong thing. Before he left, Jay was allowed to let me go, and he made sure no one in the business would ever hire me again.

The network didn't care about me. They didn't care about the story. They didn't even care enough to fire Derek—they transferred him to the skeleton crew after Derek threatened to sue for defamation. The network needed to save its image, and that meant firing the boss, O'Farrell. They brought in a clean, shiny, young exec that screamed privilege. The kind of privilege that comes from generations of wealth—not experience. I wanted so badly to plead my case. But my emails and phone calls went unanswered. The new boss worked from an office abroad—France, Morocco, Dubai, no one knew—so showing up at his front door wasn't an option either. I added his name to the list of men I wanted to see on the sex offender registry, right next to Jay O'Farrell and Derek, but shit has a way of not rolling uphill.

So, spin classes, existential crises while I brush my teeth, and Pete in the mornings reminding me of who I used to be.

No one plans to get fired, get pregnant, and resent every six a.m. class they agree to teach.

When I was blacklisted from every TV news studio, Cyclone was the only place I wasn't ostracized. Cyclone's owners—Kat and Monique—accepted me. I was already taking two spin classes a day and bought a Peloton after I got fired. Kat asked if I was interested in teaching a class. She never asked for a résumé. Getting certified was a one-time eight-hour class on a bike. I did those eight hours easy—like I'd been training for the Tour de France, but it was an excess amount of hate that fueled me. No one ever talked about the news with me at Cyclone. Never. Now hardly anyone ever recognizes me, still carrying an extra fifteen pounds of postpregnancy weight. My clothes are stained, and my hair has been absent a haircut for months now. I hardly recognize myself.

The song changes abruptly, pulling back my attention. We are now on a run, seated. I glance at the clock. Thirty more minutes to go. "Keep those pedals moving. We'll take it to second position in eight." I wish I weren't grunting. Wish my underwear wouldn't ride up my thick postbaby ass too.

"Okay, people . . ." Every thirty seconds I have to say something. It's the Cyclone formula and my job. I don't have to think—spinning, moving, pushing, yelling, keep the thoughts away, almost. "You look too rested," I say. "Let's crank that dial up to a seven. I want those quads burning by the top of this hill." I never thought I'd be a cheerleader, let alone a cheerleader on a bike.

Before I had a nine-month-old, before I ever considered I'd be a mother, I started my career on the assignment desk for the local news—three hard-fought years. Then, six more years as a general assignment reporter. Nearly ten years in, a promotion to consumer investigations—the associate-producer title that came with it was a bonus. My job was to find and create stories, and small, local online community blogs became my first source. There were the usual cliché suspects—slum landlords, police overreach and profiling. Then an all-access pass to every complaint and egregious act was granted once I was admitted to private neighborhood Facebook groups—answer a series of questions to confirm I was a local and boom, I was in. The hard stories got less attention—issues like homeless children without food at the schools. Unless a prominent white business owner called the station to bring attention to the work "they" were doing to change the situation, the story was muted. No one wanted the guilt. My time was spent sitting at city council meetings where liquor licenses were distributed to white businesses with aplomb. Street parking curfews were implemented to curtail homelessness on the main streets, where apartment homes didn't provide parking, and residential streets were awarded special permits for their blocks. I hid in the shadows of local Facebook groups under the name Shirley Smith, but then again, so many of the commenters used fake names, what was one more person in hiding? I considered myself an elite internet spy. I became the go-to person at the station to find information on anybody—fake name, real name, dating history, and what they had for breakfast; I could find it in under an hour. If I couldn't, they were likely someone who would never be found. I studied profiles. I looked for patterns in behavior, messages on social media that could be dated back ten years; anything and everything told me exactly who a person was and how a story would be told on the air. I was never wrong.

My boss threw me on as the temporary executive producer of the Special Investigations team. The previous EP had taken a leave of absence—mental health break. As EP, I was in the story. Could produce the ones that needed telling. I was the white woman riding into a neighborhood on my proverbial white horse. I made everyone believe me. I would shed light on a problem. "Trust me, I'll give them the bad guy. Tell me what happened," I'd say on the record, and people did—they told me about their landlords. The lack of hot water, pest infestations, and mold causing skin conditions. I marked the culprits, and the station branded them for life. I felt high all the time; adrenaline rushed through my body when a story broke. I wasn't afraid of consequences. I couldn't be touched. The job was mine for keeps. Until it wasn't.

I see the front door of the studio swing open—Monique. Everyone turns on my look. I swear I can hear the pedals slowing. Monique sobers a room. She's not a somber person but has the potential to remove joy from any given situation. Has a style for the posh world of boutique fitness: tattoos, stringy dyed jet-black hair. Instead of the unofficial "instructor uniform" of yoga pants and a sports bra, Monique wears skinny jeans, ankle boots, and vintage death metal tees—Slayer and Pantera have been her latest go-tos—all in various shades of faded black. It's entirely possible she's bought Lululemon pants just to burn them. Monique Pascal is the most popular instructor at Cyclone Studio. The wait list for her class is a month out. She's my boss, and not one of the girls found at Debs.

Monique owns half of Cyclone Studio. When she's not teaching, she audits. Watches other instructors—*her* instructors—and never once have I seen her on a bike. It's fucking weird. Monique isn't even her name. It's a *nick*name for Monica. Also fucking weird—in my world, that's a name change with daddy issues attached. Worst of all, Monique approaches instructors in the middle of class—rude.

I cover the mic with my hand, mid-pedal stroke, and say, "What's up?"

She looks at Jacob, makes a face, and says, "This a regular thing, now?"

"He's fine," I say. I'm panting, breathless on the bike with my legs pumping. I have too much shit going on for Monique to get me going. Besides, I've spent too much time in network-TV land to fall for that alpha-boss bullshit.

Monique glares at me as she straightens the crooked headphones on Jacob's head. "Let's put that on tonight's agenda," she says.

"Tonight?"

"Happy hour meeting. Mandatory."

"I can't—" I'm too out of breath to argue.

"Make it work, Lieberman. You bring your kid to class and make it work—bring him to the bar and make it work."

I clench my teeth and smile. If I prayed, it would be for Monique to be ripped from crotch to asshole while bringing life into this cruel world—no epidural. On cue, Jacob laughs. Loud. My riders, most of them, giggle with him. I cover the mic, give her my not-so-subtle *fuck off* eyebrows, and say, out of breath, "Happy hour sounds fantastic."

"No cheating on the bike, Lieberman." With a deft twist of her wrist, Monique spins the dial on my bike to the right. My legs seize, leaving me immobile on the pedals while Monique saunters toward the exit.

Fucking asshole.

As soon as I see Monique walk past the window and out of sight, I wrap up class.

"You're off the hook today—I'll handle the bikes." I nudge past a couple of small-talkers. "Thanks for coming! Go get those doughnuts— you earned them." I need everyone out. I pull a giant roll of paper towels from behind the desk and a spray bottle of cleanser and begin wiping the bikes—handles, seat, resistance knob. Handles, seat, resistance knob. Handles, seat, resistance knob. I sing it in my head over and over: handles, seat, resistance knob. I need to be away from the studio. I keep glancing at Jacob in his stroller, still waiting by my bike.

"Great ride, Corey." It's Ray Hunt, a regular. "Maybe we can go the whole hour next time?" He laughs at himself, but it isn't a joke. Ray is lean and tight, part genetics, part spin. His hair is nearly gone, gray and cropped close where it remains. His cheekbones defined by the shadow of his neatly trimmed beard. He looks like a mature REI model. If I were into older men, he'd definitely earn a second glance.

"Sorry, did you sign in on the sign-in sheet?" I ask. Playing dumb is always the fastest way out of a conversation with guys like Ray.

"Yeah, Ray Hunt. I come to your class every week."

I know exactly who you are. Divorced, two kids, accountant. I finish the bike I'm cleaning and go to Jacob. Ray follows close behind. I start to lift my shirt, a universal sign for most men to leave, but Ray is a creeper. He lingers to see if I'll go all the way. I scoop up Jacob from the stroller and pop him on my breast.

Ray salutes me and leaves with the sea of remaining stragglers.

I lock the front doors, grab Jacob's stroller, and head through the back exit—reserved for staff only. There, the building is secured with a keypad entry, alarmed from midnight until 4:30 a.m. Behind that door is a gated parking garage reserved for managers. My car is on the street, parked right outside the gates. The parking garage requires an additional code. Another code I had to memorize. Both codes, the door and the gate, as long as a phone number. Both a singsong in my head. Neither written down anywhere for fear someone may see them, follow me in, take Jacob, and I'd never see him again.

The blinking fluorescent lights of the gated parking garage are so trite it's as if the place were created to be frightening for a woman walking alone to her car. The building is new, sterile, and empty, except for Cyclone. A bunch of storefronts with FOR LEASE signs hanging crooked. I speed up the stroller with one hand toward the dumpster to throw out the postclass trash and make it as far as one parking space. The hairs on my neck prick up. Fear grips me tight around my chest. Yet another day I'll carry the trash home with me in the trunk of my car—and yet another anxious conversation with Evan about why I'm bringing garbage home in the car with our son.

3

"Evan." My adrenaline is on a slow drip now. Jacob squawks in the back seat. "I have a mandatory meeting tonight."

"You're yelling," he says. "Calm down." The *calm down*s are new. I remember when Evan saved his condescension for other people—stupid people. I remember when it turned me on, his intellectual diatribes at a dinner party or work function. Now his *calm down*s make me want to stick my thumbs in his eyes.

"Sorry." Not sorry at all. "I have a mandatory meeting tonight."

"Did you tell them you're busy?" His voice sounds far away over the hands-free car speakers, too far away.

"Do you have me on speaker?" I ask. Jacob laughs, giggles, maybe at the sound of his daddy's voice. "It doesn't matter," but it totally does.

"How about I come with you and make the excuse for us?"

"No, Evan, I don't need an excuse made for us." I glance back at Jacob and offer him one of my best *Mommy and Daddy are great* smiles. "I promise I'll be there for the service," I say. I hang up on my husband while he's mid-sentence defending his position, but I'm not arguing. It's not a fight. I'm not fighting for anything. And I drive toward Debs.

◆ ◆ ◆

Yellow tape, with **CRIME SCENE STAY BACK** in a font aptly named Destroy, surrounds uniformed beat cops. Outside the tape, civilians and reporters are rubbernecking at human mortality. They look like extras waiting to be called to a movie set—as diverse as the homes in a gentrifying neighborhood. I drive past.

At the edge of the park, where it is overgrown and trailless, an opening has been cut in the fence—a locals-only secret. I skid to a stop, and a dust cloud envelops the car. I turn to Jacob and say, "This is going to be fun."

The baby wrap Evan's mother gave me was supposed to mimic carrying the baby in the womb. "It's all the rage," she said. "I see the mommies in mommy-and-me yoga all using them." Mommy-and-me yoga—who can cat cow with a baby hanging from their chest? My back ached just thinking about it. No, Jacob is better off at spin class, where the playlists aren't gongs and *ohms*.

The baby wrap is a fabric nightmare. Guilt keeps me from burning it in the backyard. That and Evan loves it. He wears it like it was designed for him. I resent his ease at being a dad—playing patty-cake and singing "Baby Shark" like he's done it all his life. He loves being a father—it suits him; he was born to play the role.

"Hang in there, buddy. Mommy has almost got it," I say. The wail was imminent—it creases his face, fills his eyes. That or he has gas. "You'll like the hike. Promise." He pops. I flinch and look around. I'm not the only person who knows about this spot, but there's no one.

I imagine the wrap cutting into Jacob's fat baby thighs. He nearly fell out the bottom, once, so it has to be extra tight. Maybe he doesn't want to be closer to me. Hates me.

"You don't hate Mommy, right? You love Mommy, yes?" His deep sigh in return is the confirmation I need.

I hug him tight even though he is wrapped against me. He hyperventilates into my chest, against the rhythm of my heart. "Mommy loves you," I whisper into his soft hair.

The hole in the fence is jagged. I cover Jacob's head and duck through. Nothing sharp catches me—it's a good sign.

On its busiest days, no more than a handful of people hike Debs. A soon-to-be-lost best-kept secret in Los Angeles. Overgrowth makes the path dark, chilly too. We pass a giant rock, thick with years of spray paint. The letters blend into alien shapes—a cryptic language few can read. Remnants of a fire, black ash in a near-perfect circle, beer cans—an altar to adolescent angst. I kneel down, let Jacob hang close to the soot, touch the earth. Footprints. Jacob's toes gently dangle in the sandy dirt.

My stomach turns, hard, like someone has kneaded my intestines. My lower abdomen gurgles, and my bowels rumble. The sweats hit me fast. I clench my jaw. My breath is caught between my lungs and the outside world. I cannot get the air in. I am squeezing my insides together. The panic comes when it wants—uncontrolled. Set off by an ounce of fear, a smell, a memory of something good—that's the thing Evan doesn't understand: I can't control it.

Stand.

Walk.

Keep walking.

I wrap my arms around Jacob, quick. Pull him tight. It startles him. He spits up, or pukes—the difference nominal. The distraction releases my chest, and I breathe in deep, hitting the bottom of my lungs at last.

I wipe off the chowder-like baby vomit from my chest with my hand. And then my wet hand onto my pants. I'm now entirely covered in baby vomit. I manage to get through the debris of overgrowth and onto the actual trail. The climb is brutal after spin class. My legs feel unreliable, but my heart is strong.

This—this is the part of the investigation I know well. I'm a fly on the wall—or trail—watching and listening. There isn't any danger: The police are everywhere, the sun is up, and people are loitering around, waiting to catch a glimpse of someone or something. All eyes are on the scene of the crime. Other mothers are pushing babies in strollers up and down the sidewalks, watching and listening, collecting gossip to take back to their mommy-and-me groups. Runners remove an earbud and slow, asking those standing near what's happening. The community gathers, talks, watches—we're all in it together. The beginning of the story, the rush of excitement—I feel it coiling through me.

Close to the top of the trail, I round a bend and almost bump into a black Kevlar vest. Before the group of officers turns, I squeal out a "Good morning."

I'm too loud. Jacob turns into a human siren.

"Ma'am," an officer with a visible cross tattooed on his forearm says. *Ma'am*—being called *ma'am* makes me feel more undesirable than I already do. I smile. My ears ring with Jacob's screams. "Ma'am, you're going to have to turn back around the way you came and exit the park."

"Is everything okay? Of course it's not if you're all here." They stare. I stare back. "I'm so sorry. Can I use the bench to change this guy's diaper, real quick? He'll cry like this until he's purple. I think it's diarrhea. He's been spitting up, and—I'm sure it's gas. Maybe a BM—"

"Fine, I have four myself—I get it. Be quick, please, and take the diaper with you. It's an active crime scene, and the park is closed until further notice." The officer looks young, too young to have four kids already. His uniform fits well on his frame, his arms are tan, and his dark hair is cut close, which makes me think military.

"Wow." I feign shock at the empty diaper. Jacob giggles. He's a terrible accomplice. "Do I need a police escort back down the trail?" Cops love a mom in peril. Keeping eye contact with the young one, I tightly roll up the diaper. "Can you tell me what happened?"

An older cop smirks, eyes hidden behind mirrored aviator sunglasses—his whole look screams *asshole*—and says, "No. You'll be fine heading back out on your own. Officers are scouting the entire park."

"Seriously? My backyard backs right up to the trails," I say. I hope they don't ask for my address—more lies. "Just want to be sure I'm not in any immediate danger."

The young-looking officer says, "You'll be fine. Keep a lookout for any suspicious behavior. Keep your doors and windows locked, and pay attention to your immediate surroundings when you get in and out of your car. We need you to go, now."

"Of course. I'm so sorry." I look around where the officers are paying the most attention, taking mental photographs. I turn back to the young-looking officer and almost inaudibly ask, "Does this have to do with the two girls on the news this morning?"

He looks at me and Jacob for a brief moment before answering. "Yeah, but I don't think you have anything to worry about. You should get going." He turns and heads back to his group.

There's a small path off the main trail, narrow with tall wild grass and brush that would scratch up bare skin. I hold my breath so I can hear what they're whispering—something about lunch, a promotion someone was passed over for, nothing about the girls.

I turn back the way I came and start walking, shuffling.

"Why are you two up here? You should be down there sweeping," a new officer says as he steps up onto the plateau. "From the way they were hanging on that tree, there's no way they offed themselves. I don't give a shit if forensics calls double suicide, I'm saying, no way."

"Ma'am." An officer is next to me before I realize it. "You really need to leave. Now."

I nod and take off. Hanged. Hanging. Suicide. Murder. My thoughts twist with visions of myself—Jacob next to me—bloated, hanging from a tree. No, I do not want to die.

"How the hell did she get up this far?" I hear one of the policemen say.

I'm not halfway down before X pings me with a notification.

NELAScanBoy Tweeted:

Latest—two girls, found hanged, Franklin seniors.

NELAScanBoy Tweeted:

Early reports say double suicide not homicide. I call bullshit. NELA Unite—make them investigate these kids like they're white.

My stomach burns—acid, GERD, hiking on an empty stomach, anxiety. I lean against the closest tree and throw up—it's definitely GERD from the way it burns.

Vomit drips from the back of Jacob's head and down the baby wrap. He laughs. I pull him close, squeeze hard, and run. His head bumps my chin—support his head or his neck could break, I remember. I cup the back of his head. Bite my tongue. The metallic taste of blood coats my mouth. Sweat beads down my neck, between my shoulders. My abdomen pools with a wet warmth that fills my navel.

At the car, I laugh-cry. I don't know when the sobbing began. Jacob isn't wearing a diaper—"You're a terrible fucking mother," I say. I'm soaked in sweat and piss. I spit blood, wipe crusted puke from my mouth, put Jacob in his car seat, stuff the baby wrap, soiled, into my tote bag, and say, "I know," before spitting more blood into the dry dirt.

The hurt for the mothers of those dead girls tears at me. It chips away at a corner of my soul. It plays a nightmare in my head. It's a place exposed only by becoming a mother, by being a mother, knowing absolute pain and unconditional love exist in a moment, and for a lifetime. The pain will never end for them.

Hanged. Girls. Young. Dead. Murdered.

I put my hands to my ears. Smack them to stop the voices—can a terrible mother hang her son? "Stop," I say. "Stop." I smack my ears again. What kind of mother would hang their own baby? Could I? Would I cry out that a demon made me do it? Would it be the truth? Voices shouting over ringing ears—intrusive thoughts pull at me. The taste of blood in my mouth mixed with excessive drool and a bittersweet taste of synthetic lemons. I think I'm telling Jacob it'll be okay, but the air is thin, and it's dark now.

4

I come to in the driver's seat. Jacob screaming. I pull the rearview toward me for a look. Blood, puke, dirt, sweat, all of it on me. Baby wipes—I use half the backup container to clean myself while Jacob wails. "It's okay, baby. Mommy loves you," I say over and over, broken on repeat. All the way home.

◆ ◆ ◆

I hold Jacob in the shower. Vomit swirls around my feet. Dirt sticks to the white subway tile around the drain. I cry, again, I think. Jacob now pacified by the warmth of the water.

My stomach is electric, zapping from one end to the other. I feel like a ten-pound mallet is stuck inside my chest—full, deep breaths nearly impossible. My breath cannot reach the bottom of my lungs. My anxiety works like a wave. It starts in my legs and ends in a thick lump in my chest.

◆ ◆ ◆

My hips haven't shrunk enough to fit into anything pre-Jacob. My swollen boobs warrant suspicions of breast augmentation. I have to wear a maternity dress—none of them are flattering, either, all of them a reminder of my inevitable decline. I hate the moms in mommy groups that talk about the "miracle" of our bodies—it's bullshit. I hate the moms with mothers, sisters, family at the ready to come help. I resent them so much I refuse to go to mommy-and-me classes or join mommy groups, where all I hear is: "It's so hard. My mom helps on Mondays and Wednesdays, and I still get no time to myself." I want to scream, "Must be so hard. I have no one."

And while my mother talks about the power of prayer to help me through the early years of mothering—as a child I never even witnessed my mother go to church—Evan's mother assumed we'd hire a nanny. After all, Evan's mother had hired herself a nanny, a night nurse, and a housekeeper.

At least Jacob is asleep now. Transferring him in the car seat carrier from house to car is the easiest thing to happen all day.

York Boulevard used to have grit. Now it bustles with craft beer fronts, yoga studios, and coffee shops replete with community tables—it makes parking a nightmare.

I text Evan to let him know I'm at the meeting.

Me: Hey, I'm here. See you at service

Evan: Need me to bring a change for Jacob?

I forgot to repack diapers. Bad mom.

Me: Sure. Thanks. Oh! I left a message with the therapist.

Evan: ♥

I had not called the therapist, but owed Evan something.
I jump at the sound of tapping on Jacob's window.
I push back a scream.
It's Kat—short for Katie—which is short for Catherine. My other boss. Twenty-six years old, cheerful to the point of weaponization, with

enviably youthful breasts that complement her wardrobe of sports bras. She co-owns Cyclone Studio with Monique. I want to dislike, even hate, Kat, but the amazing woman bouncing outside my window is beyond "pretty." She is smart, kind, and interesting. Shit—I actually admire and, quite possibly, like her. Even if I do constantly compare my thirty-eight-year-old first-time-mom bod and sucked-dry tits to hers. I pull at my nursing bra, adjust my breasts back to a horizontal line across my chest. Kat makes me feel like a friend. Motivates the little bit of me that wants, needs, a push. She is genuine. A threat to no one.

"Hey, no one would tow a car with a baby seat in it, right?" I ask while getting out of the car a little too fast.

"Not if it's parked legally," Kat says, a huge grin spreading across her face.

"Is this a legal spot?" I hate being here. I feel the crunch of time, getting to service and not disappointing Evan. I do not want another lecture on the effects of hormones after giving birth. The nagging about therapy. His attempt at concern. Evan needs me to be codependent. He thrives on me needing him. There was a time I had been able to fool him into thinking he needed me, and I cling to that memory. The texts he'd send me at work, literally: I need you. I liked to wear his used T-shirts after he'd leave my place in the mornings. His vanilla-almond-oatmeal-soap scent lingering. There were times I'd wear those tees to work under a blazer, tucked into slacks, just to smell him, Evan, all day. Only taking it off after he'd seen me in it.

Desperate for reassurance, I make a quick, nonchalant pose in my maternity dress for Kat. She rush-hugs me and squeezes what little breath I have while saying something about mothers being amazing and beautiful. I'm not listening—I'm worried she's feeling all the squishy parts of my new body. I wasn't always this way. I wasn't this bad before Jacob. Nothing could intimidate me when I was on the job—never. That part of my old self, I remember clearly. I just can't access it.

Kat flashes me a sparkling white-toothed grin. "Do you need help?" she asks.

"Sorry?"

"Getting Jacob out? Do you want some help?"

"No, I got it, thanks. Don't wait for me," I say. "You go in—I'll be there in a sec."

"You sure?"

I nod.

"Okay," Kat says. "See you inside. I'll buy you a shot." She walks backward into a parting crowd and waves.

The bar is a Cyclone scene. The spin-studio crew, even here in a group of twenty strong, has split off into its usual cliques. The Dudes: meatheads with diamond-hard boners about all things physical fitness—they're all wearing fitted, solid tees and skinny jeans showcasing all their goods. The Twentysomethings: too pretty to break a real sweat, so they coach off bike while they walk around the studio in flip-flops and Instagram their classes—they're still in flip-flops and leggings but with an off-the-shoulder, slouchy sweater that reveals most of their sports bra. The Moms: Coaching multiple classes a day helps them keep off all the post-postnatal weight and proves they're still as fit, young, and relevant as their teenage children, or ex-husbands' new girlfriends. Confident or loving what spandex does for them, they are still in leggings and tanks and flex every time they bring their wineglasses to their lips. And finally, the Misfits: an awkward, albeit successful, group of instructors who seem to actually love coaching and theme rides and unpaid team meetings held at craft beer bars and are all wearing cycling shorts and branded tanks—lifers.

I gawk. Shudder. Bubble. Sweat drips from my pits, down my back, behind my fucking knees. I feel dizzy—again. I can't remember if I've eaten anything today. It's hard to tell if the anxiety is swelling, if I'm catching a virus, or if I'm just hungry. They all blend; they all instigate panic.

Who am I amid this crowd of coworkers—in a maternity dress—with my sleeping son hanging from my arm in the seat that isn't snapped into the very stroller to which it belongs? A massive tote hanging from my elbow—stained and unorganized, it triples as a diaper bag, gym bag, and purse. And it's me; I am the person that doesn't recognize me.

"Let's all give Corey a big round of applause," Kat says through the crowd, through my self-shaming thoughts, her high-pitched cheer unmistakable.

The spin crowd claps, hard, almost competitively. It's loud enough to get the rest of the bar going. Even the *can't be bothered* bartender with the waxed moustache is clapping.

"What's happening?" I think I scream it because the clapping stops too fast.

"For volunteering to assist Monique and me with the big 'Spinning for a Cure' fundraiser next weekend," Kat says.

Jacob yells—is it a word? Did my son say his first word among these vapid type A's? No, he's too young. Wait, I volunteer for nothing. Ever.

"We couldn't do it without you," Kat says.

This feels like a trap. Nice people don't set traps, do they?

"Everyone, get up off those seats. Lift your glasses and in three, two, one, drink to Corey!"

5

For a moment, I imagine what almost dying would be like—seeing a flash of the life I lived—and I believe I want this. But no. Approval—that's the snare. My trap. The need to please has caught me.

My throat locks like it's trapped in a Lycra turtleneck.

Before I can politely decline, one of the Misfits pats me on the back. What I can't tell is if the others are nodding in approval or in relief that they weren't asked to do it.

More sweat—beads of it—upper lip, armpits, under the bra, the back, behind the knees, even my feet now. My face flushes—is it perimenopausal hot flashes? Loud rumbling tumbles through my intestines.

I have to go. The sun is nearly set, and Jacob would hear his first shofar tonight. And for god's sake, two girls were hanged at Debs. Why is no one talking about it?

I can leave. Tell them I'm not volunteering. Play dumb. New-mom brain. Memory fatigue.

The Twentysomethings rush me. One by one, I struggle to hug them, one armed, using Jacob as a shield in my other.

"You really shouldn't have been daydreaming during announcements, rookie," says Diane Loeb, one of the Moms. She is so close to my ear, I feel the wetness of her words. It tickles, giving me gooseflesh.

"Did you hear about the girls found at Debs?" I say.

"Yeah. Sad. Too bad—gang-related bullshit."

It is appalling how misinformation propagates so quickly.

"I gotta go," I say.

"Where?" Diane says, too loud. Sweet whispers gone. She's like that.

"Synagogue, it's Rosh Hashanah," I say. I sound like I've been saying it my whole life.

"You're Jewish?" Monique says. She is just in earshot, and I hadn't noticed. I should have. Being a spin instructor for over two years now has made me soft—my investigative skills out of practice.

"I am, l'shana tovah." I smile and try to hustle toward the door.

"Rad, l'shana tovah," one of the Misfits says. It's Kyle—the "Yogi on a Bike," according to Kat. Kyle wears Cyclone track pants he had custom-made and a Cyclone tank top. It's over the top—double logo— even for a Misfit. He looks like a soap opera actor side hustling as a spin instructor.

"Wait," Kat says. She looks serious. Kyle has his arm draped over her shoulder. "You have to do one shot with me before you go." The shot in her outstretched hand is dark and topped with whipped cream. It looks fucking delicious. No alcohol. Kat tries to get up, and Kyle comes with her, his arm still hanging around her shoulder. Brotherly or possessive, I don't care—it's too much.

"I'm still breastfeeding," I say, lifting Jacob in his leaden baby carrier. I swear to god, there must be bricks buried in the seat. But I want it. Bad. I can almost taste the sweet cream, the burn of alcohol. Kat leans in close to my face. She smells like watermelon Jolly Ranchers and fresh laundry.

"It's chocolate milk," she says in a whisper.

I grin.

She grins.

We toast.

I throw it back—down the hatch. Fantastic. Full-fat cow's milk and heavy whipping cream without question on the list of things I don't consume anymore because of the baby—dairy sensitive. Jacob giggles and makes a face. Poopy or gassy. The conundrum now? Let him sit in his fecal-filled diaper or change him in a bar bathroom. Unimaginable choices, things I never considered a year ago.

Kat wipes cream and chocolate away from her lips with the back of her hand and says, "I'll text you about the fundraiser stuff. It's going to be hustle-hustle, with some long days, obviously fine to bring Jacob."

I can't find the words to reject her. "Sure," I say.

"Love you, girl. Have fun at church," Kat says. She moves out from under Kyle's arm and gives me a final, awkward embrace—her arms stretch around my bulk. Her hand, for a second, feels good touching me. It's been so long. I forgot that I actually do like human touch, occasionally.

"Sounds good." Jacob will ride in poop to synagogue.

6

Synagogue is a massive disappointment—the cantor is out sick. Evan, on the other hand, who has a standing appointment with his hairdresser every three weeks and a five-o'clock shadow that naturally defines his high cheekbones, looks both intoxicating and impeccable. We try to make the best of the evening by singing too loud during the Avinu Malkeinu. Jacob loves it. That's the thing with Evan—I may not have trusted dating someone so intense, but his goofy ability to sing a prayer off-key louder than the rest of the congregation was what attracted me to him. And when I say "rest of the congregation," we're talking fewer people than attended our wedding. Most folks celebrate the High Holidays at the swankier services in Los Angeles.

We convene outside after the service. This is the part that's hard to tolerate. Questions always seem to gravitate toward my dead career as a TV journalist. Even here, where community is paramount, no one is talking about the two girls found dead at our hiking trail.

"Corey, when do you plan on going back to *LA News First*? How long is your maternity leave?" Judy Lang asks. Her yellow-blond wig just slightly askew. I want to reach out and adjust it. I want her husband to gently take her aside and fix it.

"Corey's decided to take a leave to be with Jacob full time," Evan says. He's made a habit of speaking for me. We agreed I wouldn't say I was fired. But it's been three years.

"Did you hear about the two teenage girls found dead at Debs this morning?" I ask Judy.

"Gang related," she says. "I hope this doesn't become a thing."

"You hope what doesn't become a thing?" I ask. I know I'm baiting her. It may be unfair, but I need to feel something other than anxiety, and anger usually feels good.

"Gang activity, dear. Just like Courtney Wheeler said."

"I was fired," I say. "From *LA News First*. I'm not on maternity leave. And Courtney Wheeler sucks at her job." It was more of an announcement—no comment necessary. Jacob hiccups—hard and loud. And then a wail of discomfort. I lightly pat his back and say, "I better get this guy out of here. It's been a long day."

"Corey, we agreed we weren't going to tell people," Evan says. We're in the car with no escape from the conversation.

"No, Evan, you didn't want to tell people. I don't care what your USC-business-school friends think, or your parents. I fought back against a sexual predator, and you should be—"

"I should be what? Supportive? Proud? I am—I'm taking care of all of us. I've given you a life without responsibility."

"Wow."

"You know what I mean. I just want you to be happy again." I fight back tears of anger. When was the last time I was happy?

We pull into our local spot, Dot's. It used to be a twenty-four-hour diner with predictable bad coffee, burnt toast, and perfect pancakes. That was before. Evan would meet me at midnight. We'd drink too much of the shitty coffee and pound carbs while I filled him in on whatever story I was breaking. We excited each other. Now Dot's is like every other old, local spot—new hipster owners who think they shouldn't have to work so hard for a society that has failed them, plus potato-beet pancakes instead of hash browns. I admit the "global eclectic fare" isn't terrible, but there was something special in that burnt toast and stale coffee.

Jacob grabs at sweet potato fries in duck fat. Evan picks at his quinoa salad in silence, and I want to scream. It's only seven p.m. The new owners close the restaurant at ten p.m. Evan likes to be in bed before nine, and I'm not investigating news stories anymore.

My phone erupts. I look at the screen. Saturday 5:42 a.m. I've been watching the numbers change since 4:16 a.m. Friday had come and gone, and I don't remember it—feedings, diaper changes, there may have been some *Sesame Street*; it's a blur.

Kat: let's meet today for coffee!

Kat: noon

Kat: place across from studio the one with boba xo

Me: Okay. The one with the boba. See you at noon.

Kat: can't wait!

Kat: coffee on me!

I've been awake since three a.m., give or take—mothers, murder, and bad coffee on a thought loop. Jacob is next to me doing his best to eat in the side-lying position. He keeps eye contact with me while he suckles. The intimacy forces communication, so I sing Christmas carols—the only songs I know all the lyrics to by heart. I'm on "Rudolph the Red-Nosed Reindeer," Jacob's and my favorite. Evan snores just loud enough for me to start thinking of plastic bags and knives.

"How did you hear about the two girls found at Debs?" Evan asks. He pours coffee—a second cup. I hand him Jacob. My palms go cold thinking about the hot liquid spilling on my son, scalding him, ER doctors clamoring to save his skin, asking how such a thing could happen.

Trust your husband, Corey. "Hmm?" I say.

"On the news?" Evan sets his cup down and shifts Jacob to his other side.

"No." I turn away, look out the window at a broken slat in the back fence. Evan was supposed to have fixed it last fall. I wipe my hands on my pants.

"NELAScanBoy? Such a stupid handle. Why doesn't he just put *Chris Villar* like a grown-up?"

I want to scream at him—sure, and maybe his home address and phone number, and if that's not enough for someone to find him, the make and model of his car too.

"I think to protect himself from retaliation," I say. It comes out softer than the thoughts in my head. I often wonder if Evan can hear any of the resentment in my thoughts. It's stupid—he's not a mind reader—but just in case, I change the tone in my head anyway.

"You know you can tell me the truth, Corey. If you're talking to him again, tell me."

"And what is truth to you, Evan?"

"I don't want you hiding things from me," he says.

"I hike up Debs all the time," I say.

"You haven't been out there since Jacob was born."

"I was up there the other day." I shouldn't have told him, but he wouldn't know it was the same day the bodies were found.

"Did you go alone? With Jacob?"

"It was the middle of the day. Fuck, Evan. We're fine."

"Don't go alone anymore." It's an order. I don't answer; I stare at him. Evan believes, since we've become parents, that everything I do needs to be a joint decision. To Evan, motherhood means surrendering my autonomy.

"Should I just sit in the house all day? Maybe I should pad the walls for myself and Jacob."

"I'm not allowed to worry about you. I'm not allowed to not worry about you. Got it. Did you actually make that therapy appointment?" My teeth start chattering despite the warmth. My body shakes—I take Jacob from him and hold him firmly to control any physical response that Evan may notice.

"They scheduled me," I say. I can't stop lying. I can't make the appointment. The pressure of it is exhausting.

"When?"

"I wrote it down—next week," I say.

"Great. That's good, Corey. I doubt they'll put you on Prozac like your mom, but it'll be good to know what's wrong with you." Evan made a habit of using my family history against me. I blame myself for disclosing my family's secrets in the first place—a history of depression, bipolar disorders, and addiction as far back as my great-grandparents. *Generational trauma* the experts call it. I left home—drove almost three thousand miles away when I was twenty-one—to avoid catching any of the mental breakdowns that seemed to disproportionately affect the women.

"There's nothing wrong with me. I'm a new mom—it's normal. Can we just stop talking about me and therapy, please?"

Evan makes his happy monkey face at Jacob and in a playful voice asks, "How about I take you guys on a hike?" Jacob shrieks and giggles in response to his dad.

"I don't think now is great. Dead bodies."

"We can go somewhere else."

"I'm working."

"That's right. What's the charity ride for? I'm excited to tell everyone that my gorgeous wife is not just a new mom but also a budding philanthropist."

I'm mindlessly shoveling soggy cereal into my mouth while Jacob grabs at the spoon, winning a Cheerio every time. I am trying not to scream at Evan's interpretation of me, this event, my life. Ah! "It's called Spinning for a Cure. Cancer . . . maybe AIDS? I don't know. Google it." I put my bowl in the nearly full sink. A mug with the remnants of yesterday's coffee has me thinking about Kat and the chocolate-milk shot from last night. Maybe I'm not a total wreck of a human—not if someone like Kat wants me around.

"Google says it's cancer." He flashes me a wide grin as he pulls me and Jacob into an embrace. And just like that, the argument, the emotions, his emotions are gone. Soothed by a smile and an embrace, while mine sit brewing deep in the pit of me, around the edges of my brain. I want my anger and frustration at him squelched as quickly as his. It isn't fair. I want to smile, but I can't.

"Ow-ow-ow!"

"What's wrong?" Evan says.

I push away. "You squished a baby foot deep into my sternum," I say. Jacob latches his milk-covered sticky fingers into my hair and pulls.

"Shoot, sorry," he says.

"It's okay, I'm fine." I am anything but fine.

Before Jacob, before marriage, sex with Evan was easy—daily. We'd spend entire weekends in bed without needing a break. Everything was easy when it was all sex and jokes. We didn't argue. There were no heavy discussions, only heavy petting. It wasn't until our wedding night, right before we would sleep together as husband and wife for the first time, that he asked about kids. I needed a year, maybe five. I was still proving myself at work in my role as the executive producer and didn't want to be replaced while I took leave to have a baby.

"We're not in our twenties anymore, Corey," Evan said.

"I've worked too hard to get where I am in my career."

"We're talking about one child."

I swear he looked like Clark Kent back then, my Superman.

Thank god it didn't happen right away. I felt relieved. And, for the first time, I watched Evan's moods darken. They shifted like loose gravel on the trail. I wanted to please him *and* be the best at my job.

We tried, for a year. Evan became insistent. I was first to get a confirmation on fertility. With my eggs ripe and ready, Evan withdrew that summer. I'd see him sitting in his car, idling in the driveway, talking to himself. Eventually, his sperm was counted. Both of us were fine.

"I think you work too much and it's stressing out your body," Evan said. He suggested I cut back on my hours. Step down from my position. Take more vacation days.

It was October, three days before Halloween, when I started to hate sex, our relationship, the marriage. There is nothing like scheduled intimacy for building a strong foundation of resentment. Of course, through dedication and grit, the expectation and disappointment became a zygote. The pregnancy, having Jacob—it was supposed to make us right again. Channel our suffering into a utopian entanglement of love and support.

"I need to shower," I say. I hand Jacob back to him.

I grab a second mug of decaf and, on my way into the bathroom, the police scanner from the nursery. With the door locked, I turn on the shower, then sit on the floor with the scanner pressed to my ear. It's like trying to watch porn at my parents' house, shameful and exciting.

"Corey." Evan knocks on the bathroom door.

"I'm trying to shower," I respond. I toss the scanner in a drawer.

"Elsie needs to talk to you."

"Tell her I'll text her later." I don't want to deal with anybody. Not our neighbor, not my friends that spoiled us with gifts at our baby shower but haven't called, texted, or visited since, nobody. I cut myself off nine months ago from the outside world. Detached from friends that didn't understand it—I was a mom now. I owed no one anything—no one except Jacob.

"No, babe, she's here, come down," Evan says. I hear Jacob squeal in Evan's arms.

I splash water on my face and hair, throw on my bathrobe, and go downstairs.

Elsie is on the couch, arms wrapped around another woman—she's petite enough that Elsie hides most of her with the embrace. The woman—sobbing—is wearing a black long-sleeve shirt, black velour sweatpants, and flip-flops on her feet. Her black hair is wrapped in a bun at the nape of her neck. Her hands are trembling.

"What's going on?" I ask.

"This is my friend Lupe," Elsie says. "Her daughter is friends with my Dani—they go to the same high school." Dani is the youngest of Elsie's kids, a senior at Franklin High School. Dani is loud with her friends, and quiet and respectful in front of adults. She's as tall as her mom, with the same artificially curled brown bob, but about twenty pounds thinner. I like Dani. "Lupe's daughter was one of the girls found at Debs Park, Corey."

I look for Jacob. Evan has him. I look to Elsie; she doesn't make eye contact. *Hanged.* I do not want to know this woman now. I don't want the death of her child to spread to me—contagious. I do not want her in my house, her pain, her fear, her loss. Breathe, Corey, breathe. I start to count in my head up to seven, release the breath.

"I'm so sorry," I say. Blinders, a wall, my brain is working to block out the thoughts associated with a violent tragedy.

Lupe hands me a picture. A senior portrait. I recognize the girl immediately—her long, straight, jet-black hair worn down and parted in the middle. A dimple in her chin and on her left cheek, and amber-colored eyes that you couldn't help but notice. She's a stunning girl—you couldn't forget meeting her.

"I remember her," I say. "She helped me carry groceries when I was so pregnant I could barely move." I'm not sure this is true, but someone had, and it may as well have been this girl. It may have just been Elsie's kid, but it sounds good. "What's her name?"

"Araceli," Lupe says.

"The police are telling Lupe that Araceli and her friend, Natalie, could have killed themselves." This breaks Lupe. I can't imagine weeping in a room full of strangers. Elsie says, "Or they were in with some gang." She spits out the word *gang* like it is coated in venom.

"It's not true," Lupe says. "Araceli, she was going to go to Cal State. Natalie too. These are good girls. Catholic girls."

"I believe you," I say. Hearing her use the present tense makes it all seem more real, visceral, like it happened to all of us. There's a surge behind my ribs, a warning sign. I look for Jacob again, grasp at my son as Evan bounces him toward me. I see my husband in that unspoken moment and know he understands.

"You have to help, Corey," Elsie says.

"I'm sorry? I don't—?" I twist back and forth with Jacob in my arms while talking, calming myself more than my son.

"I remember you from the TV," Lupe says.

"I don't do that anymore," I say. "We can probably help with a fundraiser at the spin studio—"

"Or if you need money." Evan starts riffling around, feeling for his wallet. He sounds like an asshole. We both do.

"You're an investigator," Elsie says. "You have friends at the news stations still, right?"

"I was an investigative TV journalist," I say. "Not a detective."

I look at Lupe and Elsie. My heart aches knowing the pain Lupe must feel. I feel it, too, and my baby is safe in my arms. Elsie's face wears the marks of a woman who has been crying. I think about her daughter

Dani, Araceli's friend and classmate. It could have been Dani hanging alongside Araceli. Evan pinches my arm, snapping me out of my horrid reverie. "I'm not sure if anyone will talk to me," I say. "It's been a while, but I'll see what I can find out. Okay, Lupe?"

"She wouldn't have killed herself," Lupe says. "She doesn't know any gang people. No one will listen to me."

I wish I could go back—not just a week, but three years. Before I was pregnant. Before I was canned. Before I became this. Elsie and Lupe leave with a promise that I will do something. Evan shuts the door behind them and locks it.

"You don't have to do this. You know that, right? It's okay to send an email and leave it at that," Evan says.

"That woman lost her fucking kid, Evan. I'm not sending an email and leaving it at that. I'll make some calls, see what favors I can still cash in on."

"No, it's not your job, Corey."

"Thank you for the reminder." I hand Jacob back to Evan. "I need to get dressed."

"I didn't mean it like that." I hear Evan mutter as I head upstairs.

"I know," I call back. You never do.

We had a saying in the news: On time is late. Early is on time. Show up the night before and you might get the story first—you can't catch a thief if you're late to the crime. The boba coffee shop is across from the studio; being half an hour early isn't difficult.

The café is a square-shaped room with four long communal tables. I pick a seat and dump Jacob's diaper tote on it. Claimed.

"What can I get you, ma'am?" the barista asks. She is young. Her green hair showing off brown roots. Her apron hangs loose on her frame—a choice. A small nose stud pokes out of her oily skin.

"God, please don't call me ma'am."

"Sorry, ma'am, habit." The girl's face reveals nothing. But I know it's not an accident. Being dismissive is a rite of passage for young people.

"It's okay. I'll take a large decaf, no boba. And a shot of caffeine."

"I'm sorry?"

I take her pen—Jacob makes a grab for it—and draw a crooked line dividing the cup in half. "I want you to top off my decaf with some caffeine."

"Half caf. Got it."

The first crooks I had the pleasure of dealing with on the Special Investigations team were mail thieves that had plagued a community for at least a year. The cops were too understaffed to deal with it, and delivery persons were too underpaid. The criminals were not slick; it was an easy, opportunistic gig. From all the home–security cam footage we reviewed, it was the same couple every time. He was tall—six foot— white, shaved clean, brown hair, thirties or forties. She was medium build, dirty blond—forties. They looked like they could be anybody's neighbor, anywhere.

My camera guy and I set up a sting. We hired an Enterprise van for a day, put an Amazon T-shirt and hat on one of our interns, and sent him up to homes with empty brown boxes. After six hours of sitting and watching, we caught the guy. Turned out the guy and his girlfriend were renting a house on the corner. Two assholes who stole people's shit because they could. Our intern tackled him while we kept recording. He pinned the thief down with his entire body while I phoned the cops. It felt good. Better than good—climax good. I miss that feeling. Doing important adrenaline-rushing shit. I miss my team . . . I miss Chris.

I pull out my phone and search Instagram for Araceli while I wait for Kat. I start with Elsie's daughter Dani. I scroll through her photos, looking at their tags until I find Araceli. Photos of duck-lip pouts, short skirts, and lots of friends hugging and smiling and hamming it up for the world of social media—kids doing typical kid stuff. I use her Instagram handle to search TikTok.

"Hey, Lieberman." I startle at hearing my name come out of Monique's mouth and not Kat's.

I chose a seat for its visibility, and here I am still caught off guard. My senses are dull. Monique stands out in this modern, sterile, *trying too hard* environment, where everyone is wearing the same thick-rimmed eyewear in different colors. Fuck, I stand out like a sore thumb in mom leggings and Birkenstocks, holding a baby while scrolling TikTok.

I watch Monique's lips move but don't catch what she's saying.

"Sorry, the acoustics are so bad I can't hear you. What?" The acoustics, the music pumping through invisible speakers, the din of the crowd.

"I said, 'Hey.'"

Jacob shrieks—it rings in my ears, making my eyes water. "Hey," I reply, yelling over him.

Monique rolls her eyes, flops her macramé bag down on the table. I can make out the contents inside through the holes—brush, phone charger, towel, a pair of leggings. Her combat boots are untied; she might trip while trudging over to the counter. The barista looks afraid—her green hair childish, not punk, in comparison to Monique. Jacob grabs at Monique's purse while I continue to x-ray its contents—I add two car fobs to the inventory list.

"Jacob, no." I lightly swat his hand away. He squeals. It becomes a game—he grabs Monique's bag. I tap his hand with a "No!" Again and again and again. Happy. Jacob is happy. Happy all the time, sort of, I mean, he's a baby. "You've got nothing to worry about, huh, buddy?"

Monique slouches into the seat across from me, slurps purple boba, and scratches inside her boot. Jacob slaps the table. She looks at me like I have to do something about his bad manners. I look at her boot.

"What are you doing here?" I ask.

"We have a meeting—charity ride," she says.

"Right, shit, sorry, obviously." Jacob goes for my coffee. Monique catches the cup and places it out of his reach.

"You're a feisty guy," she says.

Jacob drools and stares. He squirms, pushing his chubby feet into all the spaces of my body where he can find leverage. It hurts.

"Yeah, he is." I grimace through a hair pull and an elbow to the lip. I dig for a toy in the tote bag, but the only thing I can find is an aspirin bottle. I put it in his hand, and Jacob shakes it with vigor. "I thought it was going to be Kat and me, that's all. Surprise." I am compelled to fill all the dead space with words. "The more the merrier."

And then, Jacob nearly blows out his diaper. It's louder than the murmur and noise pumping through the small café. Several people turn to look at me. Yes, people, my baby took a shit. The odor is instantaneous—a combination of sour milk and yogurt. "His belly has been sensitive all week," I say to Monique. I pull out Jacob's changing pad and lay it across the bench next to me as Monique stares. I place Jacob on the pad and rip off the soiled diaper, do a fast-and-dirty job with wet wipes, and snap him back into his onesie. I wrap everything up tightly and neatly, binding the bundles separately—diaper and dirty wipes in one sour ball, and clean wipes and changing pad stacked back inside the tote bag. My work merits applause—there is only judgment by onlookers.

"So, where's Kat?" I ask.

"Aren't you supposed to use bathrooms for that?" Monique says.

"There's no changing table in there, so . . ." I smile. "Did you teach class today?"

Monique's brow is damp. The baby hairs framing her face are matted to her skin. She glistens with sweat. Her face is flushed, cheeks pink.

"No," she says and swings her legs onto a stool at the table. "You have shit on your arm."

"Fuck. Thanks." I try swiping it off with another wet wipe, but the yellow glob is like dried glue. "Did you take a class?"

"What's with the inquisition?" Monique asks.

"You look like you came from the studio. That's all."

"So do you," Monique says.

She's right.

"Fair. Listen, I'm trying to make small talk, shoot the shit. That's what my dad used to say—he's not dead, we just don't talk anymore."

"What's your deal, Lieberman?" She overenunciates the syllables as if sounding it out for the first time—*Lee-burr-men*. "You want to start making more of an effort with the studio, is that it? Are you looking for advancement in your career or you want to open up your own place?"

Jesus, is this the impression she got from me? Career? The answer— an emphatic no. I want to know what Araceli was doing the night she was hanged from a tree next to her best friend. Did she scream, fight, claw at her murderer? What was her last thought before her neck snapped? I need to find out who killed her and her friend. I would get right back into my bathroom and run the police scanner for clues as soon as this meeting ended. That's the only effort I'm interested in making.

"I was shocked to hear you volunteered, Lieberman, but that's the initiative we need. Can I be honest with you?" Monique reaches around and grabs the cocoa powder from the communal coffee station and dumps it into her cup.

The rush of secrecy to come, or the caffeine kicking into overdrive, has me riveted.

"If you're comfortable sharing, I'm always open to listen," I say.

"Getting people to do their jobs, sub for classes, sign up for anything charity related, or even fold clean towels is like asking for a fucking kidney. People suck, Lieberman. We need someone like you to start taking on more responsibility."

"Like me?"

"Competent. Mature," Monique says. I wonder if she means *old*. "We need help. You don't have to answer yes. We can start with the charity ride and see how you do there. A donkey could handle the job, or even a new mom."

"Is that my official performance review?" It's clear Monique has no idea who I was. Who I'd been.

"You're good on the bike. People seem to like you. You bring your baby to class."

"Wow. Moms are impressive multitaskers—we can manage a lot at once. More than most." It's a quote from a new mommy blog I read recently—not my own words. I'm not sure it's true, but I want it to be.

"Yeah, I know, chill. My mom raised us alone. Two kids, two part-time jobs." Monique smiles a genuine smile. It's the first time I notice how bright her eyes are—a translucent blue. "So, do you have postpartum issues?"

"Huh?"

"You seem wound up a lot. You bring him with you to work all the time. Do you have some sort of postpartum thing? Like hormones and crap running amok?"

Who is this woman? Was that an accusation? I want to slap her, but I can't tell if she deserves it or if this is friend flirting for Monique. My mind goes dark like a light has been dimmed in the café. I check in with my head. We're okay, right? Yes.

"I don't know anything about that." I pick up my coffee and set it back down without drinking. My hand is too weak to bring it to my lips. "What do you and Kat want me to do for this charity ride? I don't know anything about fundraising or the charity. Well, I know it's for cancer, so that's A-plus for me." What fucking charity ride would anybody think was not A-plus? I'm an asshole.

"We need you to motivate our riders and our instructors to come participate."

I spend most days wishing I could sleep through them. My only motivation comes from getting out of the house without having to answer Evan's questions about how I'm feeling.

Monique says, "Can you call and place an order with our vendor to get more Cyclone tanks made?"

"Do you have their number or a company name?" I'm outside my body, asking before thinking. Committing to this horror without an attempt to end it.

"Yeah." Monique stares at me, expressionless, silent. "Do you want to write this shit down, or are you going to try and memorize it?"

I do not want to work with this twit full time. But I pull out a notepad and pen like a fucking secretary. "Do you have a master email list I can use to send to our clients and instructors?" I ask.

"Way to take charge, Lieberman. I'll send it to you tonight. I'll text you the T-shirt order." Monique almost laughs at my pen and notepad. I look out the window, still anticipating Kat's arrival.

"Do you think Kat's okay? It's not like her to be late, is it?" I picture a limp-bodied Kat hanging from a tree. "I'll shoot her a text." I pull out my phone. Monique snatches it.

"Don't worry, I'll wait for her. But here, I'm typing the number of our vendor into your phone so you don't lose it. You have mommy brain, right?"

Monique's form of sympathy seems to be smashing down every one of my buttons. That or she's joking. Either way, it feels like a jab with a sting that is absolutely correct. Monique is wading through all my bullshit and noticing me. I hate her. I like her, too—maybe more than ever.

"Okay, here you go." She hands me back my phone, and a list of instructions is typed out. "You're all set. I'll text you more later."

"Great." We sit there. Looking at each other. Not talking. Jacob starts flailing his arms, begging to be freed from my lap.

"You can go. I'll wait for Kat," Monique says.

I look around for a clock, something to tell me I've been here for more than ten minutes.

"It's twelve forty, Lieberman. There's a clock on your phone."

"Right—sorry, I do need to go. Thanks." I jump up, knocking over my coffee. I fumble trying to sop it up. "Sorry," I say. Clumsy, my hands foreign, alien, as if I am watching them grasp hold of my tote. I stub my toe. Stumble. Jacob and I make eye contact, have a moment in the silence between falling and not falling. I catch myself. I make surprise eyes at him. He smiles as if he weren't almost smashed by his mother. I push through the doors without looking back to check if the entire place, Monique, is laughing at me.

I drive around the block until Jacob is asleep—a puddle of snoring baby drool. I look at the clock on the center console, 12:48 p.m.—a new class would be starting soon. I park across from the studio, watching and sipping the salvaged coffee while a class of sweaty Saturday riders exits and a new batch of fresh-faced attendees files in. Everyone is smiling— excited to burn the fat. I check the studio's schedule on my phone. The next class is beginners. Kat's class. If she isn't already inside, then she will be soon. Why did she miss our meeting? Maybe I did something. Maybe she's sick of dealing with my bullshit, my baby, mommy brain. People without kids don't get it, can't recognize the inconvenience they cause when they stand us up. Change plans. Schedule mandatory meetings on holidays.

I want to see Kat walk by, catch a glimpse of her welcoming new riders to class. She should have texted. Then the image of her, Araceli, and a third girl, Natalie, hanging in a tree soothes my rage. Guilt and shame consume my thoughts now. I wish no harm to Kat. I look back at Jacob, defenseless, small, and it unnerves me. The horror of it all.

When the tinted doors of Cyclone Studio swing open, I get a clear view of the instructors behind the desk.

No Kat.

She could be holed up in the closet folding fresh towels or stocking water bottles—not showing up to our meeting, though? No text? Not her style. I want to let it go, but my lizard brain has latched on. The only forgivable excuse to leave me hanging with Monique like that would be a massive, body-altering, life-threatening car accident—on a Saturday. Evan would tell me to let it go, which would make the thoughts fester. It wasn't even that important, and Monique covered it.

I see Monique leave the coffee shop, drink in hand.

"I hope she trips," I say. "Jacob, that was not a nice thing of Mama to say. Don't you say not-nice things." Jacob, still asleep, lets out a baby gurgle. "Jacob, do not encourage my horridness. You know Mommy is a nice person. Mostly."

I put the car in drive and follow Monique. She stops at her custom blue Honda Civic. I pull up to the curb four cars back, enough distance not to be noticed. She is talking and gesturing with her arms as if fighting off a swarm of hornets. She pulls an oversize gym bag from her back seat, slams the car door shut, and walks toward me. I duck down and count to fifty.

I peek in the rearview mirror and watch her walk across the street and disappear through the Cyclone Studio doors.

I text Kat.

Me: Hey! Sorry I missed you at the meeting

. . .

7

I nurse Jacob at the kitchen table.

"Don't get involved," Evan says.

"You saw that woman, that mother sitting in our home this morning, asking for my help. Am I supposed to say no?"

"I'm not saying that. Don't get emotionally attached. Bad things happen to good people every day, and you're not responsible to fix it."

"And who is?" I ask.

We lock eyes; then he leaves the room—Evan is a room leaver. Never finishes a conversation. Gone before I can finish a sentence, thought, argument. He leaves before I can say I'm sorry, that I need this. There is so much apologizing lately. Me saying I'm sorry, him not accepting.

I grab my phone to DM NELAScanBoy so fast it startles Jacob. He clamps down and smacks me in the face.

Me: Hey

NELAScanBoy: Hey?

Me: I need help.

Me: Any word on those girls at Debs?

NELAScanBoy: Cost you dinner.

Me: When?

NELAScanBoy: I'll be in touch.

Me: Old spot?

NELAScanBoy: Yep 😉

Monique was texting and emailing me so many to-dos, my phone dings annoyingly:

Monique: Lieberman. Can you pick up a bottle of wine for our Spin & Wine Ride tonight?

Me: Red? White? Pink?

Monique: One of each is perfect. Ty.

Nothing from, or about, Kat.

◆ ◆ ◆

Chris, a.k.a. NELAScanBoy, hasn't gotten back to me. The scanner is nothing but thefts from vehicles and aggravated assaults. These were just friends or enemies beating each other up because someone called someone's mother ugly or needed money for meth. Chris never takes this long, and the wait is agitating.

◆ ◆ ◆

I met Chris when he was a production assistant on the *LA News First* assignment desk. Chris's cousin, more like a brother, is LAPD and gives Chris the 411 on crime scenes before the rest of the press has the scoop. In his off hours Chris would come back to the station and sell crime scene videos. The station manager called him a "cop chaser," a voyeur, not a "real" journalist. Chris quit the assignment desk and went solo. Sold his work to the highest bidding station and did very well. Now he's writing his own pieces for local blogs and X. More activist than journalist. He leans into criticism. Something I have always struggled with.

He was born and raised in Los Angeles. "In the barrio, Corey. You ever been?" he asked.

"Which one?" I was terrible at flirting.

After that moment, that smile, I'd catch myself daydreaming about the kind of women he was into. Who he dated, how he kissed them. How his tall, lanky frame and his smooth-looking skin felt against their bodies. In my mind, all of them were gorgeous: flawless. To fuel my fantasies, a rugged poet lived inside Chris Villar.

When I moved to the Special Investigations team, he and I made a pact: I would get his footage into the prime-time lineups, and he would get me the info I needed from his source in the LAPD—he never told me his cousin's name. That's when we began to share our fever for adrenaline, the rush that fueled our work. We were more than a good team.

When I was fired, he understood what I had done. Why I'd done it. I didn't sleep; I was depressed. Chris was the only person I could talk to about it. I called him at all hours, middle of the night, day—it didn't matter; he always answered.

Evan gave the ultimatum, Chris or him. He had to. I understood.

I missed a period. Said nothing.

Missed another. The ultimatum moot. Evan and I were starting a family.

I stopped returning his texts. Calls. The DMs. Chris had no part in my future.

Now I need him. I need a message from someone. Anyone. Chris, Kat, come on—one chime and I'd be fine.

◆ ◆ ◆

"Corey," Evan says.

I stare at him. Completely forgetting where I am.

"Corey, the bathwater is cold. Do you want me to dry Jacob off?"

"No, I got it." I pick Jacob up out of the tub and pat him off. I squish him against my chest and bury my face in the fat of his baby neck.

If I scream right now, would Evan leave? Would Jacob laugh?

"Did you email anyone at the station about the girls?"

I had, but the email bounced back. My contacts expired. I am on my own.

"Not yet." Jacob balls his hands into fists and gently taps my chest—the universal baby sign for boob. I watch his fat cheeks suck in and out as he latches. Thoughts sink their claws in, create images that rush through my mind like a dust storm, clouding everything good: my hands fumbling for a knife, running my thumb across the blade, checking for an edge sharp enough to cut my wrists—quick and clean. Suffocating myself in the car with a plastic bag after grocery shopping, buying all the right food for my son to be healthy, organic. I'm not suicidal. I don't want to die. And so I walk around scared shitless every day.

"Everyone has these passing thoughts," my gynecologist said. Why her and not a shrink? Because she'd handed my son to me in the hospital, saw that I was lost. The thoughts clung to me after that day. Weaving through my psyche. Grabbing hold until I couldn't breathe. That first month with Jacob, I would put him in his swing, go to the corner of the room, crawl under a table, clutch my knees to my chest, and count. In for seven out for eight. Then again, this time in for eight and out for seven. Always confused by the count, but focused. The numbers kept me present. Reminded me that I was still there and the thoughts weren't, couldn't be, real.

Most days, early on, I hated being alone in the house with Jacob. I'd turn on the television loud enough that I couldn't hear my thoughts. *Sesame Street.* Always *Sesame Street.* Those were the days when I'd ask Evan to stay home, be with us, his family. I showered him with guilt. Evan offered to hire Elsie to babysit me. "Think of it like she'll be extra hands for Jacob," he'd say. I wouldn't accept someone in my house watching me. I wouldn't hear of someone knowing I was losing it—that I couldn't handle being a mother.

Those days, I couldn't drive because I'd imagine turning into oncoming traffic, running a red light, gassing it into a crowd. So, I'd sit on the porch, Jacob in his baby bouncer, and listen to the police scanner. I read somewhere that holding ice helps—apparently, the brain cannot experience extreme cold and extreme fear at the same time. The heart rate slows, breath follows, all in favor of protecting core organs. The mind is supposed to shut off to keep the body alive. To date, no ice nearby when the thoughts surge and all I can see are glints of a blade and feel the plastic bag taking away my last breath. Instead of ice, I binge on NELAScanBoy's X feed and listen to the police scanner, keeping my brain focused on other people's problems. I read all the posts in the Highland Park Facebook group and all the comments— when someone makes a threat, particularly to a woman, I take to the internet to find out everything I can on them, and I leave comments, reviews, screenshots of their private FB comments on public pages for all to see. I post links to conviction records—all public, you just need to know where to look, and I do. I do it masked and cloaked—a stock image of a much older woman named Donna, since I retired Shirley. No one notices Donna.

And sometimes none of it works—I would have an exorcism if I believed it would make the intrusive thoughts go away forever. I now believe that if I never put my baby down, nothing bad can happen. Ever.

It's a struggle to continue to convince Evan to keep our knives boxed up in the attic. Plastic bags permanently banned from the house. And anything that can be used as rope, looped over a rafter—even belts—in boxes, buried under heavier storage bins I could never lift on my own.

◆ ◆ ◆

What Evan didn't know was that the panic attacks actually started a long time ago. The first one came when I was twenty-three. I went on a date with a boy I knew from my circle of friends. He and I had flirted at happy hours for months, but neither of us had ever taken the step to ask the other out. One day, he messaged me: Hey, want to do a Happy Hour without the gang?

I was ecstatic. He was gorgeous, chiseled, smart—worked in finance. I typed yes immediately.

I didn't want to look like I was trying too hard on our first date; I wore my favorite jeans, a white cotton top with flutter sleeves to show off my gym-toned arms, and a pair of blue Converse I had custom-made online. He picked me up in his very normal Subaru, and we headed to a local spot our friends were not known to frequent. The night was perfect.

I had to cover an early shift—six a.m. on the assignment desk—so I called it an early night. He feigned being bummed. Tried his best to persuade me to have one more drink, but I was firm; it was time to go.

Back in his car he asked if I minded stopping by his place quickly to check on his dog. It was on the way. I'd been there before with the group, for a holiday party. I agreed. We went inside; he closed the door. The lights were off. He steered me deeper into his house. I giggled. "Did you forget to pay your electric bill?" I asked. The outline of his playful grin teased me in the dark.

He kept guiding me deeper into his house but not talking. He was intimidatingly sexy.

"Where's your dog?" I asked.

He smiled again.

I tried to walk past him, but he was strong and blocked me. He pushed me down. I screamed; he covered my mouth. My arms were immobile; my jeans were gone from my legs. I yelled *NO!* I tried to kick and squirm and squeeze my thighs together until they ached. He pressed his mouth into my hair and whispered something I couldn't hear. I jerked from side to side.

I screamed.

I whimpered.

I begged.

When it was over, he smiled.

"Thank you," he said.

I had no tears. I had gone still.

"Why?" I asked him.

"Come on, what are you talking about?" he asked.

I pulled up my pants.

"Do you want me to drive you home?" he said.

I sat stiff in the passenger seat. My legs tightly pressed together, my body rigid; thoughts brewed in my head.

"I don't have any STDs," he said.

I wished I did. I wished I'd given all of them to him. I quietly exited his car. I said nothing as he called out after me. I didn't look back. I ran to my apartment. I locked the doors, drew the curtains, blasted the television, and threw away my favorite jeans. I called my mother the next day.

"Mom, I was raped," I told her.

"Well, you're not the first. You just have to put your big-girl pants on and keep moving forward."

I sobbed quietly so she wouldn't hear.

"I hope you're not pregnant. Kids ruin everything," she said. She said she loved me, that she had to go, my father was calling on the other line.

I never told anyone else. I got tested for everything. The clinic assured me that wasn't necessary unless I had been raped. "Test me for everything."

"Would you like to speak with a counselor?" the nurse asked. Nothing changed in her expression. Casual, cool. She'd done this many times before.

"No, I'm fine."

I never attended another happy hour with that crowd. He called once, three months later—*Unknown Caller*.

"Hey, miss me?" he said. I could hear him smiling when he spoke.

"Erase my number. Never call me again." I hung up, got a new number and a new phone, and moved.

From then on I followed *Him*, Drew Hudson, on social media like a ghost. I kept tabs on him at all times. The Notes app in my phone filled with entries—times and days he posted, people he was tagged in photos with, women he dated. I'd follow those women and note where they worked, when they eventually broke up with Drew, and if they unfriended him or continued an online relationship. I needed to know if I was the only one he'd done this to. I dug deep into online forums, searching for his name everywhere—a Women Beware website had over a hundred Drews, but mine wasn't one of them. I anonymously added him to the site. No one ever responded.

I pretended what had happened was normal, that it happened to everyone—I was okay. Then the thoughts started. Over and over in my head. That's when the first panic attack found me. So, I ran. Every morning before work on the treadmill and every night before bed. Hours and hours of running every day. It quieted the thoughts for a very long time, but I couldn't outrun them forever.

Running turned into chasing stories. I buried myself in my work. I never stopped being busy, never a moment alone with my thoughts. Then Evan—I jumped into bed with him immediately. A pattern I'd developed after Drew. Survivors of sexual assault don't all react the same.

Jacob was born. It was a bad dream every day. Until now. Two girls. Dead. In my neighborhood. They needed me.

◆ ◆ ◆

"What are you thinking?" Evan asks. "Do you want me to make you a sandwich?" He waves a butter knife in front of me.

"Can you hide that, please?" I ask.

"Butter knives now too?" He walks to the other side of the kitchen and opens the catchall cupboard.

"Not where I know it's hidden—wait for me to leave the kitchen. Hide it when you're done."

"Of course." Evan gives me a sympathetic smile that makes me feel insane. He feels sorry for me. "Do you want to talk about it?"

"About what?"

"You're lost in thought. Do you want to talk about whatever you're thinking about?" He'll keep asking if I don't say something. I don't want to talk about the murder with him. I want Chris to text me.

"It's nothing, just work—" I let it hang there, hoping it will end the inquisition. I'm thinking of Araceli. I'm thinking about what she looked like when the police found her. I can't tell him that.

He stops. "Corey, this is a good thing. You want to work, and this is a safe, easy gig."

"Right. I am not the job. The job is something I do." But that's not true.

"I'm going to head up to bed. See you up there?" he asks.

"Yeah, right behind you," I say.

Evan takes a sleeping postbath Jacob and the butter knife with him, kissing me on the top of my head.

I turn out the lights in the living room and dining room, put my glass in the sink, and open the silverware drawer. One knife—the only one I'll allow—a toddler's, purple and plastic. I hold it in my hand, teeth against my palm. Can almost see through the cheap plastic as I push it into my skin. It wouldn't take much to puncture. Just force and will.

I throw it back in the drawer and slam it shut.

8

Monday afternoon—two days since I heard from Kat. Two days since I met Lupe.

Elsie is waiting on my front steps while I squeeze into a sports bra—my work clothes. I have nothing for her—no contacts left in the news. I have goodie bags full of dollar-store water bottles and hand sanitizer for the charity fundraiser at Cyclone. I know I owe her nothing, but I want to give her everything. I don't know what to do except get the story, get the information, get what is needed. My immediate search of social media has provided no clues. I need concrete facts from vetted sources—leads I can follow. I snap the sports bra into place, take two deep breaths, and try not to think about my current career choice of teaching a bunch of oblivious gentrifiers how to ride a bike in one place until they puke. Nothing feels right, as if I'm on the bike, too—going hard, pushing forward, not moving. Elsie, though, sitting outside, waiting for my help, hoping—that is something.

"I'm working on it," I say. My sudden appearance doesn't startle her. No hello, no niceties to begin. She is here for one thing.

"Thank you," she says.

◆ ◆ ◆

The first time I did an investigation in this town was on a local Peeping Tom. Only a few blocks over from where I live now. This was during the first wave of gentrification in the area. White people were moving in literally every day and wanted to "clean up" the "scary" neighborhood. The cops were too understaffed to respond and investigate every minor infraction—a common theme I learned early. They told the neighborhood to start a Neighborhood Watch. Half the neighbors wanted to be left alone. The other half wanted to make noise. The first person I spoke to was Brian Greene. He happened to be the new Neighborhood Watch's block captain.

"Have you ever witnessed the peeping, Brian?" I asked when I confronted him at his house. He'd been working on his yard, or tan.

He paused, attempted to think up an answer.

"I don't know," he said. "Do you want some water or iced coffee?" he offered.

"No, thank you. You don't know if you've seen a man looking into windows?" I asked.

"It's hard to say—neighbors are always looking into each other's windows." He laughed. "I'd definitely like to look in your window sometime." I stared into him. "I'm kidding. It was a joke. It's a Peeping Tom, not a gangbanger. I think it's all a bit blown out of proportion. It's likely a misunderstanding. Hell, it could be a woman."

His words made my skin crawl. The way he relished in saying *gangbanger*. The way he thought a man staring into vulnerable people's homes at night was less offensive. "So why did someone report it if it's not a big deal?" I asked. "Your neighbors want my news team to investigate." I gave him my best smile. "The neighbors all confirm it's a man."

"I'm the neighborhood block captain. I take that seriously. I want Mrs. Gonzalez to feel safe when she showers at night. I want the Miller twins not to worry when they're home alone—their parents work nights," he said.

"You know the comings and goings of the Gonzalez and Miller families? What about the other residents of the block?" I asked.

He smiled and shook his head at me.

"You can do better than that, Corey."

"You can call me Ms. Tracey. I do think we can do better. I think I can catch the son of a bitch."

He shifted back and forth. "Which neighbor called you?" he asked.

No one called me. I caught it on the private Highland Park Facebook group. People were scared. Every call to the police department resulted in a drive up and down the block hours after the call was made. I was going to catch the perp and hand deliver him to the cops.

"It's not relevant who contacted me."

"I've heard the Avenues gang has been making a resurgence around here," he said. "You may want to go interview a few of them."

I locked eyes with him. "This guy knows the patterns of the residents, probably knows them personally," I said.

When I got back to the station, I returned to Facebook and looked Brian Greene up. We had a few friends in common, and he had no privacy restrictions. I dove deep looking at all his posts from the past decade plus. I found the years he attended Cal State LA and what he studied, and one comment from his college frat bro revealed he'd never finished school:

> It's fucked up you didn't get to graduate with us—that was shitty.

It was literally that easy. Everything you need to know about a person can be found online, and usually you don't even need to pay a service to find it.

I inquired with the campus police if there were any criminal records. Greene had been suspended for doing the same damn thing to girls in the dorms: peeping. He also had a sealed juvie record from high school. Reading between the redacted lines, it could be assumed more of the same. We blasted his picture all over the news. His house was up for sale a week later.

Peeping Toms are just junior murderers and rapists. It's a natural evolution from voyeurism to break-ins. Peeping is a test to see how far a perpetrator can push into someone's personal space. I can evolve too.

I'm about to teach my first evening class tonight—Monique's idea. Evening crowds are social. They hang out after class like Cyclone is running a happy hour. Small talk with childless, mostly single adults—I haven't been that person in a long time. I want to confront Kat, who I know is teaching the class before mine, so I agree.

"Evan?"

Our tiny two-bedroom craftsman, built in 1901, would never need an intercom. No matter where you stand in the house, you can hear everyone and everything. When the kitchen window is open, I can hear Elsie's dinner conversations next door. I try hard not to eavesdrop, but it isn't in my nature. They usually talk about Dodgers games on the television. There's always a lot of laughter and sometimes a spat between young siblings. The worst offense a burned dinner.

"What's up?" Evan asks.

"I'm going to go early."

"Okay. I can take Jacob," he says.

"No, it's fine."

I don't kiss him goodbye, but he stands at the front door and waves.

Instead of the studio I head to Debs first. The gates close at dusk. Giving me about thirty minutes to get back to where the police tape roped off the murder scene.

Jacob is already sleepy. I wrap him around me in the yards of cloth—washed, wrinkled, and emitting the faintest scent of vomit mixed with baby detergent. I grab my phone and set an alarm for thirty minutes and take off at a jog. Jacob's head peeks out, and my chin nearly collides with him again, but I don't slow down.

I reach the plateau and stare at the crime scene debris. Flecks of yellow crime scene tape have trapped themselves in wild succulents and September-dry goldenweed. Fire season is upon us—with dry, hot days and vacillating nights—tank top hot on a Monday, winter chill Tuesday, and back to tank tops on Wednesday. I slow down as I make my way toward a damaged tree. Raw, pulpy-looking flesh stares at me where a large branch has been cut away. I touch the space where the branch used to be, and my stomach tightens, abs flex, ribs close, breathing shallows as a wave of anxiety flows through me. I let go.

The ground near the tree appears turned upside down. As though it has been tilled. I walk slowly in a widening circle, looking to the ground for clues. I stop at a patch of purple dead nettles. Beside the nettles is a narrow space; I can make out a small footpath. One made by someone walking off the path. I walk along it. Did he drag the girls' bodies here? Did he carry them? Did they walk, single file, behind him—unsuspicious?

A second group of purple dead nettles catches my eye in the center of the path I'm following. Nettles aren't native to the area, but they are survivors. They grow despite climate, ground, predators. This patch looks untouched, while everything around it had been trampled. I kneel down to look closer and see one decapitated stem.

I walk deeper on the path; a hard right comes up quick, and I catch sight of the large parking lot opposite the Audubon parking. This lot would close soon too. There are a few cars. As alone as I feel, there are people around. I hear talking and footsteps above me and freeze. It is hard to pinpoint where the voices are coming from. I look up, and there's the fire-road trail and two women hiking back to their car.

The alarm on my phone startles me. Jacob stirs. I snooze it and head back. The girls were carried here. There wasn't a struggle. They were carried and roped without knowing it. They were probably already dead.

◆ ◆ ◆

I get to the studio at the end of Kat's class. The studio is dark. Pitch black. Terror fills me: trapped, breathless. I suck in air, almost shriek. Jacob stirs.

Then Monique's voice booms. "We're rising up in one, two, three, take it up!"

Unsteady, I lean against the doorjamb. Where is Kat?

Monique ends the class, turning the lights back on.

"Lieberman, you brought the kid. At night," Monique says.

"Is Kat sick?" I ask.

"Don't know."

"Weird, I didn't receive a sub alert," I say. I am mindlessly folding clean towels and plopping them into the basket.

"Yeah, Kat's requests only come to me and vice versa. We're the owners—we sort of have an obligation to our members to show up for our own classes or send an owner to fill in."

"I still think it's weird that she never texted me back," I say.

"It's not personal. She hasn't texted me since Saturday morning," Monique says. Her smile is forced, but it always is, I think. She gives Jacob a gentle stroke on his cheek—odd to see her touch my baby. I'm divided: protect Jacob or ignore my maternal instinct to kill a perceived threat and let her walk away. It never occurred to me that I would start to like Monique.

I pull out my phone and DM Chris.

Me: Hey, anything on the 2 girls Araceli and Natalie? When are we meeting?

Please answer. Our roles have reversed. I hate it, being a regular person asking a favor.

"Hey, Corey." Diane. The same Diane that enjoyed my discomfort at the team meeting. "I decided I needed a little ass-kicking, so I'm taking your class tonight."

We all knew Diane only came to classes when she wasn't teaching because she was lonely. Which is whenever her husband, Sean, picks up the kids for visitation. Gossip among the Moms is that Diane and her husband don't speak to each other at the pickups or drop-offs. Diane got the Audi, and Sean got freedom. They've been separated for a year now. Diane claims she didn't see it coming—Sean sat her and their kids down and told them he was moving out.

"Don't worry, I'll be here to see you every weekend. I promise." Diane repeated the line in a voice emasculating the husband that had left her. She said it was a promise to their kids, but where was his promise to love and cherish her forever? Diane had been ambushed. She said he'd smiled while he pulled a packed suitcase out of the front hall closet as if he were surprising them all with a trip to Disney. Then he left. Diane alone consoled their three kids. She was served divorce papers a few months after. Rumor is she hasn't signed the papers yet.

"Monique—why are you teaching tonight?" Diane asks.

"Kat's a no-show," I say.

"She missed my class yesterday too. I forgot to call the party girl to wake her up. Had my hands full," Diane says.

"Kat? Party girl? What kind? Unicorn onesies and gummies? Clubbing and Molly? Or, bar hopping, raves . . . ?" I ask.

What did I really know about Kat? She was in her twenties, owned a business, lived in the neighborhood—born and raised—spoke Spanish before she learned English. She was proud of her Latin heritage on her mom's side and marched against the corporate greed that was displacing people from their homes.

"Hey, Lieberman, your class isn't going to teach itself. Get out there," Monique says.

"I have that check for you, Monique," Diane says.

"Thanks, you're saving our ass right now. I can't believe Kat didn't pay it yet."

"Pay what?" I ask.

"Rent," Diane says.

"Lieberman, class, bike, go!" Monique was not interested in entertaining my curiosity.

My brain was wrapping around this new information: missing meetings, classes, not paying the rent on her business. I stare at them both.

"Go!" Monique shouts at me.

I walk to the bike, pushing Jacob, asleep in his stroller, with me. My mic on, my breath loud, no words coming out.

Diane and Monique are in a deep discussion when I look back at them. Monique looks disgusted. Diane like she's ready to get loud. Monique looks like she could be Diane's daughter getting a lecture, almost. Are they arguing? About Kat?

Missing.

Dead girls.

The visions began climbing from the depths of my dark mind: Kat running, screaming, bushes, laughter, crying, begging, blood, knives, bags. She's not sick; she's missing.

I stare at the packed room of riders and jump into my memorized routine. "Let's get ready to take it out of the saddle in three, two, one," I shout into the mic as I watch Diane and Monique walk out of the studio together.

Drenched from exertion—or angst—I look at the clock; class is done. "Thanks, everyone, good ride. Go home and order some pizza—you earned it!" Out of habit and performance, I grin. I want them out. I leave Jacob by the bike while I run behind the front desk and scan through employee paperwork. I need Kat's address. A quick drive-by

73

of her place could get me a visual. Kat could be hanging from a tree at Debs. Did Kat know Araceli and Natalie? What is their connection— is it a coincidence? Is there someone stalking women? Always. There is always someone stalking women, but these three—in the same town? Risky.

"Hey." Diane snuck up on me. "What are you looking for?"

"I—"

"I don't care. Wanna grab a drink?"

"I have Jacob, sorry," I say.

"Let's drink at your place. Got anything good?"

"I think there's an open bottle of white in the fridge from my baby shower. It's probably shit."

"It'll do. Text me your address."

I stash the studio's iPad—used to check in clients—out of sight from the large windowed front doors. "To deter robbers," Kat once put it. Were these the robbers that killed Kat? Did they snatch her from the studio when the iPad was still out?

I turn out the studio lights, and the three of us leave out the back door—Diane, Jacob, and me—trash bags in hand. The door locks when I press the alarm button—I always wonder what the cost of something like that would be for my home.

"See you in a bit," Diane says as she heads to her car.

"Wait, can you hold the stroller while I run these to the dumpster?" I'm holding the white half-filled bags. Jacob is always my best excuse, but Diane is already too far away to hear me.

The crisp night air tickles my skin. The sky, dark and clear, moon on display, the street relatively empty—it's too calm, too perfect. The neighborhood not so much suburban as it is urban, despite the heavy changes happening. On any given street, a row of houses sits—one with bars on the windows, its neighbor none, and the next one bars. Some houses are in such disrepair that squatters dwell in the shadows of their interior, while across the street a new BMW shines under the glow of twinkle lights hanging from a custom-built pergola. It is overwhelming how the contradictions exist together.

I walk faster up the unlit part of the street while the old, skinny woman who collects bottles pushes her empty shopping cart down the middle in the opposite direction. The shadows cast by the sodium-arc streetlamps make her appear sickly. I don't say hello tonight. I'm rushing, it's dark, Kat's missing.

Nothing is scarier than my own mind. Jacob squirms in the stroller. "Shh, don't wake up, sweet boy." I'm in a fucking investigation, and for this singular moment, the thought of it, my work, two girls that aren't my baby take away the obsessive thoughts about myself and my child. I am thinking only about two dead girls, one missing Kat, and who might be next.

9

I drive home with the windows down.

Diane: Bringing Liz

I pull over.

Me: Liz who?

Diane: SpinLizza.

I leave it unanswered.

I check my rearview. The elementary school Jacob will attend in a few years is behind me. The giant PTA banner hangs low between two trees and catches the breeze, swaying gently under a streetlight. I am only ten blocks from home, but the rapid pace of change occurring to the homes, the streets, the cars—I barely recognize my own neighborhood.

I pull the car up our steep driveway. Any energy I felt moments ago is replaced with fatigue. I do not want to entertain two women I'm not really friends with—I want to interrogate one about Kat. I want to go to Kat's house. I want to talk to Chris. I want to strip off my stretch pants and sports bra and trade them in for my oversize maternity sweats that are disintegrating from wear and turn on the police scanner.

I pull Jacob from his car seat and inch my way to the front door. No longer invigorated, I reach for the doorknob. The knob turns in my hand without me doing anything. I jump back, cover my mouth. This is it. I've walked in on a home invasion. I'm dead. The door swings open.

"Hi, babe!" Evan leans in for a kiss.

I start bawling.

He sweeps in to console me. I turn, give him my cheek. Grief and fear flood me. *Out of sync* comes to mind—my emotions are out of sync. My marriage—out of sync. I worry Evan will leave like Diane's husband. I worry I won't care if he does. I worry I am too awful a human being to love, be loved.

"I'm sorry, I, you scared me, and—"

"It's okay, it's been a weird couple of days. But there are two women in our kitchen dressed in Cyclone gear, and they claim to be your friends." Evan smiles impishly. My crying is normal. He rubs my back. I haven't had friends over since before Jacob was born. My friends were mostly *LA News First* folks, and I am a plague to them. "I think I'll hide out in the bedroom. Is that cool?"

I nod.

"Corey! Get in here—we're in the micro kitchen!" Someone giggles.

She isn't kidding; our kitchen is tiny. Adorable but tiny. The kitchen is all windows. One small L-shaped counter with a farm sink that takes up the entire bottom of the L. The counter space for extras like a coffee pot doesn't exist, so we use a percolator on the stovetop. "It's European," Evan said when he brought it home. We had sex immediately after that. The single-serve blender lives under the sink. Occupying the remaining open counter space is the one kitchen appliance we use every day, a toaster oven—which Evan came to the marriage with. Burn marks paint its exterior—it is overworked and toasts everything to perfection. Evan jokes I stay for his toaster oven—it may be true. We don't use the regular oven, because it aggravates the smoke alarm to the point I resent buying the house.

I reluctantly hand Jacob to Evan—giving myself a point for making an effort. Then I kiss Evan and stay there a moment past inappropriate. He's been letting his beard grow in a bit like it was when we were dating. My friends, past tense, jokingly called bearded Evan "too hot." I'd laugh, but they were right. He is gorgeous, and the beard tips the scale favorably. I run my hand over his cheek. "I like the beard." Assuring myself and him that we are good.

Three, two, one, smile. "Hi, ladies!" I say, too loud. The grin I've painted on feels like it is pulling my face apart.

Liz, a.k.a. SpinLizza, is deep into her phone, and Diane is inspecting the contents of my full sink. I immediately recognize Liz from her signature ballet bun. Most of the Twentysomethings wear messy topknots, but Liz's hair is dirty blond and tightly swept up on top of her head in a perfect ball, bobby pins strategically pushed in nearly to the scalp as insurance against any stray hairs poking out. She is fair skinned and looks much younger than her age, putting her at approximately fifteen years old in my eyes. Liz, a pro at online marketing—promoting classes, posting pictures of herself in perfect form on the bike.

Liz is still buried in her phone when she says, "Diane said there'd be wine?" It is a demand posed as an aggressive question.

"Right. I cannot guarantee its freshness. It's been in the fridge since I was childless," I say.

"And that is why I brought the good bottle," Diane says, pulling a bottle and corkscrew from her bag. "Corey, grab some glasses."

I do as I am told, enjoying the firm commands. A sense of camaraderie stirring in the space of me that usually feels scared and alone. Diane looks stunning—in this moment, standing in my micro kitchen, she could stop LA traffic on Sunset. Liz looks annoyed.

Diane's light-brown hair bounces almost surgically past her shoulders, and her skin—Christ—it holds a dewy postspin glow.

I open the cabinet and pull out three red disposable plastic cups. "I broke the last of our glasses in the dishwasher a while ago," I say.

The cups make me think of Kat, the party girl image Diane put in my head. I remember those days. Unmarried, no baby, spending money on cheap beer, wine, and street tacos or dogs. Work hard, play hard. Staying up until dawn. Sometimes, after waking up with my fourth hangover in a row, I'd decide a break from drinking was a matter of life or death. So, I'd call in sick and drive to Santa Barbara, alone in my first-edition Ford Focus hatchback. Winding along the 101 North through the San Fernando Valley, strip malls visible from the freeway until the coastline made it all disappear—just me and the ocean to my left.

I would drive up State Street and grab a sandwich and a six-pack at the supermarket, then head back down to the beach to sit in the sand and breathe in the salt air. I would stay all day, past the sunset and well into the night. Invigorated with freedom, responsible for no one. I didn't leave a note for my roommate or call my parents to let them know. Why would I? I'd been on my own forever; no one cared where I was but me. No one worried about reporting me missing. I'd shut off my phone and relish the quiet. The only place I was needed was work. And even there I was expendable.

Did Kat feel the same way? Had she needed a break and a little excursion of her own that I had turned into a *Dateline* episode in my head? She's young and free. Why couldn't it all boil down to a getaway?

In less than an hour of Diane and Liz drinking, my kitchen is a mess with candy wrappers and the carcasses of empty bags of carbs littering my countertop. Diane and Liz punchy from laughing too much. They finished Diane's bottle, and she's now pulling out an old, previously opened bottle of champagne from my fridge—a piece of foil wrapped around the top instead of a cork. Diane pours a large bit into Liz's cup.

"New game, every time Corey looks at the clock, everyone drinks," Diane says.

"That's going to make me shit faced and puke," Liz says. She and Diane start laughing. I look at the clock and down at my untouched drink.

"Drink!" Diane says. She and Liz take a large gulp. "You too, Corey. You need to lighten up."

Liz lets out a belch and says, "I'm definitely going to puke."

"No, you won't. I'll heat up some old pizza. Carbs and grease will soak it up in your belly," I say. I sound like my mother—only a drunk can teach you how to sober up when you're still a child.

My breasts are swollen. I need to pump or feed.

Diane is giving the performance of her life doing impressions of the studio's clientele.

"Okay, okay, who am I?" she asks. Her voice lowers an octave as she whines: "There are no clean towels. Can someone do something about getting me a towel? Oh my god, I cannot ride without a towel. What am I supposed to do without a towel?"

"Oh, I hate her," Liz says. "What's her name? It's on the tip of my tongue." She snaps her fingers, grasping for a name—the same way she snaps in class when she's trying to keep everyone on beat.

"Mary," I say. "It's Mary." I'm smiling—the camaraderie of hating the same person feels genuine.

"When I'm feeling really cruel, I pop over and turn up her resistance. Then I hover over her so she can't cheat and turn it back down," Diane says.

"That's so mean," Liz says, walking over to my kitchen drawers and pulling them open one by one. "Hey, where are your knives?"

"Why?" I ask. I want to slap her hand, tell her it's rude to just make herself at home this way.

I don't want to tell her the knives are hidden or why. She's gnawing her way through a taffy from the previous Halloween and is barely able to form words through the sticky taffy plugging up her mouth.

"What do you need a knife for?" I ask.

"Cut"—she nearly spits the taffy out—"pizza. Oh my *god*—I wanna do someone too! Guess who I am: I have to do something for my baby. I can't stay. My baby crapped himself. I have to go now. Wait, my baby is being a baby, so I need to go honor him as a baby."

"Got it! It's Corey," Diane says. Her laughter is contagious, and admittedly, it's funny.

I tear a piece of pizza in half and hand it to Liz. "Ha, ha, ha—that was good, Liz," I say. What an absolute asshole.

"Diane, I have to tell you something. You're never this nice," Liz manages to sputter out while laughing and sucking up pizza, taffy, wine drool from the corner of her mouth.

"I have to tell you something, Liz, honey, I've never seen you eat so many carbs," Diane says and laughs.

"Gasp, you are evil."

I look at the clock.

"Drink!" Liz yells.

"Shh!" Diane tells her as they both gulp their drinks and motion for me to do the same.

Evil. The word punches me from the inside. An image of Araceli and Natalie hanging limp—lifeless—and their mothers trying to pull them down. Their bodies already decomposing.

"You okay?" Diane asks me. "You don't have to drink, honey. We're just having fun with you."

I don't want to share Araceli and Natalie images with them—they wouldn't know the girls, only what they'd heard on the news. Then, without reason, I ask them, "What do you think of Monique?" I couldn't retract it.

"You mean, I'm so emo it hurts?" Liz says, scrolling through her phone. "She's fine, but she could dress cuter and not always be scowling and bitchy." Liz pulls away from her phone screen. She's slurring a little, but it's too early to be drunk—she's had two, two and a half glasses of wine. "Kat, though, um, yeah." Liz pretends to gag, and a mangled piece of taffy mixed with pizza dough drops from her mouth. "Oops." She puts the food back in.

"What's wrong with Kat?" I ask.

It's the first time I've heard of, or even imagined, anyone having a problem with Kat. Of the studio's owners, I figured it would have been Monique to be the one dishing out the grief.

"Kat's annoying and she plays favorites." Liz gets worked up as she speaks. "She never returns texts or emails."

This is what I don't know about Kat. This is the information I need. Maybe I've fallen out of favor with her. Maybe I'm fucking crazy and need medication to stop thinking of the worst-case scenarios as facts and to stop thinking about the same shitty person over and over and over—if Kat is as shitty as Liz says. But what if Kat is hanging from a tree right now? Begging for her life while being strung up, or surprised, silenced mid-laugh with powerful hands or a blade across the throat. No, she'd have been found. Araceli and Natalie were found right away. Just stop thinking about it, brain. Stop dwelling on this. Everyone is fine. I'm fine, Jacob's fine, Kat is fine . . . Araceli and Natalie are already dead—they're fine. They've been found; I didn't know them. It's all fine. My brain won't stop, though—it's circling images of Kat on repeat. It's relentless, and before I explode, Liz is talking again.

"Kat fired Marco for, like, no reason." Liz punctuates Marco's name with a pouty face. "She doesn't get it. She's—"

"Obtuse," Diane says, looking out my kitchen window—half in the conversation.

"Marco. Was he the one who called a woman 'fluffy and slow' on the bike?" I can't place him or see his face in my head. Kat has taken over; she is the star of the horror movie at the base of my skull.

"Well, she was fat. You don't notice the shit Kat does because you're one of her favorites," Liz says.

"She stood me up after texting me to meet her on Saturday."

Diane laughs. "I volunteered you for the charity ride. I could not let Kat make me assist her again."

Liz giggles like she already knew.

"What do you mean?" I say.

They look at each other and start laughing again. I'm annoyed and frustrated but want to stay focused on Marco.

"I'll be right back," I say. I head to the bathroom and pull out my phone. I look Marco up on the studio's Instagram page. Right. Marco. Smug and cruel. Pinched the fat on riders in the middle of class—cruel. I need to talk to Chris.

Me: Are you there?

NELAScanBoy: What's up?

Me: Have you heard anything about a female in NELA reported missing? Mid 20s.

NELAScanBoy: Not on the scanner I'll hit up my cousin on the Northeast unit. Someone you know?

Me: Yeah, name is Kat. Or Catherine. Last, Donahue

NELAScanBoy: Okay.

Me: Can you run a background check on a Marco Tan? And Ty.

NELAScanBoy: Yes. And always.

Chris is back responding to my texts. Relief sweeps over me.

◆　◆　◆

I get back to the kitchen, and Diane is crying—bigger than crying, she is sobbing into Liz's chest.

"What happened?" I ask.

Liz gives me a slight shrug and bobs her head in an *I don't know* gesture. I rub Diane's back until her breath evens out again. "Diane, can you take a sip of water?" I ask. She sips and sits up. Her face ruined, mascara staining her cheeks and the remainder of it leaving a lasting mark on Liz's white sports bra.

"I'm sorry, you guys. I feel like an idiot," Diane says. "My husband has found someone else. He's in love." She barely finishes the sentence. The crying starts again.

"Dick," Liz offers.

"He's in this running group. I guess they met there. Apparently, they've been running together since before we separated." Diane takes a deep breath. "I should have joined with him." Her hair is clinging to her damp face. "He said we don't have any common interests anymore."

"I'm so sorry, Diane," I say.

I feel uneasy. The conversation makes me picture Evan leaving me and finding someone new. Someone clean and shiny and new who does all the things he wants her to, including being a stay-at-home wife. Evan's also a runner, the kind that runs shirtless with a body that naturally produces defined abs. I'm pissed at Diane for starting this new conversation. I need—want—her to talk to me more about Marco and Kat, or just leave. I need to get online and find Kat—and Marco—myself. Are they friends? Do they hate each other? Is he stalking her? My brain is jumping around these hypotheticals—and the more I try to talk sense to myself, the more I'm panicking. The further I push the panic away, deny in my brain that my throat is tightening and I can no longer swallow, the more saliva I produce, and I strain to get it down my throat.

"Do you know who she is? We can Facebook stalk her," Liz says—her phone at the ready. She's buried in her screen again.

I watch Diane shred a paper towel into bits. I'm sweating. You don't need to stress, Corey; everything is fine, I tell myself.

"Hey, not to change gears, but did you guys see these new comments on Cyclone's Facebook page?" Liz asks. Another new conversation for fuck's sake.

"No." Diane's voice cracks through sniffles. "I'm never on that thing," she says.

"Someone is not a fan," Liz replies.

"What's it say?" I ask. Ignoring the fact that my heart is already racing.

Liz shows us her screen, and I speed-read the post:

JOIN TEAM CYCLOPATHS OF CYCLONE STUDIO FOR A CHARITY RIDE THIS SUNDAY @ NOON!

Sign up at the Studio for full details.

Xgen: Say NO to Gentrification!

NelaNoiseMakers: We don't need your overpriced hipster fake gym in our neighborhood! Give us back our buildings!

Craig: You guys are being ignorant, they didn't take your building, it's a new building and they rent space in it to provide a service for all people in the community get a life.

Xgen: Their displacement of people is wrong.

Craig: They didn't displace anyone. They raise money for local charities, man.

Xgen: You're assuming I'm a dude. You don't even know hipster.

NelaNoiseMakers: Let's picket Cyclone Studio!

NelaNoiseMakers: No one goes in or out!

Eastsiderides: I'm there, same time?

Eastsiderides: FYI posting a GRAPHIC pic below in comments. There is a beheaded dog with its head in a box on Griffin east of the Audubon entrance. Just got done hiking with my kids when we saw it.

"Okay," I say. "A beheaded dog? Really?"

"Old news. It was a coyote or mountain lion that caught someone's pet out of their yard. So gross," Liz says.

"When was that posted? Was it before those girls were found dead?" I ask.

"Earlier today," Liz said. "The girls that hanged themselves?" She took a large gulp of her drink. "So tragic. Like, we already have suicide signs up at the metro tracks. I'm not exactly excited to read them before every hike."

I look to Diane, who is still crying. "I don't have the bandwidth to deal with all this. I'm sorry," Diane says as she gets up to go.

I feel relief the night is ending at last.

"It makes me nervous," Liz says. She is still going. Liz barrels through Diane's rejection. "When I teach the six a.m. class, there's this guy hanging out front. He never has on shoes, only socks. I don't think he's homeless. He comes in and watches the class for a bit, then goes back outside."

My stomach drops.

"That's very different than a small group of protestors, Liz," Diane says. She looks shocked by this new information. "Have you told Kat and Monique?"

"I told Kat, and I asked her if she could meet me at the studio in the mornings to open, but she said it wasn't possible and that the neighborhood is fine. She said if I truly feel threatened to call 911."

"Typical," Diane mutters. She stops to blow her nose on a used paper towel. "You have to lock the front door when you're alone."

"She can't—fire code," I say. "Liz, can you give a description of what he looks like?" I snap into investigator mode; the anxiety ebbs.

"Normal."

"By normal, do you mean average height and weight, like five foot ten? Is he thin, athletic, stocky?"

"I remember he had a little belly—because he could just get on a bike and lose that."

"Liz—"

"God, okay, he was white, but like a tan white. Maybe in his thirties—maybe, it's hard to tell sometimes. He wasn't dressed homeless, except he was shoeless."

"Good," I say. "Did you happen to notice his hair color?"

"Dark, but brown, not black." Liz takes a second to think before she starts again. "He looks like a dude with something going on in his head. Kat says he's harmless. He comes in and watches her class all the time."

"Did she mention what his name is?" I ask. I demand answers from Liz. She isn't getting it—Kat isn't returning my texts; she might be missing, and this man could be a person of interest.

"No," Liz says, "and you're freaking me out even more."

I need to get upstairs to Jacob, make sure he's there, breathing. The fear I felt leaving the studio tonight—what if I was followed? What if I or my baby were next? What if Diane hadn't shown up and waited for me? I feel the bile come up, run to the bathroom, and slam the door behind me.

Ten seconds later Diane knocks. "Corey?"

I wipe my mouth and walk out. "Must be the wine. I should go check on Jacob." I smile.

"You look like shite," Liz says.

"She looks like a gorgeous, tired new mama," Diane corrects her. She embraces me. I can't get my arms up, and the bile is back. I push away. "Get some rest," Diane says. "And thank you for being there for me tonight."

Liz is already on the porch, face buried in her phone, bouncing her leg in agitation. Then they're gone. I run up the stairs to Jacob and hold my face to his nose and wait to feel his breath.

"Corey?" Evan says from the doorway. "Everything all right?"

"Yeah." His AirPods are still in his ears. Lying to Evan is easy. "Just saying good night." Nothing will be okay until Kat is found. Until Araceli and Natalie's killer is caught.

10

I lie in bed, wet. Anxiety has detoxed itself through my pores all night.

The bits and pieces of the conversation start to replay in my head. Overanalyzing my behavior, my comments, my body language could last for days.

I force myself up—the Alexa screen reads 8:07 a.m.

I throw on last night's leggings, still damp from class. The Lycra catches on the stubble of my fleshy calf. I grab one of Evan's worn T-shirts from the top of his dresser—it smells like bergamot and orange; it's so good. I slide it on over my camisole and check Jacob's crib—empty. Before my foot hits the top step, a pounding on the door echoes up the stairwell.

"Coming!" I hear Evan yell from the kitchen.

I smell coffee. I have work to do—Elsie, then Lupe's to ask questions. I need to know what Araceli and Natalie were doing the day they were killed. Where did they hang out? Who did they hang out with? And did they somehow know Kat? I need to work on their victimology as quickly as possible.

The knock comes again—Evan opens the door. I hear a man and a woman. Their voices low. Questions. They're questioning Evan—where is Jacob?

I land at the bottom of the stairs in front of one man in an out of season jacket and a woman with a badge hanging from a chain around her neck.

I grab Jacob from Evan.

"Can we help you?" I ask over Evan.

"Good morning, ma'am," the woman says—composed, a cool greeting, hair pulled back. A fitted dark blazer, sensible flats, starched button-down. "I'm Detective Lopez, and this is Detective Marks. Are you the homeowner?"

"Yes, we are," I say, my voice both firm and flat. I was used to talking to the police, liked it, almost. "May I ask what this is about?"

"Are there any other persons in the home at this time?" It's the male officer, Marks, who asks. His skin pockmarked and scarred.

"No," Evan says. He smiles at them.

"Ma'am, are you acquainted with a Catherine Donahue?"

Kat. My heart slams against every rib. Jacob whines. My stomach lurches. My chest won't open—no air—and my throat tightens shut. I can't swallow. Darkness fills the corners of my periphery. Someone, Evan, catches me as the floor comes closer and closer to Jacob and me. The officers lunge to catch Jacob. I clutch him, squeeze him too hard before everyone blurs together. I can't tell the detectives from Evan; they're all one person catching me, us, pulling me up.

I am conscious. I hear nothing but a pulsating ring in my ears.

"Breathe," someone says. Yells? It sounds like an echo, far away, urgent—filling my chamber of fear.

"In through your nose, out through your mouth, breathe, Corey, breathe." It must be Evan, has to be, right? Love. Marriage. Till death.

My face burns from the top down. My teeth chatter. I am damp with cold sweat; the shivers take hold. I hear someone ask if it was a seizure. Jacob, I hear him crying. I look for him. Reach for his sound. My vision still blurry.

I cry now.

My chest heaves.

Am I on the couch? No. I feel arms underneath me, the voices pulling me back—but Jacob is in his swing, smiling, hitting buttons that make him dance. Evan's face is too close, assessing me with his eyes; I want to slap him for looking so worried.

"Ma'am, can you hear me? Corey, can you speak?" Detective Lopez, that voice. It holds kindness and concern, but a crushing tone that wants something from me, needs it. I focus on her badge: **DETECTIVE** embossed across the top banner and **LOS ANGELES POLICE** below. I mentally trace the shape of the badge until I can see the nicks from time, faded bits that tell her story.

"I can hear you," I say. "I'll be fine." Once I'm done crying. It always stops when I'm done crying—I should tell them, but I don't want to. It's the last phase of the episode.

"Panic attack," says Detective Lopez, again the authority.

I taste my own salt; the tears won't stop.

"Since the baby was born," Evan says.

Don't speak for me. I want to scream in his face. Tell him *no*, my body has punished me since the rape, since before you. No one knows that part of me. "I'm fine," I say. "I'm being monitored by my doctor."

"You didn't look fine two minutes ago," Detective Marks says. I look up at his badge now. Far more worn than Lopez's—a bigger story to be told someday over too much whiskey and bloody knuckles. His shirt collar is almost brown from sweat and grime. Neck soft from age. Pants wrinkled from sitting. He holds a tired look, a lost energy, youth wasted on hope. I can't fault him. Under all the layers, age, grime—he's fit. No question he could take Evan out without blinking.

"I am, I assure you. I'm fine now," I say.

"Here." Evan tilts a glass of water to my mouth.

"I'm capable of holding it myself, thank you." I really do want to slap him for treating me as though I were incapable. Do they all see me as a terrible mother? The officers look to Evan, who nods. It's conspiratorial. "For fuck's sake, I am fine." I guzzle the water, hoping the action will hide my trembling. "What's wrong with Kat?" I look to Detective Lopez, who is still assessing me, my wellness, my truth, searching for something I can't give.

"Catherine Donahue was reported missing," she says.

My gut told me something was wrong, and I didn't say anything. Now the police are here. Telling me.

"These things usually turn into nothing. Person usually ends up having gone out of town, to their friend's place, and turned off their phone," Detective Marks says. Detective Lopez quiets him with a look.

"When was the last time you saw Ms. Donahue?" Lopez asks.

"Thursday afternoon." Technically it was the last time I saw her.

"Where was that?" she says.

"At a team meeting—a bar on York." There is pain in my stomach akin to contractions. "She texted me Saturday morning," I say.

"What was the text regarding? Do you know what time?"

"Early, five forty-two a.m. To meet up at noon—to discuss an upcoming event at the studio. But she didn't show. I can get my phone, show you."

The sharp pain in my stomach is relentless; I stand to get my phone but double over in pain. It's my gut talking to me. Killing me. Something about Kat.

"No need to show us your phone at this time. First kid?" Lopez asks. She writes something down on a pad she appears to have produced from thin air—it must have always been in her hand.

"Yes."

"Getting any sleep?"

"Not much." I start to cry again. Stop. Fucking. Crying.

"Hang in there. It'll get better. I have three, all teenagers now, but I remember. And the first one is the toughest. Try some Benadryl at night."

"The doctor said he can't have—"

"Not for him, for you. Five milliliters, liquid, just to get a little rest. It works."

I nod. My stomach turns sour. I jump up and run to the bathroom, without asking permission.

I flush the bile, try to see myself in the mirror, wipe my chin: There are two cops in my house looking for a missing woman. A woman that I know. There are two dead girls from the neighborhood, one of whom I also sort of knew.

"Corey?" Evan says, with a weak knock on the door. "Are you okay?"

No. I am not fucking okay.

"Yeah, I'm coming." I splash water on my face, fix the knot of hair sitting poorly on top of my head, and exit the bathroom as freshly as I can. "I'm sorry again. I'm obviously not feeling very well," I say and smile.

"Seems to me you're going to be okay," Lopez says. She hands Evan her card. "Please call me if you see or hear from Kat or if any information arises that may help."

"Yes, of course." I watch Evan pocket the card, *5 ml Benadryl* written across it. "Detective, who reported Kat missing?" I say.

"Her mother," Lopez says.

Marks takes a second to look around the room. He stops when he gets back to Lopez and nods. That is all the communication they need. I know that language well—that's the language I speak with Chris and no one else.

"Thank you for your time," Detective Lopez says.

As Evan shuts the door behind them, I pick Jacob up from his bouncy swing and hold him close to me. He pulls my shirt down and finds my left breast—the feeder. "You're staring at me," I say to Evan. The tone more annoyed than I want it to be.

"That was a big one," he says.

"I need to get some work done. I'll take Lopez's card."

"Why don't I hang on to it, and if something comes up, we can call her together. Deal?"

I won't win this fight, so I choose not to argue. "Deal," I say.

I know that a person can be reported missing at any time, not solely after twenty-four hours, as the television procedurals were so fond of propagating. But being missing is not a crime. Unless there's evidence of foul play, it's considered a voluntary missing person. I know that I have not seen Kat myself. But I have texted with her, and Monique appeared to be in some contact—hadn't she been the one to receive Kat's sub alert? What has Detective Lopez been told? I need to find out who else spent time with Kat. If she had roommates. A boyfriend.

"Corey?" Evan says.

"What?" Too abrupt. "Sorry, what's up?" I say. I try to sound more loving.

Evan pats at my chest and lap with a dish towel. "The baby spit up all over you. Do you want me to take him so you can change?"

I hadn't noticed the smell, let alone the volume of the spit-up. I snatch the towel from Evan and sop it up myself. "What if she was murdered like the other two girls?" I ask. I set Jacob down on the ground to explore.

"Your friend is missing, not dead," he says.

But she could be dead. She could be.

11

Me: Get anything yet?

NELAScanBoy: Diner later

The bathroom door eases open. "Babe, just checking if you want me to stay home from work today?" Evan is being too nice. I throw my phone onto the pile of towels at the base of the hamper and hide my reddening face with a washcloth. Jacob in his bouncy seat on the bathroom floor.

"No, I'm okay, I promise."

"Want me to see if Elsie can watch Jacob?"

"No, I'm good, he's good, we're good. I have the water running." I'm not ready to be apart from my baby, not even for an investigation. Not ever.

Evan smiles at me in the mirror, halfway in the door, half out. "Gotcha. Okay, I'll see you after work. I love you, Corey."

"I love you too." I say it and mean it, and I hope that we can show each other again.

After showering I plop Jacob in his baby walker—jungle themed with flashing lights—a gift from my mother-in-law. I rarely use it— seeing Jacob's delight makes the guilt in me swell.

I sit on the floor near Jacob, laptop open, and I type Catherine Donahue Highland Park, Los Angeles into the search. Five hits. I read them aloud to Jacob:

"Catherine Donahue Age Deceased

Catherine Donahue Age 70s

Catherine Donahue Age 20s

Kathleen Donahue Age 20s"

I click on Catherine Donahue 20s. Kat's address pops up—it's about a mile away from me. That is manageable. I can take Figueroa all the way down. I strap Jacob into the jogging stroller and head out for a run in the neighborhood, to Kat's house.

The sidewalk is jagged, crumbling from the neglect of a city that no longer takes responsibility for maintenance—Los Angeles can't keep up, not even with gentrification.

I slow my pace to a fast walk. Make my way up Monte Vista Street, smell the bread before I see the door of La Panadería. Screw jogging.

"Hola?" I say after opening the door, hearing the familiar bell ding overhead.

"Hola!" Comes the voice of Marina before I see her bobbed hair come out from the kitchen. "El guapo! Come let me see! Corey, you forgot about me." She feigns hurt. "My little Jacob, you tell Mommy she owes me visits." Marina has kept me caffeinated and my sweet tooth at bay since I moved here.

"Large coffee?" I ask.

"Sí! Of course, and cinnamon pan dulce," she says—no asking.

I nod. I know what's next: large cinnamon-flavored coffee—more sugar than coffee—with leche and warm elotito sweet bread. Like a two liter of cola to a diabetic, the anxiety bomb wouldn't be far away.

"Gracias, Marina."

I eat as I walk, my stomach accepting all of it after emptying its contents an hour earlier. I chuck the last quarter of the sweet roll in the bin, feeling guilty for wasting it and also about the extra flesh still jiggling around my midsection. The lie that breastfeeding takes off the baby weight is appalling and makes me want to choke every woman who claims it was her only fucking diet. My phone vibrates.

NELAScanBoy: 187 at Debs

Sirens wail, filling the neighborhood with a cacophony of impending doom.

Not Kat. It cannot be Kat. I start to run—I would get to Kat's house, and she would answer the door. I'm heading north while the sirens move east. Jacob cries with every bump. I run faster, determined to get to Kat's street before the sirens stop. I dodge the fruit bodegas and sidewalk chicharron hawkers, fly past dollar stores and tchotchke shops, bump tables and chairs at the new coffee houses with their outdoor seating—a violation of space to all pedestrians, especially those with strollers—sweep past the bus stops crowded with commuters and homeless alike. Time seems to slow when a flyer stapled to a telephone pole snags my peripheral. A picture of two teenage girls—young, healthy, happy-looking girls: IF YOU HAVE ANY INFORMATION REGARDING THEIR MURDER PLEASE CALL.

I hit Kat's street and climb the hill; at the top is a sweeping view of the city below. Not far off, barely shrouded in smog, is the side of Debs Park that leads to the Audubon Society. I stop the stroller at 379 Avenue 61.

Two lemon trees, drooping, heavy with fruit, frame the front window. The adjacent fig tree, gone wild in its untended state, smells almost too sweet with rot. The yard, mostly potted succulents, is clean, native, pretty. A few pebble paths are the remains of what should be a yard filled with Mexican river rock. Each elevation of the steep path to the door includes a new set of steps over which I lift the two-ton jogging stroller. Jacob jostles and screams with each one. "I'm sorry, buddy. I promise, just one more." The view is even more spectacular at the top. I knock. I pray Kat will answer.

The door opens, and I do a double take—speechless at another version of Kat. An older version of her. Brown hair and sparkling eyes showing signs of age—frown lines and puffy dark circles from crying. This is the version of Kat I could never imagine existed—sad. "May I help you?" she says.

"Hi, I'm a friend of Kat's. I was supposed to meet her here to pick up some items for the studio charity ride," I say. The older Kat starts to cry.

"Kat is missing," she says.

She looks at me and Jacob and invites us to come in. I haven't even introduced myself yet. I could be a kidnapper—I could have killed Kat. But I have a baby. The thing we're taught from the age we can walk—if you're lost, look for a mommy; she's safe.

I leave the stroller on the porch and carry Jacob. I follow Kat's mom through the front room, down a short hallway into the kitchen—like an old friend. The house has not been remodeled with the current HGTV open floor plans. This NELA home is an example of the compartmentalization of generations past. Each room fully walled off from the next, but for a door leading in and out of a narrow hallway.

"Can I get you something to drink?" she asks while she absently opens cupboards, presumably looking for glasses. Canned chipotles in adobo, a bag of pepitas, Pop-Tarts, cereals, instant mashed potatoes, dried beans, and bowls in a cupboard together. Finally, above the stove, mugs. Kat's mom pulls two down and fills them at the sink. Jacob hangs on to my left side and claws at my shirt to reveal the top of my bra. I follow Kat's mom as she quickly returns us to the front room. "What did you say your name was?" she says.

"I didn't, I'm so sorry. I'm Corey, Corey Tracey-Lieberman, and this is Jacob." I take Jacob's hand and make it wave at her. "Say hi, Jacob."

On cue he smiles. "I work for Kat at Cyclone Studio. How long has Kat been missing, Mrs. Donahue?"

"I don't know." Jacob gasses—we both laugh softly, lock eyes, take sips of water; the heaviness lifts, for a moment. "I'm Gilda." A moment of silence sweeps in, fills the space between us. I open my mouth to speak, but I don't hear anything come out. It isn't unlike the moment a hairdresser or cashier at the local Trader Joe's tells you their child has cancer. Sometimes in life there are no words. None.

"I was away over the weekend," Gilda says. She rubs her thumb over a chip in the rim of her mug. "Visiting my sister in San Diego." I bounce Jacob gently on my leg while he lunges forward at Gilda, arms outstretched—she doesn't appear to notice him. "Kat's always in and out. We're more like roommates." Gilda locks eyes with me, and that's when the ramble of information dumps itself. "I got back Sunday night—late, she was out. I assumed at the studio working, but she didn't come home that night. I texted her, but she didn't respond—there were no bubbles on the screen. I always know that means she's trying to get to me—when I see the bubbles. She's super busy, but I can sense her trying to text. She does that a lot. Starts to write, then gets busy, and forgets to send the text or whatever. She does it all the time." Gilda shakes her head. "She really does it all the time. But she didn't do it Sunday or yesterday."

"My husband does that too. I get it," I say.

Gilda cries, not bothering to wipe the wetness away. "I thought everything was fine. I thought . . ." She lets out a deep breath, then bursts into a sob, catches herself, sucks air through her teeth, and says, "She hasn't come home." Gilda stops again, looks past me, sips from her mug. "I called the police yesterday." Another sip. "They found her car parked near the studio."

"Not in the parking garage?" Monique and Kat have reserved spots inside the garage.

"Have you heard from her?" she says.

I shake my head, and Jacob mimics the movement. I want to congratulate him, but it's not the right time.

"When did she make plans for you to come here?" Gilda asks.

"Last week, Thursday." I lie without thinking.

Gilda sinks into her chair. My words, worthless strings of sounds, giving her nothing, have no value to this woman, this mother without her child. Heat fills me from the inside out—my gut screams, clawing up my spine to push, find the truth. Hug my son. Be a better person. The mother I always needed.

"And Kat's dad?" I ask.

"He died when she was still a baby—car accident. It's always just been me and Kat."

A pounding on the front door makes Gilda and me both jump. It's a hard rap, demanding to be heard. Before I'm ready, Gilda answers it.

"Mrs. Donahue." It's the voice of Detective Lopez. "May we come in and speak with you?" she asks. Her voice like honey, soft and sweet.

"Did you find her?" Gilda asks.

I'm terrified to show myself. I'm terrified not to show myself. Wouldn't it be the obvious move to come straight to your friend's house if you find out she's missing?

I walk back to the couch, still not knowing whether I should leave or stay and explain.

"I should leave," I say.

"Don't go," Gilda says.

I nod to Lopez and Marks. Lopez gives me a nod back while Marks glares at me. I put my hand gently on Gilda's back for comfort. Detective Lopez guides us to the sofa.

Detective Marks stays at the door, working the room with his eyes. I try to follow, see what he sees. I first land on a photo of Kat and Gilda at Kat's graduation. The picture sits on an antique side table next to a love-worn wingback chair in navy velvet. My eyes move along the edge of the room, searching for more; five-pound weights are tucked into a corner next to a rolled-up yoga mat. A slim blue bookcase made mostly of particle board houses shelves of paperbacks and candles, and one shelf used as a catchall is stacked high with mail, a scattering of loose keys, and a can of pepper spray.

"We found a body," Detective Lopez says.

An oppressive silence fills the room.

Detective Lopez speaks with intent, voice low.

Gilda's body rejects the news—immediately shaking her head *no*, her hands raise chest level waving them back and forth—*no*. She smiles apologetically—*no*. She stands up ready to usher the detectives out—*no*.

With Jacob tucked away on my left, I hold Gilda with my right arm. I don't know if I'm making any sound, but my mouth is open, flapping up and down. "They didn't say it's Kat." I hear myself now.

"Mrs. Donahue," Detective Lopez says. "Gilda, can you walk me through the moment you discovered Kat was missing, again?"

Gilda isn't listening. She's staring at Marks as he continues to scope out her home.

"Would anyone like a cup of coffee?" Gilda directs the question to Marks. "I'm going to go put on a fresh pot." Gilda stands to walk down the hall to the kitchen. I follow with Jacob.

"Gilda, stop," I say. We are barely in the hall, one foot still in the living room. "Gilda, Detective Lopez is asking you about Kat. It's important. You want them to find her, right?"

Gilda nods.

"What was the question?" Gilda asks Lopez.

"The last time you saw Kat—what happened?" I blurt out before Lopez can repeat herself.

"I went to San Diego to see my sister. It was her birthday. I invited Kat, but she was too busy with work and plans and a charity ride she's putting together."

"And when did you leave for San Diego?" Lopez asks.

"Saturday morning."

"Did you see Kat the day you left?"

"Yes, we see each other every morning. She gets up before me to shower first." Gilda smiles; it's a thoughtful smile. "I make us coffee while I wait for her to finish." Gilda pauses; she lets out a small giggle. "I hate driving so far alone, so I asked her to come with me. Begged her. I told her if she came, we could come back early. She said, 'Mom, you need to put on your big-girl pants and just do it. You're all grown up now.' I used to say that to her when she was a kid. She never wanted to go to school without me. She was afraid. I'd tell her to pull up her big-girl pants and be brave."

"Did you have communication with Kat when you were in San Diego?"

"I texted her when I got there, and she responded with a heart."

"What time was that?"

"Let me get my phone." Gilda turns to the side table, but there's no phone. "My phone's missing! What if she's calling me right now? Oh my god. I can't find my phone! I can't find my phone!"

"It's okay, Saturday morning is fine. We can figure the timeline out in a bit. It's okay," Detective Lopez says, jumping into the "calm-down protocol" she performed hours earlier on me. She is good.

"NO! Kat could be trying to call me right now. I need my goddamn phone!" There would be no calming Gilda down until the phone was in her hand.

"I'll find it," I say. "What's your number? I'll call it right now."

Gilda rattles off her number. I call, and the vibration of a phone leads Detective Marks to the catchall shelf. He brings the phone to Gilda, who swipes through it. Presumably looking to see if she had missed any texts, calls, emails from her daughter.

I save the number, labeling it: Gilda Kat's Mom.

"Can you see when Kat last texted you?" Detective Lopez asks again.

"Yes, at nine oh three a.m., Saturday morning. It's just a purple heart emoji. My favorite color."

"And when did you return from San Diego?"

"Sunday night."

Kat no-showed me on Saturday afternoon after Gilda had gotten her text. She'd been missing since Saturday. I should have said something. What if she were still alive Saturday and I never told anyone she missed our meeting? What if they had found her then? I feel the wetness trickle from my pits down the insides of my arms. The tip of my nose beading with perspiration. My tongue swelling in my mouth, making swallowing impossible. I need to stand and move around. Jacob grabs a fistful of my hair and yanks. It pulls my attention back to the room.

"Mrs. Donahue—" Detective Marks says.

"Gilda," Detective Lopez corrects. I can't tell if it's a tag in or a hostile takeover by Lopez.

"Gilda, we're going to need you to come down to the station," says Marks.

Gilda sits silent, nodding. Her gaze finds its way out the front window to something in the distance. I follow her stare; so does Detective Lopez. The hills of Debs Park are visible from where I sit on the couch. Past the newly renovated bungalow across the street, with its stark-white paint job and untraditional blue door. I strain my eyes, looking for a glint of yellow police tape. Stupid, considering the distance. I scan the yard across the street—decomposed granite neatly raked and a designer-landscaped garden of new succulents. The house next to it is surrounded by a chain-link fence, sun-bleached children's toys—years old—strewn haphazardly across a dead yard. I look back to Gilda. I catch Detective Marks watching me; we lock eyes for a stare down. I lose. Then back to Gilda, who is still looking out the window. I can't hear anyone breathing.

Jacob! Is Jacob even breathing?

I shake him gently and press my ear to his face. He gurgles and sucks in a breath. I try to swallow, the audible click in my throat is so loud—too loud? My mouth fills with prevomit saliva. The more I think about swallowing, the more I salivate. Finally, I pick up my mug of water and spit.

"Shit!" I say—it comes out a whisper. Jacob's oatmeal-looking spit-up has poured from his mouth onto my arm.

Detective Lopez remains completely still. Gilda hands me a paper towel. Marks is still playing the staring contest.

"The station?" Gilda asks Lopez.

"Gilda, is there anyone you'd like to call to meet us there?" Lopez says.

"I don't need anyone to hold my hand while I fill out more paperwork about my missing daughter. I need you all out there looking for her."

"I can come," I say. Jacob fusses while trying to wriggle himself free. "I can come to the station and help." I look down at Jacob, pleading for permission. "Shh, soon, baby, soon. Shh, shh, shh," I say in a whisper meant only for him.

"Good—someone wants to help the search move along faster," Gilda says. She doesn't look at me, and I wonder if she remembers my name—a stranger she met just moments ago. "Let me get my purse. Oh, and I printed a current picture of Kat. Do you have a copier at the station I can print out a few hundred to pass out?" Gilda asks the detectives.

"Yeah, bring it along," Detective Lopez says. She's being gentle, too warm when she says it.

We leave the house quiet, fussy, and disheveled—we could easily be leaving for Disneyland. Gilda and I climb in the back of the patrol car.

"Do you have a car seat?" I ask Marks.

"No car seat, but I won't ticket you for the offense today." Marks stands tall and wide. His body blocks the sun. His face is void of emotion or care.

It doesn't feel like Detective Marks is joking, but I grin despite the circumstances. I hold Jacob tight, pull his fragile body close, feel his heart against mine, hoping, needing our rhythms to sync, become one. His jogging stroller is packed in the trunk next to a neatly strapped black duffel bag and a rack-mounted shotgun. Who needs swings at the park? This is adventure. First word? Try first ride in a police cruiser.

12

The police station is quiet. Two p.m. on a Tuesday appears to be the time criminals don't get arrested in NELA. Detective Lopez and Detective Marks escort Gilda and me to the back of the station through a set of locked bulletproof doors. We are buzzed through and led around a large, open floor plan. Desks are organized in tight, orderly rows. Fluorescent lights blaze above us, emitting a quiet buzz that, once you hear it, you cannot *un*hear. The windows go from the floor to the ceiling and have the lightest of tints to them. It's very corporate, but the clients here wear handcuffs.

If I strain my ears, I can hear the artificial white noise being pumped through invisible speakers in the acoustic-tiled ceiling. The air-conditioning is arctic, dry, almost perfumed with recycled staleness.

Real police stations aren't like they are on television. There are no gorgeous people walking and talking, pretending to be busy. No Ralph Lauren suits tailored to hug perfect curves. No glossy lips that pout in concentration when listening to your story. Just a lot of people at desks staring at computers. Some streaming YouTube videos, some playing solitaire, some checking Facebook. It's like any other office building in America: worker bees at desks doing work, and plenty buzzing around. It's the energy that separates it from corporate America.

I look at every person I pass directly in the eye. My way of letting them know I'm not a criminal. It doesn't matter—they look right back and run a threat assessment; they can determine whether I'm crazy, guilty, or hiding something just by their stare, or so it seems.

I forget I'm holding Jacob. I don't notice the extra weight of him in my arms, but I always notice when he isn't with me—an appendage I must feed. They notice him too. They watch him pull at my shirt, his little fists beating on my breast, wanting to be fed. I feel the milk let down, my nipples tender in sync with his need. Not painful, but the sensation is immediate. Like being aroused, they need the release now as much as he needs the sustenance.

It overwhelms me to look around and see the real guns—pistols, actually, a fact now seared in my brain after being corrected one too many times when I was still in the newsroom—strapped to every person in the room. Their weapons on display, accessible. I can't stop from calculating how long it would take for me to go rogue, grab a gun off one of them, and start shooting before they could take me out. If I turn my back, I can shield Jacob from the inevitable spray of gunfire, but not the inevitable through and through—we'd both be goners. I look to Gilda; she can take my baby. Run away with him—a do-over.

I catch myself staring at Detective Lopez's sidearm as my fantasy continues to play on repeat. Something harder bangs against my chest, pulling my attention away from the violence. I look down; it's Jacob's head bobbing into my breast, demanding to be fed—again. Thank god for him. A mother with a baby is not a threat. At least, not a white mother, not in this country. Not yet.

I look up. Another officer has joined our party.

"Mrs. Donahue?" He is young, hair cropped too short, fresh-pressed blues, and shoes that have yet to crease. "I'm Officer Jefferies. You can follow me."

"Okay," Gilda answers. She stands perfectly straight: shoulder blades dropped back, chest up. She looks strong.

"We'll be back to meet you in a moment, Gilda," Detective Lopez says.

Gilda follows Officer Jefferies while Lopez and Marks turn toward me.

"Mrs. Lieberman," Detective Marks says.

"Corey is fine. And it's Tracey-Lieberman," I say.

"Before we head back with Mrs. Donahue, I need to ask you a few more questions," Marks says. "Do you mind?"

"Not at all." I smile as politely as I can while I say it. There's something familiar about Marks that I can't put my finger on. His general demeanor is a cop stereotype, but that's not it.

I give Jacob a squeeze, mostly for me, and I head to a room with Detective Marks.

"Thank you, Mrs. Lieberman, Corey, this is only a formality. How do you know Kat's mother, Mrs. Donahue?" Marks asks after closing the door. The room is a blank surface. The walls are white. There's a plain table with a laminate top—peeling away at the corners—and two metal chairs, one on either side of the table. Marks motions for me to have a seat. The overhead lights are fluorescent and bright, drawing attention to his skin. I recognize him now. Shit. It hits me in a series of flashbacks.

"I didn't until today. I went over to check in, to see if I could do anything."

Jacob squirms. I wish I could set him on the ground to play. A better mom would have a toy at the ready.

"You look very familiar, Mrs. Lieberman. What is it you do?"

"I'm a spin instructor. At the Cyclone Spin Studio. But you already know that."

He knows who I really am—or who I was.

"You worked for Kat and that's all?" he says. Marks is more threatening without Lopez in the room.

"It is. I *work* for Kat," I correct him. Why the hell did he say it in the past tense? Like I know she's dead. This is how words get twisted. This is why they separated me from Gilda. Everyone is going to be questioned. Watched. Listened to. Everyone is guilty until they aren't.

"Okay, Mrs. Lieberman, do you have ID on your person today?"

I rummage one-handed through the giant fanny pack around my waist—easier to run with than the tote bag. I manage to find my driver's license, a relic. The picture is twenty years old—I still look like shit. Marks stares at it for a moment.

"Corey Tracey. It took me a minute—Corey Tracey." He smiles. "I never forget a face. How long has it been?"

Detective fucking Marks. He has aged more than I would have thought, but then, so have I. He was an officer on site at a story I was assigned to cover early in my career. A tenant dispute.

Detective Marks was Officer Marks at the time—skinny, young, shiny, and new. He was sent out to the NELA neighborhood of El Sereno, the oldest community in LA, where bungalows and craftsmen compete for space, for a disturbing the peace call: a group of tenants picketing and protesting outside their apartment building in an attempt to bring attention to unlawful evictions. Officer Marks attempted to break up the protest but without authority to do so. Picketing was the only thing within their rights to do. And so the marching, the chanting, the yelling continued. I jumped the line to get a few sound bites from the tenants. I approached Officer Marks for a quote. That's when he slapped the camera out of my cameraman's hand and wrote us a ticket for interfering with an officer. We caught the slap on video and ran it on the air. *LA News First*, me—we received equal amounts of hate and praise for airing the slap, but one person emailed me regularly with passive threats to "watch my back," and a few times they emailed me violent pornography with the subject line of "Whore." I looked into Marks, had Chris ask his cousin—source—on the LAPD if he knew Marks. He did. He liked him. All my sleuthing online and word of mouth told me the guy was not my emailer. The day of the slap was just a bad day for Marks—and a bad few months for my email.

"Were you going to tell anyone you were press, or were you going to let that one skate by as long as I didn't recognize you?" Marks says.

I still want to punch him in the face all these years later.

"I'm no longer at *LA News First*. Like I said, I am a friend of Kat and her mother, and I'm here for moral support."

"Are you recording this conversation?" He pauses after asking me—what should be rhetorical required a response.

"Should I be?"

"You'll need to leave your phone with me if you plan on heading back to be with your friend."

Marks's voice makes my armpits sweat. The gun on his waist, coupled with his past erratic behavior, gives rise to my anxiety. Were I a suspect, it would be a sure sign of guilt. I hand him my phone.

"Listen, I don't want to have to be the bad guy here, but don't get involved in my case," he says.

Is that a challenge? I pat Jacob's back, and he lets out a mighty baby belch. I get up to leave Marks's office but can't help myself.

"Next time I see you, I'll bring credentials."

Through a glass window in the conference room at the back of the floor, I see Gilda at a table, leaning on her elbows. I knock. A young woman wearing a **FEEL THE BERN** T-shirt, cardigan, and a pair of Old Navy mom jeans—I recognize them because I own a pair, but she's wearing them ironically—rises from the table to greet me.

"Corey, you're still here," Gilda says.

"I'm sorry it took so long—they had me fill out some paperwork."

I find a seat at the table across from Gilda.

This is my opportunity to hear the details firsthand as the police recite what they know. I rummage for my phone in the fanny pack—fuck, is this baby brain? Marks took it. I find a diaper and a Sharpie. I pull both out, again one-handed, and set them on the chair next to me. If I can write some of the info down, my memory will do the rest. There has been another young woman's body found at Debs. No matter who she is, she was found on my trail, at my park, and so were two girls before her. I look over at Officer Jefferies. He's too young, doesn't look ready for this—I am.

"Your baby is beautiful," the woman in mom jeans says.

"Thank you. I'm Corey." I extend my hand.

"Yes, Gilda let me know. I'm Tiffany."

"She's a social worker," Gilda says.

Officer Jefferies squirms in his chair. "As I was saying, Mrs. Donahue, Detective Lopez and Detective Marks will be in shortly. They're going to walk you through the process. Are you sure there isn't anything I can get you? Water? Coffee?"

Gilda shakes her head. I smile, then look at the gun on his hip, testing the thoughts. The lurkers. Nothing. Silence. I'm good.

My pulse races, but it feels different, less confused, not muddled with fear. Excitement. That's it. The claws of this case have drawn first blood, and I like it. I check my watch: 186 beats per minute, maximum speed for endurance spinning and weight loss—also panic attacks, and I am fine. Jacob starts to fuss. The door swings open. There they are. The dynamic duo, Detectives Lopez and Marks. Same expressions from when I passed out this morning. But I'm not that person now. Lopez carries a sealed manila envelope under her arm.

"Gilda, thank you for your patience," she says.

"It's fine. I hope you haven't stopped looking for Kat, despite this other woman you've found, God bless her," Gilda says, making prayer hands and whispering an amen to God.

"This is not easy, and you've been through a lot today, Mrs. Donahue," Tiffany says, an interjection. "Would you like a moment? Maybe get some air real quick before we . . ." She is maternal and yet younger than both Gilda and me, naturally curly hair swept up off her face, ID swinging from a lanyard around her neck. She is mid-twenties, maybe close to burned out on the job, and way too mature for a name like Tiffany. How could a Tiffany look more put together than me? Better than Gilda, sure, she lost her kid. She gives Gilda's hand a squeeze, and I see Gilda squeeze back.

"No, let's get this done so everyone can keep searching for Kat," Gilda says. She sounds angry, resentful, almost certain that the body they found was not her child, that they are wasting precious time.

Detective Lopez sets the manila envelope on the table and pulls out a seat while Detective Marks remains standing. Pictures of a dead girl are inside that manila folder. Pictures of a dead girl Gilda has to identify as Kat. I know because I remember how these moments play out. Confirmation is needed because they have to stop looking for a missing woman and start looking for a killer, a suspect.

I can tell Detective Marks believes it's Kat. His disposition is a tell—he stands close to Gilda, ready to catch a possible fainting mother. They are playing it smart. They are not going to lose Gilda to grief with these pictures before they have all the information they need from her. The envelope is set aside, forgotten, not a part of the next conversation.

I bounce Jacob on my knee while I try to steady my free hand to write.

"Let's start with the last conversation you had with Kat. What did you two talk about?" Detective Lopez asks Gilda.

"Normal stuff. Work, the weekend . . . God, I don't even know—stupid stuff, really," she says.

"That's good, really good. Did she talk about any plans she had that day?"

"Yeah, yeah—she was teaching her usual beginners' class at one . . . she told me about a woman who keeps coming to the class because it's free and yet she won't sign up for any other classes. She asked my advice on how to handle it—should she tell her she isn't allowed any more free beginner classes or just, you know, let it be. Charity."

"That's good. Did she mention her name?"

"No, not that I can remember. A 'white lady, with a little extra in the middle,' as Kat put it." Gilda smiles.

"Great. That's great, Gilda. What about before her class? Do you know what her plans were for the morning?"

"She was going for a run. She mentioned she had a work meeting at this boba place she loves. Kat is a caffeine addict. She loves espresso with heavy cream and that espresso-flavored boba."

I swallow, too hard.

"The meeting was probably with Monique, her business partner," Gilda says. "That's where they usually meet."

"I was at that meeting." My stomach churns, acids take over, reflux and bile rise into my chest. Excitement has made a hard-right turn into panic. "Kat never made it."

Detective Lopez writes down my outburst. Gilda looks at me, pinning me with a flat stare. Empty of judgment.

"Where did she normally go running, Gilda? Is there a particular route she's known to take?" Lopez continues the questions.

"Yes," Gilda says. "She usually heads down Marmion Way—running alongside the train tracks to Avenue 52, where you can cross over the freeway and enter Debs at the Audubon." Gilda stops to wipe her face with a tissue. "She likes to do a loop, usually around the little pond, then head back. It usually takes her an hour. She's an excellent runner."

"Would she ever drive to Debs? For any reason? Had she driven there in the past?" Lopez asks.

"Oh sure, she's driven to hike. She would go to the opposite entrance, though. The side with the parking lot off of Monterey Road. She would drive with me, since I'm not a runner. Or, if she had a class to teach right after a hike, she might drive. Sometimes she'd go on her run straight from the Cyclone studio."

Tiffany rubs Gilda's back. Jacob has become a liability. His body falls limp in slumber. I desperately try to scribble the path Kat frequented onto the diaper while catching Jacob against my chest and throwing my head back to avoid his soft but hard skull crashing into my nose—a learned instinct from too many near crushes.

"Do you remember what she was wearing that morning?"

"Leggings—pink tie-dye ones. A purple Cyclone tank top and she had her hair in a ponytail. She always wears yoga pants and tank tops," Gilda says.

Tiffany smiles as though Gilda is funny. These are facts, Tiffany, I want to say, of the last time Kat was seen alive; do not smile. I wonder now if Tiffany is good at her job or not. Maybe she should be a kindergarten teacher.

"What about a boyfriend?" Lopez asks.

It sounds cliché coming out of Lopez's mouth. It's always the lover, except when it's not.

"Kat broke up with her boyfriend over a year ago."

"Do you remember his name?"

"Dan."

Marks shifts his weight. The manila envelope moves—the vent above it makes it look like it has a pulse of its own.

"Last name?"

"Maybe Milner . . . Milner, yeah, Milner, I think."

"Good. Was there someone new she was seeing? Was she on any dating apps, maybe?"

"I don't know. No one she's told me about."

"I need you to think of any names she may have mentioned to you. Something in passing. Think back to the conversation you had that morning before you went to San Diego . . ."

Gilda closes her eyes. I look around the room. Detective Marks studies Gilda's face, watching the quiet stream of tears pool in her clavicle.

"I don't know. I can't think," she says.

"Okay, Gilda, that's okay. I'm going to have you write down the names of all those she came in contact with regularly, like colleagues, friends that you know of or that you've heard her mention in passing. What coffee shops she frequented and lunch spots that were a part of her daily routine. The usual places anyone who knew Kat would know she'd be at. Anywhere that someone might have recognized her that day."

"Okay, I can do that."

"One more thing, did she mention if she was going to meet someone at the park that day?" This is the big question Detective Lopez has led up to gently. Who the hell was Kat with Saturday morning?

"She didn't say. I remember the news from a couple days before—there were the two girls found dead." Gilda looks to Lopez for help.

She struggles to say what she's thinking. I'm thinking it too: Did she run into the same person Araceli and Natalie did? Is that what happened to Kat?

"She wouldn't put herself at risk. Kat has always been strong willed. Likely she would have met a friend to run or hike with that day." Gilda suddenly looks beyond exhausted, bone tired. "You know, Kat was on the track team at Franklin High School. She was the captain. Fastest on the team. She also ran in college, partial scholarship. Now she's a member of a running club. She's no stranger to running around the city at all hours of the day and night. She's not afraid of anything. Sometimes she meets up with another runner. But it's not always preplanned."

Detective Lopez smiles; it's that maternal smile, a gesture. Gilda, Lopez, Tiffany—a coven of maternal energy. The same smile she gave me when she told me to take Benadryl. "Okay, very good," Lopez says. She then retrieves the envelope she brought into the room with her. An alarm screeches in the main office. It startles Jacob from his sleep and freaks me out. It stops abruptly. Detective Lopez does not miss a beat. She opens the seal while I vigorously bounce Jacob back to sleep. I just want to get through the photographs without interruption.

"Now, Gilda, I am going to show you some pictures of a young woman, and you're going to help me identify whether it is Kat or not. Do you understand what I am asking you to do?"

"Yes," Gilda says. She sits up a little straighter in the chair. Dries her face with the back of her hand, then places both hands on the table. She looks prepared to take a test.

"These photos will be difficult to look at," Lopez says. "You are going to tell me if you recognize this person as Kat. Are you ready?"

Gilda nods.

I walk around the table, stand behind her. I can smell Tiffany's perfume or soap, shampoo maybe—it's mango. The first picture Lopez sets down is a straight-on shot of Kat's face.

Gilda clasps her hand to her mouth. A small moan, muffled, comes through her fingers. There are more tears as she nods at the picture.

The second photo is Kat's profile.

Gilda nods again. Her face is wrecked. She can barely manage to look. Tiffany is holding her up, preventing her from completely slumping over in pain. Good job, Tiffany.

There is Kat, on a table, eyes closed. Her hair down, matted behind her. She is puffy, bruised. Dead.

Gilda cries from a place I hope I never have to: a deep place, a well, dark and hopeless. I've never heard a sound so guttural. Jacob wakes, quickly drowning out Gilda's crying with his own. I leave the room to quiet him. Thank you, God. Thank you for protecting my child. Please don't let my baby die—don't let my baby die. Jacob wails through my prayer, and I know I need to quiet him. I awkwardly undo the strap on my nursing bra and let him latch. In the middle of this police station. I don't care. My baby is alive, and I've got him. I hold him tight. I will never let him out of my sight.

I go back into the room. Gilda is slumped into Tiffany, sobbing. Tiffany soothing her. I soothe Jacob, soothe myself. Detective Lopez shoves the photos back into the envelope.

"Gilda—" she starts to say.

"No more," Gilda says as she raises herself off Tiffany, face red, going purple. Eyes swollen. Lips and nose puffy.

This makes it three women dead in one week, in my Highland Park.

◆ ◆ ◆

Detective Lopez brings back my phone and has me wait an hour in the main lobby before taking me home. Gilda is still back with Marks. I contemplate an Uber, but I want more information if I can get it. I snap pictures of my notes on the size-three diaper before I use it to change Jacob on the bench in the waiting area of the police department—exposing him to the public bathroom here would warrant extra vaccinations. I have seventeen text messages and two missed calls from Evan.

I need to know if Kat was alone at Debs that day. I need to ask Lopez exactly where Kat's car was found. The question I keep thinking is who knew Kat's routine and car? A stalker? A friend or neighbor? Did this person also know the other dead girls? Was it all a coincidence? I text the one person I need to hear from.

Me: Missing friend is 187 today.

NELAScanBoy: Shit

Me: You busy now?

NELAScanBoy: Yeah—7?

Me: 7

"You ready to go?" Detective Lopez says.

"Yeah, is there a trash?" I pick up the poop-soiled diaper, get a nod from Lopez, and toss it to her.

"Good arm," she says. Lopez chucks the diaper into a bin next to the bulletproof-glass-encased reception desk.

I text Evan.

Me: Getting ride home. Meet me outside, need help with stroller.

13

Evan is standing outside with his cell phone pressed against his ear. He looks a combination of worried and pissed. The same look my father gave me when I was sixteen and dropped off in a patrol car—drunk. I sit a minute longer in the back seat, Jacob in my arms.

"Thank you," I say to Lopez. "I'm going to find who did this to Kat."

"Is there something else you want to tell me about Kat? Anything that could clue me in to how you're going to do that? Why she may have been found at the bottom of a cliff at Debs?"

"No," I say. "I know what Gilda told you today." Lopez is waiting for me to say more. "Can *you* tell me anything about the two girls found hanged and why the only information that's been released is that it may be gang related?" It was worth a shot to ask. Either we bond today or we don't.

"You were with *LA News First*, right?" Lopez asks.

"And?"

"Accidents happen, Corey. More frequently than we'd like to admit. The news broadcasts more deaths than it ever used to, and yet there are still victims you never know about because no station will mention them. You know this—you better be white and pretty if you're going to make the news, let alone the national headlines. There are missing brown women in abundance. I've seen more dead bodies and sat with more families asking, 'Why do you think this happened?' than a person should in this lifetime. And I'll tell you, they don't all get solved."

I fish in my fanny pack for the Sharpie. "Do you have another card on you?" I ask. Lopez hands one over. I take it and write my cell on the back. "You probably already have it, I'm sure. But here, please call me when you have something. Anything at all," I say.

She takes the card. "Why don't you call me when you have more to say."

"You gave my husband your card," I say. Lopez reaches in her pocket again and passes me one more card. "Keep this one for yourself, Ms. Tracey-Lieberman."

I don't need to answer; there is an understanding now. I get out of the car with Jacob. When I turn around, Evan is making his way down our driveway to the sidewalk. He squeezes both Jacob and me.

"I can't breathe, too tight," I say.

"Jesus, Corey, I've been worried sick. You don't answer my calls, you send me a cryptic text, and you show up with the police officer from this morning?"

"She's a detective."

"Where have you been?" Evan asks.

"I'm sorry. I don't know where to start—"

"Try, because honestly, I don't think you get it. You don't know how worried I've been. The last I saw you this morning, you had a massive panic attack. Then you go fucking MIA!"

"They took my phone—"

"Who took your phone?"

"At the police station—"

"Were you arrested?"

"Calm down—" Oof, now I'm saying it.

"Don't tell me to calm down when I've been calling everyone we know, the hospital, Trader Joe's, everywhere looking for you!"

"I'll explain when we get inside. I need to get Jacob's stroller out of the trunk."

Lopez is out of the car and unloading the jogging stroller. Evan extends his hand. "Thank you," he says. His voice and face are giving off an impression that I read as *Thank you for bringing back my crazy wife.*

"Thank you, Mr. Lieberman. Your wife was a tremendous help today," Lopez says.

I nod in thanks toward Lopez, then usher Evan toward the house.

Lopez sits in the cruiser at the curb until we are inside, door shut. I look through the front window and watch as she pulls out a notepad and starts writing. She looks up at me, waves, then pulls away.

14

Evan looks deflated after I give him my version of events. His combed hair looks thinner. He leans forward on his legs, head down, unresponsive for some time.

"Jesus," he says.

"I know. I need to go back out tonight," I say. I hesitate. "I'm meeting Chris."

"No."

"I'm not asking you for permission."

"This isn't your job anymore, Corey. You're a mother; you have a baby who needs you. This strain on top of the postpartum—"

"You don't know I have postpartum anxiety, or depression, or anything. You can't say that, Evan. You're not a fucking doctor."

"And you're not an investigator with a news team or a story." His words hit me hard. I sit down. We're both silent until Jacob squeals—it's become a game: Mommy and Daddy yelling, then quiet. Jacob is becoming too familiar with it.

"When's your rescheduled appointment with Dr. Rosenberg, Corey?" The contempt in Evan's voice isn't subtle.

I still haven't called Dr. Rosenberg. I'm not ready to be told I'm crazy by an actual psychiatrist. What if they want to put me in a hospital? Can thoughts make me a danger to my baby and myself? Jacob would at least stay with his father, not be given to someone else, right? Evan worries about none of that. His fear is wrapped up in wondering if I would fall in love with Chris and leave him.

"End of the week," I say.

"When? I'll go with you."

"I don't need a chaperone."

Evan and I were premature. We'd been together six months, fucking for most of that time, when his lease expired. He'd been saving for a house since his senior year in college; caught in the net of what could be, we started house hunting. I scoured greater LA for furniture that suited who I'd become someday. When he carried me across the threshold into our new house in Highland Park, I held back from asking to be put down.

The first month, when we should have been nesting and filling the home with our things, I worked. Late. I made it home every night but one—nothing happened, but I wished it had.

When Chris and I weren't at work together, we were texting or chatting. The relationship consumed me. Anger settled in me when I was home and not at work.

"Are you mad at me?" Evan asked. Often. I wanted to be mean, say mean things, push him—punch him for being less than, less than Chris. It wasn't his fault. I excused my mood under the umbrella of work.

I blamed it on stress. The demand of moving too fast with Evan. I didn't love him any less. Didn't want to marry him any less. But I dreamed of Chris. Entangled in the sheets. Not sleeping. His hands on me. His body on mine, solid, the weight of it against my chest. I dreamed of tracing my fingers down his back; soft, muscular, warm. I had never fantasized about anyone the way I fantasized about Chris.

The morning I walked in after I'd been gone all night, I found Evan lightly sleeping on the couch. I tried to creep upstairs without waking him, but the house was old and terrible at cover-ups.

"Corey! My god. Where the hell have you been?" He was up, wrapping me into an embrace that left me immobile before I could feel any worse.

"I'm sorry. I didn't mean to wake you. I'm fine, really, tired," I said.

"Where have you been?"

"We had a big break in the story. Someone called in a tip. It was a rabbit hole from there." I believed myself. It was easier than I thought—besides, nothing happened with Chris. The story—a body left to decompose in the trunk of a car in residential West Hollywood—would run that morning. It was the third time in less than a year that a stolen car from San Diego had been dumped in a residential Los Angeles neighborhood. All three bodies—male—left with no teeth and too far gone to identify. I'd been tracking down the cars—when were the cars reported missing, who were the owners, where did they work, where did they park their cars? The cops and the FBI weren't talking to the press or to each other. Cartel business—the same crude markings every time. The information wasn't public, but the residents of Los Angeles had a right to know the cartel was doing business in our neighborhoods—all of them.

"Why didn't you text me?" He paused at my shrug. "I called the station—you weren't there."

"I was working at the diner."

"With Chris?"

"Yeah, with Chris. This is a big story. I've told you that."

"And so was the last one and the one before that." He didn't look at me. "What's going on between you and Chris?"

"Please don't start that again," I said. "It's work." I stepped in close. "You knew when we started this how much I commit to my job."

"It's not only about work—stop lying to yourself. We both know it."

Evan stood, silent, waiting for me to deny it or argue or make more excuses. I didn't.

"Screw this. Do you want to be with me?" he asked.

"Yes."

"Then let's set a date for our wedding."

I nodded before confirming verbally.

"Okay," I said. And we did.

I loved the security I felt with Evan. I didn't want to lose that feeling. Chris was something else. An escape.

◆ ◆ ◆

"Corey?" Evan says.

"I'm okay. I spoke to Dr. Rosenberg on the phone, and he didn't think I needed to call 911. Let me go do this tonight. I need this. I need to find who killed these women. Girls," I say.

"Jesus, fuck, Corey. None of my friends deal with this bullshit."

"None of your friends have wives that work," I say.

"Two. Two of my friends' wives chose to stay home and be the full-time parent. And you did too, remember?"

"No. No, I didn't. I was fired. And blacklisted. And depressed."

"I'm not going to rehash old arguments. I'm not going to do that anymore, Corey. I try and try, and I'm always the bad guy or the nag or the jealous husband. All I want is to read my kid a bedtime story. Have a little one-on-one time with him, with you. I'm sick of going to work with the nagging feeling you're not okay."

"Evan, I'm okay. And you're a wonderful dad. But I need to do this—it's what I do. I investigate. Please," I say.

"Hate to burst your bubble, Corey, but you are a spin instructor," Evan says. He walks upstairs, leaving Jacob with me.

"I'm sorry," I say to no one. "I thought you wanted to see me happy again." I want to make a hundred excuses—but we'd all see through them, even the baby.

15

I strap Jacob into his car seat and head to the diner, House of Pies. Technically, no one considers Los Feliz a part of Northeast Los Angeles, our beloved NELA. It is a stepsister based on proximity. Another town with a growing disparity—rich or poor, the middle lost to a void of the in-between. The streets are lined with outdoor dining. Tables covered in linens and crystal water glasses that passersby could brush their hands across. The wedge of sidewalk between the street and the diners a holding place for the queue of hungry patrons waiting. The houses, a mix of tiny bungalows and old craftsmen. Some windows are dressed with security bars, some with shiny new double-pane vinyl, black trim if the place is going for a modern-classic remodel. There are the lawns that rival junkyards, homes that need paint, some of it peeling off in sheets. Next door a house can look new, a Tesla or two parked in the driveway, an Airbnb over the garage. On other streets, not too far off, the homes are tents. The real kicker, across Los Feliz Boulevard—a mere jog away—mansions filled with celebrities look over the entire city. The mix of old, new, rich, and poor an inherent part of a misunderstood culture.

Jacob and I wait in a familiar booth, the orange vinyl starting to show cracks. One I spent more nights in than I can count. I keep an eye on the door. It's been almost three years since I've seen Chris in the flesh, but in that time, I've lost a career, gotten pregnant, and had a baby. He could have a limp, a gut, a receding hairline by now.

"Can I get you something while you wait?" The waitress is young; she looks tired, her face plain, unlike the hostesses down the street, where the queues of hip, hungry diners wait. She also likely dreams the LA cliché that most dream—one leading role could give her ingenue status and a career. One customer could be a studio executive and change her life forever. Her hair is freshly dyed, strawberry blond, but she is obviously a natural brunette. Her eyebrows and arm hair betray her.

"Yeah, I'll have a coffee, side of fries, and a slice of the berry pie," I say.

"Blueberry?"

"Perfect."

"Corey." It's Chris. Calling to me as he strides to the table like we've just been here together, like this is normal, like it hasn't been years. I'm perplexed to see him so comfortable, familiar, smiling. I notice the hostess stare and smile, too big, as if Chris were a *Teen Beat* pinup, not that she would ever know what a *Teen Beat* was. I stand and give a quick, awkward hello. Before I can extend my arms, Chris has me wrapped up in a bear hug. He smells like . . . home.

"Sorry. Not used to those hugs now. Anymore," I say. My face feels the heat of embarrassment.

"You look amazing," he says. The compliment doesn't give me the boost it used to. Now I feel on display. Vulnerable. My once-blond hair is now dishwater blond, as my mom calls it. Stringy instead of lush. Always up instead of brushed. But I'm a new mom. I have no time for myself anymore. It doesn't matter that Chris is here.

Together. Again. Finally. We both smile—awkward after so much time texting with no physical contact.

"Is this Jacob?"

"Yup. Jacob, meet Chris. Chris, meet Jacob."

My smile strains the crow's-feet that are beginning to form around my eyes.

"Sit, please. Did you order?" he asks.

"The usual," I say.

"I may need more. I've been starving all day."

His body is still lean; the cotton of his T-shirt stretches across his six-pack the way it always has. Aside from the few stray grays at his temples contrasting against the dark brown of his thick hair, he looks the same, can pass for twenty-five instead of thirty-eight.

"I'm sorry about your friend," he says.

I look at Jacob. Adjust his blanket. "We weren't close. More like acquaintances. I worked with her, well, technically for her."

"At the spin studio?"

"Yeah, did I tell you that?"

"I may have seen it on your Facebook," he says. I blush. "I never pictured you as a spin instructor, but I like it. You have always known how to command a room." He grins wide, showing a silver filling on a bottom molar among the bright white of his teeth.

I smile. Are we flirting? I can't remember what usual banter sounds like. Am I betraying Evan or just catching up?

"You should drop into one of my classes sometime," I say.

The words are out there before I can edit or call them back. An unintentional swipe right, my face turns warm.

"I don't hear from you in well over a year, and now you want me to drop in on your spin class?" He laughs. "I think we should probably slow things down a little, Ms. Tracey."

"Sorry. You're right. I'm out of touch a lot lately."

"Wow. Are you trying to *un*invite me, now?"

"No, no, no, sorry. I can give you a free pass."

If I had a mirror, I would confirm that the color of my face has changed to a splotchy fuchsia. I wish I could turn out the lights and sit with him in the dark and hide the emotions that threaten to reveal me all at once.

"I'm just teasing you. It's been a while since we've done this in person," he says. He's still smiling, beaming.

"One coffee, fries, and a slice of blueberry pie." The waitress slides my plates onto the table.

The interruption saving me from the awkwardness of our catch-up.

"Now, can I get you something, sir?" The waitress blushes at his look. Her pale skin betraying her unfairly, like mine. At least I'm off the hook—at the moment. I need the distraction too. I need to stop thinking about kissing this man.

"I'll have the same, cream and sugar for the coffee, and a burger—add cheese and extra pickles on the side—and blueberry pie with a scoop of vanilla. Thanks." Chris hands his menu to the waitress, and she blushes again.

"Did you find anything out? About Kat or the two girls?" I need us to get right into the work, or I might end up in the deep end of an entirely different pool.

"Right down to business, like old times," Chris says. "I don't have a lot on Kat. The autopsy isn't done yet, and it's really too early to say much of anything. She may have fallen or tripped. My cousin said she may have thrown herself off the edge."

"You mean jumped? Like a suicide? No, not Kat. She was an athlete. She was happy. Genuinely a happy person with way too many endorphin triggers to be depressed." I try to convince myself this is true. I know better than anyone how one bad moment can feel like jumping off a cliff.

"Like I said, this is talk. They haven't ruled Kat's death as a homicide yet, and they haven't ruled out suicide. If it leans toward accidental death or undetermined, I have to tell you it's because resources are scarce. They're not going to dive deep without sufficient evidence. The goal for the LAPD is to close cases as fast as they can. That's what they do."

"And what about the medical examiner?"

"If there aren't any signs of struggle and she died from the fall, they'll likely lean toward undetermined."

"That's bullshit." My feet are planted firmly on the ground as I say it. "She's the third death in a week—"

"Listen, listen, you also didn't know her well—you said so yourself." He pauses. I look down at my phone, then Jacob. "Far be it from me to counter your instincts. But I'm also not sure how Kat's case relates to the two girls, except for the fact that they both happened at Debs Park."

"Around the same time," I say.

"That's a coincidence and not a big one. This is a big city—there's death every day. You've been an investigative journalist almost your entire career. You know all of this."

He's right, but so am I.

"Maybe she knew her killer," I say. My breasts are leaking before I hear the tiny whimper from Jacob.

"Sorry, I have to feed this guy." I lift my top, revealing a maternity tank underneath with a corner to fold down for breastfeeding. I look up at Chris, who watches. "What?" I ask.

"Nothing. You don't have to apologize. I'm surprised you brought him is all."

"He comes everywhere with me. He's full time."

"I didn't mean that. I'm glad. I wasn't sure you would show me this side of you," he says.

"What's that supposed to mean?"

"Come on, you've always separated work and private life."

"Well, they've merged."

"Where's Evan?" he asks.

"Home. Pissed," I say. "Rightfully so. I've not been great."

The smell of burger wafts to the table preceding the arrival of more food. The three of us eat in silence. The boys inhale their meals while I pick at the pie and fries with my free hand. We wait for the unspeakable tension to subside. I can't tell if it's only me wanting Chris or if he is projecting his own feelings too.

"How do you want to work this?" Chris is first to break our silence. His words shatter the thoughts of what it would be like to be with him playing in my head.

"I need an inside source at the police station. Someone I can trust, someone who can get access to both cases," I say. "I don't want to play telephone. I want what their eyes see and what they've been told directly, at minimum. I don't have anyone left at *LA News First* to ask for favors."

"Okay. I'll see what I can do," he says. "You were at the police station today—who were the cops working it?"

"Female detective named Lopez, late forties, maybe fifty, and a Detective Marks, male, a little older. Both veterans. I may have gotten in with Lopez, but I won't know unless she calls me. I have a feeling I'll be seeing her sooner than she expects. I don't know who's working the girls' case from the hanging. I asked Detective Lopez about it—but she didn't respond. Does your cousin know?"

"Yeah, he'll know."

The energy shifts. We're back; the team is back. The mood changes—quiet spaces are no longer heavy but comfortable. Our minds focused on the work.

"I'll message you tomorrow with what I can get. Let me know what you hear from the spin-studio grapevine—other instructors. Check back in with the mom," Chris says.

"I know how to do my job." I say it more to tease than bite.

"Wasn't suggesting you didn't." Chris picks at his pie. Then says, "Do you know if Kat was seeing anyone? Romantically?"

"No, no I don't know. Her mom said she wasn't. Broke up with her boyfriend a year ago." I pull out my phone and examine the photo of Jacob's diaper. "A Dan Milner. I'll ask around the studio, though. OW!" I involuntarily shove my finger between Jacob's mouth and my nipple to release his bite-grip. "Sorry. He's a biter," I say.

"So was I," he says and starts to laugh like a little boy.

I roll my eyes. The rosy goggles off. It's time to work.

"What I want to know is what are we going to do when we solve these murders?" he asks. "I know what I want to do, and I'm not going to let these victims be swept under the rug of gang-related bullshit to preserve the gentrifiers' pockets."

"You mean white people. You can say it. We've been taking over for centuries. We are an inevitable plague on the community," I say. I am one of them. I know it.

"Then we're on the same page," Chris says. "You're white." He can't help but laugh at himself, again.

"Some things can't change." But it doesn't have to stop me from helping to get the stories of these women out there.

"You don't need to change, Corey. Just understand who you are and why you're doing this."

I am the ultimate cliché—a white savior, right? But there isn't anyone left to save. All three girls are dead. I just want to know why. Need it.

Chris pays the tab while I am distracted covering myself postfeeding. The gesture sends an unwarranted but very real spark of heat through my bloodstream. I catch him watching me again. A crush can never really cease to exist. Not until someone makes a move.

16

Before I leave the diner, my phone blows up with messages I expected were coming.

> *Cyclone:* Mandatory meeting tomorrow at eight A.M.

> *Diane:* Think we can bring our kids?

I leave Diane's question on read. I wonder if she knows I've seen her text. I question if she thinks I should be leaving my baby at home for the news that's to come at the meeting. She didn't text me that the police had been to visit her, but I have not told her or anyone else they'd visited me; we aren't that close. Obviously, Monique would know. I have to keep my mouth shut and allow everyone the opportunity to come to me with their gossip and theories—what they've heard from whom and when they heard it.

> *Monique:* I need you here at 7:15 A.M. Lieberman

My opportunity.

> *Me:* Sure

> *Monique:* Gilda called me

Me: I'm sorry

. . .

. . .

The text bubbles appear and disappear, then nothing. I pull up to my pitch-dark house and ready myself for whatever I have to face inside. If luck is at least around the corner, Evan will be asleep and not waiting up in the dark, the glow of a cell phone illuminating his rage. I tiptoe inside with Jacob clutched to my chest.

Evan is asleep on the floor in Jacob's room, in a sleeping bag. I put Jacob in his crib and leave. My talisman in his room, away from me, but I need to work. Alone. I bring my laptop to bed with me. The fear of losing my own child, a fear I have battled since he was in utero, is scratching its way to the surface. The idea that I could be the person who inflicts pain on my child, purposeful and with malice, swims through my brain like a shark—unrelenting and looking to feed. These nonsensical, intrusive thoughts like nightmares while I'm awake. And because there's nothing to wake up from, I wish for sleep, usually.

My lungs deflate when I think about breathing. I need to change the narrative in my head. Now. Quickly. I force my brain to go back to Gilda. I remember her stoicism at the police station. Her initial denial of the news. Her steadfastness when it came to seeing her daughter's body.

I play a game in my head that I call Checking in on My Demon—a symptom of the circular thoughts, one step forward, then a slip back. Do I think I will hurt my baby? The question is not a concise translation of the thought. To verbalize the darkness feels insurmountable, a feat as impossible as climbing Mount Everest with Jacob clinging to my chest—it is untranslatable fear. I cannot articulate these thoughts, and I can't stop thinking them—are there knives in the house? No. But there are—they're just hidden. And the intrusive thoughts are back.

I can't tell Evan about my brain, how it feels when ideas and images of my son, dead, circulate, brew for hours. My heart snaps like a tight rubber band, breaks into shards, and leaves me wide open.

Maybe every mother thinks, What if I can't protect my child . . . from me?

I get out of bed and start a set of push-ups to stop thinking: Three, four, five, six, seven . . . do not think of knives anymore . . . eight, nine, ten . . . do not think of death . . . eleven, twelve, thirteen, fourteen . . . do not think of your son, dead.

My heart races as the numbers get higher, and I slow down and talk to myself. "You've got this, Corey. You're good. It's fine. Think about something else." I want to rush back into his room, pull him from his crib, and sleep with him right beside me. I want to challenge the thoughts in my head. Silence them without clinging to my baby too. I sit on the bed, open up my laptop, and type Drew Hudson into my Google search. I know what will display first—his Facebook. It always does. Then Drew's company, where he was made a VP of sales. Then his LinkedIn page. Then a few Hudsons that are not Drew, and it gets broader from there. I choose Facebook. I like seeing pictures of Drew and his family. Like to see if he still lives in Los Angeles or if he's moved on somewhere far, far away.

Preferably, he would be dead.

Does he still have followers and friends? Has the number increased or decreased since I visited a week earlier? Are there other victims of his rapes keeping tabs on his social media presence like I am? Are they verbal? Are they leaving comments?

I want to write to his wife and tell her to beware. Tell their two children, both boys, that a monster lives in the house. I want to teach them how not to be like him. Is his wife testing for STDs regularly? She should be. How does a rapist get married, be faithful? It's a joke that doesn't make me laugh.

I look him up in public court filings to see if anyone has pressed charges against him. One day they will. He will eventually pin down a woman who will say no. He will take what he wants like he did from me. But she will be better than me. She will tell. She will protect other women from the same fate. She will go directly to the hospital and not let him drive her home. She will allow them to do a rape kit on her, a four-hour ordeal that makes the vulnerability she's already carrying feel like it will never end. That woman will not sit on the floor of her shower for an hour trying to rinse the evidence away. She will talk to the police. Be brave. Not question her fault in the event. She will yell from the rooftops, "Drew Hudson is a rapist!"

That woman will not need to stalk him on the internet, reassuring herself his life is nowhere near hers. She will not fear him or fear that she has to carry a secret rape around with her. Drew will remember her, even when he pretends not to remember who I am.

17

I leave for Cyclone Studio with Jacob. Evan is still in the shower. I leave him a note:

> *I'm sorry. I wasn't thinking. Can we be okay? I'm at the*
> *studio working today, but I'll call Dr. Rosenberg to see if*
> *I can get in earlier.*
> > *I love you,*
> > *Corey*

Dr. Rosenberg. A doctor from the list of two psychiatrists taking patients. The only one of two who also specializes in counseling. Both on the list are men. It has to be a man or no one, and so, it seems, I really am choosing no one at this point.

I get to the studio as the sun breaks the sky from the urban horizon—concrete and telephone wires coming to chromatic life. I punch in the wrong code to enter the parking garage, step back a moment to let it reset. My milk is letting down. Jacob yelps with excitement. I haven't pumped yet.

Fuck.

"Hold on, baby," I say.

I walk to the gate where the cars enter and punch in the same code—fingers crossed. The metal gate scrapes open; God must be real. Someone has changed one and not the other, and as early as yesterday.

Was it Monique? I look up. The security cameras are strategically placed at all angles at all entrances.

I punch in my code to the studio entrance. It bleeps red. I try three more times before the system locks me out. Once more and the police will be called, so I wait outside for Monique.

"We're good at waiting, huh, buddy?" Jacob cries for food, milk, me. I didn't realize he'd started crying—bad mother. The thoughts try to creep in. I try to ignore them with a parade of rainbow images in my head. Jacob doesn't know yet that I'm a shitty mother. "I'm your shitty mother." The look on his face I interpret as love, but it could be gas. I lift my shirt. He immediately relaxes in my arms. He feels heavier than yesterday, last night even. My arms burn under his weight. "I love you, my sweet boy," I say. He doesn't bother to look at me. "Are you sick?" I can always string together any combination of words and singsong them to him, and he smiles like I'm reciting poetry. I pace back and forth while he nurses.

Five minutes pass; an eternity passes inside my head.

I make the call: "You have reached Dr. Rosenberg's office of psychiatric medicine. If this is a life-threatening emergency, please hang up and dial 911."

I never dial 911.

"If you are an existing patient and need to reach me immediately, press two to reach my beeper. If you are a new patient and would like to schedule an appointment, please press three now."

I punch the number three.

"At the sound of the beep, please leave your name and number. I return calls same day between the hours of noon and one thirty p.m. Please expect my call at this time and answer accordingly. Thank you."

Beep.

"Yes, this is Corey Tracey-Lieberman."

"Lieberman." Monique could have scared me, but her voice isn't deep enough. "I changed the code on the doors."

"Yeah, I noticed," I say as I shove my phone back into the fanny pack I carry in my tote bag now. "The car-gate code works, so you'll want to change that too."

"Oh shit, yeah. I used the remote, so I didn't even think—damn."

I don't know what we will say next. I haven't found an article on etiquette for survivors of murder.

"I'm sorry for your loss, Monique. And I'm really sorry I don't know what to say. I'm not good at this." I play the role well—Inarticulate Human Awkward Woman.

"Neither am I, so let's leave it at that."

Monique looks different. Younger. She's wearing oversize men's sweatpants and a baggy T-shirt. I've never seen her in anything but black skinny jeans. She opens the door without giving me the code, and we go inside. Silent. Jacob still attached to my breast.

I'm on autopilot: using my elbow to turn on the lights. I kick the basket of clean towels out of the closet, ready to fold them when Jacob stops nursing. I cradle Jacob with one arm while I unlock the front doors for the rest of the team.

"What are you doing?" Monique asks. "We have an hour, keep 'em locked."

"Right, of course, sorry." I note the fear in Monique's voice.

"I didn't know you knew where Kat lived. Have you been there before?"

I am not prepared for her to ask me that. Shit.

"Once, yeah, I gave her a ride home," I say—total lie.

"Cool. Why were you there?"

"Ya know what? I went on a jog with Jacob and ended up near her house, so I decided to check on her. See if she needed anything, since she scheduled herself out sick."

"Right. I was wondering if it was because the police had been to your house to interrogate you, like they did me."

"So, you've spoken to the police?" I ask. "Honestly, I didn't want to believe them, so, yeah, I took a walk with Jacob to Kat's house. I didn't think—"

"Yeah, me neither," Monique says. "I don't even know who or how many employees the police questioned. I asked them if it was okay to have this meeting to let the team know what's going on. How fucking juvenile am I? I asked their permission. I'm the fucking business owner—I don't need their damn permission. Gah." Her words are coarse, but her tone is flat.

"Don't beat yourself up. I would have asked too," I say.

"I suppose you have to."

I don't want to lead the conversation and scare her away from talking.

"It's so fucked up. I don't even fucking know what happened. I can't even fucking believe it's happened. I mean, how the fuck does someone you know die?" Monique reaches for a tissue.

"What did the cops ask you?" I try to be gentle.

Jacob slips off my breast, asleep. I put him in his stroller and casually begin folding the towels I kicked out before. I avoid looking Monique in the eye.

"Such basic shit. Where was I, did I know who Kat was with that morning, what was the last communication we shared." She stops aimlessly straightening papers and pens on the desk and looks directly at me. "They asked me if she was dating anyone, and I said I didn't know. I honestly don't know the answer to any of their questions. I feel fucking useless."

Monique is so close I can smell her *minty toothpaste and morning breath* combo. It isn't pleasant or unpleasant, but it is too close. I turn away to check on Jacob, a buffer that makes my need for space appear natural.

"I'm obviously canceling the charity event. I need you to call the T-shirt vendor. Let them know what happened. Maybe they'll refund our deposit when they find out Kat died. Bereavement clause, right? That's a thing, right?" she asks. It is in that moment when I see that she is just a kid, really. Too young to know about bereavement, but then I suppose we all are until someone dies and we need to make arrangements.

"Are you sure we should cancel? Maybe the distraction of the event is a good thing?" I say.

If everyone could be close together, in one room, at one time, I could ask more questions—get serious while death was fresh, and it would be inconspicuous during a mandatory work event.

"Don't be stupid, Lieberman."

I let it slide.

"Why don't we do a memorial ride here on Sunday? All proceeds to go toward Kat's funeral. I'm sure Gilda could use the financial help, and it would be a way for folks to show up and mourn. Unless you think it's maybe too soon," I say.

"I don't know."

"I think people need company and support after this kind of news so they can talk out their feelings," I say.

"Yeah, it's a good idea. Well, Kat got you right. You're good, Lieberman."

The front door chimes, and Diane is there. Face puffy. No makeup. Looking too real. The clock reads 7:50 a.m. The whole lot of Cyclone instructors would be flowing in at any minute now. I unlock the doors, and Diane rushes Monique with a hug.

"Oh my god," Diane cries. Her words trail off as Monique's had before her and as every person's would who came through the door over the next few days.

"I don't know what's happening. It's a fucking nightmare. We're canceling Sunday's charity ride. Lieberman had a good idea to switch it to a memorial ride here, in honor of Kat, but I don't know what I'm doing," Monique says.

Diane nods and continues to nod until Jacob lets out a wail, followed by a series of rumbling farts. I pick him up, and he spits up all over me. The amount of which can only be categorized as a puke. I forgot to burp him. Bad mom.

"Lieberman, our bathroom is clean and has a counter. Please take care of that in there, not here." Fucking Monique.

I smile. My most passive-aggressive facial expression. I do not want to leave.

"Can you believe this?" Diane asks me as she walks into the bathroom.

"I'm trying to make sense of it," I say. I fasten a new diaper onto Jacob. "Remember the other night, at my house? You and Liz mentioned that Kat was a party girl. Do you know where she partied or who she partied with?" I ask.

It came out more blunt than I wanted, but I'm using cheap paper towels to vigorously clean baby puke off my top.

"Seriously? What are you doing?" Diane asks, a sharp bite in her voice.

"Well, I didn't pack a backup shirt for myself, so I'm trying to—"

"For god's sake, not that. What are you doing? Playing detective?"

"Sorry? No, the police asked me a bunch of questions, and I didn't know how to answer them. Like, did Kat have a boyfriend?"

"People are going to be hurting—show some grace, Corey."

Diane squints at me. She looks at me like she is warning me, passing judgment. I don't give a shit. A woman is dead, and time matters.

"Sorry, I didn't mean to sound so cruel. I'm having a hard time with this. I'm protective of this place and these girls," she says, and I believe her. She looks at herself in the mirror, too long, studies her face for a moment before moving her eyes down to her body and the clean, tight lines of her stretch pants and sports bra—beautiful in every perfect way that I am not. "The cops asked me the same thing, and I'll tell you, only you, what I told them—Kat had a habit of enjoying the one-night stand too much. I told her a million times to slow down. I was worried about her contracting an STD, though, not ending up dead. But if I'm being totally honest, I was also living vicariously through her and told her to be herself, do what she wanted. Do what felt good and not be ashamed of it. I should have been a better friend, role model . . . I don't know. I don't know. I'm a mom—I should have been more worried about her."

"You can't do that," I say. I lift Jacob off the counter. "You can't make your friend your ward. She was an adult, and she had a mother. A good mom."

"You met Gilda?" Diane asks.

"Yeah, yesterday. It's strange, because Kat lived with her mom. She didn't mention any men or parties or clubs that Kat frequented while I was there. Wouldn't she notice Kat bringing guys home? Or that she was out partying a lot?" I ask.

"Let's just say the apple doesn't fall far from the tree," Diane says. "Besides, nobody brings home a quick lay when they live with their mom. What's your interest in it? You and Kat weren't close. One of your old buddies at *LA News First* pumping you for a story?" Diane is still looking at herself as she speaks. "I remember Kat went home with a guy once who said he was separated. That was a mistake."

"Why?"

"He was separated from his wife but still living with her and their kids."

The door springs open, and Liz is standing there sobbing, snot dripping down her perfect face. Diane pulls her close. With arms around each other, they look like one heaving lump of spandex. I envy their ability to touch and be touched.

"We should probably get back to the others," I say. I slip past them and out the bathroom door with Jacob, while Diane and Liz continue to hold each other as they head to the meeting.

There's a crowd now, all the instructors standing around whispering and waiting. A few riders have shown up for class and are surprised the studio is closed. One irate woman is arguing with Monique. I step over

141

to help, Jacob still in my arms, offensive used diaper in the bag over my shoulder.

"What's wrong?" I ask.

"I've got it," Monique says. Her eyes do not leave the customer.

"Where's Kat? I don't want to deal with you anymore. I paid for this class. I moved my schedule to accommodate this class. The least you could do is honor your schedule. This is the second time this week you've subbed for the class I signed up for," the woman says. I don't recognize her from my mornings. I wonder if she's new and how new. I wonder if she is the author of some of the comments on the Cyclone Facebook page. Does her anger make her lash out in a physical way?

"It's been a weird week, and you can't speak to Kat unless you're fucking clairvoyant because she's dead," Monique says. Her voice booms through the studio.

The room grows silent, even the gossips. Those who didn't know gasp. Those who knew shed renewed tears.

"I'm sorry?" the woman says, a look of shock on her face.

"Kat's dead. Maybe you could give me a break while I figure it out, and I'll be sure to compensate you for your fucking class." Monique's voice is more sadness than her usual bark.

"I'm sorry. I didn't know. I'm so sorry." The woman continues to apologize long after the door closes behind her. The shock of the news genuinely readable on her face—she didn't hurt Kat. I quickly scan the room for someone or something that feels off.

Monique turns her back to everyone. Her small frame shakes.

I lock the doors. Then it is only us, Monique and the crew. She composes herself and stands tall and, with a certain detachment from the world, consoles each instructor that approaches. What I can't tell is if she appears fragile or guilty. Something in the room full of instructors is setting off my alarm.

When did Monique speak to Kat on Saturday? Did she meet her for a run? She looked sweaty at our coffee meeting—and she hadn't come from the studio.

I look around the room: Some are visibly upset, some are in shock, some check their phones. Who in this room would have a reason? Were any of the male instructors straight? I've met Carl's husband, Brandon's boyfriends, but what about Kyle? I try to picture Kyle and Kat in a lover's quarrel—K&K—ugh, but it isn't totally out of the question. I don't know him well. He had his arm around Kat at the happy hour.

I'd taken a class of Kyle's before I became an instructor. He taught like a yogi, soft voiced, not on a mic, lit candles for ambience, and no drills—all climbs, slow and steady. He talked about forgiveness of self and acceptance during the ride. It doesn't seem likely—I have to know who she had a close relationship with besides Monique, maybe Diane.

It's always possible she met a stranger on her run or someone from her running group is a psycho killer. Had she driven to meet a friend and parked her car in the street? Maybe the killer, her killer, put it there.

Gilda said she had seen her that morning, early—too early for someone who had stayed out all night on a bender. And I had text messages from her as early as 5:42 a.m.—unless she never went to bed at all. Would Diane make up a story like that, and so what if people aren't always who they appear to be? Sex is not an invitation to be killed, though the association of sex and murder does cloud my brain.

The cops, profilers, most law enforcement, even self-defense instructors say most killings are done by someone you know—unless it's a mass shooting by some nutjob with an agenda. But this was personal, if it was anything at all.

Then there were the two girls. Found a few days prior. Was that personal too? Hanging deaths definitely send a message.

Connection or coincidence?

The headless dog—can't leave that out, but that's too close to an obvious setup for a murder to look satanic and sacrificial, circa the 1970s occult killings—the Manson days are done.

My ears are ringing. Jacob is in my arms, back asleep. My vision is shaky, like standing too fast when you've been squatting, but instead of blacking out, everything shakes from side to side. I squeeze my eyes shut and press my thumb and forefinger into the bridge of my nose while leaning into the wall for support.

"Corey?" Monique asks.

"Yeah? Yes? Sorry," I say. A metallic taste fills my mouth.

"We good?"

I'm not sure, but my vision is evening out.

"Yeah, of course," I say.

"Can you speak about Sunday? I can hold Jacob for you. I don't trust myself not to break down right now."

"Of course, I'm happy too. But I'll hang on to him for now—he's been fussy today," I say. Monique looks at my sweet, patient, docile baby, but I can't put him down. I need him for support. Maybe Monique does too.

Monique, the strongest person I know in this room, slinks away to the front desk and busies herself with papers. I survey the eclectic group in front of me: yoga pants, gym shorts, everyone in muscle tanks with the Cyclone logo prominently displayed on the front. I smile, make eye contact, and wait for one of them to give me a tell, a clue, even better, an answer: Which one of you is a killer?

"Hi, gang, thanks for coming in this morning, and if you have to go to get to another job, please feel free to slip out when you have to." The room is silent. "As you all know by now, Kat has—" Died? Passed away? Shit. "Kat is no longer with us."

"Did someone kill her?"

I can't make out who's asking.

"Here? Was it here? Ohmygod! Was she killed here?"

It's definitely the Twentysomethings. They are loud and unorganized and need too much immediate attention.

"Calm down, everyone, please. Let's take a deep breath. In through the nose, out through the mouth. That's it. Two more times just like that." I keep my eyes open while the room of instructors shuts theirs and takes deep breaths. "Let me talk, and I will answer as many of your questions as I can. I don't have a lot of answers. No one does. Okay?" The group falls silent.

"Kat's body was found at Debs Park. We don't know what happened. It's too soon for anyone to draw any conclusions, so no one start panicking about what hasn't happened," I say.

"Oh god. Did she kill herself?" Trish asks. She is a tall, wiry Twentysomething who never coaches with a mic. Her voice carries across a room with such power it sounds like she's standing next to you. Used correctly, it is awesome; used when silence is needed—sucks.

"Trish, please let me finish. There is no indication that Kat killed herself." I believe that. "It could have been an accident."

"Yeah, but you don't even know if she was murdered, so how can you say that? Weren't those other girls killed at Debs last week?" Another Twentysomething feeding the frenzy Trish was building.

"The news said they killed themselves. Some sort of gang initiation gone wrong," Trish announces as fact.

I am about to kill Trish—manslaughter, second degree—a crime of passion. I wonder how much caffeine she injected into herself before coming to the meeting.

"Don't be a twat. This is hard. When we know, you'll know," Monique says. She appears next to me like an apparition of dominance.

"Listen, we are a team here, a family. Neither Monique nor I have the answer to the cause of death. When the police release that information, you will all know when we do."

"Are you in charge now?" Trish asks.

"No, I'm in charge," Monique says. "Corey is the new assistant manager, so listen to her."

It takes a moment to allow that announcement to sink in. "I know, this is upsetting. It's a shock to all our systems, but we're going to do the best we can to get through this as a community. For each other and our riders. Okay?" The room murmurs, most agree. I watch as two Twentysomethings I don't know well lean into each other for support. The Jocks and the Misfits all stand straight, arms crossed, expressions solemn and focused on me, a solid force. The Moms are checking their phones—likely searching Google for more information on Kat.

"Here's the plan for now. We are canceling the charity ride on Sunday. Instead, we will host a memorial ride for Kat here at the studio. The community will be invited to partake. If you need to talk to someone about anything, please know that Monique and I are here to listen." I hear Monique take in a sharp breath. But I'm looking for anyone who knows anything, and this is the best way I can make them talk.

"Classes will resume as usual, beginning tomorrow. Look for a text from me or Corey regarding Sunday." Monique sounds like herself. There isn't a hint of the distraught woman from moments ago. "Does anyone have any questions?" There's a lot of head shaking. "Okay, then you can go," she says.

I watch as the Misfits try to console the Moms and the Moms try to console the Twentysomethings. It's all a mess.

"Corey." Diane taps my shoulder.

"Hey, how are you holding up?" I ask.

"I'll be fine. I have my kids to distract me. But it's so nuts. Can I—"

"Corey," Monique cuts Diane off. She calls to me from the front of the room, eyeballing Diane.

"Sorry, I need to get over there, but hold that thought," I say.

The clock on the wall above the front desk reads 8:40 a.m., but it's ten minutes fast—purposefully set ahead so that if the instructor who is running the class falls behind, the riders would still get out on time. My phone vibrates in the bag against me.

NELAScanBoy: Gotta minute?

Me: Call you in a sec

"Hey, I've got to go take care of this guy." I motion to Jacob. "Everything okay?" I ask Monique.

She sighs impatiently and rolls her eyes. A small masochistic part of me is glad her familiar demeanor is back.

Once in the bathroom, I do a quick sweep for feet in the two stalls, determine it is clear, lock the main door, and call Chris. I look at Jacob as the phone rings. He needs to play, engage, be read to— he has a growing energy I'm not prepared for. "Maybe we can buy a sandbox or a tree swing," I say to him. He grunts, a familiar sound that is almost a word.

"Hey," I say the minute Chris answers.

"Listen, early word is accidental slip and fall on your friend. Cause of death—her neck was broken in three places."

"Do you know if they found her phone?"

"I don't—but there's nothing that suggests foul play here, Corey."

"What about her car?"

"No signs of a break-in with her car. It was parked near her work, which is not unusual. Cops aren't going to proceed unless there's cause, and right now, there doesn't look to be any evidence pointing that way."

"They're wrong. She was an avid runner who ran that path a million times. She did not slip and fall, Chris."

"I believe you."

The door to the bathroom wiggles.

"Hello? Anyone in there?" It's Liz's voice.

"Just a sec!" I call out. My voice echoes in the tiled bathroom. "Okay, let's talk in a little bit. I have to go," I say to Chris.

"Later. And, Corey, be careful," he says before the phone says end call.

I hang up. Jacob yanks the phone from my hand and sticks the top of it in his mouth. I let him keep it and unlock the bathroom door.

"Hi, can I talk to you for a minute?" Liz asks.

"Sure," I say. She walks me back into the bathroom, and this time she locks the outer door.

"I have to tell you something," she says. "Corey, my stomach hurts. I don't want this information anymore." She is now aggressively rubbing the clean counter while crying so hard her nose is running. Where there may have been makeup on her face before, now only exists plump pink cheeks from rubbing.

"Okay, it's okay. What is it?" I ask her.

"I'm Xgen. I wrote those messages on the Facebook page from Xgen. The nasty ones I told you about the other night."

"What do you mean?" I already knew it wasn't a stranger. It was too contrived—knew it had to have been an upset rider or employee, but my guess would have been that Monique was the target, not Kat.

"I was super pissed that Kat fired my friend, and then she had cut one of my classes for low attendance, and I can barely afford my rent as it is. I begged her not to, but she said she didn't have a choice. I wanted to scare her, piss her off. I don't know. I was so upset. It was supposed to be a prank, and now I feel so shitty, about all of it."

"Wait, why did you make up the bit about the decapitated dog head?" I ask.

"I didn't, that part wasn't me. That was a coyote. It was on Nextdoor too. I only wrote the stuff about the studio. I can't believe she's dead, and the last thing I did to her was awful." Snot and tears run down her face—she looks too much like a sick child. "I swear to God I didn't mean for her to get hurt or for people to take my comments seriously. I swear! It was a joke." Her voice hoarse. She throws away the paper towels and aggressively washes her hands, three, four, five times. "Do you think it could be the reason someone hurt her?" She is nearly hysterical.

"I don't know what happened to Kat. I don't know who would hurt her." I gently touch her arm with my semifree hand. "It was just a joke, right? Like when Diane volunteered me for the charity ride? A prank. Harmless," I say.

It could be that some nutjob read Liz's comments and took them to heart. Decided the world would be better off without Kat, hunted her down, and killed her. Why is Monique still breathing and not Kat? Why isn't she lying on a coroner's metal table right next to her? I couldn't see it—some fucking cyberbully managing such brutality.

"Should I tell the police? What if they think I killed her?" Liz asks.

"But you didn't kill her." I left it at reassuring but questioned everything.

With Jacob on my left hip, I pull Liz onto my right shoulder and let her cry until she is dry sobbing.

"Would it make you feel better to tell the police?" I ask.

Liz nods. She's shaking, so I pull out Jacob's muslin giraffe blanket from the tote bag and wrap it around her shoulders. She is just a kid; they all are. This was the best excuse for me to get in front of Detective Lopez again, see if she was really giving up on Kat's case so easily.

"I should let Diane know," Liz says.

"Why?"

"She knew about it. I don't want to implicate her or anything. God, what if the police question her? I don't want her to think she has to lie for me."

What else does Diane know? What other pranks have the two of them pulled? Who would be bored enough to fucking haze adults?

"Don't worry about that right now. I'll let Diane know you told me. Let's you and I drive over to the police station and let them know—maybe it can help them," I say.

Too drained to argue, Liz follows along. We leave the bathroom and go straight out the back door to my car. I text Monique.

Me: Covered in shit. Had to go. Explain later.

Monique: Seriously? Call me when you're done.

Monique's mourning period is, apparently, over.

18

When we get to the station, I ask for Detective Lopez but am offered Detective Marks.

"No. Listen, Detective Marks, she's had bad experiences with men in the past." I gesture to Liz. "Would it be all right if we waited for Detective Lopez?"

"I could lock her up right now for withholding information, you know."

"And there you have it. Bad experiences with men," I say.

"Fine, I'll see if she's on her way back." Marks leaves the lobby. I notice he has a heavy step—more tired than angry would be my guess.

About forty-five minutes later Detective Lopez arrives. Liz has been on the verge of leaving for the last fifteen minutes. She's bitten her nails so low they're bleeding—and the cop at the front desk has already given me all the Band-Aids she has. The fourth time Liz got up to use the bathroom, she came back looking more thin and frail, if that is even possible.

"Corey, nice to see you again. How's the Benadryl working?" Lopez asks me upon entering the lobby.

I look at her like she's mistaken me for someone else.

"For the sleep? Your sleep?" she says.

"Right, sorry, I haven't tried it yet."

"I see you've brought a friend."

"Yes, this is Liz Martin. She also works with—"

"Yes, Miss Martin, you were on my list of employees at Cyclone. Would you two ladies like to join me in a more comfortable room?"

Detective Lopez takes us into a small windowless office next to the reception desk. It isn't more comfortable, only more private. There is a rectangular table that works as a makeshift desk—not dissimilar to the one in the room Marks had me in alone right before Gilda and I learned of Kat's death. This time, instead of two chairs, there are three and absolutely nothing else. I sit in the chair closest to the now-closed door, Liz in the one next to me, while Detective Lopez arranges herself across from us.

"Now, how may I help you both today?" Lopez asks.

Liz looks at me. Jacob pinches my arm. "Ow, buddy. No." Jacob looks to me with fresh tears welling up in his eyes. I squeeze him tight and whisper, "It's okay, I love you, it's okay." I look to Lopez to go ahead.

"Miss Martin, is there something you know?" Detective Lopez asks. She has no notepad or pen. There is no recording device visible. I take another scan of the room, at the ceiling light and the corners, and see nothing blinking.

Liz starts with a response, but I jump her line.

"Sorry, do you want to record this?" I ask.

"If it's something useful, I will. Let me hear what the young lady is going to tell me first. Go ahead, Miss Martin."

Liz starts at the beginning with her friend's firing and all the nuanced drama Detective Lopez looks like she can take.

As Liz brings her story to a conclusion, she is in full waterworks again—guilty of harassment and probably afraid that she could be held accountable. The tears are for herself as much as they're for Kat; that much can be gleaned from her fit. The rest of what she says is garbled junk I can't make out—she may not be speaking words.

"I see," Detective Lopez says. "And *did* any protestors show up at the studio?"

"Not that I know of." Liz swats her face and wipes her nose with Jacob's baby blanket. "But do you think they could have killed her? Sometimes they write crazy-scary stuff."

"I think you've given me some excellent food for thought. I want to thank you for coming down. I know it couldn't have been easy for you," Detective Lopez says. "At this point, I don't think you have anything to worry about with the protestors. Unless you own one of the coffee shops on York or Fig. You don't own a coffee shop on York or Fig, do you?" Lopez gets a smile from Liz.

"I didn't intend to hurt anyone, really. I wanted to make Kat feel bad."

I want to punch Liz when, only moments ago, I actually felt bad for her. Had she been the bitchy reviewer of my class? Maybe I'd leave a shitty review of her class—"too much techno music."

"So, you don't think those people did this to her?" Liz asks.

"No," Detective Lopez says. "I do not think *Those People* did anything to Kat." Lopez stands. "Thank you, Ms. Tracey-Lieberman, for bringing in Miss Martin. She's been very helpful. Now, if you ladies will excuse me, I need to get back. I have a lot of paperwork waiting for me." Lopez opens the door for us to exit.

Liz walks back to the lobby. I stand in front of the detective, Jacob asleep in my arms finally, and stare at her in awe.

"Aren't you going to take her statement down? See if any leads can be sussed out?" I ask.

"No," Lopez says.

It's final.

"How can you not take every tip seriously?" I'm demanding now. Shaking with a building rage. "Don't you believe Kat was killed? Or don't you give a shit because she doesn't present as white?" I want answers to a behavior I don't understand. "Two Latina girls hanged in a tree and you guys claim it's gang related? Now, a Latina girl falls off a cliff and it's a suicide? How many girls die before the police take them for the homicides the rest of us know they are?"

"Come with me." Lopez doesn't have the same maternal smile she'd worn since I first met her. Her face is void of emotion now. I have overstepped. The tension thick after my unwelcome and possibly ignorant accusation. Another white person playing the blind hero— was it performative? I'm embarrassed, incapable of finding words to apologize. Something Chris said the night before comes back to me: ". . . understand who you are and why you're doing this." Fuck.

I tell Liz I'll be right back. Lopez buzzes us through the bulletproof doors. I'm back in the bullpen—the corporatization of police barracks.

Lopez leads Jacob and me down the rows of desks, past the conference room I sat in with Gilda, and into a smaller conference room. There are two small tinted windows—the outside is visible to us, but we are invisible to passersby. The police employee parking lot can be seen and, beyond that, all industrial buildings. The interior three walls of the room are covered in photos of the dead—mutilated bodies, each with its own index cards: dates, times, and hard-scribbled notes.

The picture that makes me want to stop and cover my mouth, want to scream, is of Emma Klapp. I reported on her way back when I was someone else. She'd haunted Los Angeles news stories for a year, longer, it seems, considering the photo. Emma Klapp, a twenty-seven-year-old, dirty-blond, brown-eyed, pretty white girl who worked in retail— fashion. She'd been at a party with friends. Nothing wild. She was sober, but tired, and lived in the apartment building where the party was held. A West Hollywood location—not the gorgeous homes of WeHo from La Cienega to Doheny, but the less popular side east of Fairfax—less night life, more Russian markets. Her friends reported she'd said good night to the room around 11:15 p.m. She was found sitting outside the party's apartment door, the cement around her covered in a dark, wet puddle; she was slumped at the waist. Throat slit. Phone and keys in her hand. No one heard a struggle. No one heard a scream. The area was notorious for pickpockets. There had been a body dumped in a stolen SUV half a block from Emma's place earlier that year. It wasn't a bad neighborhood by LA standards, but it wasn't safe either.

The street was a mix of apartment buildings and single-family rental homes—not unlike most of the city. There were always a half dozen **For Rent** signs posted up and down the streets in the area. During the day, with the sun shining, the palm trees looming above, and the bright-pink bougainvillea spreading across fences, gates, and awnings, the place looked like a sanctuary. But nothing looked nice at night under the hard glare of fluorescent streetlamps. The trash in the gutters—needles, cigarettes, condoms—was more visible. And the hedges of jasmine let off a sickly-sweet perfume that penetrated the air.

Every guy Emma had dated that year was considered a suspect and interrogated, and all were eventually released. Her online dating accounts were scoured. Every hookup and connection interviewed. No leads. A silent killer. The city of Los Angeles strongly suggested women walk in pairs after dark.

Seeing Emma's death photo on the wall is more real than the story was when we reported it. Seeing this young woman's gashed throat, the front of her blouse drenched in dark blood, is intoxicating. I want to walk into the picture. I want to look around the room, the hall, interview the party guests. I want to be there. To save her, find a weak pulse, shake her awake, resuscitate her—save the city. Why is it Emma's picture and not mine? I lived in that neighborhood around then—everyone did. I was naive and went home with a rapist once. I chased Peeping Toms and scammers and angry sex offenders. I should be on that wall—except I'm not because Emma knew her killer and I didn't; this wasn't random.

"Welcome to my Murder Board," Lopez says, walking the walls of photos like a professor, teaching me about the evils of the world. "Each brutally killed. All had someone to wonder: What happened? Why them? Do you know how many guilty people are walking around, living their lives, sucking up our free air?"

I shake my head, *no*. But I think of Drew Hudson.

Lopez says, "Too many. And this brutality will continue until I can prove guilt—no doubt." She stops and stares at the walls of death. Sounds lost, like she is still out there, in the dark—hunting for monsters—hope dying a little every day. "Most victims knew their assailants. Intimately. A spouse, a parent, a coworker, a lover. Random acts, sure, they happen, but not as often. None of these victims killed themselves. There's always a thread, and my purpose is to find it, follow it." Detective Lopez pulls a picture off the board of a child, around three, maybe four, her arms and legs twisted and broken. "This little girl's name was Madeline. Broken limbs were postmortem so the sicko could stuff her into a duffel bag. The mother, Sarah, swallowed a revolver last month."

I inhale deep and sharp because I was holding my breath, hoping for a different end.

"Did she do it?" I ask. "The mother?"

"No, but I was too late on that one too. I have more than an idea of who did it, but knowing and proving are an ocean apart."

"Who?" I ask.

Lopez shakes her head.

"I covered that story," I say.

"You and the entire state of California. Get in line," Lopez says while straightening the picture like it was a piece of art, just a bit off, hanging in her house.

I look at the boards. I recognize as many names as I don't. I look at each picture until they start to blur together. I stop on a baby no bigger than Jacob, in a crib, who looks like he is sleeping. The index card reads: *asphyxiated*. My heart jumps into my larynx. I can't breathe. I pull Jacob closer, squeeze him until he wakes. Officer Lopez pulls me away from the picture. I take a deep breath and close my eyes for a moment.

"I'm okay," I say. "Mommy's okay, baby boy, my sweet little boy. I'm okay." I hum into his head. The sweet scent of him keeping me safe in a building full of cops.

He reaches for my shirt, and I oblige. I do not want the limited vision he does have at this age to witness the photos I am subjecting myself to. I follow the board to the end; the most recent images are the two girls from Debs—Lupe's daughter Araceli, and her friend Natalie. The notes: *Hanged. Possible suicide. Possible gang initiation gone bad. Possible . . . ?*

On the table beside the board is Kat's picture and a file folder.

"Why is Kat's photo on the table?" I ask.

"She's no longer a victim," Lopez says.

"What?"

"She is no longer considered a victim of a crime at this point."

"You really believe she tripped and fell?" I say.

"No, I believe that there are a lot of unhappy people in the world, and it comes as a surprise to everyone when they take their own life," Lopez says. She's matter of fact about it.

"Not Kat. Absolutely not Kat. She was killed," I say.

"Tell you what, Corey, you bring me something real. Some tangible evidence that she was killed. A witness. Her murderer wrapped up in a pretty bow, preferably DOC orange, and I'll listen to you. Right now, we have thirty-seven victims that we *know* were murdered, and I don't have the budget or the power to look for a murderer where there is no evidence of a homicide."

"Fine," I say. Jacob lifts himself off my boob and spits up on the floor. I try to wipe it away with my foot but only manage to widen the spread. "Sorry," I say to Lopez.

"It's okay." She opens the door. "Marks!" Detective Marks turns from his desk and looks at Lopez. "Bring in some paper towels, would you? There's a spill." Marks rises from his desk without urgency and scowls at Lopez. "He hates that I'm not a Dodgers fan. Won't ever forgive me."

"Angels?" I ask.

"Mets." She smiles. "Come on, I'll walk you out."

I nod at Lopez and give Jacob another tight squeeze.

"I thought you left without me!" Liz looks like she hasn't stopped crying.

"I'm sorry. It took longer than I thought," I say. Jacob is wiggling and pawing at my face. Digging in the tote for my keys, I am accosted by the stench of everything I've been blindly stuffing in the bag for days—burp cloth, spit-up rag, diaper.

"Oh my god! What is that smell?" Liz says, still hoarse from the too much of it all.

"Don't ask," I say. "Let's just go."

"Maybe you should throw your bag away. Like, for real," she says, still covering her nose, spacing herself from me and my son.

"What do you think, buddy? Should I throw it all away? Start over?" Jacob pushes some bubbles out his tightly pressed lips, and I share a small smile just with him.

I drive Liz back to her car near the studio with all my windows down. Monique is still inside. Alone now, at the front desk.

I decide I should go in and talk to her while she's alone and still somewhat vulnerable about the entire thing, even though going back to Kat's house and talking to Gilda pulls at me. But, at this point, I have less than nothing. I don't believe some antigentrifier killed Kat, and I know she didn't kill herself. I do believe someone was with her on her hike. I do think Kat knew her assailant intimately. Maybe Monique knows something but doesn't have a clue how instrumental it could be. I park along the curb in front, a first.

"Lieberman, I didn't think you'd be coming back," Monique says as she lets me in the front door.

"Sorry, I had to bathe him, and one thing led to more things and . . ." It's best not to give a lot of details when lying because you won't remember them all later.

My phone rings—it startles me. **PRIVATE NUMBER.**

"Do you need to get that?" Monique asks.

My voicemail chimes.

"Yeah, lemme—" I look at the studio clock. 1:40 p.m. I listen to the voice message, hoping it's Lopez or Chris or someone with new information.

"Hi, Corey, this is Dr. Rosenberg returning your call. Please text me at this number so we can schedule you to come in. I do have a cancellation tomorrow if that works. Thank you."

He made it sound urgent. Usually, it takes six weeks to see a specialist.

"Someone trying to sell you an extended warranty?" Monique asks.

"Yeah, exactly." I laugh a little to sell it. Dr. Rosenberg would have to wait a little longer.

"Okay, we'll do the memorial ride at eleven a.m. on Sunday. I've already updated the website, and you should receive a text from the studio any second now—" My phone beeps before she finishes her sentence.

"Wow, you are fast," I say.

"It's better if I keep busy. I also canceled our charity T-shirt order, so we're pretty much set here."

"Hey, can I ask you something?"

Monique nods.

"I know you've already talked to the police and told them everything you know about Kat and stuff, but isn't it weird that she didn't show up to our meeting? Then a few days later posted in the system that she needed a sub? I can't wrap my brain around that. Did they tell you how long she'd been missing?"

"She didn't," Monique says.

"Didn't what?"

"Kat didn't post for a sub—I lied. She hadn't texted or called me back, which pissed me off, so I came in early to confront her before her class. She was a no-show. I feel like a fucking twat at this point. I should have called the fucking police, but who the fuck's mind goes to 'oh, my business partner is missing, maybe dead; I should call the police' just because they don't return a fucking text or miss a class—I've missed my own class before, and she's always covered me. Shit happens, ya know?" Her voice cracks. It sounds painful.

"I'm sorry. I'm so sorry. I didn't mean to upset you, of course . . . listen, nobody would have thought she was dead or even missing. We don't think crazy things like that will happen to us." Except that I do think crazy shit like that will happen. "It happens to those other people, the ones we don't know." Her head slumps on the desk in front of me. Jacob grabs a fistful of her black hair and starts to pull. "No, Jacob, no!" I scold and pry Monique's hair free from his fist.

"Could I hold him for a minute?" she asks.

Besides me, only Evan gets to hold him. Rarely at that.

"Sure," I say, before I really think about what I'm agreeing to. I pass Jacob over. It feels awkward, unsafe almost. "Listen, I know you told the police you didn't know if Kat was dating anyone, but *do* you know? Did she mention at all if she was seeing anybody? Did she have a relationship with anyone here in the studio?"

"The police did ask me the same fucking thing twice. Sorry, baby—freakin' thing," she says to Jacob and rocks him. I start shaking from the inside out. "I'll tell you what I told them. Kat broke up with a boyfriend like a year ago. He was a fucking putz. Recently she mentioned a few times that she had a date, but she didn't say much else about it." Monique pauses. "I'm not one for getting super personal. I never asked more than she offered, you know? We're business partners, not best friends." I nod this time; I do know. "I do remember her saying he may have had kids, this guy she had a few dates with. I mean, she didn't come out and say he had kids or anything—it was like she said it was his off weekend and something about coparenting. I don't know. But she was excited he was taking her to dinner somewhere swanky or something."

That matches up with something Diane mentioned about Kat sleeping with a dad. "One more thing, would you consider Kat a party animal?" I ask while reaching for Jacob.

Monique laughs like it's a joke. She looks at Jacob and makes a monkey face at him that he loves. She has a way with him; he is tickled by her expressions.

"I don't know if she partied, but she really is a homebody." Something makes Monique stop. "*Was* a homebody. It doesn't even fucking matter because she's dead."

She passes Jacob back to me, then hands me a piece of paper.

"It's the new code for the door. I'm not giving it out to anyone else yet. You and I will have to start being here during classes until Kat's death blows over—" She can't finish. "You're good with the assistant manager title?"

"Yeah." I am. It means access, and I need access.

I left Monique at the studio, alone. I fish in my bag, successfully pulling out an uncapped pen. On the back of the paper Monique gave me with the new code, I start to scribble out a list of married and single dads:

Lisa's (4pm instructor) husband Tyler Taylor

Is Amanda married? Straight? A's husband?

Ray Hunt—divorced dad

I close my eyes, trying to remember all the faces and names of the men in my morning class.

Damien—maybe married

Nathan

Mike

I put the list on the dashboard. Cap the pen and throw it in my bag. I pull out of the parking spot. I have work to do, and in a few days, we'll be memorializing a woman who, one week earlier, had us all rallying about spinning to help fight cancer. I hit the brakes.

I can't breathe.

My chest is in a vise grip.

My throat is closing, shutting down.

I can't get out of the way of the traffic.

I want out of my body; my chest lurches to escape. I need out of the car. I need to stand, walk, move. Jacob starts crying, and I can't find a voice to soothe him. The world is going dark. I'm passing out with my foot on the brake pedal.

It's quiet for a second.

My head tinges with pressure; the blood tries to get back to it. There is a tightness, a squeeze. I can't swallow and need to spit, and I am present again.

"It's fine, sweetheart. It's fine. We're okay. Mommy is okay." I start to cry while soothing my son, myself.

The car behind me lays on the horn. Jacob is purple from screaming.

I move slow; every little swerve feels huge.

I get us home and out of the car.

In the house, the quiet and stillness shake me. I lay Jacob in his baby swing, and I hide under the breakfast counter in the corner of the dining room—the sound of plastic bags and knives rings through my head. I text Dr. Rosenberg's number.

Me: It's Corey Tracey-Lieberman, I can come tomorrow.

19

Dr. Rosenberg's office is in Pasadena, a ten-minute drive. I rehearse in my head what I'll say. I'm just overly tired. New-mom fatigue. Should I have my iron level checked? My mom is *undiagnosed* bipolar, so I *don't* think we need to worry. When I exit the 110 freeway onto Orange Grove Boulevard, I lose focus.

Pasadena—unlike the vast majority of Northeast Los Angeles—is its own municipality, and it shows. Dr. Rosenberg's office is 5.1 miles from my house, but it is worlds away in a land of privilege. Mansions line the streets, the same streets the Rose Parade travels every New Year. And only 527 homeless, mostly in shelters. One exit difference off the 110 freeway and you are back in Los Angeles, staring at sixty-four thousand homeless people living in tent cities constructed along the freeway, in the parks, and on sidewalks of nonresidential streets.

Rosenberg's office is in an old Victorian mansion. The original wood floors, replica wallpaper, light fixtures, and bathrooms are simultaneously beautiful and haunting. I sit on a velvet green settee in a parlor with Jacob while I wait for Dr. Rosenberg. My phone vibrates in my hand.

Evan: Do you want me to come meet you there?

Me: No, I'm okay

Evan: I'm proud of you

Proud of me? I know he means well, but it's obtusely patronizing. I hate it. Hate myself for feeling the way I do. Every time Evan tries, I grow angrier. I don't want his pity. I want him to see *me*.

I stew. Jacob nurses. We both jump when an older gentleman with thick white hair, a trim beard, and glasses appears.

"Corey?" the man asks.

"I'm early, I'm sorry, I'm too early. If you come get me in a few minutes, it's totally fine," I say. I am not ready.

"I'm Dr. Rosenberg. I can see you now." He motions for me to follow him behind a door, down a spiral staircase that is carpeted in the same deep green as the velvet settee, and into a large, open space—a garden-level office. The size of my entire house. It is brightly lit by multiple Tiffany lamps. There are books stacked everywhere—on the floor, on footstools, and on many small end tables. The green carpet continues from the stairwell into the room and stretches from wall to wall. There are paintings hanging in abundance and leaning against each other on the floor—all framed in ornate gold.

There is a black leather sofa against the far wall next to a desk stacked with folders, legal pads, and mail. In front of the leather sofa is a wingback chair—bright yellow—an IKEA version of a classic that doesn't match anything in the Victorian-style room or house. I can smell peace in this odd and foreign place.

"Corey, why don't you take a seat," Dr. Rosenberg says.

I sit on the leather couch and sink into it like a beanbag. It's so comfortable and worn. Jacob is still attached, still sucking, refusing to break eye contact with me. I notice a large dry-erase board on the opposite wall and a camera on a tripod. Dr. Rosenberg takes a seat in the chair across from me.

"Corey, why don't you tell me what's going on."

"Okay, why don't you tell me about that camera first," I say.

"I use it for difficult sessions. With permission, of course. I'm not recording you."

"I may be difficult."

"I may record you," he counters.

I thought there would have been some preamble of pleasantries and small talk, but we're getting right to it.

"I don't want to be recorded." I look at the camera, searching for a light—red, blue, blinking. Rosenberg is up, disassembling the camera from the tripod. He packs it away in a small camera case near his desk.

"Done." He smiles at me. It's endearing, kind even. No judgment, no notes taken.

"I'm not sure what to say here. I don't know if I'm in the right place even. Should I be talking to a woman psychiatrist?" I say.

"Why don't you start with telling me why you called me," Dr. Rosenberg says.

"A friend gave me your number." He waits for me to continue. "Because my husband. He's worried. Accuses me of having a postpartum disorder."

"He accuses you, Corey? Why does he accuse you?"

"Well, I have these moments when I can't breathe. My heart beats like I'm sprinting; my throat feels like it's closing shut," I say. "Did I say I can't breathe? I can't breathe *or* swallow." I laugh; it's my nerves. "I have to spit, or I'll choke. It's probably acid reflux. My ob-gyn said it's normal. A lot of women feel this way after having a baby."

"What's happening before these moments, Corey? What are you doing?" he asks.

"Nothing. I'm just tired. I mean, sometimes I'm pouring coffee and I stop breathing. Sometimes I'm standing and the room goes out of focus and my heart starts racing. I start to have these terrible thoughts, and they loop in my head. I want to scream, but I can't, and also it feels like my heart is screaming. It just keeps going and going," I say. "I'm trapped inside my own head."

"What are those thoughts telling you? The ones that loop?"

"They're hard to translate," I say. I hear myself sighing a lot. I can't tell this man I fear I might hurt my baby, not intentionally. That I'm afraid of knives and plastic bags—that I'm going to die or try to kill myself.

"Corey, what are you thinking about right now?"

"I don't know." I feel tears burn behind my eyes. "This—that this is ridiculous. I'm fine. I'm just a tired mom, that's all. Honestly. Someone said to try Benadryl, so I need to do that." I look down. Jacob is sleep-eating. I try taking a deep breath, but the air won't hit the bottom of my lungs. I can't expand them. I abruptly stand up to try again.

"Corey?"

"I can't breathe. I want to leave."

"Corey, focus on me. What are you thinking?"

"I don't want you to take away my baby." I blurt it out. My throat burns, like the muscle has been worked to fatigue.

"Of course you don't. Is that the thought that loops?"

"No—" I move around with Jacob in my arms, still attached to my breast. "It questions whether I can be trusted not to hurt him, or myself. It's constantly testing me to pick up a knife and press it into my own wrist. Take the tip and push it into the top of my hand. Grab a plastic bag and shove my head in it." I haven't told anyone so many specific details. Tears push through; a release is coming. I am now motionless, except for the small gestures Jacob makes in my arms.

"Do you want to?"

"What?"

"Hurt yourself?" Dr. Rosenberg asks.

"No." I say it softly. And I mean it. I don't tell him I picked up a knife and held it the other day. To prove to myself that they were just thoughts, not real. That I am tired all the time. That I fight against my head every minute of every day. That I've passed out—while driving. That eventually, I cry. That after I cry, the thoughts recede, somewhat.

I sit back down and pull Jacob off my breast and hold him against my shoulder, asleep, to let him burp. I am too exhausted from telling my secrets to feel anything at the moment.

"It's all straight from a horror movie. Some psycho thriller where the mother is possessed or suffers from hysteria because she has a uterus." I stop. I can't take any of this back. I only planned on telling him I was overly tired, probably hormone related. Maybe I'd throw in a little bit about my mom being an alcoholic. But I was not supposed to tell him I was losing my mind. Was what I said enough to lock me up? I want to scream to him, I'm just kidding!

"I'm not going to hurt my baby. I wouldn't. I would kill myself before I let that happen. I would," I say. "But sometimes these thoughts make me question myself—and I think I may have to . . . kill myself so I don't hurt him. And I don't want anyone to die."

Dr. Rosenberg watches me. He says nothing. After a few seconds he sets his notepad down and stands up. He goes to the dry-erase board and starts to write:

Compulsion

Obsession

Anxiety

Trauma

The writing goes on and on in silence until the board is filled with words and lists and arrows that form some sort of diagram that reads like a map to my life. How the hell did this man get all that from the almost nothing I've said? Seeing it all like that—my head, my limbs, my body are slack instead of taut and rigid like they have been for so long.

"What I'm hearing is a series of panic attacks triggered by obsessive-compulsive thoughts," Dr. Rosenberg says, moving to sit down in his yellow wingback.

Dr. Rosenberg talks for three more hours. It isn't therapy—it is an intervention assessment. A psychiatrist, not a psychologist, and he isn't institutionalizing me; he believes me. The time is almost a total blur—I change a diaper, bounce a fit away, and burp a baby without thinking twice about any of it . . . I think I do a feeding, an automatic instinct I've lost track of. I talk a bit, then listen and listen and listen. Dr. Rosenberg asks questions, and I respond, and like a magician, he has answers. Turns out, I'm a human who has experienced trauma—buried it, buried my anger. And now at my most vulnerable state—postpartum—my brain can't cope alone with it all.

Drugs. He says I need to take drugs. Like my mother—I am being put on drugs.

"Corey, you're not crazy," he says.

I laugh. My arm is numb from holding Jacob. But I'm laughing—sad laughing, angry laughing, hysterically laughing.

"You are not going to hurt your child. You're not suffering from psychosis," he continues, despite my laughing.

But what about the things I haven't told Dr. Rosenberg: the rape, losing the career that identified me, the three dead girls whose murders I have to solve? Would my diagnosis be different?

Jacob fusses. He wants down finally, needs to explore, needs a mother to read him a book, play with giant blocks, sing him nursery rhymes. I'm lucky Evan wants to do those things with him and does—when I let him. I search my tote bag for a baby toy, a stuffie—nothing. I pull out my keys and hand them to Jacob—he accepts with enthusiasm. I'm constantly failing my kid.

Dr. Rosenberg sends in a prescription for Paxil and Klonopin and hurries us out—his goodbyes as generous as the welcomes and pleasantries. I'm to check in with him in one week.

Evan is waiting for us in the parking lot. Dr. Rosenberg thought it best I didn't drive myself. Not until the episodes—plain old panic attacks—are under control. Evan walks over to us. He came in an Uber. He is here, for me—for Jacob. The muscles I've strengthened for so long that keep all the feelings inside are fatigued from a therapy workout with Rosenberg. I don't know how to process most of it, but seeing Evan makes me feel safe. It always has.

Evan brought a fresh diaper. He also brought his perfect Kipling bag he converted into a proper diaper bag for himself. He changes Jacob, then snaps him into his car seat and hands him a stuffed dog we named Terri from Accounting. Why don't I have Terri from Accounting in my bag for Jacob? I swear I put it in my bag earlier this week.

"How did it go?" Evan asks.

"I'm not crazy, so you can tell your mom to suck it," I say.

Evan laughs. I made him laugh. I haven't made anyone laugh in a long time.

"For the record, I never thought you were crazy," he says.

But for the record, he does think there is something wrong with me.

"I'm tired," I say.

I think about Kat as I close my eyes.

20

I sleep through the night for the first time in I can't remember how long—thank you, Klonopin. I am rested and ready to go while Evan and Jacob sleep.

I need to get to Gilda's house today. I make a single cup of coffee in the French press and sip it on the porch with my laptop open. My mind races between Kat, Araceli, and Natalie. I think about their mothers. I think about Jacob—dying. About not being able to prevent it. About funerals. Small caskets. Living without him. I wait for the vise to grip my chest.

"Corey?" It's Elsie at our front gate. I didn't even hear her approach.

"Hey," I say. "How are you?"

She looks worse than unrested.

"I'm scared to let my daughter go to school. I'm sad to have to go to a funeral for a child. I hate that I'm cooking casseroles for a grieving mother's freezer."

"I'm so sorry." I am terrible at finding the words for grief. I want to make a joke about life, politics, the asshole across the street. I wish Jacob would wake up so I can deflect to him.

"I'm okay, though," she says. "Lupe's a wreck."

"I'm so, so sorry, Elsie. I've asked a friend to look into the case. He's not been able to find anything out yet."

I remember the notes from the Murder Board the other day, but I don't want to share that kind of sensitive information with her until I have something solid. I don't want to jeopardize my relationship with Detective Lopez either. "Do you know Natalie's mom?" I ask. Elsie nods. "Does she know I'm looking into this?"

"She's not all there," Elsie says and points to her head.

"Is she ill?"

Elsie shrugs.

"Those kids look after each other when their dad is at work. They have an aunt and uncle that looks in on them too. The uncle brings them meals. He's real close to the kids—they call him Tío Papa." Elsie's phone starts dinging. She pulls it from her pocket and starts to type. "That man is like their guardian angel. Natalie is—was—the oldest. She wasn't a talker—a little odd, that one. Poor thing probably would have ended up like her mother." She stops abruptly.

I can't tell if Elsie is mortified by what she has said or actually relieved the girl died before she went crazy like her mom. I am relieved it wasn't me who said it.

"The uncle's been on disability since he was knocked in the head at work. He was in construction. Been out for ten years. Basically, he's been on call for those kids full time." She stops long enough to inspect my potted succulents and prune the dead; she snaps them off the stem cleanly and tosses them into a neat pile on the ground. It reminds me of a childhood game we played with dandelions: *Mama had a baby, and its head popped off.* So violent.

"The dad travels on jobs. Sometimes he's gone for a month at a time. Also construction. Day laborer. The aunt works at Trader Joe's."

"Our TJ's?" I ask.

"Yep."

I need to make a grocery run; maybe I'll luck out and find the aunt at work.

"Can I ask you a question?"

Elsie nods.

"Was Araceli dating anyone or hanging out with anyone that was in a gang, that you know of?" I ask.

"They'd certainly have you believe that. The news and the cops."
She shakes her head. "Honestly, she was a good kid and came from
a good family. Who she dated, I don't know." Elsie sighs, deadheads
roses off my neglected bush methodically as she speaks. "These kids
would have you believe that they're okay. They bring home good grades.
They're cheerleaders, on track, in choir. They have friends. Maybe they
smoke a little weed, but who hasn't? That doesn't make them gang
affiliated. But because they're from Highland Park? Latino? They must
be categorized as gangbangers? It's not right."

"I don't know what to say. I'm sorry." And I am, but I have to rule
it out, definitively, before I can go back to Detective Lopez. "Do you
think I could talk to Danielle? Maybe she'll tell me something she won't
tell you."

I need to know if there is a connection between Araceli, Natalie,
and Kat. I have to keep the pressure on Kat's case before it's dismissed
entirely into the archives of the police catalogs as a fail. Thank god
Araceli and Natalie are still on the Murder Board—nobody has
wholly given up on them yet. It's hard to process one kid hanging
herself. But two?

"Yeah, she's home now. No school today. Skipping."

I leave my laptop out of sight on the floor of our gated porch and
take my coffee with me next door. When we get inside, Danielle is
curled up on the couch under a pink flannel blanket peeking out at
the television. From the outside, the home looks like a massive old
farmhouse multiple families could live in. Once inside, the walls and
ceiling collapse into narrow rooms and low ceilings. The home was
built in the late 1800s, meant to sleep in after a full day spent outside
farming. There was no farmland left in sight, unless you count the
orange tree, potted, in the front yard of their house.

"Hey, Dani, how are you?" I ask. She sits up when she notices her
mom isn't alone.

"Hi," she says, sounding as deflated as she looks.

"Corey, can I get you a refill?" Elsie asks.

"That would be great," I say, though my cup is still near full and sipping at it helps my nerves. Elsie leaves for the kitchen, and I plop myself down on the couch next to Danielle.

"I heard about your friends," I say.

"Who hasn't." It isn't a question. "My mom said you were helping."

"I'm trying to. To be honest, I'm not really in the business much anymore." I pause. I want her to lighten up, to understand this is me trying to help. I want her to read the questions in my mind and just start talking. My arms empty, I have the feeling I've forgotten something. A baby crying? I look down. My nipples are leaking.

"Do you want a towel?" Danielle asks.

"Sorry, it's Jacob. My milk, when you breastfeed you—"

"I know. My friend has a baby. Do you want a towel?"

I nod. She'll turn eighteen in a month or two and already has a friend with a baby. I had friends with babies at that age. But she also has friends who were murdered. I think about Kat. We have more in common than we should today. I need to get home to Jacob. Danielle comes back with a towel. I blot my chest.

"Listen, I don't have a lot of resources anymore," I say. "I'm going to ask you something, and I need you to tell me the truth. No one will know but me. I won't tell your mom. I won't tell the police. I want to help if I can, okay?" She shrugs. "Do you know who Araceli was dating? Was she hanging out with anyone new or that you didn't know?"

Danielle, on the verge of tears, shakes her head no.

"She dated a guy a while ago, like in eighth grade, like forever ago. He's a year older than us. He never actually graduated, but he'd be out of school now, you know?"

I nod. "Did she start seeing him again recently?"

"Sort of, I think. He'd been hanging around a lot before school and after."

"Waiting for Araceli?" I ask.

"No, he was selling."

I nod, again letting her know that I'm listening, know what she meant.

"He was always teasing Araceli, like, 'Look how cute you got. I shouldn't've never let you go.' Nothing bad. I just didn't like him for her," Danielle says.

"And Araceli did?" I ask.

"She was always defending him. I think she loved him in a way. I don't actually think he would hurt her. He's stupid, but he's not a bad person. I don't know who he sells for, but they can't be good because he's been by the school lately with his face messed up."

"Did you tell the police any of this?" I ask.

"Yes. They know him. They don't do anything. I told them about Araceli and him dating, and they took it to this whole new level. Saying that she's involved with a gang. Like, his gang, or something. It's not true. She liked that he called her pretty."

"And . . . ?"

"And a couple of times she asked Natalie and me to come with her to meet him at a movie or to get food. He was cool about it and always paid for us. He's actually really nice. Just stupid. Please don't tell my mom."

"I won't. Do you know where he lives?" She shakes her head. "Can you tell me his name?"

"Nando Alaniz."

"Thank you. I'd hug you, but . . ."

I look down at the circles of wetness the milk has made around my breasts. We both giggle. Elsie returns with my mug. It is cold. She looks at me, and I can see remnants of the tears she's wiped away. She hugs her daughter hard. We know she heard everything, but none of us would speak about it, ever again.

I walk back to my house and sip my cold coffee. I have two people to visit today: Gilda and Nando.

Evan and Jacob are waiting for me on the porch. Evan is showered and groomed, wearing his slim-fit navy corduroys and a soft pink fitted button-down. I see my laptop, now closed, rests on the porch table instead of the ground.

"Good morning," I say.

"Good morning. How is it over there?" Evan asks.

"Fine, I was visiting with Elsie."

I look at Jacob's sweet smile and set my mug down so I can scoop him up.

I whisper in his ear, "Never lie to your mama, sweet boy. Always tell me the truth. Always tell me where you are. Always let me save you, please."

Evan wraps himself around us both and squeezes hard.

"I have to get to work—late," he says and squeezes harder. It feels like a team hug. Like we are a team, again, maybe.

21

I feel no panic. Has to be the Klonopin. I'm taking it every six hours to stay ahead of the attacks. Like Dr. Rosenberg recommends. A quick read on the internet about Klonopin and panic attacks tells me I'll be on it for the next three weeks until the Paxil kicks in.

I can't find Nando Alaniz in any directory online. No social media accounts. Nothing. A digital ghost. I need Chris. He could mine for this guy.

Me: Hey. Can you find an address for me?

NELAScanBoy: Shoot me the name

Me: Nando Alaniz. Maybe it's short for Fernando? Went to Franklin. Maybe 19 maybe 20. He's a dealer.

NELAScanBoy: I'll keep you posted.

Me: Ty

◆ ◆ ◆

This time, I drive to Gilda's instead of run. Dr. Rosenberg told me exercise is the best natural cure for anxiety and the thoughts that jump out of the darkness and assault me—I call bullshit. If that were the case, I wouldn't have been to see him because I've been teaching spin class for months. Besides, I need the car in case Chris comes through with Nando's address.

I park in front of Gilda's house, Kat's house. There are flowers and candles on the sidewalk. A neighborhood vigil.

Gilda's car is parked in the street because Kat's white Honda is in the driveway. Strange to see it like that, innocuous and ordinary. A car I never would have noticed before, but now it screams at me. I try to remember Kat behind the wheel. Did I ever notice anyone else driving around the area in a white four-door Honda? But, as cars go, it's invisible. A fucking Amber Alert would lose that sedan. But here, as I stare at it in the driveway, the driver dead, it is a howling banshee. I imagine Kat jumping in and heading out after giving her mother a wave goodbye. I stare at it through two songs on the radio. I'm aware, but I'm frozen. Sitting. No urgency anywhere in my body. Is this the pills too?

Jacob whines. A whine telling me to get out or to start driving again. I could sit still like this for the rest of the day. Definitely a new and unfamiliar feeling, and I don't hate it.

"We're going, dude, right now. Hang on," I say to Jacob.

I lose track of when and how I get from the car, with Jacob and my bag, and onto Gilda's front porch, but here I am, loitering. I pace by her front door. Look to the street. No one is around to see how intrusive I'm being. I knock and wait. No one. I knock again. It strikes me I don't know what Gilda does or where she works.

I follow the driveway around to a tiny backyard that looks a lot like the front yard. Gilda kneels beside a painted flowerpot with a bag of soil beside her. I am lightheaded—is this a side effect too?

"Gilda?" I announce myself with almost too much caution because she doesn't respond. "Gilda?" I say again a bit louder. Nothing. She must be ignoring me. I walk closer. Earbuds are stuffed into both ears. I tap her on the shoulder, defeating all efforts not to alarm her.

"Oh my god, Corey. You scared me!" Gilda says.

"I'm sorry. I should have yelled louder, not come up on you like that. I'm not thinking straight."

"I'm not either," she says, waving away my apology. The statement falls flat between us, no emotion in either direction. "The doctor put me on Prozac, and Xanax for sleep. It's not working great."

She looks okay at first glance, but on closer inspection she is the furthest thing from it.

Christ, what do I look like?

"I'm sorry, I'm rambling," she says. "Want a cup of tea or coffee? I also have three refrigerators' worth of food stuffed into one. Let's go in and feed you." I shake my head and start to decline, but she insists, "Please, you'll be doing me a favor. If Kat were here, she'd probably be taking trays of it into the studio." She pauses, more of a stop. A look flashes across her face. "If Kat were here, the food wouldn't be." It is a matter of fact. The reality she is steeped in from now on: an empty home that was once filled with her heart, her life, her daughter. A refrigerator of grief food the constant reminder until that, too, runs empty. It makes me think of Elsie preparing food—casseroles, more grief food, for her friend.

"Yeah, let's go eat," I say. Jacob giggles in agreement.

We eat pan dulce treats, tamales, and lasagna. I feel sick after eating so much heavy food but can see that it is providing some comfort for Gilda.

Gilda starts to cry. "They said that she may have killed herself. I keep asking myself, What kind of mother doesn't notice her kid is suffering like that?"

I shake my head. Careful not to interrupt.

"It took a long time to get over losing Kat's dad. The grief never goes away—you just learn to live with it. I'm not sure I can a second time. Kat was the only reason—"

"I don't think she killed herself," I say. "Gilda, I want to figure out what happened to Kat."

"Don't you think I do?" Gilda's tears are transforming into rage. I can feel the heat she is emitting. "Tell me, what would a former *LA News First* reporter do?"

I nod—of course she would recognize me; she wasn't twentysomething.

"I have a few connections, and I'm looking into the case of the two girls that were found at Debs before Kat."

"Do you think there's a connection?" she asks.

"No. I don't know. I don't think so." I don't sound convincing as someone who can help at all. "Would you have a problem with me investigating Kat's death?"

Gilda, hands cupped around her mug of tea, stares into the hot drink, avoiding me. After a long moment of silence, she says, "Kat never asked you to come over that day, did she?"

"No."

My confession is met with a brutal silence. If not for Jacob cuddled in my arms or the Klonopin numbing me, I would say something.

"I want to bury my daughter. I can't stand her body sitting in a cold refrigerator. She needs to come home now."

I look at Jacob, try to imagine how I'd feel if his body were stuck at a morgue, in a small refrigerated box. I shudder, but my heartbeat is normal. My throat—open. The magic pill.

"If she was killed, I'll find out," I say. Gilda isn't looking at me—I wonder if it's the Xanax she's taking, if it's made her so calm she isn't feeling the surges of emotion, anxiety, panic she must have.

"Hearing someone say it out loud, that she was killed, is harder somehow than my brain whispering it to me all day," Gilda says.

"I've been beating myself up that I didn't check up on her after she missed our meeting Saturday." Relieving myself of the guilt I've been feeling. Do I want Gilda to forgive me too?

She looks at me and asks, "Did you kill her?"

I take a moment. The bluntness of the question. Why, how, what would make Gilda ask me that. I hesitate, again, before I answer. "No.

No, I couldn't." Jacob pulls a fistful of hair from the side of my head. I want to smack it out of his hand. I don't. I massage his fist open and continue. "No, but I should have told the police right then. Maybe she wouldn't have died." I'm not sure it's true or that I even believe it myself.

"She was probably already dead," Gilda says.

I stare at her. Her comment surprises me.

"That's what they say about missing women and children. They're usually killed within the first hour of being taken. If she was taken—and I hope she didn't suffer any fear at the end," Gilda says. She sounds passive about it all. It has to be the pills.

But Gilda is right. And the fall killed Kat. Our meeting was scheduled for long after whatever she had planned for that morning. It's selfish of me to want a dead girl's mother to console me. Absolve me of my guilt.

"Do you think she drove her car to Debs that day to meet someone? Or do you honestly think she went on a solo run before teaching classes all day? Think hard about her patterns," I say. I need to know if Kat actually drove to Debs and met someone she knew that morning. And if so, did that person drive Kat's car back to Cyclone and abandon it there after killing her? Or, did Kat meet someone at Cyclone Studio and then end up at Debs? Why would she tell Gilda she was going for a run? Did she start her run at Debs? What was Kat hiding from her mom?

"Don't you think I have been? I'm not an idiot. I'm a schoolteacher. I educate everyone else's children every single day. I teach safety to my students. And here I am with a dead child." Gilda looks like she's going to crumble. I don't want her to think I'm diminishing her value. Blaming her for her daughter's death. I'm pushing her too hard.

"I didn't mean to imply . . ." I say.

"I know you didn't. It's everyone. It's all of it. I'm sorry—I haven't slept. My whole life is a fog right now," she says.

I wonder if crying has become a reflex for Gilda like it has for me.

"I'm sorry, I think you should go now," she says.

"Gilda, please, let me do this."

I coo to Jacob to break up the intensity of the moment.

"If I had to make a guess, she would have driven to Debs. But, she didn't. And, she told me she was going running before teaching classes." Gilda takes a sip of her tea. The dark circles under her eyes are also puffy today. "Maybe she drove to the studio and met up with someone and carpooled to Debs. With who, I don't know—please don't ask me to think. I gave a list of names to the police already. But, if she had been with someone, what happened to them? Kat wouldn't be stupid enough to meet a stranger and carpool. It doesn't make sense, Corey," Gilda says.

"And she has gone for a run from the studio to Debs before? You know this?" I want to eliminate as many possibilities as I can, if possible.

"Yeah, of course, just usually not before teaching. Too exhausting," Gilda says. She looks like she needs a nap. I cannot tell if she's processing the information she's giving me like I am.

"Okay." I take a beat to observe Gilda, make sure I haven't pushed too far. "Her car was found at the studio, right?"

Gilda nods.

"I noticed it's in your driveway now," I say.

"I had it towed here from Cyclone," Gilda says. "Listen to me, Corey. There wasn't anything from the autopsy that suggests foul play. The ME is certain—they're not marking it as undetermined, or homicide. Once that's done, it's over. Accident or intentional—she fell. At the end of the day, no matter what, my baby fell and broke her neck."

"Why tow the car?" I ask.

"The police didn't find the keys on her body, and I can't seem to locate them either. I asked Monique to check at the studio, but so far, they're missing. So, I had it towed."

"Could they be locked inside the car?" I ask.

"Maybe. I haven't looked. I can't bring myself to. Seeing her things around the house, her laundry, I folded it and put it away in her drawers. Her toothbrush . . ." Gilda trails off.

"Gilda, I need you to find the key," I say. She continues to nod. I'm ready to go out and break the window. My phone chimes, and Jacob grabs for it in my hand.

NELAScanBoy: Found him.

NELAScanBoy: He's in HLP AVE. 49 #429

"Gilda, I have to go," I say.

Jacob's teething leaves a pool of saliva on Gilda's table and my leg. I wipe the table with my hand and then my hand on my dry leg.

"Can you look for the key? To Kat's car?" I ask.

"Yeah, I'll look for it now."

I fumble with Jacob, the tote bag—my hands wet and sticky, but I have a burst of energy from this new information. I have a clear focus.

I pull the Sharpie out of my tote bag and write my number on a paper plate. "Call me when you find it, and I'll come right back," I say.

22

Avenue 49 isn't far. Nothing is in Highland Park. "He's really nice," Danielle said. A nice guy. Probably still lives with his mom and dad. Probably doesn't even have a driver's license yet. Probably just a kid. I was closer to my house than Gilda's now. Nando is nearly my neighbor.

I pull onto his street, looking for house number 429. It is one of the few streets left that has managed to avoid a makeover. All the homes are small and tidy. The street is quiet but lined with parked cars. I pass house number 425. The next numbered house is 431, so the unnumbered house in between has to be Nando's. I wonder what happened to house 427. There isn't a parking spot in sight, so I pull into the driveway.

Boards cover broken windows. The doorframe is bent and gives the illusion the door is crooked. The front yard is a concrete slab with a few determined blades of grass pushing through.

The effects of my Klonopin are dissipating. I should take another preventatively, but the fogginess and paralysis of brain function the Klonopin causes are becoming more apparent as I sober.

"Okay, buddy, you and Mommy are going to go knock on that door."

Jacob looks at me and gurgles like this is a fun activity. "I need you to act super cute, okay?" I say. I have been neglecting his playtime all week. Selfishly putting my needs ahead of his. He needs time to practice standing, pulling himself up, but I'm not ready for it. He needs to play with the little plastic chair that sings when he sits on it—he needs to sit on it. I need to read him *Snuggle Puppy!* and *Guess How Much I Love You* so he knows I "love him to the moon and back." Sing him Raffi songs, let him watch *Sesame Street* instead of making him listen to the police scanner with me. But hell, this is mommy-and-me time too. He's not sitting in some day care with ten or more kids sucking on shared toys and waiting for his turn to be held. I'm showing him the world in real time, not a fantasy some children's author imagined. Jacob and I are living.

I fish in my tote for Terri from Accounting, Jacob's favorite stuffed animal, but come up short again. I swear I put it back after leaving Dr. Rosenberg. I open the bottle of Klonopin and pour the contents into my bag, replacing them with yogurt puffs. I screw the top back on and rattle it at Jacob—I'm proud I didn't just give him the pills to shake this time. He delights in snatching it from my hand and shaking it with vigor. I pull him, and the makeshift rattle, out of his car seat and leave my tote bag in the car with the door unlocked for a quick escape. I put my keys in my fist and ready myself. I knock on the door. It looks as though it may fall off its hinges. It takes less than a minute for someone to answer—a young man with a mustache. His arms tattooed from left wrist to right. A series of pictures intertwined—a story. It's beautiful. He smiles. "May I help you?" Polite.

"Hi, is Nando here?" I wonder if he is Nando.

He gives me a once-over, still smiling.

"Sure, one minute, please." He turns from the door and yells. "Nando! Door! Tina." Tina—also known as meth. I want to correct him. I am not looking for meth. Do I look like I'm looking for meth? I do a quick inventory of my appearance. I think about the recent uptick in suburban housewives using meth. Do I look like them? Do I look like the mom on antidepressants? Probably, yes. I shift my body sideways, turning Jacob away from the door.

"I don't need Tina," I say. He looks at me and smiles more. "Just Nando."

At that moment, a much younger guy appears. He has great hair. No visible tattoos. A crisp white T-shirt and jeans. His eyes are a beautiful hazel color. Aside from the light bruising around his right eye and the cut on his lip, he looks ready for college. Not what I would expect from a local meth dealer. But then I've only ever met one other meth dealer—a guy that used to live in our house. He came around looking for someone else right after we bought it. When he didn't find them, he asked if we needed any meth. Same as the kids selling magazines, but this guy wasn't in khakis. He was unwashed, his clothes too baggy to be his own, a mustache that looked drawn on. A few weeks later he came back again, same clothes, asked if we needed our lawn mowed. Evan let him mow the strip of grass between the sidewalk and street and paid him twenty bucks. Elsie told us later he'd been picked up by the cops—larceny. Released on bail and found dead a few days later—shot in the head from behind. I think about him more than I like to.

"Are you Nando?" I ask.

"Who sent you?" he asks.

"I knew Araceli."

The guy that answered the door pulls Nando back inside. "Get the fuck outta here," he says.

I try to back up, but there's nowhere to go except down a step. I stumble. Hit the ground with both feet. Jacob starts to whine, and I know leaving would be smart, but I stay.

"I'm here because of Araceli's mom. I know Nando was dating her."

"Who are you? Ain't no *police bringing their baby to work* day."

"I'm not the police. I'm just a mom who was asked by Araceli's mom to find out what happened to her dead daughter. Unless you know something about her death, I'd like to talk to Nando."

I'm shaking violently on the inside, but the pill keeps me in a mild paralysis. My fight-or-flight instinct mute. Jacob lets out a small frustrated wail. I try to comfort him with small bounces on my hip as I say, "It's okay, Mommy's here. It's okay."

"Or what?" he says. "You're not the police—you have no business here."

I keep my voice low and flat, almost a whisper, to simultaneously soothe Jacob and the situation. I turn sideways so my whole right side is between Jacob and the man at the door. "There's no 'or what.' Do I look like I'm going to 'or what' you? What are you, twenty? Where's your mom? Don't you think she'd want to know what happened to you if you died in a park hanging from a tree? Do you have something to hide? I know I don't scare you. Do you think you scare me? I have thoughts of killing myself every fucking day since I pushed a nine-pound baby from my body. I have thoughts I will kill my own child. I live on the brink of complete self-destruction. Every. Goddamn. Day. Do you? No. I don't think so." He stares at me. There's still plenty of daylight. I know he's not going to do anything here or now, but I want to vomit. "Let me talk to Nando, and then I go away."

We stand there, staring at each other. His former manners all but forgotten. The investigator in me all but taking over.

Nando pushes the guy aside and comes out. He whispers something I can't make out. Jacob's wailing gets louder. If anyone on the rest of the block were home, or gave a shit, they'd be on their porch watching, or peering through a window.

"It's okay," Nando says. The guy retreats into the house, leaving the door ajar.

"Do I know you?" Nando asks. He puts his hand out toward Jacob and wiggles his fingers. Jacob grabs hold of it with both hands, dropping the pill-bottle rattle, his cheeks wet, and he giggles at Nando puffing his cheeks out and crossing his eyes in front of his nose. Have I ever connected with my son the way Nando is? Engaged in goofy faces to make him smile? My child is bonded to me through breasts, but this kid, this Nando, instantly bonds with him through a simple gesture. Shitty mother, shitty mother, shitty mother.

"You're good with kids, huh?" I say.

"I have a lot of nieces and nephews." Nando's hazel eyes are still locked with Jacob's. "You didn't answer me before. Do I know you?"

"I don't think so," I say. "I'm a new friend of Araceli's mom." I wonder if he recognizes me from the news, but I doubt it—he's too young. "I was hoping you would talk to me about Araceli. Maybe about what happened to her?"

It's a big ask—this kid has every right to freeze me out and not speak, especially if he is hiding something.

"I loved Celi." He breaks his gaze with Jacob to wipe his eyes. Jacob reaches for him, but I clutch his hands. "She was so special. Smart. She was really smart, you know? Book smart, street smart. Life smart."

Jacob wiggles in my arms. I sit down on the step. Nando joins me. Christ, he's young. He retrieves the makeshift rattle from the ground and passes it back to Jacob.

"When was the last time you saw her or talked to her?" I ask.

"Maybe like a week before she died. She broke up with me."

"Did that make you mad?"

"Nah, I wanted her to. She was too good for me. I wanted her to stay on track, go to college, be somebody better. She's not like me. She didn't grow up like me. I told her if she didn't break up with me, I would never be able to let go of her. I wanted her to leave me, see? I wasn't mad. I was so damn proud of her."

Jacob yelps—his attention-seeking sound. He's happy and wants to touch and feel and be noticed. I nuzzle his cheek with my nose. Take a big inhale of the top of his head. I may not ever be the mother he needs or deserves. I could never leave him, but he would grow up and leave me one day, and that would be it, because I could never leave him. In this way I understand Nando completely. And I wouldn't be mad at Jacob for leaving me. I wouldn't be mad at him if he grew up and hated me. I'm a mess; he deserves better.

"Sounds like you really loved her."

"It's bullshit what they're saying about her."

"What is?" I ask. I know what he's going to say.

"That she was wrapped up in some gang bullshit. That's not Celi."

"I know. What about her friend Natalie?"

"Nah, that chick didn't even talk. Her mom is real messed up. She was lost without Celi. Like, Celi protected Nat like a little sister. Natalie wouldn't do anything to piss her off, and gang shit?" He shakes his head. "No way."

"I don't want to hurt you, Nando, but I want to ask you a tough question. Was Araceli seeing anyone else, that you knew of?"

"I don't think so, but I went MIA. I couldn't be around her and not be sad."

"Do you know if Natalie was dating anyone?"

"No." Nando is laughing now.

"Why is that funny?"

"You didn't know Nat. She was a kid. Like, she wasn't like that. She was just—she was a kid is all."

"Did Araceli ever mention anyone she was having a problem with, or Natalie had a problem with, maybe at school? Something she would only confide to you?"

"She was a good person." He chokes, then swallows—burying his grief like a man. "Her dad was hard on her, but that's because he loves her. Her AP English teacher gave her a lot of grief. Made her stay after a lot to work on her essays. Never cut her slack, but Celi defended her a lot, so I guess she liked it."

"Can I ask you a personal question?"

"Shoot, what'd you think you were already doing?"

I laugh.

"Fair. But why did you show up at the school with a beat-up face? Looks like you're still bruised."

"Like I said, I didn't want to go back to that school and see Araceli—it hurt too much to see her. So, I didn't make my nut. I got in trouble. Lessons learned. I'm back there now."

I nod.

"You're a good guy, Nando."

"I'm all right."

"Is this what you want?" I gesture toward the house.

"For now. This is my family. Those guys in there? They're my cousins. They feed me. They house me. I got no complaints. I miss the shit out of Celi, though. Sad and shit every day."

I believe him. I don't think he has any answers about Araceli's death.

I shake his hand, and we part ways at the porch. I strap Jacob into his car seat and pull myself into the driver's seat. I start crying. How could I bring Jacob here, like this? What was so goddamn wrong with me? That a couple of dead girls makes me feel more alive than I have in a long time. That the death of a friend is giving me a reason to live again? I can't work for Kat anymore at the studio, but I can work for her now. For all of them. Maybe this is the way back to me—my job, my life.

A crew of guys has gathered at the gate to Nando's backyard and watches me. Bile climbs up my throat. I swallow, and it burns all the way down to my gut. I put the car in reverse and floor it, barely missing a parked car. I shake. I need to pull over. What was I thinking, talking to his cousin that way? Thank god for Nando being a nice guy. I pull over and take out my pills. One to stay ahead.

Next stop, Trader Joe's.

23

I stare across a row of parked cars trying to remember how I got here—Trader Joe's with the Polynesian arches in the parking lot and strategically spaced palm trees. I drove, yes, but I remember nothing. Not one turn.

In the store with Jacob—his carrier strapped to the shopping cart—I look for a woman I don't know from Eve. I text Elsie.

Me: What's Natalie's aunt's name?

Elsie: Betty

I put bread in my cart, bananas, hummus, cheese. Domestic bliss at its finest. Nothing in my cart has any thought put into it, or meaning. I'm grabbing and dropping while I look at name tags. I sample the new prebagged salad—it tastes like prebagged salad should taste.

"This is great. Thank you," I say.

"You're welcome. I added our precooked grilled chicken and done," says the Trader Joe's woman. She grins like an emoji—the standard TJ's flirt every store member commits to across the country.

"I'm so sorry, but can you tell me, do you know if Betty is working today?" I ask.

The woman looks down at her cutting board and tosses the bowl of shredded lettuce and chicken cubes.

"She's in the stockroom working," she says.

"Great. I'm an old friend. I was hoping I could say hi. Is there any chance you would grab her for me?" I gesture to Jacob. "She's been asking to meet the baby."

The woman looks at Jacob and smiles.

"You know what, it would probably cheer her up. Let me go get her for you."

I park my cart next to the coffee bean–grinding station, the aroma oily and bitter—delicious. There's a Trader Joe's employee in his Hawaiian TJ's button-down stocking teas while Jacob and I wait. It is methodical, the way he uses his box knife to tear through the shipping packaging.

"Can I help you?" a woman asks. She's carrying a blackboard and a used box of gel markers.

I quickly glance at her red name tag with a name printed in white, **BETTY**.

"Betty?"

"Yes?"

"My name's Corey. I'm a friend of Elsie and Lupe."

Betty is tall and curvy—not what I expected, but then I hadn't really expected anything. I can't tell if her lashes are real or fake, but they are like long-legged spiders reaching her eyebrows, thick and gorgeous. Her hair is down, a scrunchie on her wrist.

"Right. Lupe mentioned—I'm not sure what you're doing or think you're going to do that the police aren't already doing."

I want to tell her what I told Brian Greene, the Peeping Tom, that the LAPD has the lowest ratio of police officers to residents of any major city in the country. Translation—there are only nine thousand active police officers serving all 503 square miles of Los Angeles. That means there is one officer to every 433 residents. One person responsible for the safety and well-being of 433 people at any given time. It's a gamble, determining which call warrants the most immediate response. And which cases then warrant investigating and how much.

She looks me up and down, my stretch pants, my stained tank top, my baby. "My niece is gone. Please don't make this harder on our family than it already is. Her father and brother, not to mention her mother."

"No, no that's not my intention. I'm only trying to help," I say.

"Help how, exactly? The girl was troubled. Easily influenced and troubled. She hung herself. She wasn't happy. You know about her mother? She was her mother's child. We want to bury her and mourn and move on."

"What makes you certain it was suicide? There were two girls, don't forget. Araceli was with Natalie."

"Don't remind me."

"I'm sorry?" I say.

"Araceli was a bad influence. She's the one that had Natalie talking about the family. Spreading lies. Making up stories about everyone. I'm sure the whole stunt was just to get attention. Probably didn't think they'd actually die." She sets the blackboard down against the shelf of coffees, along with the markers. The board lists new items, but it's the artistic penmanship, calligraphy-like, that is doing the selling.

"Wow. I had no idea. Can you tell me what sorts of things Natalie and Araceli lied about? What were they saying?" I ask. "I would like to be able to give Lupe some closure." Jacob snorts, then sneezes. He sneezes six more times, until there's more fluid on his face than inside his nose. Betty passes me a tissue from her pocket. "Thank you," I say.

"This girl convinced Natalie to start locking her uncle and me out of the house. Said she didn't need our help anymore. That we're self-serving." She stops talking. The pause is long. Thoughtful. "Natalie had a lot of anger inside her. Growing up with a mother who stays in bed all day. Cries all night. It got to her."

I did know a little about that from personal experience.

"Did you stop going over?" I ask.

"No, my husband, Joe, is the reason those kids get up and go to school every day. He's the reason their mother is fed and cared for. He's the reason *they* get fed."

Betty's anger and resentment are palpable.

"We couldn't have kids ourselves, and we consider them like our own. It hurt me when Natalie didn't want us to be there anymore. And it didn't matter anyway—we have our own keys."

"I heard that Joe was hurt—it was a work-related accident?" I ask.

"I'm not sure how that's relevant."

"I'm sorry—it's not. I just heard about it and was curious how he was doing."

"Oh, well, thank you. That's thoughtful, but it was years ago. Some scaffolding fell on top of him. It caused some brain trauma, but he's fine. Better than the doctors thought he would be. He can walk, which they assumed he wouldn't be able to do. It's a miracle. He didn't lose any of his cognitive skills. I worked doubles to pay for all the physical therapy he needed, and it was worth it." She looks at me. I sense she's proud of that. "Whatever they told you about him, whatever Natalie told them, it's not true. Joe loved Natalie like a daughter. He would never hurt her."

"Teenagers are known for their moods and shitty commentary," I say. Betty gives me a weak smile. "May I ask what Natalie was saying?"

"The police already have the statements, so it's not new information. Natalie told the school nurse that her uncle touched her, forced himself on her. She claimed she was pregnant. I'm telling you, she was troubled. You ask me—she didn't want the boy she was sleeping with to get in trouble, so she accused us. The little tramp had Child Protective Services at our house. My husband was grilled for hours." Betty looks over at the shelves of tea—her avoidance of me a tell. She reaches for a box, studies it. There are no tears, no sighing, just averted eyes. She knows as well as I do that Natalie wouldn't have gone around falsely accusing her uncle of sexual assault. Betty knows who she married. Or her suspicions were confirmed when Natalie finally spoke up. But why is she still protecting him?

"We can't even have children. We tried for twenty years. It's all lies," Betty says.

Yes, Betty, you are lying.

"I'm so sorry. I cannot imagine how traumatic this has all been." I stroke Jacob's cheek. He smiles and speaks to me in gibberish, sounds that are more like words than ever before. *Tramp*—the word more revealing of Betty's character than Natalie's. "One last question, do you know the name of the boy?" I ask.

"Who?"

"The boy Natalie was dating?"

"Of course. I was ready to charge his ass with statutory rape. He's nineteen. Natalie was only seventeen. I was so mad. She begged me not to."

"What's his name?"

"Fernando Alaniz. He's a high school–dropout punk. Natalie was so much better than him. I didn't even know she was interested in boys. Never saw a sign of it."

My throat is dry. "Thank you. Thank you so much for your help." I stumble on the way out.

Betty walks over.

"I'm fine. Just a little dehydrated." I wave her off. I say goodbye and thanks, again.

I get to my car and sit with Jacob on my lap—he crawls into the passenger seat and pulls himself up the window. Passersby wave, and he waves back. He *waves* back. "Buddy, you're waving." A milestone. I need a book to record this in. I should write it down for later, but my hands are shaking too hard to write or strap him into his car seat.

This sure as hell sounds like motive and a cover-up. Who is lying—Betty, the uncle, Nando . . . ? If CPS found the claim to be unsubstantiated, like Betty said, then Lopez may not even be aware that a call was ever made. The police and Child Protective Services are two separate agencies. Without criminal charges, there's no reason for them to communicate. And backlogs with CPS have long been accepted as status quo—part of agency culture.

Fuck.

Who do I still know in Child Protective Services?

"It's time to go, Jacob. Let's get you buckled in your seat, before Mommy ends up on the wrong side of CPS."

24

"Smells good in here," I say when I walk through the door and am hit with kitchen warmth and garlic. I didn't expect Evan to be home.

"I got off early, thought I'd make us a nice dinner," he says. Evan takes Jacob from me, gives him a head kiss, and dances off with him, back to the kitchen. He is playing Phish and finding rhythm where I hear none. Jacob delights in being spun around and sways in the arms of his dad. Evan's face is equally lit with joy.

I grab my phone from inside my tote while my hands are free. I type as Evan and I speak. "That's sweet. Is it almost ready?" I ask.

Me: Hey

NELAScanBoy: Hey

Me: I met with him.

NELAScanBoy: Nando?

Me: Nando. Do you have a CPS contact? Diner in an hour?

NELAScanBoy: Whoa. Maybe. That works

Evan says, "It can be, you in a hurry?"

"Yeah, I need to head over to the diner." I wait for the argument I am sure is coming.

"Okay, do you want to eat when you get back instead?"

I stare at him. I rely on the familiar script here, and Evan is changing it.

"Sure, I—that would be great. You don't have to wait for me," I say.

"I can wait. Do you want to feed Jacob before you go?"

"He's not hungry yet. I'll just do it there."

"Actually, I thought you could leave him with me this time. I haven't seen him all day. I'd like to spend some time with him."

Here it is. The new script. Evan, brilliant Evan, has found a new way to fight.

"You know I'm going to take him with me, so let's not do this, okay?"

"Should I come with you too? I can watch Jacob there. We're in the middle of reading *Don't Let the Pigeon Drive the Bus!*"

"Evan, it's work. You were here with me when that woman, that mother, sat here and asked me to help. You didn't come swooping in and say no to her."

"Okay, Corey. So what role do I play in this then? What do I do while you take our child every night to go save the world?" He's trying to control his volume because of Jacob, but his tone is clear.

"Be supportive. Let me go to this meeting without hassle and be here for me when I get back. Do not give me grief." I am begging him.

"Is that what Dr. Rosenberg told you to say?" he asks.

"What? No. I didn't even—"

"Never mind, just go. I'll be here. Waiting."

Evan hands Jacob back to me and goes upstairs. I hear the bedroom door shut. I turn the burners off on the stove. I hate winning when it means I've lost in the long run. I go to the bathroom with Jacob and freshen myself up as best I can. My hair will have to remain in a knot on top of my head, too dirty for anything else. I pull a tinted lip balm from my tote bag and find a wadded-up diaper from days ago—thankfully just a pee pee. I drop it in the waste bin and spray air freshener in the room, inside my bag, and on my clothes before I leave.

❖ ❖ ❖

As is our way, I get to the diner before Chris. I settle into our booth, and immediately Jacob is hungry. I open my shirt for him. As he latches, the waitress takes one look and spins around to help a different table. "Well, at least you get to eat," I say. Jacob's sweet face stares back at me.

"Hey, sorry, I couldn't find parking," Chris says, dropping into the booth. It's like he's appeared out of thin air. I didn't notice him or sense him coming at all.

"No worries, I just got here. Haven't even ordered," I say. He flags down the waitress that ignored me moments ago, and she stands awkwardly looking only at Chris.

"You hungry?" he asks me.

"Starving." I didn't stop to eat all day. "Can I get a grilled cheese and soup?" I ask the waitress, who stares at her pad.

"Nice choice. I'll have the burger, fries." He looks at me mid-order. "Do you want pie?"

"I could eat pie."

"And a slice of berry pie, à la mode."

My phone vibrates and chimes in my bag. I dig it out one-handed, swiping my hand against something wet—hopefully baby wipes rather than something that would wait to be cleaned until I forgot about it.

Gmail: GoFundMe . . .

Dani started a GoFundMe campaign to assist with funeral costs for Natalie and Araceli. I wonder when their bodies will be released for burial. Jacob is asleep on my breast, so I gently pull him off and cover myself.

"You look distracted," Chris says.

"I'm hungry," I say. I can't think. My energy, and with it my clarity, is fading. The tightness in my throat is back. Our food comes. I'm sweating. I can't eat. I'm too warm. I dig in my bag for my new prescription. More wetness—I look into the bag, a leaking water bottle—the Klonopin is at the bottom. Loose from dumping them out earlier to make a rattle for Jacob. I collect as many as I can, one-handed, and pass the pill bottle to Chris.

"Can you open this?" I ask. I have one hand free, the other holding Jacob, the baby I could hurt. Do I want to hurt my beautiful baby? No. Shut up, shut up, shut up. The knife on the table stares at me, and I stare back, begging it to stop calling me. Chris empties the yogurt bites from the bottle and hands it to me. I pop a pill in my mouth and chew it—hoping it would make it work faster. The bitter powder coats my tongue. I pour the pile in my hand into the bottle, and Chris recaps it for me. We sit in silence. I can feel Chris looking at me, but my eyes are down. I don't want him to actually see me crying. I feel relief knowing the Klonopin will shut my brain off soon enough. The repetitive thoughts will quiet.

"I'm okay, I promise," I say. "It's just some postpartum stuff I'm dealing with."

"Okay. Take your time. I've got all night." Chris takes a swig from his water glass, then sets it back down in a puddle of condensation. I watch as he traces water on the table into happy faces until I am ready to eat and talk.

"I'm good," I say. Just barely, but knowing the pill is in me is almost enough to calm me down—and avoid a full-blown panic attack.

"Good. I'm starving. Let's eat." It's that easy with Chris.

Not with Evan. It would start with mostly genuine concern for me. And my response, "I'm fine," would be taken as an affront. I would then have to listen to Evan again explain how much weight he carries being the breadwinner, the caretaker of our family, a father and husband who feels the pressure of making sure we're perfectly tended to all the time. It would be an hour more about exhaustion from his job. The one he works for nine, ten, sometimes more hours a day to make sure all the time he took off to care for me in my postpartum stage won't reflect poorly on him at his performance reviews. There's never any mention of the financial value I provide our family by staying home with our child.

After the last bite of pie is eaten and the entire day recapped, Chris orders himself a coffee.

"Do I have to say it?" Chris asks.

"What are we talking about?"

"Nando isn't the father."

"Sure. But was she even pregnant at all? I don't know. And if she was—is there a possibility she was still pregnant when she was killed? The aunt said they couldn't have kids. A bit open to interpretation—can she not have children or him?"

"I'm waiting on my guy to call me when the autopsy is done. They'll know and likely have done a paternity test, if there was a fetus."

"I'm worried about any other kids in the house right now—siblings of Natalie's. The uncle could be doing this to them too."

"God, Corey."

"I know." I pause to look at Jacob. "Can your guy get us the uncle's and aunt's alibis for that night? I'm positive they were questioned."

"Yeah, of course." Chris types quickly into his phone and then looks at me. "But why Araceli? Why would they kill Araceli?" he asks.

"Because she was Natalie's best friend," I say. "Because she knew too much."

"You have to talk to the mother—Natalie's mother," Chris says.

"I know. I also have to work on Kat's case." Kat is dead in a morgue. A charity ride for her funeral expenses only two days away. Her mother at home feeling she failed a depressed daughter. I have trouble concentrating. It's unshakable—it's the medicine taking control. I have to grab hold of one thing and follow it, but that possibility is nearly moot. I flag down our waitress.

"Can I get a coffee? Can you bring one of those pots to the table for me? Thank you," I say.

"Corey, maybe you shouldn't drink coffee if you're feeling anxious."

"I know what I'm doing, one cup. I just need to balance the fogginess from the medicine."

Jacob gasps and coughs. I look down. He's rolled over, now teetering off the edge of the booth. Shit. I pick him up and hold my face to his nose. His breathing is normal. He stirs awake, then asleep again. I almost did it, hurt him, and while my reactions are muted, dull, slow. I'm numb. The Klonopin could sedate Jacob as well—but it excretes in such low levels I don't have to worry if I'm taking one a day. No, that's the Paxil. One a day. How many Klonopin have I taken today? It's one every six hours, as needed—staying ahead of the attacks. I can pump and dump or opt for formula—if I'm overly concerned, according to Dr. Rosenberg. The negative stigma around formula—even at nine months old—is engrained into my brain. If I don't breastfeed, I'll cause irreversible psychological damage. If I don't take the medication, couldn't I be causing myself irreparable mental damage?

There is little my body is willing to give when all the functions are turned down from the Klonopin. Chris reaches across the table and takes my hand. I am unable to emote—I sit expressionless, all feeling shrunk down into a single cell, that cell pushed into an unused corner of my body—silenced. I hope it will kill itself—or the Klonopin would snuff it out.

"It's okay," Chris says. "Jacob is fine. Everything is fine. You're okay, and so is he."

I wipe my face with a rough diner napkin—I realize I'm crying. I can't put Jacob back down. He has to stay in my arms now, where he is safest from everything. Two deep breaths. The waitress is back with coffee, and I guzzle it. Take another deep breath and plow ahead.

"Here's what I know. Those girls, Araceli and Natalie, they're still on the Murder Board," I say.

"The what?"

"The Murder Board at the NELA precinct. Natalie and Araceli are on the board. Kat's not on the board, which is bullshit. She's in a folder on the table, maybe a desk now. Shit, maybe already in the filing cabinet. But it means the police do not believe Kat's case is related to Natalie and Araceli. Otherwise she'd be on the board with a possible **SERIAL KILLER** note next to Natalie and Araceli."

Chris squeezes my hand, the one he's still holding. I think about all the times we never kissed. Every pulse on me starts to beat like a loud bass against my skin. I smile and will the Klonopin to keep my fair skin cool and not warm to pink. Worse, red. I want to go back in time and actually do all the things I only thought about doing with Chris. Back in time before the baby and the marriage.

"Maybe we should take a break," he says.

Jacob gives a small whimper. His face scrunches up; any minute it would be a wail. I pull my hand from Chris's and open my blouse, stop—no. I dig in the tote, feel the water-dampened bottom and then the soft nipple of a pacifier. The moment is already fleeing. If I can just get Jacob to take the pacifier, maybe I can rekindle a second of it.

"I'm sorry, let me settle him and—"

"I think we should call it a night. We can talk tomorrow. I can talk to my cousin more—he's on nights right now, so it's good. I'll find out if they're even watching the uncle. See if he has a contact at CPS," he says.

The moment is completely gone.

"Yeah, good idea. I can focus on Kat tomorrow. I need to go back and talk to Nando again. If Araceli was protecting her friend, she confided in someone."

"I'll come with you this time."

"I don't think so. Not a good idea. The baby and I aren't a threat, and now he knows me. I'll be all right," I say.

Chris walks me out to the car and waits while I put Jacob in his car seat, fussy and tired. His phone vibrates, but he ignores it. I wonder if it's a girlfriend. Or another woman journalist waiting for him at a bar, not a diner, to work on a story. We walk around to the driver's side door to say goodbye. He grabs my hand. I hope he pulls me in, wraps me to his chest, and squeezes, the way he used to. He always hugged for keeps—he never let go until you did first. And I remember always letting go a little too soon. I never wanted to overstay the hug—letting go in the past felt like the safe move. Like not saying I love you first. But tonight, he grabs my hands and cups them inside his instead of a hug.

"Corey, will you tell me if you need help?"

"Yeah, but I'm fine. I'm on new medicine, and it's got to kick in, and I'm adjusting to this new role—mom." I want to cry and tell him no, I'm not okay. I'm a fucking mess, and I want you to kiss me, and I want it not to matter to Evan.

"If you need to talk, I'm here for that. It doesn't have to be work all the time. We can be friends again too."

"Aren't we?" I ask. "Friends?" He squeezes my hands tighter, or maybe I'm the one squeezing. Clenching my hands inside his. "I'm not myself right now," I say.

"You're as much you as you've always been."

I can't tell if I move in toward him or he moves in toward me or if we've been standing this close the whole time, but suddenly I hear his pulse, hear him swallow, hear his lips open and close while he speaks. I'm fixated on it all.

"I should go," I say. "Jacob is so tired."

He doesn't let go of my hands, and I don't pull mine away.

He bends down and comes toward my face. "Get some rest." I feel the heat rise in my cheeks. Then, his lips are on my forehead. "I'll talk to you in the morning."

I fumble into the front seat of my car and leave, Jacob whimpering in the back.

25

I wake up with a buzz just before Evan's alarm clock, but Evan's not in bed. It doesn't matter. I have an agenda for the day—Nando. I look at my phone; there's a message from Chris:

> *NELAScanBoy:* Aunt Betty is Uncle Joe's alibi. They were home all night.

No solid alibi, abuse allegation—what is Lopez waiting on?

Evan's in the kitchen already as I walk in.

"Morning," he says. "Can I feed Jacob for you this morning?"

"Yeah, thank you." There will be no breast milk this morning—I'm worried about the pills. Baby cereal and butternut squash mash from a plastic cup with a smiling sun on the label. "Did I tell you that tomorrow is the ride at Cyclone for Kat?"

"Yeah, it's on my calendar. I don't think I'm going to go, unless you need me," Evan says. I want to tell him to come. To just be there for me. Not fixing me.

"No, yeah, of course—I'm sure I'll be busy dealing with people, so that's fine," I say. All the tension and animosity between us is gone. A flat, nonresistant energy left—or the Klonopin in my system is halting my brain from its usual overanalysis and subsequent feelings. "I've got some errands to run today—pick up more waters and energy bars." And stop at Nando's to find out what he really knows about Natalie's uncle.

"I really want to come and support your work, Corey. I do. I have to go in to the office for a couple of hours to make up some time on some projects that are due," Evan says. "I wish I could be here more with you and Jacob. I don't want to be an absent father or a workaholic husband. I promise I'll make it up to you. We'll take a beach day soon."

I nod in support. "You're a great provider, Evan. No one can ever say less." I know that's what he is bred to be—provider, hunter, gatherer. The burden of the patriarchy he grew up in. I just don't remember him being this cut and dried about our roles. Not when we said "I do."

He takes a seat in front of Jacob's high chair and airplanes orange and beige spoonfuls of mushy food into his mouth. Half the food successfully makes it in; the other half falls back out—Jacob is still lacking sufficient teeth to gate the tongue and food inside his mouth. I watch the way Jacob connects to Evan and Evan to Jacob. For Evan, Jacob isn't part of a new routine or a new job—he's a part of Evan's life when it's convenient. He doesn't have to worry about his freedom. His happy hours and work lunches are not determined by a nap schedule, diaper change, or breastfeeding. It's easy for him—motherhood is not his burden.

I wait for Evan to get in the shower before I pack up Jacob and leave. I make a left onto Monte Vista Street—one block, two blocks, three, and turn. One more left—into Nando's driveway. I take Jacob back to the kicked-in front door and knock. The street is more desolate today—one whole side is near empty of the parked cars that were there before. A house down the way has three children playing in the front yard—it looks like tag. No one answers, so I knock harder. I may not have even knocked the first time, but I did this time. My knuckles hurt.

A woman answers the door. She is older than me: gray hair, wrinkles, wearing a muumuu, and wearing it well.

"Is Nando here?" I ask.

"Yes. Why?" Jacob smiles, revealing a newly crowning baby tooth.

"I was here the other day. I just want to ask him something, if that's okay?" I don't know if the woman is his guardian or what, but she appears protective and worried. "I'm not the police," I say.

"We don't do that at this house. No drugs. Do you understand?"

"Yes. No, I'm definitely not looking for drugs. I'm an investigative . . . I used to be an investigative reporter. I'm only here because I'm helping—"

"Nana, I got this," Nando says as he comes up behind the door.

They speak in Spanish. I listen without comprehension. After all the years I've lived in LA, I should be able to do better than this.

"Jacob, my man, how you doin', big guy?" Nando says. He rubs Jacob's cheek with the side of his finger and makes silly faces at him until Jacob giggles uncontrollably. "Did you solve your case?"

"I don't know, Nando. I really don't know. I think you lied to me," I say. Nando looks at me. I can see darkness in his otherwise happy demeanor.

"How so?"

"I went and saw Natalie's aunt."

His shoulders drop. He takes a seat on the stoop.

"Pinche puta," he says. "She doesn't know shit because she doesn't want to. She's pure evil, man. And she's loco."

"If you want Araceli's death to be resolved, then you have to tell me everything you know," I say.

"You don't get it. You live here, but you don't live here like I do. We take care of our own in Highland Park."

"Don't say that to me, Nando. Listen, you're just a kid. You wear grown-up sizes, you face reality every day, you hustle to survive, but listen to me—whatever it is you think you're going to do, don't do it."

"Fuck this." Nando looks small. "I don't need to hear this from you."

Nando is right. He doesn't need to hear it from me. I will never know what it's like to grow up in this community. It's unfair to ask him to understand. When I was his age, I was hanging out at frat parties and worried about midterms. I've made a mistake: He is not a child; I was at nineteen, but Nando isn't.

I change my tone. I'm pleading now. It's unfair of me, but I am scared. "You want to spend the rest of your life in prison?" He doesn't respond. "You want your Nana to die with you locked up? Is that what you want?"

"Fuck this," he says again. He covers his eyes.

Jacob starts to cry.

"Shit, little man. I'm sorry. It's okay." Nando gives Jacob his fingers. Wiggles them like kelp off the Catalina coast. Jacob grabs at them. "Can I hold him?" he asks. The Klonopin has me incapable of saying no. I'm passing Jacob to Nando without thinking.

"Be careful," I say.

Nando looks at me and smiles. "He's good to have around, right? Like you feel some shit, then you see him and it's better?"

"Sort of," I say.

"I need to get out of this place," he says.

"If you don't want to talk to me, then talk to Detective Lopez."

"They think I'm a suspect. It's too late," he says.

"That's not true. It's not too late."

"Do you know what that piece of shit did to her?"

"The uncle?" I ask.

He nods.

"Yeah. I think I do," I say.

"He kept getting away with it. That puta wife of his kept bailing him out. I told them when they questioned me."

"You told the police?" I ask.

"Yeah."

"Was Natalie pregnant?"

"Wait—what?" Nando looks surprised.

"Natalie told the school nurse she was pregnant. Did you know about it?"

Still holding Jacob, Nando stands up and punches the porch wall, leaving a dent. I jump up, yell, and grab for Jacob. Nando's grandmother is at the window shaking her head. My heart is racing. My hands claw into Nando's arm.

"Let me have my baby, Nando!" His grip around Jacob is strong. He pace-stomps on the porch before punching the wall again.

"Nando, give me my baby," I say, calmer but demanding. Jacob screams and yelps, alarming Nando, who looks scared and surprised.

"I didn't know it was like that. I swear to god, I didn't know." He covers his eyes with one hand. "He probably wanted her to have it so he could steal it from her. I told them to wait for me. I told them I would help them. Araceli begged me to stay out of it. She didn't want me to get into any more trouble. That's why she left me." Nando wipes at his face, damp with tears. "Damn. He killed them for that baby."

"Did you tell the police everything you know?"

"I told you, we take care of our own," he says.

"I don't know what that means, Nando!"

"Tell Araceli's mother I got this." Nando hands Jacob to me. "You shouldn't come back this way, Miss Corey. It's not safe for you." He looks at Jacob. "He got your eyes." He pauses. "Ears too." Nando goes through the bent doorframe and closes me out of his world for good.

It feels like seconds later when I pull up to the curb outside my house and call Detective Lopez.

"Detective Lopez, it's Corey Tracey-Lieberman. Please call me as soon as you get this, it's time sensitive. I have new information regarding the girls hanged at Debs. Today, now, ASAP. I have a source; he has firsthand knowledge. I don't want to go to the press with this information, but I can—and I will. Again, it's Corey Tracey-Lieberman."

I wait for her to call me back. I stare at my phone, watching the numbers change. The screen lights up with news updates, like who is divorcing whom in the world of celebrities. I look at Jacob asleep in his seat, spit bubbles forming on his lips. I look at my house, on the little knoll, green with brown trim. I look back at the clock; twenty-seven minutes have passed, no callback from Lopez.

I feel a sharp pain in my lower right abdomen, my liver. Is cancer the cause of all this and not postpartum bullshit? Do I have to add hypochondria to the growing list of paranoia? I can't go down this road. I need to not feel this right now. I take another pill. I have to finish the errands I told Evan I was running.

Evan is waiting with dinner again and open arms when I walk into the house. He has a bottle of breast milk I pumped months ago and froze ready for Jacob, and it all looks like a perfect, normal, happy setting. Even I'm happy to be here, or I'm too foggy to feel otherwise.

"Hi, I didn't expect you to beat me home again," I say. I drop my tote bag on the floor. Evan walks over and kisses me, and I lean into the kiss instead of fighting it. "I have to go back and get the bags from the car." I finished all the errands I needed to run, a first.

"I thought that it may be nice to start a new family tradition of eating dinner together on the weekend. I'll try not to go into the office as much, give you a little break from Jacob so you can do something for yourself." Evan takes Jacob from me and starts to bounce him. "Why don't you start eating? I'll get the bags with my main man, Jacob."

"Okay." I nod. I get myself a plate of Bolognese and take it into the living room. I eat while I watch my phone for Detective Lopez's call. I eat and think about Nando. I eat and think about Araceli. I eat and think about Chris. I eat and think about Kat. And I eat while trying to piece everything I've seen in the last few days together. I eat until I forget that I'm eating.

I'm on the couch, an empty plate on my lap and no Evan or Jacob in sight. I'm disoriented. I can't remember where I am, who I live with. Is my mom here? I know there's a mom that lives here, a woman. I don't know what house this is and if my sister lives here too. I instinctively start counting one, two, three—I'm the woman that lives here. Everything is flooding back but just a little beyond my grasp still.

"Hello?" I call out, can't quite get my bearings. "HELLO? HELLO!?" Am I alone? I shouldn't be alone, right? My breasts hurt. My right nipple is leaking. I check my phone. I have messages. Evan is running down the stairs—Evan! Yes. Me, Evan, and Jacob.

"Babe, what's wrong? Are you hurt?"

"Where's Jacob?"

"I just put him down."

"How long have I been home?"

"Maybe thirty minutes."

"I spaced out. I think I fell asleep for a minute, and I couldn't remember where I was or who was supposed to be here."

"It's okay. It's okay. I'm here. You're okay," he says, putting a hand on my shoulder. I touch him to make sure he's really here. Real. I scratch my arm to make sure I'm not still dreaming. I can't shake the feeling. I'm shivering, but it's not cold. "Did you take a pill?" Evan asks.

"Yes."

"Okay, maybe this is a side effect. We'll keep an eye on it."

"Is Jacob asleep?" I ask.

"He is. I'm going to get you some water."

I reach for my phone. One pill makes even the slightest quick movement difficult, but two pills make me feel like I'm running through deep water, and my reactions are slow. I'm aware of the delay and can't force faster movement. It's strange and concerning but, in reality, so much better than another panic attack, and that scares me, a lot.

NELAScanBoy: Kat's phone was found with the body. They had forensics on it. It was clean.

Shit.

"What?" Evan is back with my water.

"I can't catch a break with this story," I say.

"Stop, please, I don't have the mental strength. I love you, and I think you need to stop with this. You need to rest." He hands me the glass of water. "Just for tonight. Turn off your phone, please. For me."

I turn the sound off on my phone and set it on the table.

Evan sits on the couch and pulls me toward him. He kisses me, and I let him. It's too much work to say no, and I want to feel something other than scared and broken. "I love you," he says.

It's been months and months since we've been intimate. "I love you too," I say. The words are part of our routine. They are familiar, easy; it's all safe, and I'm not ready to lose him. I'm not ready to be alone, single, jobless, with a baby. Tonight, I need to feel safe. I push everything else away: Kat, Araceli, Natalie. They will be there when we are done. They will still be dead.

After sex, Evan falls asleep and I sneak into the bathroom, my safe space. The window looks out over the neighboring houses, city lights, and the mountains, which are all illuminated by tonight's giant moon. I sit on the floor, door closed, and lean against the mint green antique sideboard that works as our linen cupboard. The black-and-white checkered tiles are uneven and bumpy on my bare feet. The sloping ceiling makes the room feel both huge and cozy at the same time. If it were big enough to move a reading chair into, I would. I unmute my phone and open my laptop. The messages and alerts come to life.

Ding. Ding. Ding.

I turn the volume down so Jacob doesn't wake. I have a message from Chris, hours old.

NELAScanBoy: Corey—you disappear?

It's too early, or maybe too late, depending on the person, to text back—I don't know Chris's schedule these days, so I go for it.

Me: Sorry. Going to go see Natalie's mom today after spin.

LA News First streams on my laptop:
"A woman has been taken into custody late last night in the Northeast neighborhood of El Sereno . . ."
"the Clippers . . ."
"a new drug . . ."
"Can you tell us what the weather has in store for us today?"

NELAScanBoy: Want company?

Me: You could make her nervous. Can you get me the address?

NELAScanBoy: Will send shortly.

My fingertips tingle. I press my head to the floor and let the tile cool me. I stare at the alerts on my phone. I have voicemail. Nobody leaves voicemail. The transcription won't load, so I play it.

"Corey, this is Detective Lopez. I received your message. Thank you for your continued interest in this case. This is an active investigation. I cannot comment on an active investigation. If you'd like to come down to the station tomorrow morning, I'd be happy to have a conversation with you."

I look at the time. It's five in the morning. The night a blip. Today is the charity ride.

26

Jacob and I wait at Lopez's desk at seven a.m. Her desk is part of a quad. Two are bare—empty. My eyes dart around the space looking for clues about her. The one that sticks is a picture of Lopez with grown-ish children and a man I assume to be her husband. He isn't unattractive, but he doesn't pop the way Lopez does—he's a background guy. I want to open her drawers, see if she keeps packets of instant oatmeal or nutrition bars.

"Ms. Lieberman," Lopez announces from behind me. "I hope you haven't been waiting too long. My night and my morning were more exciting than I had anticipated when I called you last night."

"So were mine," I say. We smile at each other. "So, who are your suspects for the hanging case—the two girls from Debs?"

"You know better than to ask that," Lopez says. She almost laughs.

"Natalie's father?" I ask.

"On a job in San Jose."

"The uncle?" I ask.

She scowls, a bit of humor behind the eyes as if to say, again, "You know better."

"He did it," I say. "A weak alibi, an allegation against him made by Natalie herself—"

"Thanks for the intel, Sherlock."

"That uncle, Natalie's uncle, killed those girls," I say. I'm shaking—but it feels good because it's with anger instead of fear. And Lopez is basically confirming it. "You know. Why haven't you arrested him?"

"And what evidence did you bring me?" She answers my question with a question.

"Haven't you done the autopsy? Natalie was pregnant with his baby. Do a paternity test on the fetus."

"Natalie wasn't pregnant."

No—that isn't right. Natalie's aunt—why . . . my stomach drops. I bounce Jacob vigorously to mask my shock. "Why did she tell the school nurse she was?" I ask.

"Who told you that?"

"I am not revealing my sources," I say. "You want my information, you're going to have to give me something in return."

"You love your baby, Corey?"

"Of course." Where the hell was this going? I shift in my chair, defensively.

"You love being a mom?"

"I think you're about one word away from offending me," I say, trying to break the tension in my gut.

"Stop trying to be a detective. Go be this beautiful baby's mother."

"Holy shit. Is that what they told you when you had your first kid? When you applied for detective? What about your second and third child?"

Lopez takes off her blazer and sits down. "I wish they had; then I wouldn't be in the position I find myself, telling families about their dead children." Lopez stares at me as she speaks. It's working—I'm uncomfortable. "Are you sure you want this story? Because there is no happy ending. If I were you, I'd be damn sure before I opened that door."

"I'm not looking for happy endings. I'm looking to stop a monster from raping, and potentially killing, more children."

"Fine. Off the record, but you don't write this story until I tell you—otherwise I will find a reason to lock you up. You will not come in here and get another word from me on anything if you betray me. Crystal?"

"Crystal," I say. I'm not writing stories anymore, but Lopez, Marks, none of them need to know that.

I put Jacob over my shoulder and extend my hand. Lopez takes it. She gets up and leads me back to the Murder Board room.

"Natalie wasn't pregnant," she says.

"Okay," I say.

"Natalie's brother is her uncle's son. He's been raping Natalie's mother for years. She was diagnosed with muscular dystrophy about ten years ago. Her husband hasn't been home more than a weekend a month since. The uncle helps support the family financially—he won a very large settlement after his accident. When she ended up in a wheelchair, he started coming over more to help."

"I don't understand," I say.

"Let me finish, and you might."

I nod.

"Natalie's mother never pressed charges. She's pretty much gone at this point, and the uncle started to turn his needs onto . . ." She put her hands up.

"Natalie."

She nods and continues. "She'd been conditioned, Natalie. Araceli found out what was happening. Started staying at the house so he couldn't do anything. She was in the way—"

"So, he needed to get rid of her—"

"Natalie must have fought back, and both girls ended up on a tree."

I ball my fists. Choke down the desire for revenge and let the hairs on my body settle before saying, as calmly as possible, "Why hasn't he been charged?"

"The only concrete thing I have is the unlawful removal of two dead bodies. The girls were dead before they were strung up on the tree."

"How?" I ask—I want to know and don't because what if the thoughts latch on and whisper about new ways I could possibly kill someone, myself. Fear kicks me in the chest.

"Blunt force trauma to the head."

"Both of them," I say. Lopez gives me the nod. "And you can't get him for that?"

"I'm working on it."

I smile to myself. I haven't lost my skills—we need more evidence, and that has never been my job before now.

"I need to find the murder weapon, or the DA won't take it on," Lopez says. "Also, I'm going to need you to stop talking to Nando."

"What?"

"Fernando Alaniz. You're going to have to stop talking to him. Putting ideas in his head. He's not a bad kid—yet—and I want to keep it that way."

"But how did you—"

"I have my sources too."

"What about Kat?" I ask.

"There is no case, Corey. You need to accept that."

"You're wrong. I'm going to show you."

"I wish every victim had a capable advocate working for them. Prove me wrong. Bring me something, and I'll listen," Lopez says.

It isn't the first time I want to punch a cop. Bring her something? A dead body wasn't enough?

Lopez walks me out. On the way we pass Detective Marks coming in. He nods his hello and goodbye at once. As soon as I'm out, I lift my shirt and let Jacob eat. I sit on the edge of the retaining wall outside the station while I breastfeed. I watch as people come and go. I look at Jacob. I think about Natalie. The little boy who still lives in that house.

But I have to get to Kat's memorial ride first. Three victims, one Corey—that's still more investigator per victim than most. If everyone had an Evan supporting them, maybe every stay-at-home mom could work on a case and there'd be far fewer left unsolved.

27

I left the house so early, I can't remember if I took a Klonopin before driving to the police station or if it was the night before. I dump the bottle of Paxil into my hand and count them, twice, to confirm that I took one of those—I only take one of those a day. The Klonopin is as needed, but until the Paxil kicks in, I'm supposed to stay ahead of the attacks—about one every six hours. My prescription of twenty-five is dwindling. My chest is tight, but my head is clear and not heavy, and I want it to stay that way; I need it to. I throw the Klonopin back in my tote, along with the Paxil. I hope knowing the Klonopin is near will be enough to prevent any attacks.

Jacob is calmer than usual, sleepier than usual for this time of day. I worry the meds are in his system, slowing him down too. I'm trying to minimize the breastfeeding, but sometimes it's the only thing that can soothe him—and me.

Monique appointed herself to lead the memorial ride. Every instructor who had ever worked at Cyclone Studio showed up at eleven a.m. to help, to mourn, to talk. There are more riders than bikes. The studio is so packed the crowd's spilling out to the sidewalk and side street. It is the exact kind of showing I expected. Old people die, and there's barely anyone left to mourn them. Young people die, and the entire world thanks God it isn't them and packs a place to show it.

Jacob is strapped onto me in the baby wrap (more stained from spills in my bag than from wearing it with him) while I help people with their bikes or a drink, or I take their money and put it into an envelope that will be handed over to Gilda later. If the event weren't for Kat's funeral, it would be considered successful. But it's a memorial for a twenty-six-year-old found dead and abandoned at the bottom of a hiking trail. Can you measure success by the turnout for her funeral? Popularity, maybe.

Diane is walking in the front doors with a man I haven't seen before. He's cute. Younger maybe or maybe just really handsome.

"Hi, Corey," Diane says as she walks toward me and Jacob. She hugs us both tight. I worry Jacob will be smooshed. "This is Sean."

"Hi. Sean?" I extend my hand to him. Do I know him? I try to picture him on a bike in my class or at the counter paying for a bottled water, but it isn't coming to me.

"I'm Diane's ex-husband," he says.

My brain flips through files of information to confirm what this man has just said. I am more puzzled. I cannot get the information straight.

"I'm sorry for your loss," he continues.

"Thank you. I'm sorry, it's been a very long morning," I say. I can't process meeting Sean here, today, now. "How are you doing, Diane?" I try adjusting my attention.

"I'm okay. I still can't believe any of it. I've been more freaked out than I thought I would be, so Sean's been staying over with me and the kids."

"Corey!" It's Monique calling me from the podium.

"Go, I'll handle this," Diane says, grabbing the envelope from me.

"Thanks. Bikes are full. You just need to take the money and put it in the envelope." I explain the simple task like it's complicated.

"Money, envelope—got it."

"It's nice to meet you, Sean."

If I didn't know they had been married, I wouldn't believe it. Diane is gorgeous. The way you picture a woman looking to be cast on a reality television show. Sean is rugged, full head of wavy sun-blond hair, young, but not a polished Hollywood hunk—he's real, attainable . . . like Chris. I always pictured Diane married to an older version of Evan.

I push through the crowded room to Monique. Mary is there, stretching. Ray Hunt has come. Liz assists some newbies with preride stretching. "Be sure to hinge at your hips," I hear her say.

I finally get to Monique. She's arguing with another instructor.

"Kyle, put on the goddamn shirt. I'm not going to keep telling you, you cannot ride shirtless," Monique says.

"You're being a bitch. Nobody cares but you. Why?" Kyle asks.

"What's going on?" I say.

"Corey, can you get Kyle a new Cyclone tank? I've got to start this ride," Monique says.

"Fuck you, Monique," Kyle barks.

"Why don't you and I talk outside," I say to Kyle. Kyle was all over Kat at the happy hour the night before she disappeared. He's not a dad, or married, but there was definitely chemistry between them. Did they hike together the next day? Did she turn him down on the hike—tell him she was with someone else?

"No, I'm good," he says. Monique is already on the podium when Kyle yells to her, "It should have been you at the bottom of that cliff, not Kat."

Monique flies off the podium and tackles Kyle to the ground. The baby wrap catches on Monique's headset and nearly pulls Jacob and me into the fray. Sean, Diane, and others are pulling Monique off Kyle while Mary, of course fucking Mary, dials 911.

Sean pushes Kyle out the front doors, and Diane leads Monique outside, away from Kyle. I snatch a headset from the front desk.

"Okay, everyone, not to worry, emotions are high all around. It's a small misunderstanding, trip and fall." I feed the crowd excuse after excuse until the room goes back to full activity. "Who is ready to get this ride started?" I say. I'm rewinding a now-fussy Jacob back around my chest tightly in the baby wrap and jump up on the bike. "Let's do this for Kat," I say.

A minute into the ride I climb off the bike and order Liz to take over. "I'm going to see what's happening outside," I whisper off the mic.

Outside, a police car and fire engine have arrived. I walk over with a screaming infant fastened to my chest. Jacob's crooked headphones are pulling on his little wisps of hair. "I'm sorry, Mommy can fix it," I say, adjusting them and then rubbing the side of his cheek with my finger.

"Corey, thank god, can you please tell them what happened?" Diane asks. "Everyone is going to be arrested if this isn't cleared up."

"Yeah, tell them how she physically attacked me," Kyle says.

Monique is sitting on the back of the fire engine, separated from her antagonist—could he do something to Monique? Is he violent?

"Were you a witness to the altercation, ma'am?" an officer asks. His sunglasses are dark, so I can't see his eyes. I wonder if I've noticed him at the police station in the past week. But everything about him, his haircut high and tight, height five foot ten—he could be a storm trooper—I can't tell him apart from any of the other uniformed officers at this point.

My upper lip is starting to sweat. My heart pounds hard against Jacob on my chest. There is a low buzz turning into a sharp pain in my ear.

"Ma'am?" the officer says.

"Yes, sorry, one second." My pills are inside the studio in my tote. I need to walk, jump, peel the skin off my body. I burst into a set of jumping jacks until my mind releases me. Everyone quiet now and watching. Jacob's head an inch away from nailing my chin. I stop.

"Yes," I say, slightly breathy. "This man, Kyle Rogers, is now a former employee of the studio, and he attacked this woman. To be completely transparent, emotions are high today. We're hosting a memorial ride for our recently deceased owner," I say.

"That's bullshit! She attacked me! Look at the scratch marks on my chest." Kyle is in a full screaming tantrum now—long gone is the meditative yogi leader I have experienced in his classes.

The cops look at Kyle, nearly three times bigger than Monique. "Let's all try to get along, folks. Sir, it's time for you to leave, maybe find a new place to ride bikes."

Kyle starts walking down the block, muttering a few "assholes," among other less-kind names. The cops make sure he's in his car leaving before they say, "Are you sure you don't want to press charges?" They ask Monique, who shakes her head. "Well, if you have any more problems, just give us a call." And then they leave in their patrol car.

The rest of the team heads back inside.

"Thanks," Monique says to us—Diane, Sean, me.

"Come on, no need for thanks. That guy is a douchebag," Sean says. He and Diane head in first.

"Hey." I grab Monique's arm. "What's the deal with Kyle?" I ask.

"He's an asshole," Monique says.

"Were he and Kat, like, a thing?" It's worth asking the question. "Are you going to be safe?"

Monique shakes her head.

"Kat wrote him up for inappropriately hugging and kissing team members, twice. Once more he would be out. He's a dick. And he's out."

"So, he had beef with Kat. Did he have an altercation with her too?" I ask.

"Kyle was teaching Saturday morning at another studio in Santa Monica. He didn't kill Kat—he's just an asshole," Monique says.

I knew it couldn't be that easy, but I hoped for just a moment.

◆ ◆ ◆

At noon Monique starts a second ride for all the folks who didn't get a bike during the first ride. A few instructors had brought wine, and the local business owners from the shops up and down the street bring whiskey and more. The bakery brings doughnuts, and Dot's Diner brings a smattering of everything, including beet hash. It turns into an eating frenzy.

Jacob is becoming restless and fussy, but I keep him locked to my chest. I don't have the energy, or patience, to be present while he struggles to crawl on the floor. I need to observe everyone in the studio—especially now as the crowd thins.

"Hey, why don't you let me hold the rug rat for a bit. You know I have three of my own, right? Nothing bad has happened to them," Diane says, coming up next to me.

"Thank you, I do need to get something from my bag." I let Diane hold Jacob while I dig around my tote for my pill bottle.

"Prozac?" Diane asks as I pull out the amber container with the white childproof cap.

"No. God, no. Just a Klonopin," I say.

"Same difference."

I stare at her, rebuking the accusation as I pull out a pill. "I can take Jacob back," I say.

"It's okay, I'm not judging you. I've taken my share of pills: Xanax, Ativan, Prozac, Wellbutrin."

"No, I wasn't saying you were, sorry. I only take it when I feel a bit of anxiety come up," I say. I am not ready to admit to the Paxil. I do not want to be classified as a long-term, daily pill popper.

"I usually take one or two with a bottle of wine." She laughs.

I shove the pill back in the container and throw the container back in my bag. I take Jacob from Diane.

"Well, if you're not going to take it, can I have it?" she says. The look I give her must be steeped in contempt because she quickly puts her hands up and says, "I'm kidding! Come on, let's get this place clean the way Kat would have liked."

"I'm going to walk around, say goodbye to people first," I say.

Some folks are huddled together. Others crying, or laughing. Some act like nothing has happened. No one is coming off as suspicious here.

No signals for me to snatch and track down. Sean, sitting by himself drinking a beer, waves me over.

"Hey. Uh, Corey, right?"

"That's right."

He takes a sip of his beer, examines the bottle like it's the first time he's ever seen it.

"It's weird drinking a beer in a spin studio," he says. "Feels like I'm back in high school. Breaking some rule just to break it."

"That what you did back then?"

"Well," he says, "it's what I wanted to do. I had an image in my mind of myself that was different than the reality, that's for sure."

"When is that supposed to go away?" I ask. I smile, politely, not big.

"You are asking the wrong guy." He lets out a harmless chuckle. "I thought I was finally getting it right—turns out I was wrong."

"Maybe you'll get it right this time." I stop. "I'm sorry, that was inappropriate and none of my business. Wow." My face heats under his gaze.

"It's okay, maybe I will."

"So, did you know Kat?" I ask.

My breasts are full. Bordering engorged. I have to pump or feed Jacob before I start leaking. I mindlessly lift my T-shirt, revealing too much of my breast, and pop him on. If I had a Klonopin before the police station, it's nearly out of my system by now. Sean didn't look or even seem to notice.

"A little. I took a few classes in the early days, and of course, I knew her through Diane," he says.

I sit down beside him and readjust Jacob. Sean's beer looks good. Jacob suckles. It's like an echo in my head, the rest of the room a dull murmur. People are saying their goodbyes. Sated, they've done their duty; all ready to move past the trauma of death.

"You okay?" Sean asks.

"What?"

"Are you okay?" he repeats. It's almost a whisper.

"I think so. Are you?"

"Your baby—" Sean leans in toward me.

I look down. Jacob has fallen asleep feeding and is sliding out of my lap. Sean scoops him up from my arms and gently rocks him.

"Oh my gosh, I'm so sorry. I—I—did I fall asleep?" I ask. I feel a draft and realize my shirt is still lifted a bit. I pull it down and look around the room. No one is interested in what just happened but Sean.

"Is this your first?" he asks.

I nod. "I don't know what happened," I say.

"You're in the zombie phase. With our first baby, Diane and I would alternate nights. It must have been four, maybe three in the morning. I was on duty. Anyway, I'm up rocking her, our daughter, I'd had three maybe four hours of sleep that *week*, and I decided, okay, I'll rest my eyes. I drift off and wake up to a loud thud. I'd rocked her right out of my arms and onto the floor. She's fine—she's on the honor roll now. After that, Diane and I were glued to that kid until she went to kindergarten. Honestly, we still do, you know, treat her extra special ever since. But it does get easier."

I force a smile.

"I've been told," I say. "My mom said she dropped me a hundred times, and I'm definitely not fine." I let out a soft laugh. It feels good.

"People are hard to kill," Sean says. He passes Jacob, still asleep, back to me. "It's why something like Kat is so shocking. There's this running group we were both in. I'd occasionally see her out with the group. Everyone seems like something they probably aren't."

"You were in Kat's running group?" I ask.

"Well, it's not Kat's running group. It's a community-wide group, open to the public. There's a group organizer, and over a hundred locals join in on runs weekly." He scans the room and lands on Diane. "Diane's joining the group. What about you? Are you a runner?"

"I was," I say. I was a treadmill runner, but did it matter? Sean may be an unknowing witness.

"You should come out some time. It's a good group of folks. There's always someone ready to meet up, and there are scheduled group runs. Safety in numbers."

Safety in numbers, until one of them pushes you off a cliff.

"We're actually going to run in honor of Kat this week." I stare at him, trying to read something in him. "You should come," he says.

"Yeah, I should," I say.

"Great, I'll send you the Facebook invite—Corey Tracey-Lieberman, right?" He shoots me a smile I would have overreacted to in my younger years. I give him a nod. He finishes off his beer. "I should go find Diane," he says.

"Yeah," I look at the studio clock, 1:25 p.m. I need to get to Nando. "I should get this guy home. Thanks for the assist, before."

"It gets easier, I swear," he says and leaves to find his estranged wife—Diane. I wonder if Evan would show up for me in a crisis if we weren't together anymore.

"Lieberman," Monique calls to me from across the room. She motions for me to come over. I stand up with Jacob and look around at the loiterers as I walk over. "Thank you for helping. This was good. You should go home. That guy looks drunk," she says and points to Jacob.

"Yeah, we're going to take off." I look around the near-empty studio once more. "Hey, have you seen Diane?" I ask.

"I see her leaving through the back door right now. With the guy she came in with." Monique points behind me to the door that leads to the garage. I catch it closing behind Sean.

"Have you ever met him before?" I ask.

"Yeah, he used to be a regular. I thought for sure he'd have auditioned to be an instructor, he was here so much. But it's been a while. Maybe because they separated? I don't pay attention. I told you. Anyway, he looks like every other hipster dad. I don't notice 'em," Monique says.

"No, he doesn't. He's way better looking—and not remotely hipster," I say.

"You know I'm gay, right?" Monique says.

"You know that doesn't matter, right? He's hot." I smile at her as I say it. "Is he younger than Diane?"

"Lieberman, are you looking for a new baby daddy or what?"

"Curious, that's all. Feeling the need for some lighter conversation."

"Okay, fine, yes, he's hot. Yes, he's younger than her. They got married when he was twenty-three and she was thirty-three and knocked up. There was some scandal she'll tell you about with his folks early on, but that was all a long time ago. I was fucking surprised to see them here together, okay? Can you go now?"

"Yes, thank you." I hug her through Jacob. "You okay to lock up?" I ask. There are a few Misfits cleaning up who would wait for Monique to lock up. The day still young.

"Yeah, I'm good, Lieberman, I'm good. But don't ever hug me again."

I sit in my car and think about Kat. All the lives she touched. The mystery man she may or may not have been dating. Does he know she's dead? Has anyone told him? Who would have told him? Would he be at the running-club memorial?

Detective Lopez—does she know who Kat was dating? About all the men Diane said she'd slept with? Does Lopez have Kat's cell phone?

I pull out my phone to check for messages and automatically start texting Chris.

Me: Hey I need to figure out who Kat was dating

NELAScanBoy: Any leads?

Me: No, can you find out if the police still have her cell?

NELAScanBoy: Did you ask her mom?

Me: Asking you first.

NELAScanBoy: Okay, give me an hour

I drive down the street listening to Jacob babble. My chest starts to squeeze.

A thought begins to emerge. You could throw your baby off that cliff.

I pull over.

Am I crying?

I don't want to take a pill, but I fear not taking one.

Sharp knives in the drawer waiting. I see in my head the drawer open, the brown wood-handled steak knife. Thin, dull teeth but the tip sharp enough to draw blood.

"Shut up. STOP!" I hit the side of my head with my open hand. "Leave me alone already!"

I find the Klonopin. Fuck water. I chew it down. The bitter chalk coats my teeth once again. I turn on the radio and sit there. Jacob screeching.

"Please, baby, please, I'm so sorry. Mommy loves you. Give me a minute, please." I start to cry. Not just a little but a lot. My face is wet from the pour of emotions: tired, frustrated, scared, angry, sad. I watch the minutes on the clock: 2:02, 2:03, 2:04, and the voice gets quiet. Six, seven, eight, then gone. I gather the courage to try summoning the demon in my head. "Knives, plastic bags, guns . . ." Nothing.

My eyelids are heavy. I feel nothing but lethargic. The nothing is relief—nothing. Why was I so afraid of taking the medication? I can't remember, and it doesn't matter. The voice is gone. Even the whisper of it at the back, lurking there all the time, is gone right now, and I am free.

28

I'm not going home—I'm going to find Nando. I check the clock—2:30, plenty of daylight left to show up at his house. Driving his street, I see a car pull out of the driveway. It's him. I U-turn and follow. About two miles through Highland Park to the Garvanza district, right behind the old 99-cent store, he stops at a small white house that needs new siding and paint. Otherwise, it looks like most of the homes on the block—historical craftsmen and bungalows. Garvanza is part of the HPOZ, historical preservation zone. It's hard for the flippers to get the permission needed to update the homes with trendy paints and loud doors. Mauves, custardy yellows, and muted greens are the only options. Nando is walking up the stoop of the dated white bungalow when I call to him.

"Miss Corey?"

"I was wrong," I yell. I'm grabbing Jacob from the back. "Wait!"

"Listen, the uncle—"

Nando hits the deck. I cover Jacob with my body.

"Run!" Nando screams while getting up and running through the front door.

"Fuck!" I run with Jacob. I don't know if I'm running toward or away from the shots. I think Jacob is crying or laughing. I don't know; my ears are ringing, not from the gunfire.

I run inside the white bungalow and grab for my phone. "Shit, where are we?" I say.

"It's Natalie's house," Nando says.

On the floor is a middle-aged man bleeding from his shoulder and his abdomen. A small-framed, ill-looking woman is in a wheelchair—aged beyond her years, with a gun in her lap.

"Nando, call 911," I say.

A little boy, who looks to be about four, peeks around the corner and stares at us.

"I can't," Nando says. "I can't use my phone." I shove mine into his hand.

"Are you Natalie's mom?" I ask. The woman stares. I can't tell if her shaking is part of a condition or because of what is happening. "Can you tell me your name?" I say. I force patience into my questions while my gut pushes bile up into my chest, and Jacob, undeniably now, cries. My shirt gets wet, warm, and sticky in response. Jacob grabs my face, a chunk of my cheek pinched in his nails—too long. Bad mom. I forgot to cut them this week.

"She can't talk much," the little boy says. "Her name is Ann."

"Is she your mom?" I ask.

"Yes."

I nod at him and smile while Jacob shrieks. His face deep red from his screams.

"What's your name?" I ask over my baby crying.

"Mateo."

"Do you know Natalie?" I ask.

He nods and says, "She died."

The room starts spinning around me. Jacob's crying is reduced to a tinny wail in my ear. I blink hard to keep the darkness at the edges away. I need a pill—no time.

"I'm not going to hurt you, Mateo, okay?" I lift a sobbing, hiccupping Jacob up in front of me. "See, I have a baby. I'm a mommy. Did your mom teach you to find another mom if you were in trouble?" I ask.

"Araceli did."

Thank god.

"How old are you, Mateo?" I ask.

"Six and a half."

"Wow, you're a big kid." I inch closer to him. Jacob's head slumps onto my chest—exhausted from the excitement, crying subsiding to a whimper. "Mateo, do you have a television somewhere in the house?"

"Yeah, in my room."

"Oh my gosh, you are so lucky. Do you want to watch some TV?"

"I want to stay with my mom." He walks over to the wheelchair and climbs up into the woman's lap, pulling her arms around him.

"Miss Corey, I have to go." Nando says, stepping back inside from the porch—pushing my phone into my free hand. "The cops are coming." Nando gently rubs Jacob's back and says, "I'll see you soon, little man, promise." I know we'll never see each other again. "Please don't—"

"You were never here," I say.

Nando splits.

I watch a man in his late forties, dark hair, muscular arms, eyes closed, bleed out, and no one in the house moves to help him—I don't move to help him. I watch a woman in a wheelchair invisibly console a child who absorbs the trauma like he is watching an action movie.

The sirens are close. I put my arm around Ann's shoulder. I feel the twitch of muscles when her hand moves an inch around Mateo. The gun next to the boy, who snuggles closer to his mother. It is almost too much. I want to take the gun away, but I'm afraid of it, or myself, of the evil it possesses. I don't understand how she pulled the trigger when she can barely pull her arms around her child. "It's going to be okay now," I say to them both, to myself, to Jacob.

Mateo looks at Jacob for a moment, then turns his face into his mother's chest and cries.

An officer, gun drawn, walks in the open front door with several uniformed young cops right behind. Everything happens quickly now. I am escorted out of the house by one of the officers—they all look alike in their uniforms: dark hair, closely cropped; muscular; sun-kissed skin—and I'm led to an ambulance.

"I'm fine," I say.

"Ma'am, we'd like to check your baby's vitals," the medic, a thin-lipped, unsmiling woman says. She looks shapeless in her ill-fitted white short-sleeve button-down.

"He's fine—we weren't hurt. We were in the home after the shooting occurred."

Despite my continued objections, both our pulses are checked and our ears. Jacob wakes after briefly passing out, and now I can feed him.

"Wrong place, wrong time, Corey," Detective Lopez says. She sits next to me on the back of the ambulance.

"When did you get here?" I say. "And I didn't see anything. I got here after it happened. Maybe it was the right time."

"Okay, well, I'm going to need you to tell me what you saw when you got here."

I relay everything to Lopez exactly as I saw it. I leave Nando out of everything. After I repeat the story to her twice, she lets me go. I strap Jacob into his car seat. Find my bottle of Klonopin and chew one down. Then another before I drive us home. I try to recall how many pills that made. I want to get the woman's eyes, the boy's face, the dying man out of my head.

29

I'm home. In bed. Shaking. I don't know for how long—I look out the window, and the sun has moved sides. I took too many Klonopin. How many? Three. I took three today. Yes. I'm allowed to stay ahead of the anxiety—a pill every six hours as needed, short term, can be addictive. I should slow down.

Jacob.

I run to his crib. He's sitting up babbling. I smile at him, and he pulls himself up into a wobbly stand on the balls of his feet. His knuckles hold the lip of the crib's frame in a death grip, and he beams a smile at me. One that exudes pride in his accomplishment. I stare at him in amazement when Evan calls out.

"Corey?" Evan calls again.

Can I answer? Be the wife I'm supposed to be after what happened?

"I'm coming," I yell back. I have no idea how my voice sounds. I grab the baby and deliberately touch my foot down on each step while holding the stair rail. I don't want to float away.

"Hey, you look like you got some rest," Evan says. I can't tell if it's a joke. "I missed you this morning."

"Where've you been?" I ask.

"I went for a run in Angeles Crest. I feel amazing." He looks at me funny but keeps on. "I tried calling you, but your phone's been going straight to voicemail."

"Shoot. Can you call it? I don't even know where it is."

"It's going straight to your voicemail—I just told you. Did you just wake up from a nap?"

"Yeah, sorry. Here, hold Jacob, let me go check the car." I run outside. Elsie is there, washing hers like she does every Sunday. I have no sense of time—shouldn't it be late?

"Corey, I was going to come by in a bit," Elsie says. "I have news." I can't. Not now, if ever.

"I know, I already know. It's terrible, I am so sorry, Elsie. For your friend, for everyone—but I need my phone. I can't find it." I push past her, get to the car, and find the door unlocked. Was I robbed too?

"I have your bag," Elsie says.

"Jesus. I'm a mess. Thank you." I stuff my tears into the back of my throat.

"What's happening? You left your bag on the top of your car, and you do not look well, sweetie."

She wants to say that I look hung over, strung out. I can see it all over her face. I did black out, in a way, because I don't remember what happened between the shooting and waking up shaking in my bed.

"I think it's a touch of the flu, to be honest. I had to race into the house—my stomach. I think it's passing now," I say. "Just in case, stay back a bit." It could be true. My stomach is cramped and nauseous. "Have you heard from Lupe?" I ask.

"No, why?"

"I think I was confused. I only meant that I don't have any news yet, and I feel bad about it all." I dig in the tote for my phone. It lights up with messages. Chris, Evan, and Gilda. "Can we talk later? I don't feel great."

"Of course. I'll make you some broth. You look terrible. Get some rest. Please."

I think I smile.

I pull up the messages from Chris first. I want to read them as much as they want to be read.

NELAScanBoy: Corey, call me.

NELAScanBoy: I drove past your house, your car is there, so I am assuming you're fine. Call me.

NELAScanBoy: I have something. Call me.

Monique: Lieberman new schedule is up.

I listen to my voicemail.

"Hi, Corey? It's Gilda, Kat's mom. I found the key to her car. Well, the spare. She had locked the other one in the car, like you thought. That is very Kat, actually. Anyway, I'm not sure what I'm looking for, to be honest, and I was hoping you'd come over. Maybe we could go through it together?"

Oh shit, Gilda.

I am sitting on the front porch staring blankly at my phone. I think about Evan and Jacob and the thought that I could lose them both. My life over in a split-second decision to run into a house with gunfire. I feel the vomit coming now and heave into the thorny rosebushes. I get up to go inside. Evan is holding Jacob in one arm on his hip while he scoops jarred pureed chicken into a neon-green baby bowl. I grab him around the waist and press my face into his back.

"I love you," I say. "I love you and our baby so much."

Evan turns around and says, "I love you too." He kisses the top of my head. "Listen, I'm sorry for everything." My god, what does he have to be sorry for? Pushing me to get help?

I don't tell Evan about the shooting. He hands me Jacob and leaves to go change out of his sweaty running shorts. He's happy.

I send Gilda a text that I would be at her house within an hour. We would go through the car together. After I drain my breasts. There's just enough light outside to make the evening errand normal to Evan.

◆ ◆ ◆

I drive to Kat's house—screw running.

Getting out of the car with Jacob is exhausting. My body moves like it's weighed down with sandbags. Carrying Jacob was a workout not on the pills; these days, on the pills, it feels nearly impossible. I have to sit down on the curb to fasten him into the baby wrap.

"Corey?" It's Gilda coming down her front walk.

"Yeah, I just needed an assist from the curb to get this stupid wrap on," I say. I don't just look hungover, I actually feel it. My body atrophied. I have cottonmouth, and my nose is acutely aware of Jacob's current diaper or gas. In the back of my head—guilt from the shooting and fear Evan will find out. My lie like an affair. He'd take Jacob and leave me.

"I hated that thing. I hated every woman that made it look easy and comfortable to wear," Gilda says. "Here, give me your hand." She pulls me up. I nearly fall forward.

"Do you think I could have a glass of water?"

"Of course," she says.

Jacob looks at me like he knows what is happening to me. He grabs my cheeks and kisses me, then smiles. I almost die on the spot. "I love you so much, buddy."

"I have about a dozen casseroles left. Are you hungry?" Gilda says.

I wipe away the tears no one sees but my son and say, "I am, yeah."

We sit down at Gilda's round kitchen table. The food is already out, and she passes me a plate. I spoon cheesy casserole potatoes and a cream-of-something casserole with green veggies onto my plate.

Gilda says, "I stopped taking the pills today. I didn't feel right. They fogged my head. I couldn't get up and shower. Between them and the depression I feel, well, it's a trap."

"I feel like I'm moving in slow motion," I say. "I'm not sure I want to take mine either. Then I feel the panic come, so I shove them down my throat. Too many, sometimes." It's more of an admission with the hope of forgiveness and redemption attached.

"There's no good choice. Either feel the insurmountable grief or feel and think nothing. Kat would tell me to smoke pot if she were here." Gilda clears our dishes, too full for a second round. "I'm going to go back to work next week. I need to be around the kids. Detective Lopez called me. She wanted to check in—see how I was doing."

"What did you say?"

"I told her I failed my daughter, and I hoped that the LAPD wasn't failing her too."

"Gilda, you did not fail her." Jacob squeals, delighted; his unity is noted. "Let's get this car open."

I don't know if Gilda is aware of the memorial ride we held earlier. I don't know if Monique invited her. But I don't want to talk about it. About the room full of people mourning her daughter's short-lived life. I don't have the strength.

We rummage through Kat's car for ten minutes. It is pretty clean and nearly empty, aside from a car key left in the middle console. The trunk is littered with outside debris from a pair of running shoes that had been dumped muddy and used. There is one sunshade, a few empty reusable grocery bags, sunscreen, and an extra pair of socks.

Jacob lifts a pair of sunglasses from the back seat.

"No, buddy, give those to Mama," I say.

"Huh, those don't look like Kat's," Gilda says. "Let me see them." Gilda examines the glasses, then puts them on and rips them back off. "These aren't Kat's."

"How do you know?" I ask.

"They're prescription."

"May I see them again?" Jacob tries to rip them away from Gilda, but I manage to get them on first. "Are these men's glasses?" I ask. Jacob continues to try and rip them off my face, his tiny fingers smudging the lenses. "They look like athletic glasses."

"How do you know?" Gilda asks.

"I used to own a pair similar for mountain biking. These bands are meant to grip around the head so they don't bounce off when you're riding, running, whatever," I say.

"They could easily belong to a friend," Gilda says.

"Do you mind if I take them to Cyclone and see if anyone claims them?" I ask.

"Sure." Gilda sits in the passenger seat of the car. She runs her hand between the seats, comes out with a receipt from Arco gas station, a french fry, and a hair tie—mundane parts of Kat's forgotten life. Gilda looks lost. "I'm so mad at myself. I don't know what I thought we'd find in here. I was hoping for a letter. I was hoping for something from Kat that said goodbye." She looks at the receipt. "There's nothing but her life."

"I'm sorry, Gilda."

"I need to mourn her, and I can't do that if I don't accept what happened and that she's not coming back."

"Gilda—"

"It's not healthy for me. And look at you. You're a new mom. You should be happy and enjoying this time with your baby." Gilda looks at Jacob. "It all goes by so fast. You should go home and hold him, Corey. Never let him go. Make sure he knows how much you love him every day."

"Gilda, I don't want to—"

"No. It's time you go. It's getting late. I'm done." Gilda looks tired, I'm tired, Jacob is a baby that needs me to tell him it's time for bed.

Gilda looks at the hair tie of Kat's she's been holding. She doesn't wipe away or try to stop her tears. I've made this woman experience this pain right now. I insisted she look through the car tonight. I watch grief come over her in waves of deep sobs until dehydration takes over. Gilda and I are in two different groups of motherhood now, and I will never understand her pain.

"I'm going to take the glasses," I say.

"Corey—"

"I'm so sorry, Gilda," I say. She hugs me tightly before I leave with my baby and the sunglasses. I watch her go back in her house and close the door as the sun sets behind Debs Park.

30

Instead of home, I go to Cyclone Studio. Classes for the day resumed after the memorial ride. The last class for the night should be finishing up. The new schedule Monique posted has Diane teaching and Monique covering the front desk. I get a parking spot right in front of the doors. I have a new perspective of the street from this spot. A small tan building with blue doors stands one building down from Cyclone Studio. A small sign lit up by the streetlamps reads MONTESSORI PRESCHOOL: PARKING IN BACK. There are no other indicators that the building is for children—certainly not the bus stop bench in front that needs a paint job or a bleaching, advertising same-day cash loans. Before I go in, I text Chris.

Me: It's been a day. I'll tell you everything later.

I don't wait for a response. I get out of the car with Jacob, asleep in my arms. I drape a blanket over him so he doesn't wake from the lights.

"Lieberman? What the hell are you doing here? Miss me?" Monique asks when she sees me at the door. Her delivery—deadpan. Neither inviting nor revealing. Typical Monique.

"Has anyone called about a pair of prescription glasses?" I ask. Keeping my voice low. Can I ask Monique to do the same? I hate being shushed by mothers with sleeping babies.

"Corey." Diane walks in from the bathroom and embraces me in one of her signature post-Kat's-death hugs. "The memorial ride was a huge success. Not my class that just ended and only one person showed up to." Not the way I would describe a memorial ride—a success. Diane looks at the glasses folded in my hand. "Oakleys? Sean has a pair exactly like those. But his are prescription."

I sit down on the bench, take a deep breath.

"You look a little green," Diane says.

"Yeah, I think I need some water," I say.

Diane runs to fetch a bottle. Jacob stirs.

"Here, I'll trade you, baby for the water," Diane says.

I nod and hand a sleeping Jacob over. I get the lid off the water, take one swig, and can't swallow. Back into the bottle it goes.

"I'll take him back now," I say. Jacob stirs at the exchange. "How is Sean?" I ask.

"I don't know, good, helpful. This has affected me more than I would have thought." Diane moves behind the desk and begins folding towels. "I think he sees that, and he really wants to be there for me and the kids."

"I thought he was living with someone else, like, a new girlfriend?" I say.

"No, he wanted to get my permission to introduce the kids to his new girlfriend, but she's out of the picture now, and he's back. I mean, it's crazy, ya know? He's been giving us his undivided attention. Things are better now than they ever were."

"So, you never met the woman he was dating?" I ask.

"The *girl* he was dating? No. Never."

"Right, she was twentysomething . . ."

"Yeah. She probably didn't want to be saddled down with a few kids that weren't hers. Come on. Would you want an instant family at twenty-six?"

How old was Kat, how old was Kat, how old was KAT?

"How did you say they met?"

"Running. Did you know that's how he and I met back in the day? We were both doing a 10K. Prepping for the LA Marathon. It was this thing we did together, running. The fact that he met her the same way is—"

"Coincidence," I offer.

"Shitty." Diane slams a folded towel onto the stack she's created.

"Are you reconciling with him?" I ask.

"Why are you being weird?"

"I am being weird. I'm sorry. I had a long day, and . . . anyway, I'm glad he's there for you."

"I get it. This has been fucking surreal."

Everything is coming into my brain in rapid-fire response—just like it used to. I'm quick on my feet. My responses are fire. It's not a mirage; I'm me in action.

"Maybe this is one of those tragic life experiences that can save a marriage. Save my marriage," Diane says.

"Gross," Monique says.

I'd forgotten Monique was there. She'd been buried in paperwork and too quiet.

"Did Sean give up his apartment?" I ask.

"Not yet. We're using it as a pied-à-terre away from the kids. It's the only good thing to come from this. I hate that my friend dying brought my husband and me back together, but the universe is funny that way. You know?"

Monique interrupts. "Hey, happy hour was over hours ago. I want to get out of here, so if you're done chatting, let's go. Lieberman, you can leave the glasses in the drawer."

"Good idea," I say but slip them back into my tote. "Hey, the running group that you and Sean belong to," I say to Diane, "he mentioned they were doing a memorial run for Kat. I'd love to come. Sean was going to send me the Facebook info but hasn't yet. Can you shoot it to me?"

"Oh, sure. I didn't know you were a runner. It'd be great to have you in the group. I'd love the company."

"Ladies, let's go, let's go," Monique says.

On cue, Jacob lets out a long, loud rumble. "Shoot, I can't drive with him like this. You two go. I'll lock up. I'll be fine." He's unaware that he's once again proven to be the best partner, but I'll keep telling him, and one day he'll know.

"You sure, Lieberman?"

I nod. "Look, my car is right there in front. Don't forget to send me the Facebook invite, Diane," I say.

"Doing it now," she says. The door closes behind them. A notification on my phone chimes. I lock the door and go through the employee records for Diane's address—it's right there, in the L's, for Loeb.

31

Jacob is asleep in his car seat when I pull up to our house, and, shit. Chris is out front waiting in his car. I definitely can't bring him in the house, and if Evan sees my car outside, he'll wonder. I pull up alongside Chris.

"Get in," I say.

Chris gives me a look of concern.

We drive around the block and park. The Metro Gold Line train runs along Marmion Way, splitting the street in two, and I park the car facing the tracks. Jacob loves watching the train on walks—but I had one nightmare he crawled out of the stroller and in front of the gateless train tracks, and that was it. Now we watch only from the car, and I pray the thoughts won't tempt me to drive in front of it. There are big signs at all the crosswalks aimed to stop suicides, but according to Dr. Rosenberg, I'm not suicidal—I'm just scared shitless all the time.

"We're only two blocks away from Nando's house," I say.

"Corey, my guy—my cousin saw you at Natalie's house today. He saw you." Chris reaches across the center console and hugs me hard. "Corey, you could have been seriously hurt—or worse. I told you to wait for me."

"That was today? I'm losing my sense of time." I pull out of the awkward embrace. He reluctantly lets go. He smells good. I don't want to know how I smell.

"He talked to you. Thinks you were experiencing shock. Corey, what were you doing there? I hadn't even gotten you the address."

"I followed Nando and—"

"Wait. Nando was there? That's not in the statement reports."

"No, he had nothing to do with any of it. I told him to get out of there when we heard the sirens coming."

"This is messed up, Corey."

"Stop. I know. He didn't do anything, and if you read the reports, then you'd know the mother shot the uncle."

"No, she didn't. She doesn't have the motor use. The kid shot him."

The chill of the information makes my spine tingle. I watched the woman in the wheelchair unable to move enough to hold her small child . . . Did I know and just pretend that the truth wasn't real?

"Corey?"

"Huh." Chris is shaking my shoulder, saying my name again and again.

"Corey, are you listening? Can you hear me?" he says.

"Yeah, I can hear you." I look over my shoulder at Jacob—asleep. Images of Mateo holding a gun, pulling a trigger twice fill my head.

"Corey, the kid, the boy—he's going to be okay. His dad is on his way. He might already be back."

"Sure. And the years of intense therapy will be paid for by the state, right?" I say.

"I'm trying to find something positive here. You can't change what happened to him any more than his father can," Chris says.

"I know." I look at Chris. He's studying me—waiting for me to make the next move, change the subject, anything. "I know who killed Kat. I have his sunglasses in my bag."

"Slow down. What?"

"They met in a running group. He was—is someone else's husband at the studio. I think he left his wife for Kat or something, I don't know, but he pushed her off that cliff."

"Speculation. Proof or nothing," he says.

Fuck proof, I know he did it. I want a confession from this asshole. I say, "Nothing, but I'm working on it."

"Working on it how?"

"There's a run for Kat. He invited me to come join."

"Wait, what?"

I shrug.

"Alone?"

I hadn't thought it through. "No, there's got to be like a hundred people in the running group," I say.

"No," Chris says. "You can't go alone."

I'm never alone, though. Jacob is always with me.

"I need confirmation on those glasses, and a confession would be nice too," I say.

"I'll be there," he says.

"Where?"

"The run. Christ, Corey, straighten your shit out."

"We can't go together—" I say. He's never spoken to me like this. He's scared.

"Fine. Separate, but together."

My phone is practically buzzing off the dash. Chris looks at it. I grab it and see about six messages from Evan. Did I forget to tell him I was leaving the house when I went to Gilda's?

"Listen, I have to get going."

"Why is your hand shaking?" Chris asks.

I look at my hands. Sure enough, my body is betraying me again. I latch on to my hand and hold it still. Catch my breath, hold it too. My eyes feel like they're shaking.

"I'm fine, just a little chilly," I say. "I have to get home . . ." Change a diaper, pump my breasts, kiss my husband hello, and join a Facebook running group.

32

Evan's car is no longer in the driveway when I get home. It's late. I can't imagine where he'd go.

"Evan?" I call out when I get inside the house. No answer. I go upstairs and put Jacob down in his crib and sit in the rocker next to him with my laptop. I open Facebook and pull up the invitation from Diane to join the running-group page. I accept. There are photos separated into folders organized by the year. I look through last year's folder for any pictures of Sean and Kat together or pictures of Sean wearing sunglasses.

By the time I get to the second album, I'm bored from looking at people I don't know. Faces are blurring, and I catch myself falling asleep. I decide to look at Sean's page—private. Shit. Kat's page—postings are all about Cyclone Studio. Nothing to glean from either of their social media accounts. I google running groups Highland Park, CA 90042. The group has additional accounts on other sites, including Meetup and Yelp—both have over two hundred members.

"You're home," Evan says.

I jump.

"You scared me! I thought you were out. Where's your car?" I ask.

"I parked in the street—closest spot was at the end of the block. I was trying to leave the driveway open for you."

"Didn't you hear me calling for you?" I ask.

"I dozed off, I guess."

"I didn't see you—" I start.

"I was in our bed."

Didn't I check there? "Sorry," I say. "It's been a day."

"Yeah, and I feel like I haven't seen you, or our child, much. Do you want to tell me anything?" He couldn't know anything more than what I've been telling him, nothing, but something is different in the way he asks tonight.

"Diane, from Cyclone, invited me to join this running group she's in. They're doing a run to honor Kat, and I thought I'd go."

"Maybe I'll go with you."

"Yeah, sure, I'm looking up the details now," I say. I can't keep telling him no.

"How are you feeling?" he asks.

"I'm tired, but otherwise good. Yeah, I think the medicine is helping."

"I think so too. I'm really glad, Corey. I'm going to go shower."

Evan leans down and kisses my cheek. Guilt wells up inside me. Had he asked me if I thought we'd make it—I'd say I don't know.

I hear the shower start while I add the run to Evan's and my mutual Google Calendar. The Kat-and-Sean search has resulted in nothing. I tiptoe out of Jacob's room. I need food—cake, cookies, doughnuts. Evan is great at not keeping sugar in the house—the pantry is stocked with protein powders and baby food, so I settle on one of Jacob's teething biscuits.

Evan's phone alarm buzzes nearby. I go over to shut it off. There are some missed texts from his mom and an update message from an app called Follow Me. I open the app. Staring back at me is a log of my locations since that morning.

Fuck.

I nearly throw the phone but pick up a glass from the kitchen counter instead and smash it into the sink. It shatters.

"Corey?" I hear Evan yell.

"Everything's fine. I accidentally dropped a glass in the sink."

I close the app and leave the phone on the counter where it was.

I'm not ready for this fight with Evan. The complete violation of privacy. His lack of trust. I'm pissed. I cannot deal with him now—the benzos not totally flushed from my system, with the day I've had, the shock I may be experiencing. First, no more pills.

I go to bed after Evan is asleep. I will confront him in the morning.

I barely slept. Got up before Evan and Jacob and cleaned up the broken glass in the sink from last night.

"Corey, have you seen my phone?" Evan asks while I feed Jacob a bowl of funky-smelling infant cereal.

"Why does this baby cereal smell rancid?" My tone is more accusatory than inquisitive.

"It's organic. I don't know. It's fine. Can you focus? My phone—have you seen it?"

"Yeah, I think I saw it last night." I walk over to where I found it before. There is a new message from Follow Me. "What's this Follow Me app? You have mail," I say.

"It's nothing, just in case my phone gets lost," he says.

"Cool, can you show me how it works? Maybe I should download it."

"I don't actually think it works that great. Too complicated, so I'm probably going to delete it. I love you. I'll see you tonight." I wonder if he's practiced that lie. It was so easy for him. He leaves without a kiss for me or Jacob. A first. Such a basic tell. He definitely isn't cut out for investigative work, but he is a smoother liar than I'd have thought.

I pack Jacob up, and we head to Diane's house. Before I leave, though, I want to fuck with Evan.

Me: Going to Diane's for coffee. I love you.

I drive in a large circle around the neighborhood. I drive north on Avenue 50 past Lolita's Café, an upscale breakfast spot opened by locals, and Castro's Pizza—a neighborhood holdover from the eighties and nineties. The outside of Castro's is hidden by canopies and security bars—the kind of security measures that deter the new generation of Highland Park clientele.

I turn on Milo Terrace and then San Rafael Avenue and park outside the house we nearly bought. A corner lot, like ours now, but with Saltillo-tiled stairs that lead up to a dark blue-gray bungalow with giant blue agaves neatly outlining the yard. It had a fireplace and a third bedroom that was staged as an office when we looked at it. But the thing we don't have, and it does, is a backyard with a wall of giant cypress trees. I take a deep breath and drive around a little more. Stopping at Baltimore Street Elementary. I watch the kids at recess running around the cement top yard, the sun beating down, no coverage, no grass, no sandbox—screaming with delight regardless.

Evan's app should be alerting him like crazy with my erratic route. One last errand—Starbucks—then Diane's. I grin to myself, thinking about Evan in a meeting, his phone blowing up. Happy Monday, babe.

"Jacob, let this be a lesson to you, buddy. Do not mess with Mommy." I check on Jacob in the rearview mirror. He looks at me and spurts out a new sound. An almost word. A button on the end of my warning.

33

Diane lives on the "good side" of NELA, which is real estate bullshit for white: north of Colorado Boulevard in Eagle Rock. There are no signs in Spanish. No one is walking the street with a pushcart and bell, selling chicharrones with chili and lime. There isn't a single taco truck hanging around at lunch hours on that side of town. We share a Trader Joe's, and that's about it.

I pull up to Diane's house with two large coffees, two giant cookies, and a growing baby. I hope the offering will get me some answers or, minimally, the baby will get me in the door.

I pull Jacob out of the car, asleep, and balance the tray of coffees and cookies as I walk up the immaculately landscaped front walk of Diane's classic Spanish-style home. The roof is clay tile. Well kept. Stunning, for a roof. The walkway is paved with bricks. The lawn sparkles. The trees: one avocado, two lemon, a lime, peach, and fig look mature, along with the house. Before I make it up the front walk, Diane is at the door.

"What a surprise!" Diane says, coming down her front step. She meets me with an awkward hug, considering all the items I'm balancing.

"You said you were having a hard time. So, I brought treats," I say.

"Is that coffee?" Diane asks.

"It is." I smile like a beauty pageant contestant—so big it hurts a little. I don't know how to play Diane, complete transparency or dumb flirt. She's tough and doesn't take bullshit. I need her to feel, at least, like she is steering the conversation. "Cream and sugar, right?"

"You are good," Diane says.

Jacob kicks his feet in excitement and knocks the coffee tray. "Oh shoot!" Coffee spills down my shirt. "Can I use your bathroom?" Once again, Jacob gets me what I need—inside Diane's house.

"Oh, sure. Where are my manners? Let me take Jacob. I miss holding a baby," she says. Reluctantly, I pass Jacob into the arms of a woman I suspect of knowing, and possibly covering for, a killer.

"Oh, and there's a chocolate-fudge cookie in there with your name on it."

"The bathroom is the second door on the right. I'll be in the kitchen with this guy when you're done—just walk around until you find us." Diane continues to walk through her house, leaving me in her foyer to find the bathroom. She never looks back.

I head down the hall toward door two on the right. I stop at the first door and take a peek—coat closet. There's a hall table with a stack of mail I flip through: mail addressed to Diane and Sean Loeb. How long were they separated—a year?

I hear Jacob yelp from somewhere else in the house, and I drop the mail and go.

I find the kitchen and run in. "Is Jacob okay?" I manage to hold back the panic as I ask.

"Oh yeah, he wanted down, but I'm not sure when I had the floor mopped last. I know how delicate you are with him, so I had to say no." Diane is speaking directly to Jacob. Jacob is eating it up. "How are you doing, Mama?"

"I'm tired," I say.

"Me, too, but Monique asked me to take over all of Kat's classes this week," she says. "But you already know that, *assistant manager*."

"Yeah, I saw the schedule. Are you okay with that?" I say.

"I guess. I am trying to work on my relationship, though. I definitely want to be home more at night with Sean now that we're doing this." She motions to the house, the lawn, the neighborhood—rebuilding a world with her ex-husband.

"I have all of Kat's routines memorized. Even her scripts: *Everyone's body is a temple of its own design. We don't function alike, so we don't ride alike. Be you on the bike. Close your eyes and ride the path of your own journey, not your neighbor's.* I actually wrote that one for her." She chuckles, more to herself than to me. "Hey, I'm going to spice mine up a little," she says and shakes her coffee in front of me, with the hand not holding Jacob. "I've got whiskey and Baileys. What's your preference? I like the combo myself." Diane winks.

"Why don't I take Jacob from you? He gets so heavy after a minute," I say, and instead of waiting for her to offer him, I pull him out of her arm, and I smell the whiskey on her breath. This won't be her first drink today.

I watch her pour a third of her large coffee into the sink and replace it with Woodford Reserve and a dash of Baileys, stir it with a butter knife, and replace the lid before taking a gulp. She then snatches my cup off the counter and pops off the top.

"No. No, sorry, I'm good. I'm still breastfeeding," I say.

"And you're on benzos? They can damage your baby as much as alcohol, worse even. You must be pumping and dumping?" Rosenberg said it was fine, hadn't he?

I scan Jacob's face, looking for signs of damage.

"You look like you need it, so I'm adding a splash—for flavor." Diane's splash is not conservative, but it's only Baileys.

"So, where's Sean?" I ask.

"It's Monday, babe. He's at work."

She is drunk; she's using *babe*. "What does he do?" I ask.

"Real estate." Diane says it with a hint of contempt.

I rock Jacob in my arms, but he's not tired. He's awake, and he wants everything. Freedom, playtime, entertainment, the park. I shove my hand deep into my tote bag, feeling around for a bottle or squeeze pouch of yams, until I land in yet another puddle of wetness—bigger than the last purse-puddle I felt—and find an ill-closed wet wipes container as the culprit. Then I feel something hard—sunglasses from Kat's car. I pull them out and settle on letting Jacob latch on to my breast—I'd let him suck for a minute, no harm.

"Oh, hey, you mentioned last night that these may be Sean's, so I thought I'd swing by with them before someone scratched them or, you know, took them." I hold up the glasses sealed in a ziplock bag, preserving evidence or fingerprints.

"Hello?" comes a voice from the front door.

"Sean?" Diane calls.

"Yeah, I'm just in and out. Forgot something," he says.

"Hang on, can you come here? In the kitchen."

"I really don't have time for this, Diane. I told you, in and out." He comes into view dressed in a navy blue skinny suit and appears taken aback by my presence. "I'm sorry, I didn't know you had company."

"Hi," I say.

"Corey, it's so nice to see you again. I wish I could stay, but I'm showing a client a building and I'm late."

"Babe, Corey found a pair of sunglasses, and I thought they looked like yours," Diane says. "The pair you've been complaining you lost— since you can't see in the sun." Drunk Diane sounds resentful.

I hold them up for Sean to inspect.

"Sorry, I wear prescription. Probably not." He shrugs. "Ladies, I'm going to see a client." He starts to walk off.

"These are prescription," I say. "No one's reported any missing at the studio, so I drove them over."

He stops, back toward me, while he looks at Diane.

"Stop being weird, Sean. Try them on and see if they're yours. You probably left them at Cyclone during the ride," Diane says.

Sean waits while Jacob unlatches himself and goes for nipple number two. I pull down my shirt over my used breast, then pass Sean the glasses. They look at home on his face.

"Maybe they are mine," he says, taking them off almost instantly.

I absently reach for the glasses—my evidence.

"Well, I think I'll hang on to them this time," Sean says. He chuckles politely—it's charming. He's boyish, his personality cute, and I see how disarming it is, he is.

"Of course," I say. I stumble. Catch the edge of the counter with my hand and press my weight into it for stability. Sean's eyes land on mine. I hold his stare. Too long a gaze to speak first. I want to call him out in front of Diane. Ask him—did you kill her? Did Kat beg for her life? Did you watch until she crashed, or did you cowardly run off?

"Thanks, Corey. I guess I left them during the ride."

"Did you and Kat—" I say, but Diane comes in loud and urgent.

"God, I thought I remembered you complaining about losing them weeks ago. Didn't you call and ask if they were packed inside one of the kids' overnight bags?" Diane says while she pours more whiskey into a near-empty large coffee cup. "Maybe Kat found them during a running meetup and brought them back to the studio for you. No telling how things make their way back to their owner, am I right?"

"Nah, I'm sure you took them by mistake, Diane, and left them, seems more likely." Sean looks at his wife. "I'm leaving. I'll see you tonight. Corey, thanks for finding these." He is gone without a kiss goodbye for Diane.

"I've been pretty shaken up over Kat. I can't eat. I can't sleep. I'm a fucking zombie," she says.

I take a large sip of my coffee. The Baileys made it sweet and thick, sticky in my mouth.

"Hey, did you ever figure out who Kat was dating?" I barely manage to spit it out. "Maybe Sean knows? Maybe the running-club folks?"

"Well, she definitely got around that group. I got to hear all the details. But no. I don't think it was very serious, whoever it was. Sean wouldn't know."

Diane grabs the bag of cookies and starts to pick at the bits of chocolate and nuts that are piled high. There are more bits than cookie, and like a bird, she pecks at it with her fingernails one morsel at a time. Instead of putting them in her mouth, she throws them in the sink.

I watch her strip the cookie clean. Turn the now-naked disk over in her hand. She scours for more to dig out—an unearthing. I am digging too. I will scour if I have to. "Do you think someone killed Kat?" I ask.

She laughs. Not a typical big Diane laugh. Something more authentic. I have pulled her out of the deep and back into the present with me.

"Like, murdered?"

I nod, full of anticipation for the perfect answer.

"No way. The police said it was an accident."

"Ow!" I shriek and reflexively swat at the thing that bit me. Jacob cries. I almost cry in pain and guilt. "Mommy is so sorry." I hug him and squeeze him until he sniffles. I look down. My nipple is bleeding. "Do you have a paper towel?" I ask.

Diane fumbles. I notice her hands shaking. She hands me a wet wad of them.

"Do you ever take a break?" Diane asks.

"What do you mean?"

"From Jacob. I've never seen you without the baby. They need breaks from us as much as we need breaks from them." Diane takes Jacob from me and says to him, "Isn't that right, big guy? Do you know the 'Itsy Bitsy Spider'?" Diane sings to Jacob while using her hand as a spider to crawl up his belly. He laughs and sputters out sounds in response to her. They are having a conversation—a baby-appropriate conversation. I would not be surprised if Jacob's first word is *murder*.

"I had a biter, too, by the way. It was the worst." She strokes Jacob's chubby, soft arm. "I'm not some tragic housewife, okay? I love him—Sean. It really is that simple. When I said 'for better or for worse,' I meant it." Diane looks at the clock. "Shit, I have to go get ready. I'm teaching class in an hour."

I smell the whiskey on her breath again.

"Do you need a ride?" I ask.

"I'm fine." She hands Jacob over to me. She walks us out of her house. Kisses me on both cheeks, hugs us both too hard—then closes her front door.

She knows. She knows what Sean did.

34

I drive away from Diane's house, stopping every few blocks to ensure the app on Evan's phone continues to beep at him. Sun pours through the windows, making me uncomfortably warm. I have a sense I'm being followed. The car is silver, gray, maybe white—nondescript—too far back in my rearview mirror to see well. When I stop, it stops. I turn left, right, left, left, right. It's probably a coincidence. I look in the rearview, but now an SUV is behind me. I head toward an unmarked dead end—notorious in the winding, hilly streets of our neighborhood. I pull over to the curb and drop my head in my hands and take a deep breath. I lift my head and shriek.

"What the fuck are you doing?" I scream through the closed window. Evan is standing next to the car.

"Roll your window down," he says.

"Are you following me?" I ask.

"Corey, I'm sorry. I was worried," Evan says.

"First you put a tracking app on me and now this? This, Evan?"

"Tell me whose house that was you were at—"

"It was Diane's, asshole." I roll my window back up and speed off so fast I blow through a stop sign. A cop car shows up in the rearview. Dammit. I pull over before the cop hits the lights. The police cruiser pulls over behind me and waits. I turn off the car. I'm thankful Jacob is sleeping through it all. I check my mirror. The cop pulls into the road and up alongside me. He motions my window down.

"Everything okay here, ma'am?" asks the officer.

I don't recognize him—they're all starting to look like the same person: Jefferies, Marks, this guy. "Fine, thanks, just taking a moment."

"Have you been drinking today?"

"No," I say. Then it occurs to me that I have Baileys in my coffee, thanks to Diane. "Is there a problem, officer?"

"You blew through a stop sign a few streets back. I noticed you appeared distracted on your route."

"Yes, sorry, I have an infant in the car. I was a little distracted. He's sleeping now, but I pulled over to find his pacifier." Was lying this easy for Sean too?

"Consider this a warning. Be more careful. Keep your eyes on the road."

"Thank you," I say. "It's been a long week." I give my best facial performance—once an on-air talent, always an on-air talent. I wait until the cruiser is around the corner and out of sight before I pull back onto the road. I feel shitty thinking it, but thank god I'm white and not being dragged out of my car at gunpoint.

I head home as fast as I can. I'm fifteen over the speed limit and not slowing down for yellow lights. I need to get home before Evan. I have a rush of energy, an adrenaline bump that has been missing for years. I blow through another sleepy stop sign two blocks from our house when I see the police lights go on behind me this time, before I hear the siren.

SHIT.

I pull over and dig for my wallet this time. There is a knock on the window.

"Ma'am, please roll down the window," the officer says through the glass.

"Hi," I say. It's the same cop or his identical twin.

"Ma'am, are you aware that you blew through another stop sign doing at least fifteen over the limit?"

"Were you following me?" Too wrapped up in my own head to notice. I giggle to ease the tension. "That's not really a stop sign, officer."

I end up laughing as I say it. I'm not flirting. I'm desperate. I try to take a deep breath. I try to feel my lungs expand to the bottom, but they won't. I feel hollow. "I live here," I say; it comes out impatient. "That stop sign has only ever functioned as a yield." I pull my bag into my lap. My heart is racing. I think about Kat plummeting to her death—did her heart race? I can see my pulse beating in my wrist. I need to take a pill before I lose it.

"Ma'am, keep your hands where I can see them."

"Sorry." I'm gasping for the breath to speak the words. "I need to get my pill." I pull out diapers, and wet wipes, and pacifiers. "I think I'm having a—" I stop breathing. Or I'm holding my breath. I have tunnel vision—I hear Jacob wake and shriek. I am being pulled out of the car.

"Ma'am, can you hear me? Ma'am?"

"Yes, yes, my baby. Can you get me my baby? Someone get me my baby!"

"Ma'am, do you have a heart condition?"

"No, I have a postpartum condition."

After ten minutes of observation and discussion, I sit on the curb of the sidewalk. My keys have been confiscated, and I am forced to wait for Evan, who is jogging from our house to get Jacob and me. We sit in silence while the officer writes me a ticket for running a stop sign and for driving ten over the speed limit.

"I am not citing you for driving under the influence. However, postpartum drugs are not considered lifesaving, and your condition is not considered life threatening. I don't want to see you on the road like this again," the officer says, scolding me in front of Jacob and now Evan, who has just arrived—perfect timing.

What a joke. My privilege got me off, but my prescription drugs were incriminating me.

It's the second time in less than a week that Evan has seen me with the cops. The officer hands me a ticket and Evan my keys. I want to yell at the cop that I am not the threat—Kat's murderer is. And, if anyone cares, I know who he is.

◆ ◆ ◆

"I yielded at the stop sign," I say. "You do that all the time."

"Yeah, but I don't get caught," Evan says.

I laugh, but I'm mad at him for tracking me.

"Listen, maybe you shouldn't be driving," he says.

"Don't tell me you're taking that cop's side," I say. "Thank you for the patience with your fucked-up wife. I think I got it. It was one stop sign."

"It was two. I saw you speed through one when you ran away from me."

"I didn't run away. I drove away. And that's your fault. I was pissed. You've been following me and spying on me, Evan. I don't suppose you ever thought about the fact that that is a crime? It's called stalking."

"I'm not stalking you. I'm a worried husband. A month ago, you said you were having episodes while driving. Yet you insist on driving all over town with our baby. How would you feel if the situation were reversed?"

"Ah, but it never will be because you'll never be his mother."

"I wish you'd stop playing the mom card on me. You're right. I'll never know what it's like to carry a child, to go through labor, have postpartum anxiety. But you know what, Corey, you'll never know what it's like to start a life with someone only to find out they'd rather be with someone else. You don't know what it's like to be shut out of a relationship with your wife and your child. I'm sick to death of your self-pity. You're selfish and honestly, if it wasn't for Jacob, I wouldn't still be here trying. I love Jacob as much as you do. I swear to god you're even selfish about that."

His words stun me. They're like a slap to the face. Like I'm being plunged into an ice bath. Evan pulls up to the curb in front of our house. He puts the car in park and gets out, then takes Jacob out of the car. I stay seated on the passenger side. Unable to find words or the will to move.

"For the record, that app is me needing some control over what happens to my son." Evan delivers his last blow—he walks away without me, just Jacob.

I find my legs and follow after him. "No! It is intrusive, Evan. You never talk to me. You tell me what you need from me, but you never ask what I need. Did you think I needed my partner to become my parent and micromanage my life?"

"No, Corey, I thought you needed a doctor to tell you what kind of mess you've created and help guide you back to me. To me and to Jacob. I'm going to be in the next session with Dr. Rosenberg and you. I want to make sure you're being honest. And that's final."

35

Elsie is sitting on our porch listening, watching us fight. I still don't know if I can tell her what happened with Natalie's mother.

"Can we talk for a minute?" she says.

I'm numb from the fight with Evan.

"Sure," I say. I see Evan through the screen door. He shrugs, and I don't understand what he wants. I focus on Elsie. "What's going on?" I ask her.

"The news," she says. "I can't believe it."

"The news?"

"That Courtney Wheeler said it was an Avenues initiation."

"Courtney Wheeler? What do you mean? When did she say that?" I ask.

"This morning. It was a total of thirty seconds." Elsie paces the length of the porch in long strides.

Evan comes out with Jacob in a new baby carrier strapped to his chest. The kind of carrier I wanted and didn't get. He's got two glasses of water with him.

"Thank you," I say to Evan. Jacob reaches a hand out toward me.

"Mammma" comes out of Jacob's mouth.

I look at Evan—back to Jacob.

"Did you just say *mama?*" I say to Jacob. I look at Elsie. "Did he just say *mama?*" She smiles at me. "Say it again, Jacob. Say *mama,*" I beg him. He reaches for me, frustration showing in his expression. I see joy and pain on Evan's face. I grab Jacob's outstretched hands and tell him, "In a minute, baby. Mommy will be in, in a minute." I give Evan a nod, and he retreats into the house.

"Do you want to sit?" I ask Elsie. All I can think about now, though, is that Jacob said my name. As awful as I may be as a mother, I'm still his mama.

Elsie sits. "Araceli's mother and father are setting up a scholarship in her name," she says. "She was so smart. She would have devoured college, and it was important to her. They want to give that chance to another child. I thought, maybe you could ask some of your friends at the station if they would do a piece on it—since they wouldn't respond to Lupe when she asked. Shine a light on good people."

"I don't have any friends left over there," I say. In fact, I cut every nonwork friend out of my life after the rape. And after being fired, there weren't any work friends left either. I had neighbors and Evan's friends' wives. Then the people at Cyclone. Elsie looks let down. "Have you heard anything about Natalie's family?" I ask.

"No. I was at Trader Joe's earlier—apparently the aunt has taken a leave of absence." Elsie takes my free hand and squeezes it. "You look tired," she says.

"I am."

Evan comes back out with a plate of cookies.

"Would you mind if I excused myself?" I say. "I think I need to lie down."

"Want me to come with you?" Evan asks.

"She's fine—let her go rest with her baby," Elsie says. "New moms need all the rest we can give them."

I take Jacob from him and into the house with me. "I am Mama, baby. I am Mama," I say. I take him with me to the bathroom. He's warm and wiggly and smells like baby. I pull my phone from the waistband of my pants but can't remember when I put it there. I close my eyes for a minute trying to think what to do next. My phone vibrates in my hand. I look at the message—it's an unknown caller.

Unknown Caller: Hey team! Thanks for signing up for the Run for Kat! Click the link for details and map of the upcoming event.

A moment later a voicemail appears—I never heard my phone ring. *"Hi, Corey, this is Dr. Rosenberg. You missed your follow-up appointment this morning. I'd like you to call me back as soon as you get this so we can reschedule."*

I hadn't scheduled my follow-up with Dr. Rosenberg yet. I needed to but hadn't gotten around to it. I open my calendar on Google and look—nothing. I open Evan's calendar: There it is, labeled Corey's Shrink Appointment.

"Evan," I yell from the top of the stairs.

He comes into view. "Yeah?"

"Did you schedule a Dr. Rosenberg appointment for me?"

"What?"

I run down the stairs with Jacob. "Did you schedule an appointment with Dr. Rosenberg for me?" I ask.

"Yes, but it was when you were acting irrationally, and I was worried. I canceled it."

"You had no right." I stare at him, holding back hot tears. I refuse to cry.

"I think it's time I go," Elsie says. She's still on the porch. I don't care if she hears the whole conversation.

"You had no right to make an appointment for me with my doctor behind my back. If you were worried, you could have talked to me, asked me to schedule one."

"You're being irrational now. Blowing the whole thing out of proportion. It's not that big of a deal. I'm your husband."

"I want you to leave," I tell Evan.

Elsie is already out our front gate and gone from sight.

"Fine. I'll go for a walk, give you some space to cool down." Evan grabs his jacket.

"No, I want you to leave. Go stay at Tobin's, or someone with a wife that isn't me. I can't look at you anymore. You've been spying on me, following me, calling in doctor appointments behind my back. I don't know who you are," I say.

"No, Corey, you don't know who you are anymore. You said you wanted this." Evan motions around him. "The family, a house, domesticity. You said you wanted me." He stops, but he's not done. I know his patterns. "I need a little air to cool down."

Evan walks out the screen door; it slams shut behind him.

Jacob starts crying.

My breasts throb in time with his wails. I nurse him on the couch, just the two of us.

After more than twenty minutes, he passes out on my left breast, larger than the right because I always forget to alternate which breast to start with.

I carry Jacob into his room—once my office, which was light and airy, with white walls and a sisal rug. Now it looks like a Pottery Barn Kids catalog.

The last two months of my pregnancy, I was in the hospital on bed rest and monitoring, thanks to my uterus going into early labor. Evan and his friends' wives—the stay-at-home moms—decided to surprise me with a nursery makeover. The room looked like it had been staged for selling. The walls were navy blue, gray, and white striped—a nautical theme. **J-A-C-O-B** in big blue wood-block letters arched across the wall above his crib. A gray chevron-patterned tepee took up one corner of the room. Bookshelves were lined with nostalgic children's books that Evan reads to him—including too many Dr. Seuss books, thanks to Evan's mom. My sisal was replaced with a high-pile cream rug that felt like a velvet blanket underfoot.

I look at Jacob asleep in his crib and notice how much he looks like Evan—more and more every day.

I call Dr. Rosenberg's mailbox and leave a message:

"This is Corey Tracey-Lieberman, and I'm just calling Dr. Rosenberg because I don't think the medicine is working fast enough. Can you call me back? I think I need to talk to someone."

Then I text Chris:

Me: Are you busy?

My insides feel like a possessed corset is squeezing my ribs tight around my lungs, but I decide not to take any more pills. I need clarity more than calm.

I run to my purse, pull out the Klonopin, and dump half the bottle in the trash—the other half I keep for extreme emergencies. I sink to the kitchen floor, pull my knees up to my chest, rest my chin on them, and rock back and forth.

The house is quiet without Evan. I never realized how much space he consumes. And it's dark—I haven't thought about it before, but I never turn on the lights; Evan does. I also never collect the mail or water the plants. Those are Evan jobs. I load the dishwasher, but he always reloads it—I don't mind. He unloads the dishwasher too. I clean the counters, but he replaces the sponges weekly.

I get up from the floor and start pacing. Waiting for Chris to text me back. I can't stop thinking of all the things I don't do, and Evan does. I let him do those things, ignore them until they become his business. How does he stand me at all? He's right. I don't know who I am anymore. I've changed—maybe that is the problem. But I can't be who I was.

NELAScanBoy: Hey—slow work night

Me: Evan left.

NELAScanBoy: He'll be back.

He will be, but I don't want to be alone in the quiet house, and I can't leave because of Jacob—and I need company.

Me: Can you come over?

NELAScanBoy: Yes

Chris appears hesitant when I answer the door. His usual toothy smile is replaced by a closed-mouth grin. His arms are crossed over his chest. He hangs back from the door a good foot—he looks more on his way out than on his way in.

"Come in, please," I tell him and head straight for the kitchen.

I search the cupboards for something to offer but fall short and come up with stale rice cakes.

"Corey, what are you doing?" Chris says.

"It's really quiet when Jacob's sleeping," I say. "My head gets really loud."

"I bet. You get used to someone else's noise: footsteps, breathing, swallowing." He stops to eat a rice cake. "These are so gross."

"I know. I'm sorry. I think I'm supposed to go to the grocery store, but . . . Are you hungry? I can do Postmates."

"I'm fine," he says while choking down another bite of old rice cake. "Do you have any news?"

"That's usually my line, isn't it?" I laugh. It seems the only person I've laughed with in weeks is Chris. "Do you have any updates on Natalie and Araceli? I heard Courtney announced it was gang bullshit. How the hell did that happen?" I ask.

"I know. They're making it go away."

"Who? Who is making it go away, and why?" I already know the answer, but I want to hear someone else say it.

"Corey, come on. Two brown-skinned girls killed by a family member? That's not news; that's sad. Where's the story for *LA News First*? Where's the path of white women raped and left for dead? Where's the serial stalker, celebrity overdose, celebrity suicide in the story?"

"How do we fix it?" I ask.

"I'm working on it."

"Fine. Then, talk this out with me so I know I'm not crazy. Guy leaves his wife—he claims he wants more 'me' time. He meets a younger woman: beautiful, no kids, no commitments. She can spend all her time focused on him. Eventually, this younger woman wants to meet the kids. The ex-wife vetoes that request real quick. The ex-wife also refuses to sign off on the divorce, sort of holding the guy hostage from living a life he thinks he wants. On a hike or a walk at the top of Debs, they argue. The younger woman decides she's out. It's all too much work. The guy begs her to stay. She won't. He snaps. Pushes her, maybe by accident, and she falls to her death. It looks like an accident or suicide, or accidental suicide—fuck it. He moves back in with the wife to show the world what a good guy he is. The only thing anyone should be worried about now is how long it takes him to kill the wife—fucker might not even bother to make it look like an accident." I sound like an episode of *Dateline*. "Have you heard anything more from your cousin?"

"Kat's body is scheduled to be picked up by the funeral home tomorrow," he says.

"Dammit."

"Does the mom know about the sunglasses?" he asks.

"She was there when I found them. It's when she told me she was done with investigating and wants to move on." I look at the plate of rice cakes. "Promise me we won't let Courtney Wheeler deliver the final word on the two dead girls."

"Her thirty-second blurb isn't the end of their story. You need to write about it, though. Write about the community. Write about all of it. The people, the gentrification, the crime—all of it. People still respect your work." He takes my hand. "I have a guy at the *Eastsider Times*—you write the story; he'll publish it."

"I don't know." I think about what Evan said before he left— that I don't know who I am anymore. He's right. I think about what Nando said—I live here, but I don't live here the way this community does. They take care of their own. I know what he means. Sometimes where you work, the job you do, is your community. I know what I want—I want to be back with my team, investigating the crimes in my community.

"No, you write the story, Chris. People need to hear it from you. This is your community—it's different coming from me. It should come from someone they trust."

"Are you sure—this is as much yours as it is mine."

"I'm sure. I'll fill in all the blanks for you. I'll tell you everything that went down word for word," I say.

"Okay. I've got to get a few things to the station before the late show," he says. "Walk me out?"

I leave Jacob asleep inside the house and walk Chris out to the porch.

I try to swallow—it's hard and loud. My teeth chatter.

"Are you cold?" Chris asks.

"Guess I should have grabbed a coat," I say. He steps in and takes my shoulders.

He's so close to me I can hear the click in his jaw when he speaks.

"Corey, are you happy?" he asks.

"I'm working on it."

I anticipate it but don't expect it and am taken aback when he kisses me.

It's different from the pecks Evan and I barely exchange, maybe because there is no baggage attached. I expected to feel something, but I'm numb.

I pull back, afraid Elsie or Pete will see us. Or Evan coming home, up to our porch, me kissing Chris.

"I'm sorry," I say. "I shouldn't have—"

"You didn't. It was me."

"I'm sorry, you should go."

I leave Chris on the porch and go in. Lock the door behind me and wait to move until I hear the front gate close.

36

Evan is still gone when Jacob and I leave for the studio in the morning. The new Cyclone schedule has me teaching multiple early-morning classes, but not usually the one I'm headed to today. I drive cautiously, looking for squad cars and stop signs. I make it to the studio without speeding.

Monique is already here—but there is no one at the front desk. The music is loud. Jacob is louder. My son is not going to be happy in his stroller today. I pick him up and bounce him on my hip and whisper in his ear, "I promise I will give you everything if you just help me get through today, okay? I love you." My words mean nothing. He is no longer an infant—he needs more from me than promises. He needs action and full-time attention.

I wave to Monique. All the classes have had low attendance since the memorial ride for Kat. It will be a miracle if the studio survives. If it doesn't, it will be chalked up to big investors pushing out small businesses in the neighborhood—not the death of a woman.

The front door chimes. Diane walks through, looking like she is still trying to get out of bed. She's a mess. Her hair greasy. Dark circles color the skin under her eyes. She wears a baggy chambray button-down over her Lululemons. I look at the clock. Fifteen minutes until class. A few riders file in behind Diane.

"Nice of you to show up, Diane. You shouldn't have bothered. I called Lieberman in to cover," Monique says.

"The cops came by. They requestioned me and questioned Sean," Diane says.

"What?" I ask.

"I feel sick. I haven't been able to sleep. I'm a complete mess, and now the police are in my home questioning us." Diane stops and looks down at the wedding band and diamond ring she never removed from her finger. "I finally get my husband home, and we're invaded by police and death. It's not fair."

"I thought the police said it was an accident," I say. I haven't called Lopez with the sunglasses or the affair I suspect Kat and Sean of—where could this be coming from? Chris's cousin?

"It's all so messed up," Diane says. She cries while the few riders ready themselves on bikes.

No one appears to notice. The music still too loud.

"This is bullshit. Diane, I can't shut the place down because you're mourning—there's rent and obligations," Monique says.

"You could show some emotion about this whole fucked-up thing, Monique. Maybe the cops should be questioning you and not Kat's real friends," Diane says.

"I have a class to teach," Monique says. "Asshole." And she's gone.

I turn my attention back to Diane, but she's left. Gone without a word. I watch Monique get on the bike, a first for me to see. Headset adjusted to her head. I guess I'm not teaching after all.

Fuck.

I step outside with Jacob and my bag. I dig through its contents, struggling to keep Jacob on my hip and single-handedly scoop out Lopez's business card from the day she drove me home. I find it: **Detective Lopez NELA Division**. It's wet and mushy from all the wet-wipe leaks, but legible. After leaving Lopez a voicemail, I save her number and toss the soggy card.

The class ends, and none of the riders linger like they used to. Jacob snores in my arms. I squeeze him a little too tight—the world can't crush him yet. Just me. Diane slumps back through the front door with a large boba.

"Monique, I'm sorry," she says. "I was being selfish, and you don't deserve that—especially now." Diane approaches Monique, arms extended, but Monique isn't giving it to her.

"Lieberman," Monique says, "can you take over Kat's Monday noon ride?"

"Probably." I don't want it, but now is not the time to say no.

"Good. Let me know by tonight. Diane, I'm giving you Saturday's beginners' class."

Diane gives a sarcastic grin, then says, "Fine." And leaves abruptly.

"Lieberman," Monique says.

I'm at the door, ready to chase Diane. I need to know who, why, what the police said to her and Sean. What did they suspect—if in fact they were still calling it an accident? Did they have evidence of him and Kat? A witness, fellow runner at Debs that morning?

"Yeah?" I say.

"So, you'll let me know, right, Lieberman?"

"About?"

"The schedule? The class?"

"Right, yeah."

She doesn't look up.

"You can go," she says. "There's no one signed up for the next class."

Monique stays focused on the paperwork in front of her. I silently grab Jacob's stroller from behind the counter and glance at the paperwork Monique is reading:

RENT AGREEMENT

I leave the studio without saying another word. My phone buzzes with a private number. "Hello?"

"Hi, Corey, this is Dr. Rosenberg. Is now a good time?"

I jump in the car with Jacob. "Yeah, thanks for calling me back. I think there's something wrong with me." My eyes burn as the wetness starts to spill from them.

"Corey, the medicine isn't going to work right away. You're putting too much pressure on yourself to be fixed, but you're not broken. Your brain needs to readjust. You're smart, and you are capable, and you need to remind yourself that it's temporary. Can you come in next week for a session?"

"Yeah. Yes, please."

"Great, I'll send you a confirmation. Now, Corey, remember it takes thirty seconds to change a thought. When you find yourself spiraling, I want you to think of something else. A good memory, a book you loved, a trip you want to plan, and follow that thought instead. Okay? Can you do that for me, Corey?"

"Yeah."

"Good. And if you need me again, please page me with 911, and I'll call you back within five minutes."

"Thank you," I say. "Dr. Rosenberg, I'm scared. All the time."

"I know you are. But you're going to be okay. Do you trust me, Corey?"

"I do. Thank you." I hang up the phone and look at Jacob. I'm so happy to be here right now with this beautiful baby. My baby. He sleeps with one arm over his head—always. I snap a picture of him with my phone. "I love you so much, Jacob."

I finish plugging Jacob into his car seat base and slam the door shut. I jump a mile high when a man approaches me from behind in socks, no shoes. He doesn't appear homeless—his khakis are clean and ironed. His face shaved. A button-down, loose, but not ill fitted. He could be a salesman in Hawaii and nothing would appear odd, except he's shoeless, here, in NELA. Liz's shoeless man.

I put my hand in my bag for something hard or sharp. I find my keys and squeeze them into my fist.

"Do you work there?" He points at the studio.

"Why?" I'm not trying to be polite.

"Do you know the girl who died?" he says.

"Did you know her?" I answer with a question. I'm not telling this guy shit and want to keep him talking because that means he's occupied.

"She was my friend." His hands ball into fists at his sides. His face reddens.

He stares down at his socks.

"What happened to your shoes?" I ask.

"They hurt my feet, so I took them off."

"Do you know who might have wanted to hurt Kat?" I ask.

"You know, this is my corner. I'm safe here. Bad people don't like me. Most people are scared of me."

"What sort of bad people?" I ask.

"You're Kat's friend," he says. "Be careful."

Then he walks down the block in the opposite direction.

"Wait! What's your name? Who are the bad people? Are they the ones who hurt Kat?" I call to the guy, trying to get him back and talking, but it seems he's done with me, and I can't chase him—Jacob's in the car.

I jump in the front seat and quickly lock the door. I dig through the tote for my phone. Nothing. Shit. I sweep my hand under Jacob to see if it fell in the seat while I was snapping him in. I get out of the car and look on the ground. My phone buzzes—my phone buzzes in my hand. Get your shit together, Corey. I lock myself back in the car with Jacob and text Liz.

Me: Liz, can we meet before your class? 2:30 studio?

Liz: Ugh. I hate being there early. Sure, but don't be late.

Me: Promise

Liz: Bring coffee

Me:

37

I go back to Debs. I want to see if I can feel Kat's presence. I haven't felt it anywhere since she disappeared. Her energy a void at the studio and her home.

◆ ◆ ◆

I'm at the spot where Natalie and Araceli were found. Police tape is still stuck to a few trees. The surrounding area is decently raked, for evidence. The branches Araceli and Natalie had hung from are removed and fresh stumps left behind. I wonder what will happen to the stuffed bears, candles, cards, and posters that friends and neighbors have brought—a memorial to the girls. Who would come and collect these things when the bears turned moldy and the candles rolled around in the wind? Would the scraps just become litter? Would Lupe want to come and take any of it?

I pick up a few of the cards and sit on a large rock. I unfasten my top and nurse Jacob while I read the sentiments the mourners left for the girls: classmates who couldn't believe it; strangers saying prayers to God for their souls; others cursing them for hurting their parents with their selfish act. It's gruesome and morbid. I don't want Lupe to find them, so I pick up the rest of the cards and notes.

"Ow!" I gently swat Jacob's bottom that is tucked inside the wrap. "Stop biting me." I snap my nursing bra closed. I need to shut Operation

Breast Milk down because it's becoming lethal. I make a mental note to investigate biting. I look around for a trash bin but know it's futile; the closest bin is in the parking lot, a real issue for those who bring dogs.

"Miss Corey?" I hear from behind me. I spin around so fast I lose my balance and grab the victimized tree for support.

"Nando?"

"Yeah, it's me," he says as he emerges from the brush. "I just came to leave this." He wiggles a rainbow-dyed narwhal doll in his hand. Jacob lights up.

"It's good to see you," I say. "Are you okay?"

"Yeah." He brings the doll closer to Jacob, who is kicking his feet into my hip bones with enthusiasm. "You like that, little man? You like it?" Jacob squeals with delight and drools on his chin reaching for the doll.

"Not for you, baby, that's for someone else," I say. I'm talking to my baby. I do talk to my baby. How often do I do that? Maybe I'm not horrible. Maybe that's the drug talking.

"Nah, she doesn't need it. Can he have it?" Nando asks.

"That's very sweet of you."

"Araceli loved narwhals and unicorns—she was such a girly girl," he says.

"Hey, my son apparently does too."

Nando laughs before he falls silent. He looks up at the freshly cut branches.

"You know, nobody treated me as good as Araceli did in my whole life. She saw me as more."

"I'm sure she was right to," I say.

"Yeah, she would say that too. I signed up to take classes for my GED. My cousin's gonna help me out. Maybe get a college degree. I'm good with numbers. I always thought I might like to be a CPA or something."

"Nando, that's awesome. It sounds weird to say because I'm nobody, but I'm so proud of you. If you need anything, I'm always around."

"Yeah, well, my cousin lives out in Azusa, so I'm gonna move in with her. But thank you. You're a cool lady. You might actually be one of us some day. A lifer here."

"Thank you, I think you're pretty cool too." I laugh. I want to hug him.

Nando gives Jacob and me a fist bump goodbye. I hope I see him again someday—not here, though. I hope he leaves this place for good. Comes back with that degree.

I head up the trail a little higher, looking for the spot Kat must have fallen from. I know I can't get down to the spot she landed—unless I fall too. It's too dense with brush, and there's no path. That's why no one saw her right away. I'm looking for more yellow tape bits but have yet to come upon them.

I have thirty minutes before my meeting with Liz. I need to head back down to my car.

I expect Kat's reserved spot in the parking garage to be vacant when I arrive, but it isn't. There's a shiny black Tesla with a child's booster seat in the back parked next to a custom blue Honda Civic. Diane and Monique must both be inside.

I slip in the back door quietly. Thank Jesus and God that Jacob is dozing in my arms. I stay in the back, hidden from view, and listen.

"Fuck it, I don't give a shit," I hear Monique say.

"Listen, I'm sorry Kat's gone, and I wish I could—but it's just not possible right now, honey," Diane says.

"You were willing a week ago to put up a third of the studio. You think I'm a bad investment? The whole thing was contingent on Kat being around?"

"No, that's not it, and that's not fair. I was putting up the money I was getting in the divorce settlement. Now that I'm not getting divorced, I don't have it."

"But he does! Tell him. Let me pitch to him. I don't understand why this has to change anything. You wanted to be a partner five minutes ago!"

I cough.

Diane jumps. "Corey. Dammit. You scared me."

"You're like a fucking ninja with a baby, Lieberman," Monique says.

"I didn't mean to interrupt," I say. "What's going on?"

Monique lets out a forced sigh and says, "Diane was going to buy a third of the studio and become partners with Kat and me. The contracts were drawn up and ready to sign."

"Yes, but the situation has changed," Diane says. "For all of us." Diane looks even more tired than earlier, if that's even possible.

"Hey, do you want to take over Kat's share of the gym, Lieberman?" Monique asks. The sarcasm is apparent, but if I said yes, I think she'd be on board.

"Monique, stop. Just calm down for a minute. Let me talk to Sean."

"Really?" Monique asks.

"Really. But I think we should revisit the terms. If I do this, I want 51 percent of the business, not a third. Are you going to be able to cover the rest? The whole reason you two came to me in the first place was to take on a third because you couldn't carry as much as you were," Diane says.

"I'll make it work. Gilda has offered to help me," Monique says. Hearing Gilda's name makes me feel guilty. "Lieberman," Monique says, "your kid is crying. Can you not hear him?"

I look down at Jacob—he's whining. I did not hear him. I'll make a note of that on my list of side effects the medication may be causing. Right next to—kissing an old crush. I don't want to think about that now, but I haven't stopped.

"Sorry, I was just thinking," I say, and I set Jacob on the counter and keep my hands on his waist. My hips ache from carrying him.

"Put him on the ground—let him loose for a bit. You're always holding him. He needs a little space," Diane says.

"Why are you here?" Monique asks.

I had not expected them to be here. I had not expected anyone to be here. I had not expected to need to make up an excuse. I'm here to snoop on you both, but you've ruined it.

"I left my cycling shoes." With my mommy brain and all, I thought that should be enough for Monique.

"You don't just leave them here like the rest of us?" Diane asks. I shake my head and start to look around for legitimacy. My shoes are in my tote bag under a wadded-up baby blanket, a spare onesie, and a large tub of Aquaphor. Thank god for all the baby crap hiding my truth.

"I'm going to look in the closet. Maybe someone shoved them in there," I say. I take my tote bag and set it out of their line of sight on a bench. I pretend to rummage through the storage closet, looking for a black pair of Shimano, Velcro, cycling shoes. The same pair everyone wears. It would be impossible to know if a pair were yours unless your name was on them. "Found them!" I snatch a pair belonging to some instructor, maybe even Diane, and hold them up for Monique and Diane to see.

"Great, you should put them back so they're here for your next class. It's stupid to carry them back and forth," Monique says.

I nod and put the shoes back. Liz would be here any minute, too early for her class, and ruin my excuse. I would be outed as a liar.

"We're leaving, Lieberman. Walk out with us," Monique says.

"Right behind you. Just have to get Jacob." He'd crawled behind the desk. I stall and let him try to pull himself up on the desk chair.

"We can wait," Diane says.

Shit.

I pick Jacob up—he throws a massive fit. It's a struggle avoiding his flailing arms. I take two tiny fists to the mouth. His face purple and red. "I promise, it's just for a minute."

I walk out with Diane and Monique. "All right, I'll see you later," I say. They are both in the garage parked next to each other. I head out to my car on the street, open it, and set Jacob inside in his carrier, unfastened. I toss in my tote bag, then pull myself up into the driver's seat. Monique leaves, driving right past me. I wave, but she doesn't notice me at all. I wait a few more minutes to confirm Diane has had time to leave.

I pull Jacob back out of the car—in his carrier—and tiptoe-run back to the parking garage entrance.

38

Diane's car is still there, but she isn't. Did she go with Monique? The employee door is unlocked, and the alarm is off. I slip inside, begging Jacob not to make a sound.

I skirt around the bikes to the front desk, but I don't see her. I set Jacob's carrier on the counter and walk over to the storage closet.

"Diane?" I ask while pulling open the door.

"JESUS CHRIST!" Diane clutches her chest. "FUCK, Corey. Are you trying to kill me today?"

"I'm so sorry. I had to come back again. I didn't realize what time it was, and I wanted to see if Liz could cover a class next week, so I thought I might as well just wait here instead of going all the way home and texting her because she's teaching in a bit and—"

"I get it. Fuck, my heart is racing."

"What are you doing?" I ask.

"I left my phone."

"In the closet?"

"No, I was grabbing a water bottle. What's with the interrogation?"

"Weird place to leave a phone is all," I say.

The phone starts ringing. She motions for me to keep quiet. "Hi, honey, what's up?" She walks to the front desk, picks up a pen, and starts to scribble. "I'm on my way. No, feed them whatever there is. I want us to show up together later." Diane hangs up the phone and tosses it in her bag. "I need to get home."

"Was that Sean?" I ask.

"Yeah, we're still finding our footing."

Diane looks distracted.

"He's had such a temper lately. And the police talking to us felt like a goddamn interrogation. If I didn't know they'd already determined it an accident—well, I would have thought Sean was some kind of suspect, which is ridiculous. I'm trying so hard to make coming home easy for him, but every day things seem to escalate. It's brutal—the timing is bad."

"Why would you think that? Kat and Sean barely knew each other, right?" I ask. I lead the conversation, hoping this time she doesn't accuse me of being insensitive.

"I think the police are just questioning a lot of people that had contact with her—they're in the running group, and I work here."

Diane wouldn't be this upset if she believed that.

"Maybe you and Sean need a break," I say. "Can he sleep at his apartment?"

"I've asked. He won't leave."

If Diane knows about Kat and Sean, would she have informed the police of the relationship? Was the police visit Diane's doing?

My heart speeds up with each thought. I check in with the evil in my head—knives, swords, murder—nothing. I push forward.

"Did you ever get the name of the girl he was seeing? Look her up on Facebook? Do a little recon?" I ask.

She shakes her head. "It just infuriates him when I ask. He says the 'b' is out of the picture." She grabs Jacob's hand and plays with it. Jacob smiles and pulls his hand away with a laugh. "I should go. We'll see you tonight, at the run, right?" she asks.

"Yeah, I'll see you guys tonight." I plan to ask Sean straight out— were you fucking Kat. And did you kill her.

Liz walks in the minute Diane opens the back door to leave. There's an awkwardness between them.

"Hey, thanks for coming early," I say.

"You didn't tell me she was going to be here," Liz says, avoiding eye contact with Diane.

"I was just leaving," Diane says. It's tense. I didn't notice any friction between them at the memorial ride. I suppose the "prank" on Kat left a rift. Good for me, bad for Diane.

I follow Liz to the front desk, where Jacob is still nestled in his carrier. She drops her bag, keys, and water bottle. Jacob is working on a teething toy. One that looks as gnarled as a dog's rawhide ear. Diane follows us.

"Diane, I thought you were leaving," I say.

"Right. I was. Liz?" she says.

"Yeah?"

"Are we cool?" Diane asks.

"Fine."

It's weird and quick, and Diane leaves.

"Is she upset with you?" I ask.

"Just Diane being Diane," Liz says. "What did you want to talk about? Where's my coffee?"

"I met that man, the shoeless one," I say. Fuck, I had promised coffee and completely forgot. "I forgot the coffee. I'll make it up to you. Promise. Coffee on me all next week."

"I don't trust you'll remember. Make it a coffee gift card," she says, typical Liz. She slips out of her sweatshirt and folds it neatly. "Yeah, he's been around a lot more lately. I told the police about him too. I found out he lives down the street in the assisted-care facility. Did he tell you his story?" she asks.

"No, tell me," I say.

"He's harmless, after all. A car accident, I think, left his brain a little scrambled. Monique told me. Kat had started volunteering at the facility once she knew his story. I mean, it really takes a community to look out for one another, you know?"

The early riders, ones who want a specific bike, start filtering through the door, more than were at Monique's earlier class.

My mind is on fire. Breathing is an obstacle. I grab the bottle of Klonopin and take one without water. I wave bye to Liz.

"Don't forget the gift card," she says and waves back.

I leave to get ready for the run. I'm about to catch a killer.

39

I drive the most direct route home. It's three p.m., and I have to get ready for the run tonight. My phone dings. I glance down. A text from Evan. I feel my face turn hot and red. I've cheated on him. I pick the phone up to look.

Evan: Are you on your way home?

I reach down to set the phone back in the cupholder. In the moment it takes my eyes to look down, I hear the horn of an oncoming car. My head jerks up to see a car coming right into me. I swerve back into my lane as quickly as I must have drifted over. My phone lands on the passenger-side floor instead of the console. "It's okay, buddy," I tell Jacob. "Just a little boo-boo—it's okay." My hands shake at two and ten on the wheel.

I see the lights, and I hear the siren of the police car behind me pulling me over. God dammit—no texting while driving, because obviously you'll swerve into another lane and kill yourself and your baby. Jacob is quiet.

I turn back around and see the officer from yesterday standing at the window. I read his name tag this time—**VILLAR**. I roll down my window. "Officer Villar, you are following me," I say.

"License and registration, please." I fish in the tote bag for my wallet, which is at the bottom, beneath my cycling shoes and a musty, damp towel I don't remember taking. I pull out the pieces requested and smile. "Do you know why I pulled you over?"

"Are you Chris Villar's cousin?" I ask.

"Because you were swerving into oncoming traffic."

"Technically, I was setting something down and accidentally swerved. I wasn't actually driving intentionally into oncoming traffic." I hand the documents over. "Is Chris having you follow me?" I ask. Wow. First Evan, now Chris. Jacob starts to fuss. He's hungry and tired, and it has already been a long day. He flails his arms and Hulk opens his harness.

"Is he not buckled into his car seat?" Officer Villar asks—he's shorter than Chris. Bulkier too. His hair cut close, like most uniforms'. I see the family resemblance at the mouth. Same teeth. If I hadn't taken the Klonopin, my heart would have burst out of my chest already.

"He was, I swear. I would never put him in the car unbuckled. I'm sure Chris would have told you I'm a good mom." I would cry, but the damn drug has dried out all my tears.

"Are you on medication today, Corey?" he asks.

I want to lie, but if he looks in the car and sees the pill bottle, I will be done. If I tell the truth, I don't know what will happen; he'd take me in for child endangerment? I'd get off on a fine and another warning? He'd call Chris? I don't know the law for these circumstances.

"Yes, I had a Klonopin earlier today, but my doctor said I am fine to drive with caution."

"I'm going to need you to turn off the car and hand over your keys, now." Officer Villar isn't testing the situation; he is the situation. I do as commanded and step out of the vehicle at his behest. "I'm going to need you to turn around and face the vehicle."

"Are you arresting me? Is this necessary? I'm fully willing to go with you. Call Chris—I am not a liability here. I should report you for stalking." I try to remain calm as the hard, heavy metal handcuffs are tightened around my wrists behind my back. Jacob is staring out the window at me. He's crying, confused, begging to be held. I want to overreact, but I'm too medicated. The muscles in my body are slow and heavy. "What are you going to do with my baby?" I ask.

"He's coming with us."

I'm gently guided to the police cruiser while Officer Villar carries Jacob in his car seat, sans base, to the squad car. He gently helps lower my head so I can balance getting in.

I walk into the station, unhandcuffed now, carrying Jacob. We pass through the pen of desks. The station is very quiet. It appears closed for business. I scan the room for Detective Lopez.

"Where is everyone?" I ask.

Silence.

I'm taken back to the room where I sat with Gilda the day we learned Kat was dead.

Once in the room, Villar tells me to sit down, and he leaves. Jacob and I are alone. I sit on the floor with him. I watch him tentatively crawl away from me. He looks back, like he's making sure I'm okay.

"I'm good, baby. I'm good," I say. He gurgles back at me. "Say *mama*," I urge. When he reaches the end of the table, he turns around and comes back, happy. "Do you want to play patty-cake with Mama?" I take his hand in mine and start rolling his arms. "Roll it out, roll it out, and mark it with a *B*." Before I can finish, the door opens.

"Do you know why I brought you in?" It's Villar.

I stay on the floor playing with Jacob. My body so light and relaxed I could take a nap. I really haven't gotten the hang of how the Klonopin will react with my system yet.

"Chris is concerned about me?" I say.

"Chris asked me to keep an eye on you, yes. Do you know you were driving erratically? Jesus, your baby wasn't even buckled in properly."

"I'm legally—" I start. "Never mind—am I under arrest?"

"No, you're lucky it was me who pulled you over."

"You pulled me over because you were following me without cause." I see Officer Villar squirm. "I'm sorry," I say. "You've been helping us, and I'm appreciative. I don't like being watched. Followed. Spied on."

"I'm not arresting you. I'm doing Chris and you a favor." He slides my cell phone over to me from across the table. "Call Chris to come pick you up."

I text Evan, not Chris.

He looks at me, and I read disappointment. His uniform fits well, as if he was born to wear it. The kind of cop whose job has come to define him. "Listen, Corey, I do not care that you are suffering. Women like you are a dime a dozen. Your privilege, your Prozac, your wine— your lives just so hard. I suggest you clean yourself up, get right in the head before you do something that you cannot undo. I don't want to arrest you, but I can."

I swallow hard to keep my *fuck you* to myself. He's our informant—I don't want to lose him. Shit, I know if I weren't who I was, the situation would have been different. Emergency placement found for Jacob. Weekly visits with him and the resource family he would be staying with. A white family who couldn't have a baby of their own, secretly praying I couldn't keep my shit together so they could keep my baby forever.

I nod. Thoroughly scolded, humbled, and pissed. My pills are prescription and legal, so is my driving while on them. I hate this man—I hate Chris for having him follow me.

"I got it." I play along. He isn't telling me I'm a bad guy—yet. Just a bad mother.

There's a quick tap-tap-tap on the door, and Lopez enters.

"Corey Tracey-Lieberman, why do I keep seeing you around this place?"

I sigh with relief. "Detective Lopez," I say.

"I can finish up here, Officer Villar, if you're done," Lopez says. Villar nods to me and then to Lopez and exits.

"Corey, what are you doing here?" she asks.

"Applying for a job?" I say. I am met with silence. "It's a mistake." I can't tell her Officer Villar is our informant.

"Yeah, that's what everyone says."

"I was driving home. I looked at my phone, and he brought me in."

"That simple, huh?"

"It really is."

"Listen, I don't want to sound like an asshole, but you're white, in case you forgot. Nobody is just bringing you in for a minor infraction."

Hearing Lopez say it catches me off guard. "I'm on antianxiety medicine. It looked like I was driving erratically. But I was reading a text. And I admitted to being on pills when Officer Villar asked."

"Maybe you shouldn't be driving," she said.

Everyone has an opinion.

"Did you get my message earlier?" I ask. "You didn't call me back."

"We've combed through Kat Donahue's phone. Her house. Her network of people. Unless you have video of her being pushed, or a recorded confession, I don't know what else could prove anything. Do you have a video of her being pushed?" Lopez asks. She actually sounds sincere.

"Why did you question Sean and Diane Loeb earlier today?" I answer her question with a question.

Lopez looks at me; her brows pull close together. She is surprised by the question.

"You owe me information," I say. Didn't she? Didn't we make a deal?

"Unless you have something concrete for me, it's time to go. Mr. Jacob looks tired," Lopez says.

She pushes her chair back to leave.

"No, I have sunglasses," I say. I don't move.

Lopez looks me straight in the face. "Sunglasses?"

Why did Lopez look surprised when I asked about the questioning today? Diane said they were interrogated. She specifically said she *and* Sean were interrogated.

"Sean Loeb's sunglasses. I found them in Kat's car. They were having an affair," I say. My insides tight, urgency races through me. My pulse is overwhelming, like when riding up a steep climb.

"Can you confirm this affair?" she asks.

"I'm working on it."

Lopez nods.

"I'll get a confession too," I say.

It was going to be a long, uncomfortable run tonight.

She looks at me and Jacob. I look at Jacob. My baby looks at me. "Come on, I'll walk you out."

When we get to the lobby, Lopez says, "Get yourself a bus pass." She can't slam the door behind me, but I think she would if she could—she's getting harder to read.

I walk out of the station with Jacob. Evan is waiting curbside. Without a word, I pop Jacob in the back seat and climb inside next to him. Evan doesn't say anything, either, not until we are moving.

"You shouldn't have been texting while driving," he says.

"I was reading *your* text, not writing one. But, honestly, I think it's fair to say they were overreaching. Being hauled into the station over a small moving violation?"

"Agree, but at least it was only a warning. Corey, I don't think you should be driving with Jacob in the car for a bit. It's like you're marked now."

"That seems to be the general consensus." I roll my eyes. "You actually think I'm endangering our child." The hurt in my voice is nearly indistinguishable from the rest of my emotions. The pills did that. They're working hard to keep everything neutral. I can feel the fight happening inside me.

"God, Corey. I don't know what to believe anymore. I'm in the fucking dark all the goddamn time. You're never home. Our baby is always with you. Your therapist knows more about what's going on from one session than I do living with you. Fuck—fuck—fuck!" With each fuck he slaps the steering wheel.

Evan swipes at his eyes with the back of his hand. Then promptly replaces them both at the ten-and-two position.

"Where did you sleep last night?" I ask.

"I didn't sleep." He takes his eyes off the road for a moment and looks at me. "I went to the Sheraton in Pasadena." I look at him still watching me. His eyes are puffy, his facial hair more a beard than end-of-day stubble. He looks about as rested as he did after our first date. We'd gone for drinks. That turned into dinner—which turned into a frenzied make-out session in the back seat of his very practical, understated like him, Honda Accord. Which turned into watching the sun rise over the Pacific Ocean in Malibu. That first night I knew I loved him.

40

"Did you put the jogging stroller in the car?" I ask Evan.

"Yup, and waters and a bottle so you don't have to stop and nurse."

"Thank you," I say. We've barely spoken since the car. The tension thick enough to squeeze my lungs like an overchlorinated pool.

"I'm not going to ask you to talk about last night right now, but we need to have a discussion, Corey. I can't continue to live like this," Evan says.

"I don't want to fight with you, Evan. Yes, let's talk later. I'm sorry," I say as I look through and feel in my bag for my phone. I need a recorded admission of guilt.

"Are you listening to me?" he asks.

"Yes, I said I don't want to fight, you said we need to talk, I said I'm sorry. I'm multitasking. I can't be late."

"You care more about this dead girl than you do us," he says.

His words are powerful because he's right. I've always cared more about the job—it's not just about solving a case. It's understanding the processes that prevent victims and families from getting justice. How our laws and systems don't serve all people, and how all police districts aren't created equally. It's the deep digging for answers that give clarity and hope and bring about change. I thought that's what attracted him to me in the beginning.

"Do you want to come with us?" I ask.

Evan looks taken aback, his eyes wide, and then a simple "Yeah."

◆　◆　◆

York Park is crowded with runners. Too many to count. It's good to see that there are other couples with babies and jogging strollers—we won't stand out too much. Evan and I find a spot a half block down from the park. I tuck Jacob into the stroller with a blanket, and Evan tosses in a pacifier Jacob hates—I swap it out for the one he loves. I did, not Evan. I smile to myself. It's not supposed to be a competition.

We jog down to mingle. I see Chris. He saw me first. I don't wave or acknowledge him, but we make eye contact.

"Is that Chris?" Evan asks.

"Corey!" I spin around when I hear my name and see Diane and Sean walking up on Evan and me. Diane grabs Sean's hand. She's wearing a color-coordinated outfit—a matching pink sports bra and leggings. She looks better than she did earlier. Her ponytail full and glossy. Lips shiny, mascara, and maybe bronzer. Sean looks irritated. He looks around when other runners call his name and gives a quick nod or wave but otherwise stays focused.

Diane introduces Sean to Evan.

"The last run I did was a 10K two years ago. I'm about to feel my age, I think," Evan says. He's an ace at throwing himself right into things—friends, conversations, karaoke. He's perfectly handsome, athletic, outgoing. No one would ever suspect Evan of adultery, let alone murder. Evan is so well balanced he'd never need to take medicine for anxiety or be told he was a bad father because of it. My shortcomings make my disdain for my husband relentless.

"It's been a helluva week," Sean says.

"Yeah, you can say that again," Evan says.

"Want to pace together?" And just like that, Evan's in.

"That leaves you and me, good," Diane says. "My whole damn body is tired."

"We can all pace together," I say. I cannot let Evan run off with Sean. I need to be with him. If Evan fucks this up—no. I only have myself to blame.

"Evan, I want to pace with you too," I say.

"I'll set a good rhythm for us," Diane says.

Then someone on a megaphone cuts off our conversation.

"Okay, runners, listen up. Tonight's route is east on Avenue 50 up to Echo, over to Avenue 52. and we'll follow it around to the Audubon entrance of the park. The park has left the gates open for us tonight. If you can't run the climb, you can head over to the Greyhound Bar and Grill on Figueroa, grab a beer in Kat's memory. Got it?"

I push the stroller up closer to Evan, who is small-talking with Sean and another guy who has joined them.

The groups all nod or holler "yeah," and it's go time. I look around frantically to get an eye on Chris. I can't find him.

"Evan," I say, "let's all try to run together." I repeat myself. I need a confirmation from him. He isn't paying attention to me—typical. There are new people all around him now talking with Sean.

"Corey, it's fine. Let them go together. It'll be good for us to be able to chat," Diane says.

Fuck.

I smile.

Fuck. Fuck.

There's a sharp pain behind my left breast.

Fuck!

I turn on my phone's recording app, then place the phone in the stroller caddy that stretches across the handlebar.

"Evan," I say. Yell, to get his attention. "Why don't you take the stroller? It's too heavy for me to push the whole route. And we can follow you guys until we slow you down?" My whole body starts shaking. My stomach is nauseous. My hands grip the push bar like a steering wheel coming down a steep incline.

"Are you sure?" Evan whispers in my ear. "Are you sure you're okay with me taking Jacob?"

"Yeah, I'll be pacing you, and we can trade off and on, okay? Stay close." I bend down to kiss Jacob. He is sound asleep, as he should be. My skin hurts. Evan kisses the top of my head. I can imagine him believing this is progress.

The four of us stay together for the first mile. It's pleasantries, superficial friendliness, and a lot of silence and breathing. Sean speeds up, and Evan stays with him, pushing the stroller with ease. It looks like Sean is running away from us. Diane picks up her pace to catch up to him, but he just pushes harder. Evan looks like he's barely trying, easily running whatever speed Sean sets.

Without Jacob on me or the stroller, I feel physically light. I'm nearly floating. Running is easier than I remember. My lungs open; the air digs deep trenches in my chest.

We are nearing the park entrance, and Diane grabs my arm and slows down to a jog. Evan and Sean are silhouettes far out in front.

"Evan," I call out, but my voice is lost. He's too far ahead.

"Do you mind if we walk?" Diane asks.

I'd have to race to catch up to them now.

"I haven't been here since Kat," Diane says.

"What do you mean?" I ask.

"I used to hike here with Kat. She'd work off her hangovers, and I'd live vicariously through her stories."

"I didn't know you hiked together," I say.

"How would you? You and I never really talked until recently. When Sean left, I was in a pretty dark place. Kat and I would hike before Saturday classes when my nanny and kids were still asleep in bed—which I technically consider to be her watching the kids." Diane laughs at herself.

"Is that when you and Kat got close?" I ask.

"No, that's when we started to drift apart. I was busy trying to mend my family. Keep us together. She was too young to understand. She cared more about living in the moment and short-sighted happiness."

"I get that," I say. The evening climb is well lit thanks to the full-ish moon. Now I can see that Diane has the same puffy eyes from earlier in the day. Her skin sallow now that the makeup has sweated off from running. I notice her outfit doesn't match as perfectly as I thought; instead it's two different pinks trying to match and failing.

"Kat and I were a lot alike. She reminded me of myself when I was her age. She was like a sister, a little sister, to me. I wanted to help her with the studio and with dating. She wanted a family. Lots of kids," Diane says.

Her watch lights up her wrist, and I can make out a bruise, the purple oval shape mimicking a thumb print and—more faded, almost green now—a larger circle that could be the rest of a hand.

"That's odd for someone who partied all the time. Especially when she wasn't very monogamous," I say.

"What?"

"You told me before that Kat was a party girl," I say.

"Right. Well, monogamy and family are not mutually exclusive." Diane takes a stretch break. I follow. "Kat wasn't who I thought she was," Diane says.

"How so?" I ask. "I regret never having the opportunity to know her as a close friend."

"Don't be. She'd stab you in the back if you gave her the chance."

"Kat?"

"It doesn't matter. I shouldn't speak poorly of the dead. I'm sure she'd defend herself if she were here. She always had a reason," Diane says.

"Are we talking about anything specific?" I ask.

The air is chillier the higher we climb. My teeth start chattering. A few runners at a time pass us by.

"First, I had to deal with all of Sean's bullshit, then Kat's, then Liz's, now Monique's. I'm just tired and venting. Sorry."

"Evan and I are going through a rough patch too," I say.

"Good thing Kat's dead or she might have pounced on Evan. She did like dads."

My breath catches in my throat. I try to breathe—but each intake is too shallow. My head is light because I'm losing oxygen. My lungs burn. I know this dance. I start to count in my head—one, two, three in. Then out. My lungs begin to unclench.

Diane slows her pace more. The gap between us and other runners widens.

"Is there something you want to tell me?" I ask. It comes out strained, but it helps get the air back into my body when I talk.

Diane is consuming air like it's a cleansing shower. Her arms spread wide as she throws them up and back into a deep stretch behind her. She is graceful and agile. She walks to the edge and looks down. I follow her. There's nothing visible below. I need to keep Diane talking.

"It's obvious that Sean loves you, Diane. He came home to you. You can let the rest go, can't you? The only days that matter are the ones out ahead of you," I say.

"Was that in your horoscope today?" She starts to jog up the trail, and I follow.

"Hey, we're off the path."

She doesn't answer me. I continue to follow. It's dark, but I have a vague sense of where we are from previous hikes.

Still, my mind races with images of me falling. My neck breaking on the way down. Jacob growing up without me. Knowing his mother died and left him. Bad mother.

"Diane, can I borrow your phone real quick? I want to check in with Evan."

She ignores me. I am on my own.

I reach the end of the path. Diane's ahead of me in warrior pose. A formidable figure under the moon.

"Evan's probably worried. Did I tell you how overprotective he is?"

"Sounds like he loves you," Diane says. My eyes continue to adjust to the darker light. There are no other runners in the area. "Come here, look at this view," Diane says.

"Okay, but then I could really use a drink. And my body is way too out of shape for all of this," I say. I force a laugh. I've never felt physically stronger.

"Promise."

I think about that night at Drew Hudson's—his dark house, the teasing, the uncertainty replaced by fear. I think about all the things I wished I'd done. Said no when he asked me in. Said no when he asked me to come over. Left the moment he didn't turn on the light or when I didn't hear a dog bark. I followed him into his house. I teased back. I played along, and then it was over. I could have prevented it from happening, but I didn't. And here I am again.

I hope Evan finds my body quickly.

At the edge, the brush opens up to a view of the entire city. It's no longer dark. I can see below. The ground has been cleared. Leaving what looks like a hole. It's cold at the top, like standing in the shade in winter.

"Isn't it awesome?" Diane says, more of a proclamation to the universe and stars.

"Yeah." My teeth chatter hard, making it nearly impossible to speak. "Diane, is this where Kat fell?"

"It is. This was her favorite spot. Every Saturday before the beginners' class. It was our thing. I really loved her." I can see tears streaming down Diane's face. Her body leans into the sadness.

"Were you with her the Saturday she fell?"

"It isn't what you think," Diane says.

"What do you mean?" I ask. "The police said it was an accident or suicide maybe—that's all I'm thinking."

"Don't lie." Diane steps closer to the edge and looks down. "I didn't kill her. She fell."

"How?" I ask.

"She wanted to hike. She knew I had found out about her and Sean. Don't pity me—she pitied me—just don't." My expression is as blank as I can muster while Diane continues. "Kat wanted to explain it to me. She 'didn't mean for it to happen.' It was 'an accident.' How do you accidentally fall into bed with someone else's husband? No, your friend's husband. Do you know? I don't. How does that happen?" She breaks her gaze from the edge and looks at me. "Answer me, Corey."

"I don't know. I accidentally kissed a friend yesterday. I wish I hadn't. Maybe that's what she meant," I say.

"Stop. Don't help her. She told me her feelings were too genuine and deep to call things off. Can you fucking believe that?"

"She was young," I say.

"She was young. I told her that. I told her that my feelings were also genuine and deep, three fucking kids deep. *A ceremony to love each other no matter what* deep. She cried. She had the audacity to cry to me. She tried to explain that Sean had called the whole thing off multiple times. That he wrestled with coming home to me and the kids or staying with her. That she told him, if he wanted to go, she would support that. But it had to be his decision. Oh my GOD!" Diane looks up to the stars. "The nerve of her!" Her yell rattles the silence.

I stand still. I listen for people, anyone who may also come to this spot. I listen, but all I hear is my heart pounding and Diane moaning through more tears.

"I told her to break it off. I told her our friendship depended on it. That my family depended on it. She was ripping us all apart, and how could she, a child, even begin to understand what she was doing," Diane says, her nose ugly-running. Her body heaving for breath through sobs.

"Does Sean know?" I ask.

"Corey, she tried to hug me. I pushed her away. That's all. I pushed her away, and she was gone."

My vision starts to blur. My chest is rubber band tight. There is a din in my ears.

"Corey?" I hear Diane say through my tunnel of panic. She lunges for me. I fall back—a short drop to the ground.

There's a rustle on the path from where we emerged moments ago. Diane squints toward it.

"I'm okay," I say, too loud. Covering. Hoping it's Chris or Evan—that they haven't given up on their stalking of me yet. I bring Diane's attention back to me.

Diane looks completely deflated. Her body empty of the secret, like being expunged of a virus and needing to find a way to rebuild.

I hear a stick snap. Animal, or Chris—God willing. I force myself to keep going with Diane.

"Diane, she fell. Why didn't you call the police?"

"I have children. She was having an affair with my husband. Who would believe I didn't push her off?"

Diane pushed Kat off that cliff. Intentionally or not, she pushed her off that cliff. Kat's death became a greater burden for Diane than the affair Kat had with Sean.

I hear the static of a walkie-talkie. Then a familiar voice—Lopez is here?

Detective Marks and Officer Villar now stand feet away on the trail, and Lopez approaches Diane and me. Looking back, I can now see Chris standing near the blue and red lights on the fire-road trail. Where we are, the moon is the only thing lighting the path, which makes the trees appear to be thick, ominous giants. Little glowing bugs buzz past or stick around, pecking about my face.

Diane heaves a sob. Lopez stands next to her and speaks softly—I can't make out what she's saying, but I'm sure she's not suggesting Diane take Benadryl and it will all go away.

Diane sighs and wipes her face.

Diane is looking at me while Detective Lopez stands beside her. She says, "Kat brought me out here to tell me that she and Sean were moving in together. That she wanted to tell the kids together, the three of us, so it wasn't awkward for them."

"Why did you go?" I ask.

"What do you mean?" Diane says.

"Why did you say yes to the hike?"

"I don't know. Maybe I did want to push her off a cliff."

Diane turns toward the edge. She stands there, her arms open, daring the breeze to turn into wind and pull her off. The darkness is brutal—the fall from the edge looks like a black hole.

Lopez isn't in a position to grab her; if she moves, Diane will likely drop off the edge.

"Diane, come on. First glass of wine is on me," I say. She doesn't respond. "It's okay, Diane. You didn't kill her. It was an accident, like you said. You couldn't have predicted what would happen. You were a good friend."

"What if I willed it to happen?" she asks.

"You can't—that's not a thing," I say.

I walk to the edge and stand next to her—Lopez nods at me; I hope it means she'll grab me and not let me fall. "Did I ever tell you about the voice in my head? The one that tells me I could kill my baby?" I ask her. "But I don't. I don't—it's just an intrusive thought, Diane. You didn't kill her; you said it yourself." Saying it out loud makes me want to laugh. It's so absurd—I would never. "Diane, we have kids. I have a baby. Don't make me do this. Get it together and let's go."

It takes what feels like forever but is only a minute longer, and Diane is away from the edge. Detective Lopez reads Diane her rights. Diane stands up straight. She holds back her tears now. The emotion is in the past, and strong Diane is here to take the blows. The three of us make our way down the narrow path to the fire road and Lopez's car.

Diane gets into the vehicle, and Lopez closes the door.

"Ms. Tracey-Lieberman," Detective Lopez says.

"Yes."

"Good work." She extends her hand to shake mine. "Do you need a ride?" she asks.

"I think I'm going to walk back, if that's okay with you," I say.

"I'll need your statement. First thing in the morning." Lopez walks around to the driver's side of the car.

Lopez and Marks get in the car and drive off. I stand there for a moment and watch Officer Villar talk to Chris, then follow Lopez in his squad car.

◆ ◆ ◆

Chris and I are about half a mile from the park's exit when we finally speak.

"That was something," he says.

"Yeah, it really fucking was." It's about another mile to the bar. "Thank you for being there."

"I've always got your back, Corey." He stops, and I look at him.

"I know. You're a great friend." I pause on that word.

"And the kiss was a mistake."

He stayed with me the whole run. Never left me.

"I think I need to walk alone the rest of the way. Is that all right?" I say.

"Yeah. It is." Chris comes in for a hug. After the kiss, after Diane's story, I have guilt. He flashes me a smile and then takes off in a jog. I start walking toward the bar, alone for the first time since before Jacob. It's strange and good. The heaviness in my shoulders, gone. My head light. It's easy, like floating.

I stand still and call to the demons in my head, but they're gone—for the moment. Sleeping. Hopefully hibernating for good.

"Corey!" I turn around, and Evan is running up behind me with Jacob in the jogging stroller.

"I'm okay."

"What happened?" I see fear pass over his face. I pick up Jacob, sleeping, from the stroller and hold him close for a moment before gently setting him back down. I wrap an arm behind Evan and begin to tell him everything, from the beginning, as we walk back home as a family. No matter what, we will always, forever, be family.

Epilogue

I come to Kat's funeral alone. Jacob and Evan need time alone together, and so do I. Progress. It's been a month since Diane's confession. A month after Gilda had originally been asked to retrieve Kat's body. Lopez has received permission to investigate further based on Diane's confession.

I see Sean in the last row sitting in a pew alone. I grab the seat next to him.

"I'm sorry," I say.

"Me too." His reception of me is awkward, bordering on cold.

"I didn't see you at last week's run."

"Well, my soon-to-be ex-wife is on bail, pending a trial for involuntary manslaughter of my girlfriend, who was a beloved member of the running club. I don't think I'm going to be well received there anymore."

"Did you know?" I ask.

"Stop. I've got nothing more to say, and I mean it. The goddamn media haven't left me alone."

"Fuck the media; tell me. I want to know if you knew. Did Diane blackmail you to stay with her? Or did the pain of you both losing someone you loved so much bring you back together?" I ask.

He looks down at the program in his lap.

I see Gilda walking toward us from the front. "Tell me," I say.

"I didn't know," Sean whispers. With that he gets up and leaves before Gilda can have him forcibly removed. I don't believe him.

Diane already gave her first interview, where she waxed poetic about being a mom and how protecting her children was the most important factor in her choices that day. The fear of losing them was so paralyzing to her that she didn't call for help. It turns out losing your children, no matter how you lose them, is devastating. She was already receiving more airtime than Kat.

Chris wrote the story for the *Eastsider Times*—a critical look at the lack of funding for investigations of murder within the NELA Latino communities. He focused the story on the two girls, Araceli and Natalie. Two promising Franklin High seniors murdered. The evidence of homicide buried. Labeled as gang related—by a source inside the LAPD. An investigation was promised. Chris wasn't done. He wrote about the media's bias: Over two hundred Latino victims of murder in Los Angeles in the past year—and most of them the media wrote off as gang related. Chris is changing the narrative.

I slip out after the eulogies from Monique and Gilda and head to Dot's Diner. I grab a booth in the corner and order coffee. It's still a new feeling being alone, without Jacob, but it's just for the day. I have to remind myself, just the day. I've been on the Paxil for five weeks now and managed to cut back to one Klonopin a day, max.

"Miss Corey," Nando calls from the door. He walks over and slides into the booth. I grab his hand and squeeze it.

"Nando, I'm so glad you came."

"Of course, you said it was about Celi."

"Yeah, it is, but we're just waiting for someone else. Do you want a coffee?" I wave the waitress over.

Elsie and Lupe walk in and sit down just as the waitress leaves.

"Nando?" Lupe asks. Nando nods. "I'm Lupe, Araceli's mother."

Nando looks on the verge of tears.

"Araceli wrote an essay about you her teacher thought was quite remarkable. She thought very highly of you, and so do I." Lupe clears her throat—she allows her tears to rain down silently. "We've started a small college scholarship in Araceli's name, and it would mean the world to her, to me, if you would be the first recipient."

Nando, Elsie, Lupe are a mess. I pass them napkins. I want to hug them all. I want to cry with them, but the Paxil leaves me an emotional desert. Nando would be taking his GED exam in a month and already has an application completed for Pasadena City College.

I pay for everyone's coffee and leave them to talk, work out logistics. I have two more stops to fill my day before I get to be with my baby again.

I get to the NELA precinct and ask for Detective Lopez. I wait on the bench I had to change Jacob's diaper on just a few weeks back.

"Corey Tracey-Lieberman, if I didn't know better, I'd think you worked here. Where's Mr. Jacob?"

"With his dad today."

She raises her eyebrows.

"Shall we go into my office?" Lopez asks.

"You mean your Murder Board room?"

"Listen—" she starts.

"Actually, I think you should start listening to me."

"Corey—"

"No, you wanted to write Kat's death off. You did write it off. And those two girls? You didn't give them justice, a six-year-old boy had to. Now he's separated from his mom while she's sitting in a hospital waiting to die. Think about that the next time you tell me to go home and enjoy being a mother."

"Corey—"

"Don't, I might lose my thought—Paxil does that to me."

"Corey, you did a good job. Let's talk."

I leave the station and feel vindicated. It's a rush. I have a plan—and it starts with Chris. I'm going to put together an online neighborhood-news resource with a daily live news report. I'm going to have a job—as an independent police consultant working directly with Lopez. I know I have to figure out where things stand with Evan, but I can't face where I think things are headed just yet. I want to get home to Jacob, my mama-saying Hulk, but I have one last stop to make.

I get to the diner, and Chris is there waiting—pie and coffee on the table. I slide into the booth across from him.

"I have so much to tell you!"

He grabs my hand under the table and squeezes. He smiles at me, and I think I melt a little.

I have time to tell him all about my plans later. For now, we can just eat our pie. And then I'll get home in time to put Jacob to bed.

Author's Note

I didn't intend to write a book about a woman with postpartum anxiety and obsessive-compulsive disorder. I entered grad school with every intention of finishing the book I had applied with—a dark comedic novel with a criminal twist about a single woman's life, told through notes, emails, and texts, with the many, many roommates who shared her space through thirty-five years of life. However, every time I sat at the computer, instead of working on a second draft of that book, I found myself writing Corey's story.

I shed a lot of tears for Corey while writing her journey. She isn't perfect; she's human. She's struggling with many of the challenges we all struggle with—especially after having a baby. Not everyone is in a position to call on friends or family to come and bear some of the burden of new parenthood. I saw a meme recently that said the biggest parenting flex isn't how smart, beautiful, or talented your kid is—no. The biggest parenting flex is having grandparents that help without being asked; it's having friends who show up with a casserole after you give birth. There are too many folks that can't say they have that in today's world.

Maybe that lack of family and resources is partially responsible for the high percentage of women suffering from postpartum anxiety and OCD. Clinical psychologist Dr. Sarah Allen writes that "About 3–5% of women experience postpartum OCD, so although it is not talked about as much as postpartum depression, it is pretty common."

In fact, a new study out of Australia says the percentage of women suffering from postpartum anxiety and OCD is closer to 30 percent, compared to postpartum depression, which affects about 4 percent of postpartum mothers. And I know a thing or two (or more) about it, because I suffered from it too. Yep, I had severe postpartum anxiety and OCD (and more panic attacks than I care to remember). I had a great doctor who was able to identify the condition, and I didn't have to solve any murders during my panic attacks, just how I was going to finish graduate school.

Corey's story is more than just a thrilling crime novel or a battle with postpartum anxiety. It's also about this beautiful community that still functions like a small town within a large city—Highland Park in Los Angeles is the center of old traditions, where neighbors really do look out for each other. Where they keep their front doors open so neighbors can walk in and visit. It is generations of family living together and insular enough to keep older generations speaking the language of their mother country comfortably. I wanted to share that place with readers, so they know that even in a vast city like LA, this community exists. And I wanted to shed some light on the myriad pressures of gentrification and how violence against women is treated to this day.

This book brings this all together in ways I wasn't quite expecting. Because I really wasn't expecting to have a protagonist who is fearless at a murder scene but terrified of her own child's cry.

This book contains discussions of suicide, sexual assault, rape, and struggles with mental health. If you or someone you know is struggling, there is help. My hope is that this book makes you feel seen and heard instead of triggered and that you come away with a sense of community and belonging.

If you are struggling and need assistance, you can reach out to the Crisis Text Line. Text HOME to 741741 to connect with a volunteer crisis counselor, available twenty-four hours a day, seven days a week.

Acknowledgments

Writing a novel is an incredible journey, and it's one I could not have completed without the support and encouragement of many wonderful people. Writing can be lonely, or you can have the unconditional support of generous people who believe in you and step up to read every draft and sentence change you make over six years. That's how long it can take to write the first novel. That is how long it took me to get here.

First and foremost, I owe my deepest gratitude to my extraordinary agent, Dara Hyde. Your belief in this project and your guidance through the postwriting process have been invaluable. Your keen insights and dedication made this book better than I could have imagined. And to Charlotte Morrissey, I am so glad you are on the team! Thank you.

To Alexandra Torrealba, thank you. Thank you for seeing the vision in my book. Thank you for understanding Corey. And thank you for that first call. I will never forget your words. Thank you forever. Thanks to the entire Thomas & Mercer team. Ali Castleman for stepping in and watching over this project. Michelle, Alicia, and all the editors at T&M, thank you for your beautiful editing notes. I cannot say thank you enough to everyone at Thomas & Mercer. There are no words.

To my incredible husband, Jason, your patience, love, and understanding have been my anchors. Your support in both the quiet moments and the hectic ones has meant more to me than words can express. And, to my beautiful son, Jack, you are always my inspiration and motivation.

A special thanks to Tod Goldberg, the very best teacher and mentor a writer could ask for. Thank you to Oliver Brennan and all my MFA pals, whose contributions have been crucial in the development of this story. Whether through brainstorming sessions, invaluable feedback, editing, or just lending a listening ear, your input has made a significant difference.

To my friends and family, thank you for your constant encouragement and belief in me. Your support has been a source of strength and motivation. You all read every draft with enthusiasm and support—both Corey and I don't know what we did to deserve you. When they say it takes a village, they are not kidding. Your enthusiasm for Corey still makes me cry with joy. I will never forget the initial reactions you each had when you finished reading the novel. I thought, wow, if these are the only readers I ever have, I've won. Second to none, all of you.

I want to thank Dr. Jane Estes and Dr. Alex Beebee. Thank you. You helped me heal and get to the place where I could write this book and speak about the journey of panic disorder without fear. You answered every time I called scared and confused. I wish everyone a care provider like you two.

And finally, to all the readers out there—thank you for picking up this book. Your enthusiasm and support mean the world to me. I hope my gratitude for each of you shows in the stories I tell. I see you, and I thank you.

With heartfelt gratitude,

Jaime

About the Author

Photo © 2023 Joanna DeGeneres

Jaime Parker Stickle is a writer, actor, podcaster, and professor of film and television at Montclair State University. She is the creator and host of the true crime investigative podcast *The Girl with the Same Name* as well as the hilarious podcast about side hustles *Make That Paper*. Jaime lives in Los Angeles with her husband, son, and fur babies.